AN UNOFFICIAL ROSE

AN
UNOFFICIAL
ROSE

By

Iris Murdoch

" Unkempt about those hedges blows
An English unofficial rose "

1979
CHATTO & WINDUS
LONDON

Published by
Chatto & Windus Ltd
40 William IV Street
London W.C.2

★

Clarke, Irwin and Co. Ltd
Toronto

ISBN 0 7011 0984 X

First Published June 1962
Second Impression June 1962
Third Impression September 1962
Fourth Impression July 1966
Fifth Impression March 1971
Sixth Impression February 1979

Printed in Great Britain by
Redwood Burn Limited
Trowbridge & Esher

To
MARGARET HUBBARD

Contents

PART ONE

Chapter One

I am the resurrection and the life, saith the Lord: he that believeth in me, though he were dead, yet shall he live.

FANNY PERONETT was dead. That much her husband Hugh Peronett was certain of as he stood in the rain beside the grave which was shortly to receive his wife's mortal remains. Further than that, Hugh's certainty did not reach. The promise meant little to him that the priest had uttered. He did not even know what Fanny had believed, let alone anything concerning the possible consequences of her beliefs. After more than forty years of marriage, and although his wife had not been a mysterious woman, he had not really known what was in her heart. He looked across the open grave. The tiny coffin opposite to him, under its pile of sodden roses, was like that of a child. She had shrunk so much in her last illness.

Fanny had had few friends. Yet the gathering at the graveside, under its receding rows of black umbrellas, was a large one, and the family itself accounted for little of the throng. In the chapel, during the dreary singing of *Abide with me*, Hugh had been too dazed to note who was present and who was not. Now he began a little to look cautiously about him. Fanny's peevish architect brother was there of course, the one who had inherited the pictures. He looked so transparent now with thinness and age that it was hard to remember that he was her younger brother; Fanny herself had been so plump and busy, such a bouncy little person, till the cancer came. Then there were the others, his own people, Fanny's and his people. His son Randall and Randall's wife Ann stood nearest to him; and half opposite, little figures in navy blue raincoats, were two of his grandchildren, Randall's daughter Miranda, and young Penn Graham, Sarah's eldest son and now Hugh's eldest grandchild. Dear Sarah was in Australia with her husband and Penn was there, as Sarah had put it in her long emotional cable, "to represent the love of all the Grahams". What a rotten time the boy had had, Hugh reflected. It was almost indeed as if he had come for Fanny's death-bed. They had even forgotten his fifteenth birthday. Poor Fanny had been looking forward so much to seeing him on this long-promised visit; but by the time he arrived she had become too deeply concerned with her own last things.

With so much rain it was hard to tell who was weeping. For those who, like himself, felt it indelicate to raise an umbrella in the presence of death, external nature provided a semblance of that tribute which, from a warmer spring, the heart could not or would not offer. Hugh had no tears. But Penn was certainly weeping. Hugh looked at the boy. He seemed slight and childish in his school mackintosh, his little thin face all red with grief, as he stared down at the raindrops fretting the pool of water in the pit below him, and thrust his knuckles regularly into his eyes. He had scarcely known his grandmother, but because she was his grandmother he had loved her, and he sorrowed now with a complete sorrow as at an utter loss. Hugh envied the completeness. All the same there was something frail, almost sentimental, about the boy. He was quite unlike the tough Australian grandson of Hugh's imaginings. Given what the boy's father was like, they had all been prepared for something roughish, but not for this rather pathetic elf.

Hugh looked at Miranda. She too appeared younger than her age. She must surely, he reminded himself, be fourteen now. Or was she? It was shocking not to know. Her very pale freckled face, so like her mother's, wore a paralysed self-conscious expression. She was not crying. She looked steadily upward above the heads of the mourners, determined not to catch the eye of her parents, and as if absorbed in some long calculation of her own. Now and then with a nervous hand she patted the unaccustomed little black hat which covered her red-golden hair, her bright hair which fell usually in big separate locks like a cap of autumn leaves, hidden

now except where a few rain-darkened ends clung to her neck. She
was to Hugh a totally mysterious little girl.

The other person who was really crying was Ann. As she was
on Hugh's deaf side he could not hear her sobs, but he could feel
against the sleeve of his overcoat the convulsive movements of her
shoulder. He gave her a quick sideways look. Her eyes and nose
were red, but the rest of her face absurdly retained its usual waxen
paleness so that she looked like a rather damp clown. A wet scarf
covered her hair, which had been, when Randall married her, so
flaming, but which had faded to a pale ginger now on its way to
becoming a sandy grey. She had loved Fanny; and Fanny had
loved her too, in her way. "Such a *serious* girl", Fanny had said of
her at first, a little timidly, a little suspiciously; and timidity and
suspicion had always remained to temper their good relations, for
Fanny was never very far from thinking that Ann thought her a
fool. But Fanny had believed in Randall's marriage, had believed
in it right up to the end, seeing no danger signs and noticing no
deterioration; and perhaps that very belief had helped to keep Ann
and Randall together.

*We brought nothing into this world and it is certain we can
carry nothing out.*

It was true that Fanny had brought nothing into this world. On
the other hand she had had plenty of things waiting for her when
she arrived. It was many years now since Hugh had stopped
wondering to what extent he had married for money. Plump rose-
red Fanny had somehow so much made one with her rich art-
dealer father and the great family collection that it made no sense
even to ask whether he had married her for the pictures: and by
the time the pictures went away to the boorish brother and the
collection was dispersed Hugh hardly wanted them any more. Except the Tintoretto. That he had always wanted, and his wish had
been rewarded, since Fanny got the gem, the Tintoretto. Perhaps indeed he had married her for the Tintoretto, as in a curious muddled
way it had sometimes seemed to him in his dreams when his poor
wife and the picture became strangely identified with each other.

For man walketh in a vain shadow, and disquieteth himself in vain: he heapeth up riches and cannot tell who shall gather them.

Hugh hoped that the children were not too disappointed about Fanny's will. She had left everything to him and nothing to them, which was characteristic of her and perfectly right. Yet Randall had shown resentment enough when Hugh paid Penn Graham's fare to England, as if it were already Randall's own money that was being wasted. Hugh hoped there would be no unpleasant discussion. It was true that Sarah and Randall both needed money: Sarah to feed her increasing brood, and Randall—Randall for his freedom. The rose nursery, Randall's creation, still brought in an income. But Randall's heart was no longer in it: heaven knew indeed where it had fled to by now, that most volatile organ. Hugh reflected that perhaps it was better after all that his son should not be wealthy, should not, anyway, be wealthy yet. They could wait, both of them, they could wait for what was left of Fanny's cash.

It would not be very long. Old age, which when he had been younger had seemed a coloured prospect of broken wisdom, a condition like that of a late Titian, full of great melancholy shattered forms, now presented itself, when he was on the brink of it as a state, at best, of distraction, irritation and diminished dignity: his rheumatism, his indigestion, his weak legs, his deafness, the perpetual buzzing in his head. On the brink of it was indeed how he now from day to day imagined himself. To picture himself passing that limit would be to admit into his imagination the reality of death; and this even now he could not do. Fanny had not done it, up to the end; and as Hugh well knew, her spiritual adviser, the rector Douglas Swann, had not been able, in the course of many visits, to bring himself to steer the conversation round to the state of her soul. Fanny had not been equipped for the seriousness of mortality, and one had felt, in the midst of grief, almost embarrassed for her in this respect.

When thou with rebukes dost chasten man for sin, thou makest his beauty to consume away, like as it were a moth fretting a garment.

His own beauty, such as it was, had certainly consumed away

14

some time ago. Others of his contemporaries had done better, he reflected, as he looked across at his old friend and rival Humphrey Finch. Humphrey, for instance, had kept his hair. He stood now in a respectful attitude under his umbrella, his enviable head with its thick white mane soberly bowed, while his eyes rested thoughtfully upon Hugh's grandson. Humphrey was a quick man and Hugh was a slow man; and although Humphrey's career had come to an untimely end after an incident in Marrakesh which even the British Foreign Service, with its wide tolerance of eccentricity, could not overlook, Hugh still felt that Humphrey had been the more successful of the two. Hugh's own career in the Civil Service after he had decided, or rather discovered, that he was not a painter, had been if not exactly meteoric at least exemplary and such as could pass as distinguished. Flattering words in high quarters had attended his retirement. Yes, he could pass as a distinguished man, just as he could pass as a good husband, and few would ever know anything to the contrary. But the terror and the glory of life had passed him by.

Hugh shifted his gaze to the neighbouring umbrella under which he made out the unusually fashionable hat and unusually subdued face of Humphrey's wife Mildred, who although she had not been particularly fond of Fanny had produced for the occasion a look of highly reflective melancholy and even a few tears. She was leaning, not upon her husband's arm, but upon that of her handsome younger brother, Colonel Felix Meecham, who held the umbrella high above her and contrived, even with both arms thus occupied, somehow to stand at attention. "Poor Mildred", as she was called by those of her acquaintance who knew, as indeed who did not know by now, the scandal of her husband's sexual preferences. Yet Mildred was not a figure to pity: Mildred, whom Hugh had kissed passionately once, he remembered, on a summer evening over twenty-five years ago, when they were both already sensible middle-aged married people. He wondered, as he watched her dab her eyes with a small handkerchief, whether she still recalled that curious incident.

The days of our age are three score years and ten.

Fanny had not lived out her appointed span. The cancer came sooner. And he himself had yet another three years to go. Well, Fanny had lived, she had married a distinguished man, she had borne children, she had loved her husband and her children and her grandchildren and her cats and dogs. She had been, he supposed, happy. She had not been altogether cheated. Hugh recalled the last funeral he had attended. When his eldest grandson Steve, Randall's boy, had died of polio Hugh had felt a frenzy of anger and misery which was quite unlike the resigned grief of today. Steve's death had been something gratuitous and wicked, and Hugh had raved at the universe in vain to find a place to pin that wickedness down.

Nothing had been right since Steve died. Randall had been reeling drunk at the funeral and said later that Ann "had never forgiven him". It was rather perhaps that he had never forgiven Ann, upon whom by some insane and fantastic logic he had seemed to fix the blame of his bereavement. Drunk he had been at the funeral, and drunk he had been with increasing frequency ever since. Doubtless he had loved in Steve and lost in him his own immortality, his own more radiant self, for the boy had resembled him to a singular degree. Where had it come from, Hugh wondered, all that charm? Not from Fanny certainly, and not from himself. He was a slow man and he had no charm; it is a thing that one knows. What they all remembered now about Steve was his charm, and not that he had been, like his father, "impossible". Yet those who, like Steve, like Randall, compel love, also for just that reason, Hugh reflected, merit the love they compel. While the worthy and deserving ones, such as Ann, are, by a terrible justice, unloved. Hugh had long ago ceased feeling guilty or even puzzled that he did not love Ann. He liked and respected and admired her, but there was no compulsion of warmth. Yet, when she was young and her hair was as red as Miranda's Randall had loved her; and perhaps, it had been hinted in the village, Douglas Swann, though serenely married himself, loved her now in a way that was the tiniest bit more than pastoral.

PART ONE

By shifting his head slightly Hugh could see behind Ann the pious profile of Douglas Swann, and seemingly superimposed upon it, in his sidelong glimpse, as in a composite photograph, the handsome face of Clare Swann, her prominent eyes ablaze with curiosity and life. Since Fanny had been moved, two months ago, to the clinic in London, Douglas Swann had come up from Kent several times to see her, and today they had both come, which was very good of them, considering how busy they were, Hugh reflected with irritation. At least he was being spared the experience of having Swann conduct the burial service. Words of such terrible weight are best not profaned by those whom one has caught out being, if not positively frail, at least certainly absurd. With added annoyance Hugh recalled that he had promised to drive the Swanns back to Kent after the service was over. How much, how very much now, he did not want to go back to Grayhallock, to the big unspirited house and the acres of dreary roses. But there was such a lot still to be done there, so many tasks, so much sheer tidying up, now that poor Fanny was gone. Well, it would all be done, and then he would be free. He would be free. Ah, what did that mean?

Thou hast set our misdeeds before thee: and our secret sins in the light of thy countenance.

It was just as well he reflected that most of his own *were*, fortunately, secret. Yes, he had passed as a good husband. No one had known about Emma Sands. He had got past. Perhaps it was just this which should be, when his own time came, engraved upon his tombstone: he got away with it, he got past. His career had been successful, his marriage had been successful. No one had known about Emma: that is no one had known much or anything for certain; and people notice so little and they forget. Fanny had known, of course; but Fanny had been so incredulous, so puzzled, so unable to cope in her thought with the irrational violence of that episode, that she had later made it, in a way, as if it had never happened. She had seemed to forget it utterly; and this too Hugh could hardly forgive her. Because he had spared her the details, she

17

had never known how nearly she had lost him. Or had she, he wondered fruitlessly and for the thousandth time, so nearly lost him? He was, when all was said and done, a conventional man.

His mind had run this course many a time until he knew every turn and cranny of the reasoning by heart. Surely it was not for Fanny's sake or for the sake of the children that he had not then gone away. The children had been nearly grown up; and as for any real bond with Fanny, so great a fire would have frayed it in a second if he had let things rip. But he had not let things rip. Was it for pure convention that he had sacrificed that marvel? Perhaps. Was it because of the department? Was it because he had had·no money of his own? Perhaps. Or was it for some demon of morality which, he knew, would have given him, later, no peace? Yet morality, as it subsequently seemed, was neither here nor there. No great store of spiritual energy had been liberated by his sacrifice; and his action, too high doubtless for any context which he could sustain for it, appeared to have had merely a destructive effect. He had passed years in a resentment against his wife which had gradually deadened his tenderness into pity and his pity into a dull resigned companionship. Their marriage had become a hollow frame. It was for that solid but echoing framework, its painted exterior so bravely held up to the world, that he had given up the peril of a great love.

Though Emma Sands had been Fanny's childhood friend, Hugh had seen little of her in the early years of his marriage. Emma had been away school-teaching, first abroad, later in the north of England. Then she came to London; and Fanny, who always feared bluestockings, had treated her remarkable friend with a mixture of timidity and casualness: and Hugh had seen Emma as awfully nice, awfully clever, but awfully absurd. Then he looked again. From the moment when, in Emma's dark over-furnished flat at Notting Hill, he had with a burst of illumination which came quite suddenly, and with a deep prophetic groan, taken her into his arms, until the moment when he had walked away down the long corridor in a coma of misery, had been a space of two years. It sometimes seemed to him that that time had been his only real life, and what began and ended it his only real actions.

Emma had never married; and Hugh had not met her since, though he had, at strangely regular intervals, seen her: distantly at a party, in the National Gallery, from a passing bus. He had occasion, of course, abundantly to know of her, since it was after their parting that she had begun to write the detective stories which had made her by now so famous. By this inconvenient fame, if by nothing else, her image had been kept vivid and even unnervingly up to date. Hugh was aware too, and this was more disturbing, that Randall, somewhere in the mysterious private maze of his London existence, had run across Emma. What his son and his former mistress made of each other he did not know. It was a subject from which he averted his mind.

We commit her body to the ground; earth to earth, ashes to ashes, dust to dust.

Hugh fell silent in his thoughts. He was aware, in the greater stillness of attention round about him, of the steady sound of the rain, as for a brief moment all present seemed to confront the mystery of their last end. They muster steadily, the dead. Yet in such a scene the dead person is defenceless, outfaced by the sturdy solidarity of the living. Hugh had wished to think of anyone but Fanny. Now for one moment he saw her, perhaps for the last time, face to face. He saw her sitting up in her bedroom at Grayhallock, playing patience on the counterpane, her cat Hatfield curled purring in the crook of her arm. He saw her face lifted to his, after the doctor had gone, in an entreaty which both sought and feared the truth. And in those last drugged delirious days at Grayhallock, before they took her to London, there had been the endless questions about the swallows. Oh God, the swallows. Had they remembered to open the doors of the loft for the swallows to come in? Would the swallows come again at all, would they ever come again? Perhaps they would never come. Had they come yet? Had they come? Hugh had told her truthfully day after day, no it was too early, they had not come yet, they would come soon. But today again they had not come. And poor Fanny had been moved to London before they came. Perhaps he ought to have lied to her about the swallows.

The relaxation of the dying hand. He jumped to feel Ann's clasp upon his arm. She had been saying something to him. It was all over. He had seen the coffin awkwardly descend into the watery pit and heard the earth fall upon it. It was all over. He turned stiffly about and let Ann lead him slowly into the quietly shifting crowd. The priest who had performed the ceremony murmured something inaudible to him. Douglas Swann came up beside him and took his other arm. He was an old man being led away. This was what was conveyed to him by Ann's gentle pressure, by the bowing, melting, solicitous, curious crowd. He shuffled along, seeing in front of him now the gate of the cemetery, the rows of cars outside in the road. Douglas Swann was putting up an umbrella over him and making some remark about the rain. In another moment or two he would be out again in the ordinary world.

He turned round to know if Randall and the children were following, and saw like a shaft of light through a cloud a momentarily opened vista between the rows of dark figures. Something at the far end of that vista arrested his attention for a second before the opening was closed again by the movement of people toward the gate. Two women he had seen like bats clinging together, their glasses glinting under the black canopy, two women facing him in grotesque stillness down the rainswept vista. One of them was Emma. Hugh stopped. The vision had gone, but as if to confirm its reality he caught sight of the intent averted face of his son, and his son's hand descending after a gesture of greeting. Hugh stood still for another moment. Then he set his feet in motion.

He passed slowly along the line of cars. He passed Randall's Vauxhall and Felix Meecham's very dark blue Mercedes. Here at last was his own clumsy capacious Standard Vanguard. *O spare me a little, that I may recover my strength: before I go hence and be no more seen.*

PART ONE

Hugh staggered slightly as he came towards the car. Ann was still tugging his arm and insisting that she should be allowed to come with him and drive the Vanguard. Close behind them Clare Swann was absently humming *Abide with me*.

Chapter Two

"I THOUGHT this lot for the refugees," said Ann, "and these perhaps I might offer to Nancy Bowshott. What do you think?"

They were sorting out Fanny's things. Ann had been very firm that they should do it at once and get it over, and Hugh supposed she was right; though when it came to it he could hardly bear it. At the funeral he had felt unreal and detached while Ann sobbed. Now when he wished to give himself up to a small frenzy of grief Ann was being calm and busy and practical. That was just like a woman. All the same he was deeply grateful to Ann, grateful to her for having insisted on having Fanny at Grayhallock, for having insisted on nursing Fanny. Without Ann the last six months would have been for him an almost unendurable torment.

It was Sunday morning and they had all been back at Grayhallock for three days. Some pale sunshine made the soaked garden glitter and the steaming spongy lawn warm to the touch. More distantly, between the beech trees, the bleak lines of spiky rose bushes could be seen, sloping away below the house, scattered with a confetti of multi-coloured points; and below and beyond there stretched toward the invisible sea the flat pale green expanse of Romney Marsh, crossed with reedy dykes and dotted with distant sheep and presenting to the eye toward a bluer horizon a remarkable number of tree-shielded and variously shaped church towers. It was still early in the month of June.

"And I thought we might give some little thing to Clare as a memento," said Ann. "She was so terribly good to Fanny."

"Whatever you think best," said Hugh. "But what about you and Miranda?"

"Somehow I'd rather not," said Ann, "for myself. I thought perhaps Miranda might have some of the cheaper bits of jewellery, if you didn't mind? I remember a painted bead necklace—"

PART ONE

"Why ever should I mind?" said Hugh irritably. "Everything belongs to the family. Naturally I assumed you'd have all the jewellery. There's no point in sending it out to Sarah."

"But some of it's valuable—"

"Oh, for God's sake, Ann," said Hugh, "don't make a fuss!" Everything to do with money and possessions was so depressing. He knew Ann was incapable of resentment, but how tactless she was all the same. This was no moment for scrupulous counting.

He sat down on the bed. It had been odd, coming back into this so familiar room in which he had seen the season change from winter to spring, and now finding the bed all folded and flattened. There had been the mornings when he came in fearing to find Fanny dead. And there was Fanny's poor old dressing-gown still hanging on the door. Ann had given her another one for going to London. Of course he had loved his wife. Any idea he might have had to the contrary was romantic and irresponsible and absurd. That was what was hollow. His marriage, whatever its short-comings, had been a real living thing and not an empty shell. He had imagined that now, when it was all over, he might have felt, all the same, a sort of relief. But what came to him instead was a quite new sorrow, a dreadful sense of her absence. He kept missing her, searching for her. But she was nowhere now.

Ann kept turning over the heaps of clothing and going through the pockets. The action had an air of thieving absurdly at odds with the plain humble expression of face which she had put on for the sad little scene. There was not much to find. There had not been much to find in the desk either. Poor Fanny had had no secrets. She had been a woman without mystery. There had been no darkness in her. And Hugh, as he looked at intent Ann, pale shabby Ann with her short lank ginger hair pushed back behind her ears, reflected that she was, after all, in this way, not unlike Fanny. Both he and his son had married women without darkness.

"I hope Randall won't mind our deciding things without him," said Ann.

"He'd better not mind!"

On their return to Grayhallock Randall had retired to his room and had stayed there in a sort of voluntary state of siege. Nancy Bowshott, the head gardener's wife, brought him up his meals; and Miranda reported that he emerged each day at dawn, armed with secateurs, to cut the newly opened bourbons and gallicas. Ann had apparently not set eyes on him. Hugh, who had seen his son's ménage under strain before, had refrained from comment.

"I suppose he hasn't changed his view about coming to Seton Blaise?" said Hugh.

Seton Blaise was the Finchs' house, some ten miles distant from Grayhallock. Mildred Finch had rung up on the previous day to invite them all over to dinner on the Sunday evening. Randall had refused to have anything to do with the invitation and was reported by a giggling Nancy Bowshott as saying that he had no desire to be patronised by that horse in human form. He thus designated Colonel Meecham. Ann had then told Mildred that they could not come to dinner; but Mildred in turn had made her promise at least to bring her depleted party over for drinks at six o'clock.

"No," said Ann. She hitched up her skirt and began folding the clothes. She added, "I'm so glad Penny will have a chance to see Seton Blaise. He ought to see a real English country house. It's a pity Mildred and Humphrey weren't here earlier on. It would have been a nice change for him after the chaos here."

"Our chaos is ceremony to him," said Hugh. "And you know he thinks Grayhallock is terribly romantic!"

What a mess they'd all between them made of Penn's visit. He was to have spent a term at an English school, but they had bungled the arrangements and then it was too late to get him in; so that since his arrival in April he had been simply hanging round the house, helping Ann with the washing up, running errands for whoever was looking after Fanny, and generally acting as a rather bedraggled page to the long sad event which had lately proceeded to its end.

PART ONE

"It's true that he sees no evil," said Ann.

She sighed while Hugh attended for a moment to the more sinister aspects of the chaos to which she had referred.

She stopped her folding and went on, "Poor boy. You know, I hope he doesn't feel that all the time we're comparing him unfavourably with Steve—"

Hugh got up. He was always pained and amazed at the free way in which Ann was able to refer to Steve. "I don't see why he should feel that. No one has particularly talked to him about Steve, so far as I know." There was no Peronett grandson now. The name would live on only as the name of a rose.

"All the same, children are so sensitive—He's a funny little boy. I shall miss him when he's gone back."

Yes, thought Hugh, you are lonely, you are lonely, poor Ann. He looked at Ann's greenish-yellowish eyes, widened now and misted with sad thoughts. He apprehended her with what he knew was but a perfunctory pity and but a vague good will, poor Ann incarcerated here with spiteful mysterious Randall, and only her enemies Nancy Bowshott and Clare Swann for company. How soon, he began to wonder, could he decently go back to London?

The sense of unhappiness at Grayhallock had been, since his return there, almost intolerable to him. The house was a melancholy one at the best of times, and had always seemed to him, if not exactly hostile to Ann and Randall, certainly indifferent to them. It had never, he felt, taken them altogether seriously. It had known quite other things, and there were times, especially at night, when one could feel it thinking about them. Grayhallock was only partly an old house, it had few pretensions to beauty, and such pretensions as it had to grandeur were now gentle and absurd. The long central portion of the house with its tall windows and yellow stucco and wide semicircle of steps dated from the early eighteenth century. In the nineteenth century it had been acquired by a linen manufacturer of vast wealth from County Tyrone, who had given it its present name and a pair of lateral battlemented

25

towers. He had also added an ornate glass porch over the steps, a vast mushroom-shaped conservatory, and a red-brick kitchen annexe: excrescences which, in spite of Hugh's protests, Ann and Randall had never seen fit to remove. While within, the house always seemed to Hugh to be both dark and damp, centred, as round a vast atrium, about the cold stone-flagged still-room, full of rain-soaked overcoats and rows of muddy Wellingtons.

"Well, that's that," said Ann. She put the last garment on to the neat pile and patted it. "Now I must find Miranda and tell her to change for church. Thanks so much for helping me, Hugh."

Ann's Christian piety, though doctrinally a little vague, was unwavering, and, Hugh conjectured, unreflective. Randall, who did not share it, tolerated it; but had been much less ready, as he put it, to see his daughter 'godded'. Miranda, however, to the surprise of some, though in so many ways her father's little girl, had so far continued firmly in the faith of her mother. Hugh himself, undramatically and again unreflectively, had no faith. Religion lay far behind him with things he had forgotten.

He got up with relief and followed Ann in the direction of the drawing-room. As he emerged into the corridor he apprehended, like a cold breeze, the presence of Randall in the house. He wondered, as he felt it, with such a presage of unpleasantness to come, blow upon him, with what icy authority it must now be touching the shrinking soul of Randall's wife.

The drawing-room was a long room with three big windows hollowed and upholstered with shabby chintz window-seats. Beside the front porch, it also had the view of the beech-fringed lawn. The lines of roses were out of sight now below the hill, and between the towering beeches there was only visible the blue and white swiftly moving sky which before a brisk north-west wind was descending across the pallid chequered Marsh in the direction of Dungeness and the twenty miles distant sea. The room, which apart from Randall's bedroom was the only 'serious' room in the house, was pleasant enough, its panelling a faded green, its furniture of a battered elegance, old miscellaneous 'finds' in lesser antique shops. The thick fawn carpet was scattered with a dim glow of threadbare rugs, which although 'if perfect' would be treasures, were now almost impossibly, manifestly, imperfect. A huge rosewood bookcase held the family library: rarely disturbed now since the younger Peronetts were not great readers.

Miranda was curled in one of the window-seats with three of her dolls propped up opposite to her. She was raising her finger as if to admonish one of them, and paid no attention to the new arrivals. Hugh was permanently disconcerted by his granddaughter. He could never, for instance, decide how far to humour her air of childishness. Miranda had always seemed younger than her age, and yet managed to combine her Peter Pannish demeanour with a knowingness which made Hugh sometimes conjecture that it was all a sort of masquerade. Yet it would be absurd to think this. The child, after all, in this respect curiously resembled her father. Randall was certainly a Peter Pan; and it was hardly fair to raise an eyebrow at Miranda's undiminished passion for dolls when her father still kept by his bedside the woolly toys of his childhood. They were both of changeling blood.

In appearance, of course, Miranda was the living image of Ann, and indeed 'living' was the right word, since the same features glowed in the child with a difference which made the resemblance inaccessible to a casual observer. Miranda was as pale as her mother, but her face had the transparency of marble where Ann's had the dullness of wax. Miranda's hair fell consciously about her, and about her brow and eyes, in straight bright strands like a mop of red and golden tassels, while Ann's neglected hair, which grew in just the same way, was something limp and string-like to be thrust back unheeded. Yet Ann was handsome still, with her strong face and her direct green glance, if one could only see her: which, as Hugh reflected, perhaps hardly anyone could any more. It was, he reflected too, Ann's own fault if she had become invisible.

"Where's Penny?" said Ann.

"Haven't the faintest," said Miranda, rearranging the three dolls.

Miranda was a weekly boarder at a school not far from Gray-hallock and spent her week-ends at home. During these times she did, as far as Hugh could see, nothing. She had even, as a result of a serious fall two years ago, lost interest in the Swanns' pony.

"Is he in his room?" Penn occupied one of the top tower rooms, above Ann's room. Miranda occupied the corresponding room in the other tower, above Randall's room.

"As I don't know where he is I don't know whether he's in his room," said Miranda, still *tête-à-tête* with the dolls. This was one of those moments which made Hugh wonder.

"Ah, well," said Ann.

Her philosophical treatment of her daughter also caused Hugh surprise mingled with irritation. He still experienced a recurrent desire, which he had not always, he thought with satisfaction, inhibited when she was smaller, to slap Miranda hard.

"I was just wondering if he'd mind drying up while we're at church."

"I'll dry up," Hugh heard himself resignedly saying. He detested the housework which Ann kept shamelessly hinting he might help her with. Penn already did more than his fair share of it; Miranda, in Hugh's opinion, less.

"Oh, that's terribly sweet of you!" said Ann. "I'm afraid there's an awful lot. Then perhaps Penny could lay the table, if he turns up."

Penn was excused church of course, his father being one of those who could scarcely credit that any rational person still believed in God. Not that there was anything wrong with Jimmie really.

Ann was telling Miranda it was time to go and change for church, while Miranda, her slim tartan-trousered legs curled under her, continued to commune with the dolls.

Hugh wandered away down the long room and touched guiltily in his pocket the fat letter from Sarah which had arrived two days ago and which he had still not nerved himself to read properly. It had been posted before the news of Fanny's death. He glanced at it, gathered that all was well in general and that Sarah was going to have another baby; but he had not settled down to plough through the details. Sarah wrote such enormous interminable letters; heaven knew how she found the time, with four children and another on the way. What is more, she relentlessly expected an intelligent commentary in return, and complained if she didn't receive it, so there was no use skipping. Hugh loved his daughter dearly, but he had never got used to her marriage. Sarah had met Jimmie Graham during the war, when he was a fighter pilot in the Australian Air Force, and she was in the WAAF. Jimmie now worked in the ICI works in Adelaide. Hugh had only a faint conception of what he did. She was terribly happy of course. But all the same.

Hugh pushed the letter deeper into his pocket and withdrew his hand. He looked idly at Ann's desk. It was covered with piles of printed cards saying that the Peronett Rose Nurseries much regretted that, owing to shortage of staff, they could not receive visitors this summer. It was a mystery to him how, in these recent years, Ann had managed at all. Randall's small genius had made the nursery, of course. It was his patient work which had produced the series of new roses, most of them now well known, by which the name of Peronett would be remembered. The younger Randall had been, in his way, a remarkable horticulturalist. He had met Ann when he was studying agriculture at Reading University, where Ann was reading for a degree in English. He had communicated to her his science; but the flame of his originality he could not communicate. Randall was in the end more artist than scientist, and had nothing of the commercial. Hugh recalled his saying once of Ann, "She doesn't really love the roses. She regards them as a chemical experiment." Perhaps the great days of the nursery were over. Yet it was on Ann's science and Ann's business sense that it depended now.

Hugh looked at himself cautiously in the big gilt rather battered cupid-encrusted mirror that soared over the mantelpiece. With a slightly guilty shock of recognition and detachment he saw a tall, stout, stooping man with a dome of bald head surrounded by a thick and longish fringe of brown-grey hair. The round surprised deprecatory eyes were of a limpid brown. The flesh surrounding the eyes had darkened and sunk, and here especially the death's-head was visible. Mortality was there; yet at the same time Hugh could see his younger face present still with a cherubic complacency, alive and spirited, superimposed upon the jutting skull. And if he could see it so touchingly and so yearningly present, perhaps another might see it too.

He had tried not to think about Emma Sands, but of course it was impossible not to. The figure he had momentarily seen at the funeral had certainly been Emma; and he only rescued himself by the reflection that her presence was in bad taste from the reflection that her presence was almost sinister. But Emma had never been afraid of bad taste. She was a person who did whatever she wanted. It was a little later that Hugh reflected that Emma and Fanny had been great friends in childhood, and why should not, at such a distance in time from either object, that childhood friendship be as real to her now as the venomous jealousy with which Fanny had later inspired her. Yet this thought was disagreeable too.

His mind returned in an obsessive way to Randall's mysterious salute. Something in that gesture suggested to Hugh that Randall was not surprised at seeing Emma. Randall was not surprised, Randall was in Emma's confidence. There was something here which if he attended to it would be perhaps intolerable. He tried not to attend to it; and his grief for Fanny, returning to him now in the house where she had suffered so long, came to him with a kind of healing intensity. He burned himself with that pure pain. But he knew too that he had been touched by something, some leper touch, which would work out its own relentless chemistry, ignore it as he might.

It was odd the way he had kept seeing Emma through those years: seeing her, but never speaking to her. It was as if some god designed that he should not forget. Yet, in a way, he had forgotten. The wound had healed, the anguish had gone, in the end, as he could never have imagined it would. It had never crossed his mind, once the first terrible time was over, to try to see Emma again; and this not because of any sense of duty, but because of a steady failure of inclination, a steady diminishing of appetite. When, at the regular intervals appointed by the god, he had espied her from the top of a bus, glimpsed her, always in the next room, at a picture exhibition, seen her back disappearing into a shop, and once passed her unobserved on an ascending escalator while she descended on the other side, he had felt an extreme but quite momentary shock. He had thought of her as belonging to the past.

For nearly two days now he had known that he would have to talk to Randall about her. What he had seen made it imperative. But it was an unpleasant, even distinctly alarming, prospect and he had put off doing so. Randall had been seventeen at the time of the affair with Emma. He had certainly known a little about it at the time. He had doubtless learnt more since. But the name of Emma had never come up between them, and it was only indirectly that Hugh had learnt, and had tried to forget it at once, that Randall was sometimes to be seen at Emma's house.

What Randall did in London was a mystery to all. In the last few years, and especially since Steve died, he had taken to spending more and more time in London, where he kept a little flat in Chelsea. Ann had increasingly taken over the management of the nursery, so that by now Randall, who even dared to complain about it, seemed more like a privileged lodger than like the master of the house. At some point in this process Randall had given it out that he had decided to become a writer; and shut up in his tower room he had in fact written four plays, none of which Ann or Hugh had been allowed to see. Part of his time in London had doubtless been devoted, unsuccessfully, to getting one of these plays put on. But it had gradually and imperceptibly become fairly evident to Hugh that Randall must have a London mistress. He wondered how evident it was by now to Ann.

During Fanny's illness Randall had spent much more time at home and had behaved in a fairly orderly way, and it had seemed possible to Hugh that the bad patch was now over and that his son might settle down again with his wife and child. Randall's behaviour since their return to Grayhallock had not been exactly reassuring; but it was too early to tell, and what Randall would do next was anybody's guess. Hugh had avoided 'speaking seriously' to his son about his treatment of Ann or indeed about anything else; and he occasionally wondered if this were not, on his part, a grave failure. He certainly ought to speak to Randall sometime about the drink. That the other things were bad might liberally be thought a matter of opinion, but it was no mere matter of opinion that the drink was bad. These were unpleasant thoughts. And Hugh knew, which was another unpleasant thought, that only the spur of a quite personal and selfish obsession would ever make him overcome his reluctance to be frank and direct with his boy. Under the pressure of such a spur he now writhed in the direction of a decision.

"And this afternoon perhaps you'd make another search for Hatfield," Ann was saying. She did not like people to be idle. Hatfield, Fanny's cat, had run wild since her death and disappeared into the fields.

"He's gone right away, Hatfield," said Miranda. "He won't come back ever."

"Yes he will," said Ann. "Bowshott saw him last week quite close to the house. And the milk I left out got drunk up."

"My hedghogs drank that milk."

"Anyway you try and find him, and take Penny with you. You're neglecting Penny."

"He wouldn't come back with me," said Miranda. "He doesn't like me. He's a one-woman cat."

"Well, off you go to change, it's after ten-thirty. Which doll are you taking to church this time? Is Poussette the lucky one?"

"That's not Poussette!" said Miranda scornfully. "That's Nanette! You always mix them up." She uncurled herself and began to make for the door, trailing the doll in one hand.

Half-way there she stopped and turned back to Hugh. "So sa
I never remembered to ask Granny how that card trick was done,
the one where you hit the pack on to the floor and the card you
looked at first is left in your hand."

The door banged behind her. Avoiding Ann's eye, Hugh settled
down to read Sarah's letter.

Chapter Three

᷍'T stand for it a moment if I was your missus!"
᷍n't you, Nancy? And what would you do about it,
would you beat me? Why, I believe you would!" Laughter followed.

Pausing on the stairs of the tower, Hugh recognised with distaste Nancy Bowshott's voice issuing from the half-open door of
Randall's room. He hated this familiarity with the servants, he
hated everybody knowing that all was not well.

Ann and Miranda were still preparing for church, and Hugh had
nerved himself, before further reflection should make him once
more hesitate, to go to see his son, though he had not decided what
he would say to him. The nervous urge to confront Randall had
suddenly become strong.

Hugh retired, coughed, and went noisily up the remaining stairs.
He knocked and put his head round the door. Nancy Bowshott, a
plump girl with a great deal of chestnut hair and a discontented
face, who was credited with having a brute for a husband, hastily
put down a glass upon the table. She picked up her dustpan, patted
the neat tight handkerchief out of which her mane bulkily emerged
at the back of her head, and looking a little red, slid past Hugh with
a murmured "Good-morning". Hugh entered and closed the door
behind him.

Looking a little like something by Hogarth, Randall lounged
behind his table on which were to be seen a bottle of whisky, two
glasses, three bowls of roses, a pile of notebooks, some scribbled
sheets of paper, an overflowing ashtray, a banana, a half-eaten
biscuit, a pair of secateurs, and an original volume of prints by
Redouté which had cost Randall a very large sum of money at
Christie's. Without a coat, displaying striped braces, his crumpled
collarless shirt open at the neck, he surveyed his father with an air
of benign and meditative encouragement, like an Abbot giving
audience. The room smelt of alcohol and roses.

"Well, Randall," said Hugh.

"Well, Father," said Randall.

Hugh's relations with his son, uneasy in the latter's childhood, impossible during his adolescence, and embarrassed in the early days of his marriage, had unaccountably improved of late. Hugh was not sure whether this was due simply to an increasing need to replace Sarah, or whether it was not connected in some subterranean way with the deterioration of Randall's relations with his wife. This last suspicion caused Hugh some uneasiness; and there were moments when he detected, in his still shy and reserved dealings with his son, the merest touch of an unpleasant complicity.

"I was just wondering," said Hugh, "whether I could persuade you to come over to Seton Blaise with the rest of us this evening."

"Well, I don't think you can," said Randall, tilting his chair and still benign. "I don't like those people and they don't like me, and I don't really see why I should expose myself to their bloody disapproval."

"All right, all right," said Hugh. Did they disapprove of Randall? He didn't know. Mildred, with her long tolerance of Humphrey and her skill in defending him, was surely not a censorious woman. Mildred: he thought of her for a moment. Yes, he remembered kissing her, but he could not recall the details, except that it was summer.

Quiet in Randall's attention, Hugh crossed to the window and looked out. From the tower it was possible to see over the tops of the beech trees and over the nursery garden which looked from here like a set of embroidered squares with the roses showing against the bare earth, as it followed the plump arc of the sharply falling hillside. Near to the foot of the hill arose the short spiky spears of a sweet chestnut plantation, and beyond it a little patch of woodland, where the wild cherry was but lately over, half veiled a group of conical oast houses in a blur of green. The village, hidden under the other spur of the hill, showed between luxuriant elms, golden-yellow now in the bright sun, only the slim upper part of the church spire. Beyond again was the far-receding level of the

Marsh, its grassland, its willows, always a little paled and silvered. Hugh gazed at it, almost invisible to him in its familiarity, and heard up above his head Miranda bounding noisily about her room and singing in a tone that was meant to be heard *Auprès de ma blonae*. She had a pretty little voice.

"I've had a letter from Sarah," he said. "Would you like to see it?"

"No, thanks," said Randall. He added, "Letters from Sarah give me a pain. She's treated me like a composite entity ever since I got married. She begins 'Dearest Ann and Randall', and ends 'With love to you both from us both, yours Sally'. As if 'love' could mean anything in a formula like that. And as if my dear brother-in-law had ever felt any emotions where I was concerned except amazement and contempt."

"Which you reciprocate."

"A meaningless man from a meaningless place. I suppose Sarah's all right?"

"She's pregnant again," said Hugh.

"God, not again!" said Randall. "Anyone would think they were bloody Roman Catholics. There's Jimmie, and Sally, and Penny, and Jeanie, and Bobby, and Timmie, and now there'll be Baby too. ~~Jesus Christ~~!"

"Ah, there's Penn," said Hugh looking down. He saw the boy emerge from the beech trees and drift across the wide space of lawn, his hands in his pockets. He seemed aimless and lost. The poor child was naturally a bit overwhelmed by England. Hugh hoped that he was not in too much of a daze to recall the drying up.

"What a pity that boy's got that accent," said Randall.

"I wish they'd sent him to a proper school, as I suggested," said Hugh. "That might at least have civilised his voice." Hugh had pressed Sarah to send Penn to a boarding school in Australia and had offered to pay the fees. The offer had been refused, with confused explanations from Sarah behind which Hugh could hear Jimmie's voice exclaiming that he was not going to have his son made a bloody snob of.

Randall, who disapproved of money spent on the Graham family, was silent for a moment, and then said, "He wants to be a motor mechanic anyway," as if that removed the scandal of the accent.

Miranda, dressed for church, erupted into the room, shot a quick glance at Hugh and ran to her father. Randall's face was illuminated. He swung his chair round and Miranda precipitated herself on to his knee, locking her arms tightly about his neck. "My little bird," he murmured, and his hand descended her back. Hugh turned away.

Miranda, after hugging him in silence for another moment, drew herself off and bounded out of the door. Randall looked after her smiling.

Hugh contemplated his son. Randall was certainly good-looking. He had a big imposing sensual face with a large nose and large brown eyes. His straight dry brown hair was copious and showed no traces of grey. His mouth pouted with sensitive humorous hesitation as if he were perpetually suspending judgment about a funny story that was being told. Only a slight moistness at eyes and mouth, a slight pale plumpness of cheek, aged him a little and touched his vitality with a faint shadow of indulgence and excess.

Hugh absently picked one of the roses out of the nearest bowl. Randall preferred the Moss roses and the old roses of Provence to the metallic pink of his own creations. Hugh looked at the rose. The petals, fading through shades of soft lilac, and bending back at the edges so that the rose was almost spherical, were closely packed in a series of spirals about a central green eye. He said to Randall, "Are you drinking too much?"

"Yes," said Randall. He got up and joined Hugh at the window. They both looked out.

While Hugh was hesitating about whether and how to pursue the subject they saw, far below, Ann and Miranda emerge from the porch and set off along the wide band of gravel that lay in front of the house. The two, hatted and gloved, seemed to trot with a conscious demureness. The men watched them go. There was always for Hugh something a little weird in the sight of Miranda on her way to church.

Hugh could smell Randall's breath now. He twirled the rose and tried to think of the right words. "I suppose you're worried—about Ann and so on?"

Randall made a violent inarticulate exclamation. "Worried? Christ!"

"What's wrong, really?"

"What's wrong? Everything's wrong." He was silent for a moment and then said thickly, "She just ruins me. She—she destroys my footholds."

Hugh became aware that his son was positively drunk. He said a little sarcastically, "Footholds? So you're climbing *up* are you?"

"Up or down it makes no difference," said Randall, "so long as it's away from her." He still stared at the place where his wife and daughter had disappeared. "Or rather," he said, and his stare became vaguer and his voice softer, 'it is, for me, up. Up to where I can move about, up into a world which has some sort of structure. Ann is awfully bad for me, you know."

"Bad for you—?"

"Yes. I ought to have people around me who have *wills*, people who take what they want. Ann has no will. She saps my energy. She makes me soft."

"If you mean," said Hugh, "that Ann is unselfish—"

"I don't mean that," said Randall, speaking faster. "I'm not interested in *that*. For someone else she may be a bloody little angel. But for me she's the destroyer, and the destroyer is the devil. She's got a kind of openness which makes whatever I do meaningless. Ah, I can't explain."

"If you mean she discourages you from writing—"

"She doesn't directly discourage me from anything. It's what she *is* that does it. And it isn't just writing either. Can't you see me fading away before your eyes, can't everyone see it? 'Poor Randall,' they say, 'he's hardly there any more.' I need a different world, a formal world. I need form. Christ, how I fade!" He laughed suddenly, turning to face Hugh, and took the rose out of his hand.

"Form?"

"Yes, yes, form, structure, will, something to encounter, something to make me *be*. Form, as this rose has it. That's what Ann hasn't got. She's as messy and flabby and open as a bloody dogrose. That's what gets me down. That's what destroys all my imagination, all the bloody footholds. Ah well, you wouldn't understand. *You* managed all right without fading away. What's it matter. Would you like a drink?"

"No, thanks. What do you—?"

"I'm suffocating here," said Randall, pouring some whisky with a shaking hand into one of the glasses. "And I can't stand the mess."

"Well, why don't you—"

"Ann's a hysterical woman."

"That's not true, as you perfectly well—"

"Never mind," said Randall. "Sorry, my nerves are all shot to pieces. Do have some whisky, for Christ's sake."

Hugh accepted some and sat down opposite Randall, who had sunk back into his chair looking blank and limp, the rose pendant from one hand. Hugh took a good gulp of the whisky. Some of Randall's momentary wildness had communicated itself to him, and as he gazed across he felt a thrill of pleasureable vitality which seemed to have little to do with the slumped figure of his son or the violence foreboded by those recent words. He looked round Randall's room where a powdery sunshine mingled the strewn books, the faded chintz, the cushions, the coloured prints, the china, of this rather feminine apartment into a pastel-shaded pot-pourri. He braced himself. "Was that Emma Sands I saw at the funeral?"

Randall jerked himself up. He thrust the rose back into the bowl. He smoothed his hair, looked away, looked back and said, "Yes, she was there. You saw her?"

"I caught a glimpse of her," said Hugh. "Who was the person with her?"

"A girl called Lindsay Rimmer, I think. Her secretary, companion person." A careful frown deadened Randall's face. Without losing Hugh's gaze he tilted his chair back against his divan bed, and reached out to where on the Welsh coverlet, geometrically figured in blue and white, Toby the toy dog and Joey the toy rabbit nestled shabbily together. He got hold of Toby and brought him on to his knee while he awaited Hugh's next remark.

"You see Emma occasionally?"

"Now and then, you know."

"Where does she live now?"

"In Notting Hill Gate," said Randall. He added, "In the same place."

A deep quietness had fallen between them during these exchanges as if other sounds in the room had been stilled.

Hugh was silent while Randall stared at him with his deadened watchful face and fondled the toy dog. The silence lasted long, trembling hideously with what might be said. It was a subject which could be named but could not be pursued. Yet the very name set the echoes ringing.

Hugh shivered and got up. "Ah well," he said. "I'm sorry you won't come to Seton. Now I'd better do that drying up if young Penn hasn't."

Chapter Four

"IT's good of Felix to be so kind to Ann," said Hugh.

He was standing with Mildred Finch in the big bow-window at Seton Blaise while Mildred arranged in a blue porcelain bowl the old-fashioned roses which Ann had brought her. Outside across the lawn, under the shadow of the huge cedar tree, Ann could be seen sitting on a seat with Mildred's brother. Here the sun had dried the garden and the open window let in a warm rich smell of mown grass and satisfied earth. The dark green shadows of the trees were just becoming fatter and longer and the colours more intense with a hint of evening. The glossy surface of the slow stream, like dark lacquer, could be seen beyond the cedar, disappearing from view where a thick clump of bamboos almost hid the little eighteenth-century bridge. In the foreground near the house Humphrey, thin and elegant in white shirt sleeves, inspected the flower-beds, occasionally casting an eye to where across the stream in the grove of chestnuts Penn and Miranda could intermittently be seen running: two strange half-grown creatures, uneasy with each other, unable to rest and yet unable to play.

"Yes, he's a kind-hearted boy," said Mildred absently. She thrust a white-quartered green-eyed Madame Hardy in between two lilac-shaded pink-scrolled Louise Odiers and stood back to admire the result.

"All the same," she said, "I must admit no one arranges flowers like Ann. I hope she'll do the flower-arrangement competition at the Women's Institute again this year! It always gives me a special pleasure to see her beat Clare Swann hollow."

Hugh, who was feeling very tired and more than usually troubled with the buzzing in his head, which today sounded like a perpetual distant murmur of voices, said defensively, "Clare's been very kind to us." Mildred's mild but almost universal malice depressed him sometimes.

"Why wouldn't she be?" said Mildred. "It costs her nothing and satisfies her curiosity. But however much she clicks her tongue, she wishes really that poor Douglas was a wild violent man like Randall."

Was Randall a wild violent man? Hugh did not know. He sat down on the arm of a chair and contemplated through the window the back of Humphrey's pure white copiously furnished head: deplorable but happy Humphrey.

"Do you think Randall is going to leave Ann?" asked Mildred. She added two Belles de Crécy to the left hand side of the bowl.

"No, certainly not," said Hugh. "He makes a fuss, but he'll stay. Ann irks him, but only Ann consoles him for it." He resented her casual curiosity. But he was not just putting her off; he believed what he said. He had seen his son like that before. He shifted his view to the scampering children across the stream. He recalled for a moment Randall's curious words of this morning: *I need a different world, a formal world*, and *You managed all right without fading away.* For a second, obscurely, he found himself envying Randall. Then it occurred to him paradoxically that perhaps Randall envied him. Randall saw him as a man who had overcome his difficulties.

To prevent further discussion of Randall he said to Mildred, "How's Beryl?" That always set her off.

Beryl was the Finchs' daughter and only child, never apparently forgiven by her mother for not being a boy. Beryl, now in her thirties, was the principal of a teachers' training college in Staffordshire. Hugh, at their rare meetings, had liked her, appreciating her evident cleverness. He had been, he felt naïvely, unable to decide whether Mildred's show of contempt for her daughter was sincere or not.

"Always the same!" said Mildred. "That girl will never marry. She's always being the self-conscious vanguard of something or other, and men hate that. I suppose there wasn't much chance for her to be normal, with Humpo as queer as a coot all his life. But I doubt if she's the other thing either. I'd like to think she had *some* fun." She stripped a papery pink and white Rosa Mundi of its leaves and thrust it into the centre.

Hugh was constantly shocked at a liberality of speech in Mildred which bordered, he sometimes felt, on the vulgar. Of course, he had known her a very long time, ever since Humphrey, then his fellow-student at Cambridge, had produced her as his fiancée. Humphrey had got a better first and Humphrey had made a richer marriage. Hugh contemplated her now. She was not exactly a feminine type herself. Not feminine as dear Fanny had been. Mildred had an acute face of a powdery paleness, tightened and much marked about the brow and eyes by quizzical horizontal lines, as if bound about by fine threads. The white skin of the cheeks by contrast had now a soft old look. The very blue eyes and the mouth were long, amused, often sarcastic. Her hair, a yellowish grey, had a short sensible cut which quite failed to control or even offer suggestions to its natural fluffiness, and her coiffure, never the same from day to day or even hour to hour, had often a positively unkempt appearance; for Mildred was not always impeccably turned out. Yet she was the handsome, clever, bustling Mildred still. And his mind groped again for details of that kiss; but he could still remember nothing except that it was summer at Seton Blaise and he had kissed her. That had been just before the Emma business started; so perhaps it was not surprising that the record had been erased. Mildred had known Emma too, long ago; they had been eccentric lady students together, with beribboned straw boaters and chaperones and skirts that brushed the ground. But they had quite lost touch later, and Hugh was satisfied that Mildred had received no confidences touching himself.

"I think that'll do, don't you?" said Mildred. She put the bowl of roses carefully on the mantelpiece. "It's not up to Ann's standard, but it's not bad for poor me. Now, where's your drink? No more? Well, let's pretend we're an ancient pair, shall we, and take a turn on the gravel?" She took Hugh rather formally by the arm and led him out toward the garden.

Everyone had felt relieved at coming to Seton Blaise. After the

43

slightly damp, slightly sinister, and more than slightly Randall-ridden atmosphere of Grayhallock, Seton Blaise seemed a haven of innocence and warmth. Here the summer was more established and more complete. The pretty Queen Anne house, with its pitted rosy-red bricks and its blunted grey stonework stretched its bland length with a certain luxuriant confidence, surrendering itself to the garden whose proportions were perfectly attuned to its own. There were no large views, as Seton Blaise was low-lying, surrounded by water-meadows. But the little park afforded its own vistas: the avenue through the chestnut grove to the lake, the turn of the river, a miniature reach, between the cedar tree and the bridge, the lawn sloping, with little copses of feathery shrubs, toward the main gates. The place was small, but beautifully composed; and seeming to have everything it appeared neither large nor small but merely perfect. Hugh had coveted it once; but that too belonged with needs and longings that had died.

He crossed the drive with Mildred. The very dark blue Mercedes stood at the side of the house, its handsome glistening form standing out in the more intense evening light against a long bed of yuccas and tree peonies. As Mildred led him diagonally across the lawn in the direction of a distant deck-chair, he saw that Miranda had ceased her scuttling and was hovering about Ann and Felix. As he watched he saw her throw a big armful of grass mowings on to Ann's lap. There was distant laughter. Outlined against the heavy leafy chestnut boughs, which at this point almost swept the ground, Humphrey was talking to Penn on the far side of the stream. Watching them as they moved off Hugh remarked, perhaps for the first time, a certain coltish grace in the boy. The pair disappeared between the chestnuts in the direction of the lake.

Mildred reached the chair and sank into it. Hugh sat down on a rug on the grass beside her, averting his eyes while she adjusted her skirt. Mildred often managed to have some untidy piece of petticoat showing. He poked gloomily into his ear in a vain attempt to mitigate the buzz. "Sorry, what did you say?"

"I said, 'Hugh, come with us to India'," said Mildred.

He looked up with surprise. "India? Are you going to India?"

"Felix and I are," said Mildred, "or so we hope. I can't get Humpo to come. He wants to go back to Rabat when the weather gets colder to stay with an old diplomat friend, and doubtless for some other fell purpose. Felix is between jobs at the moment, as you know. His next one is probably recruiting Gurkhas. He adores that. And I thought I might travel out with him. It would be such fun if you came too."

"How kind of you!" said Hugh. "But I'm afraid I couldn't possibly—" Then he reflected: in fact there is absolutely nothing to stop me.

"Nonsense, dear," said Mildred, with the quiet assured smile of one knowing his thought. Her long intent blue eyes were alight with humour and with a familiar air of friendly bossiness.

Hugh laughed. He rubbed his bald head. "Of course it *would* be possible. And I think it's an attractive idea. But it would cost a great deal. And I think I ought to stay here to—to keep an eye on things, you know."

"Don't give me these Civil Service answers, Hugh dear," said Mildred. "You've got quite enough money to spoil yourself and still leave those children more than's good for them. And we shall be taking to our beds forever soon enough. And as for keeping an eye on things, 'things' being Ann and Randall I presume, you said just now that you thought there was nothing to fear. In any case, you know quite well there's nothing you or anyone can do for those two. Leave them alone and they'll come home, bringing their tails behind them."

Hugh was silent. The idea was certainly tempting. He had never travelled much. Fanny had detested foreign travel. And to be free, to get right away. Yet did he really want to travel with Mildred?

"We'll see the Taj Mahal by moonlight!" said Mildred. "Why not?"

"It's a tragic country. It would make you sad to see it, Mildred."

"Don't be so stuffy and old," said Mildred. "It's a wonderful exciting country. Did you know Delhi was Humphrey's next assignment when that Marrakesh thing happened? It would have been his first big job."

Hugh had not known this, and he reflected that if he had never for a moment thought of Humphrey's broken career as a tragedy, that was a tribute to Humphrey.

"I bought so many books on India," Mildred went on, "practically a library. Then when we didn't go I was so terribly disappointed. I've never really got over it. I've had a thing about India ever since."

And if it had never occurred to him to think of Mildred as capable of disappointment, as capable indeed of being put out by anything, that was a tribute to *her*.

"I don't have to decide now, do I?" he said. "I doubt if it's possible. But I'll certainly think about it."

"Of course there's no hurry!" cried Mildred. "Felix's job isn't even definite yet. I thought we might go by boat, you know, if Felix still had a bit of leave left. That would be a nice rest for you. But anyway, think it over. And now, let's walk to the bridge, shall we, before dutiful Ann starts hurrying back to her spouse? She's already stayed longer than she threatened to."

Hugh got up stiffly. India. Why not? As Mildred said, their travelling days would soon enough be over. Yet in the sudden whirl of possibilities which her suggestion had evoked he felt that somewhere, though he could not at the moment discern it, there was an authoritative reason why he could not go.

"The midges down by the river are something dreadful," said Mildred. "Let me give you some citronella to keep them off."

She picked up a little bottle from beside the deck-chair, and, reaching up, dabbed some on to Hugh's neck. The strong curious smell invaded his nostrils; it invaded his mind. Mildred took his arm again and they began to pace slowly toward the river. The smell of the citronella troubled Hugh exceedingly. What a muddled state he seemed to be in today. Why was that particular smell in that particular place so oddly disturbing?

They reached the grey humped bridge with its two tiny semi-circular arches and its crumbling balustrade yellow with lichen. From the middle of the bridge they looked back down the little reach where a blue haze of forget-me-nots, growing out of the water, tangled about the verge of the tall flags and bulrushes which almost hid the lawn from view. The clump of slender bamboos, their thickly crowded stems as straight as spears, their drooping delicately fingered tops even on such an evening never still, enclosed the view toward the house. The robust chestnut foliage leaned to touch the stonework on the other side. The little sheet of murmuring water was screened and private.

Hugh leaned on the parapet and looked down. He descried in the sunny water the long waving tresses of the green weed. Then moving his gaze, and by a change of focus, he saw just below him in the stream the reflection of himself, and of Mildred who was leaning close beside him and also looking down. With that, and with a wild rush of distressed emotion the memory came up and he recalled the kiss. It had been here, exactly here, and at just such a moment when they had both paused and seen their reflections in the glass below them. They had seen their reflections; and then, as if prompted by those shades below, turning to each other, with a naturalness, passionately and in silence they had kissed. It must have been the citronella that made him remember; and he some-how knew, though he could not see it with the eye of his memory, that on that evening twenty-five years ago Mildred must, in exactly the same way, have dabbed the citronella on his neck. But the kiss, that he saw again in all its detail.

Hugh gazed. Their two faces, in the blurred reflection, looked young again. Then with a start he moved away from the parapet. Mildred was looking surprised at his abrupt movement. He could not, he felt, credit her with remembering. The accident of the citronella had been a charm which had worked for him but not for her. For a moment he was disappointed. Then he was relieved. They began to walk back toward the house.

Ann was coming across the grass now, vigorously pulled by

Miranda, laughing and trying to talk to Felix who followed just behind her.

"Ah, they're going—" said Mildred. She slowed down, and Hugh mended his pace to hers.

"Hugh," she said, "may I come and see you in London soon? I shall be there mostly for the next few weeks. I haven't seen the Tintoretto for such a long time. That would give me such pleasure."

"You are very kind to me, Mildred," said Hugh. "I'll give you a ring in London, shall I, and we can fix a day."

"And, Hugh—do come to Vishnuland."

He was feeling thoroughly disturbed, and anxious only to take his leave. India, yes, he would think about that. And in the not altogether painful turmoil of his spirit he tried again to discern what the reason was, the powerful reason, why he could not go. *O spare me a little, that I may recover my strength: before I go hence and be no more seen.*

They turned the edge of the house, beside the very dark blue Mercedes, in whose shining flank he saw reflected Ann and the tall figure of Felix Meecham who were following close behind. Miranda, who seemed to be more merry and prankish than usual, had raced ahead and was trying to swing on the door of the Vauxhall in a way which would do it no good.

"Did you see Emma Sands at Fanny's funeral?" he said suddenly to Mildred.

"Ah—" said Mildred. "My old college chum. Was she there? No, I didn't see her."

"Yes, she was there," said Hugh. "Odd, wasn't it. I mean, she hadn't seen Fanny in years."

"Emma always showed shocking taste," Mildred murmured. "Except perhaps once. Now if you'll excuse me I must go and find those two babes in the wood."

This speech, which left Hugh with intimations of more knowledge than he had credited her with, was the last which, on that occasion, she vouchsafed him *tête-à-tête*.

Chapter Five

"**O**F course most of these things are rather too young for you," said Ann. "Steve just never threw any of his old toys away." She opened the door of the big cupboard.

"You're sure you—" Penn murmured. He stood awkwardly behind Ann, stooping with an air of ineffectual helpfulness, while she rummaged in the cupboard.

It was the following Saturday. After breakfast Ann had asked Penn if he would like to look through Steve's old room to see if there was anything there that might amuse him. She couldn't think why she had not thought of this before, she said.

Penn was fascinated and troubled by this suggestion. Steve's room, still so called, the first-floor room over the front door, next to where Grandma had been, which was now only occasionally in use as an emergency spare room, had always been an object of somewhat eerie interest to Penn. He had never entered it before.

He looked round it now while Ann began to spread out the contents of the cupboard on the floor. It was a big room, airy and plain and modern, not like most of the cluttered-up rooms at Grayhallock. It had a big window and a window-seat and the view of the beeches. Still, it wasn't worth a dash compared with his own tower room. His tower room was much smaller, only half the size of the lower tower rooms which Ann and Randall had, and a third the size of this room. But it was so marvellously high up, with windows on both sides so that he had what he called the light view and the dark view. The light view was the south view toward the invisible yet somehow present sea over the flat faded Marsh where low aeroplanes continually nosed in toward Ferryfield Airport, and this could not be seen at all from Steve's room. The dark view was the northern view over a big hop field which he had watched become in these last months the greenest thing he had ever seen, to another darker plantation of mixed conifers beyond, as if the North

49

itself were coming into their backyard. He wondered why Steve had not had the tower room. Perhaps he hadn't been let. In those days, he had gathered from Nancy Bowshott, there had been 'living-in servants', and perhaps one of these 'servants' had occupied the undignified but wonderful little room.

"Well, it's a lot of junk really," said Ann. "But do just root about for yourself, Penny. Those are Steve's books in that bookcase. And the cupboard's all yours. I'll leave you to it, shall I?"

Penn, who was Penny in Australia but preferred to be Penn in England, knew that Ann called him Penny out of the kindness of her heart to make him feel at home, but he wished she wouldn't, especially since Miranda had said mockingly, "But it's a girl's name!"

"Thank you so much, Ann," he said. "Please don't wait. I'll just look round. If you're sure you don't mind——"

"Of course I don't mind!" said Ann. She looked at him in a sad affectionate way. "I wish I'd thought of it before. It's a *good* idea. Though I don't think you'll find much. It's child's stuff." She lingered at the door. "Penny, are you *sure* you want to stay with Humphrey in London?"

Humphrey Finch, who had been very nice to him last Sunday, had said he'd be glad to have him to stay in London and show him round. Everyone had seemed rather dubious about this, which was odd, as they'd been saying for ages, though without doing anything about it, that it was a pity he wasn't seeing anything of London. Humphrey Finch was nice, but Penn was sorry he hadn't been able to talk more to Colonel Meecham who had an M.C. Seton Blaise was nice too, but it hadn't got towers like Grayhallock. What he had liked best was the lake where, while Humphrey questioned him about his family, he had seen a kingfisher cross the water like a metallic blue bullet.

"Yes, I'd love to go, if that's all right."

"Well, yes, fine," said Ann. She still lingered. "Ah well. I must go and do the bonfire."

Penn closed the door firmly behind her. He was not at an age to be indifferent to loot. He felt, in any case, moved and excited, indeed thrilled in a dark way, at the idea of looking at Steve's things. His cousin whom he had never met, nearly two years his senior, had been an object of veneration to Penn from long ago, filling in his thought the place of the elder brother for whom, over-provided as he was with younger siblings, he frequently yearned. He had so much looked forward to meeting Steve one day, upon the constantly talked-of but constantly deferred English visit. He had imagined that, somehow, they would do remarkable things together. He had been exceedingly shaken by his cousin's death. It had been, indeed, his first experience of mortality.

He decided to look at the books first. The results were disappointing. Besides Shakespeare and all that, there were a large number of books on birds, but nothing about aeroplanes or ships or motor-bikes. Well, there was one book about *sailing* ships. And there was a book on veteran cars which looked promising. He put that on one side. Books about climbing there were, only Penn who had no head at all for heights was not interested in climbing. There were some boys' school stories and adventure stories, but no science fiction. There were two rather technical books about horses, but Penn, to the scandalised amazement of his English relatives who imagined Australians were always galloping across endless plains, was not able to ride a horse, and had no desire to learn, in spite of the offered loan of the Swanns' pony. The rest seemed to be mainly text-books, Latin grammars and such. There were a few Penguin novels, but they looked dull English tea-party stuff.

He turned his attention to the contents of the cupboard. Steve had evidently not shared Penn's passion for electrical gadgets. There was nothing electrical to be seen at all, except for an electric train set of *very* simple design. There were several mouth organs and several sorts of pipes of different sizes, but Penn had no musical talents. There were a number of teddy bears and things which he treated with stiff detachment, and quantities of board and counter games. There was a chess set, but Penn was not acquainted with chess. A box full of whistles and screws puzzled him until he decided they were devices for imitating bird calls. There was a big electric torch, but the battery was dead. There really seemed to be nothing at all that was worth taking away as loot. He opened a final big wooden box. It was full of the largest number of lead soldiers he had ever seen.

Penn had always had a passion, never by his impecunious family anything like fully indulged, for lead soldiers. He had wanted to be a soldier himself until he had decided more lately that he wanted to be a motor-mechanic, or as, ashamed of his cowardice, after realising that his English relatives for some reason disliked this phrase, he now termed it, 'an engineer'. Not over-bright at school, he had usually managed to get good marks in History because of a passionate interest in matters of weapons, uniforms and machinery of war, to which a few other facts about what was going on managed to adhere. He delved into the box.

Black Watch, Rifle Brigade, the Blues, the Royal Marines, Gurkhas, Sappers, Scots Greys. He began to set them out on the floor. Then he stopped. "Child's stuff," Ann had said. He looked at the soldiers and sat back on his heels. Of course, he never played with soldiers now at home. He even stood by in a good-natured way while Timmie and Bobby mis-called, ill-treated and broke up his once-precious battalions. He began to put Steve's soldiers back into the box. Then he was taken by a sudden rush of emotion as if, he didn't know why, he might even weep.

Penn had so long and so desperately looked forward to coming to England, he had scarcely admitted to himself, let alone to his family, that when the time came to leave home he could hardly bear it. The aeroplane flight and the excitement of arriving had consoled him of course. But since then everything had been depressing and disappointing. Grandma dying had been so awful. And he found his English relatives alien to a degree which, he felt, they themselves quite failed to realise. He was perfectly aware, of course, that they all felt that his mother had married not exactly beneath her, but, well, unsuitably, regrettably. He was aware more obscurely that they were all, well, a little disappointed in him. He was not a patch on Steve, of course; he was prepared to admit this himself. And if his Uncle Randall sometimes seemed positively to dislike him, it was perhaps only natural, since Penn was alive while Steve was dead.

He had not minded, what they reproached themselves about most, their not having got him into a school. He was really rather relieved about this, since what an English school suggested to him most of all was the idea of being beaten: an experience which he had never had and the possibility of which he regarded with a mixture of fear and thrilled awe. He had not minded mooching about at Grayhallock—he was better at amusing himself than they imagined—though he would be sorry to go home without having seen a bit more of England. But he was depressed by the countryside which they all thought so pretty, and constantly exclaimed about instead of taking it for granted. He disliked its smallness, its picturesqueness, its outrageous greenness, its beastly wetness. He missed the big tawny air and the dry distances and the dust; he even missed the barbed wire and the corrugated iron and the kerosene tins: he missed, more than he would have believed possible, the absence of the outback, the absence of a totally untamed beyond.

He was not able, and this was what depressed him most of all, in any way to settle down with his English relations. Grandpa and Ann liked him of course, and he was fond of them, but it was all so awkward. He could not see into their ways. It irked him that even Ann, who was so kind, did not treat Nancy Bowshott as an equal. This instance of class-prejudice so constantly before his eyes incited him to such a degree that he had adopted an air of ostentatious affability and mateyness with Nancy: until he became aware that she thought he was flirting. After his alarmed withdrawal, coldness set in between them. This hurt him very much.

The strained and precarious relationship between Ann and Randall, which he had been quite unprepared for, was also a constant source of pain and surprise. After his own noisy argumentative affectionate family it seemed to him scarcely credible that two married people could continue on such terms, being so cold and mysterious to each other and so *silent*: he was shocked. Randall had now been in a state of sulky retirement in his room for about ten days, ever since they had returned from London, and no one seemed to think it particularly odd. Ann did not run to coax him out. She just accepted his sequestration. At home somebody would be *laughed* out of such childish conduct! It was all so *irrational*, he thought, using one of his father's most favoured terms of abuse. Yet whenever he thought of Randall there brooding up above in his room, he shivered. He was afraid of his uncle.

As he squatted in Steve's room in the wet green light in front of the big box of soldiers he thought with renewed longing of his own home, the lovely new-built bungalow at Marino, with its multi-coloured roof under the shadow of the great dry rustling blue gum tree: so clean and airy and modern, with its floors of precious jarrah wood and its lemony peachy garden. They had only lived there a year, since his father's promotion, and he had not got used to the wonder of it yet. Before that they had lived in Mile End, nearer to Port Adelaide, and made do with a week-end shack at Willunga. But now it was like a holiday all the time, with the sea filling half of space, and the white sand below, and the uncleared gum above, and the cries of galahs and kookaburras to wake you up in the morning. That was a real place.

As he put a few more of the soldiers back into the box he caught a glimpse, through the interstices of the jumbled figures, of something else lying at the bottom. He unpacked again carefully until he could thrust his hand down. What he drew out was a very beautiful modern dagger, a soldier's dagger, the kind that really meant business. The leather sheath, from which two metal chains depended, was dark and supple, and the instrument came out of it with sizzling sweetness. The blade was as bright as a mirror and terrifyingly sharp. Now this was worth having, this was real loot. He stood up and brooded delightedly over the dagger, trying the edge and the point with his finger. He examined the hilt. It was black, beautifully enamelled, and within a circle near the top was a small white swastika. It must have been a German officer's dagger. He let it drop from his hand and it stuck trembling and quivering in the floor boards between his feet. He restored it to its sheath and thrust it into his pocket. It was a most sinister thing, and he loved it.

He repacked the soldiers and put the other things back into the cupboard. He picked up the veteran car book. He could feel the dagger heavy inside his pocket, touching his thigh, imparting power. He felt himself lifted to a higher plane of detachment as if some little movement in the mysterious and irreversible process of growing up had become momentarily perceptible. He looked down at the wooden box of soldiers. He was a free man, his own judge, and he would do exactly what he pleased. He decided to take the soldiers to his room.

He emerged into the corridor with the box under his arm and closed the door behind him. The long corridor, known for some reason as 'the gallery', was rather dark, since the big northern window which was supposed to light it had been walled in when 'that Orange vandal', as Grandpa called him, had built, across the once handsome stairhead, a mean draughty little room for some 'servant'. The light now came from the two extremities of the house, where in a whirl of ornate white-painted metal banisters, the two circular staircases rose to the towers, and a cold light streamed down from above. Penn could not now, as he emerged, help glancing about him a little guiltily. He saw, with a certain chill, that Miranda was sitting on the stairs which led up to her own tower.

His little cousin was an unsolved problem to Penn. He could not have imagined her beforehand, and indeed he did not try; but he had brought nevertheless in his luggage a special piece of affection labelled with her name. He was made at the first overtures to feel a simpleton, and this gift had never been delivered. Yet *what* in her thus defeated him he did not know, as he watched her, remote as a cat, playing with her dolls, and realised with shame that he did not even know her age and did not now dare to ask. She was certainly not a bit like Jeanie. The grown-ups seemed to expect them to play together, but her company made him uneasy, and the nearest they got to mateyness was on occasions when she teased him into excitement and then snubbed him for being rough. She was, and this he took for granted, a superior and special little girl. She was a green sprite, something composed out of the green watery light of England. But he was not at all sure that he liked her.

She was sitting sideways on the stairs, her feet tucked under her, leaning her head against the banisters, as if she had been waiting for him to come out, while two of her dolls with legs dangling sat on the stair below. The little cold group of strange beings regarded him. Sitting there quite still, beyond the dusk of the corridor, picked out in the light from the staircase windows, they seemed like something in a play, at some moment when the main character is immobile at the back of the stage; only now their stillness in the chilly light in the dreary cage of the staircase suggested some jumbled and senseless drama in a dream.

Penn felt disconcerted, and thought at first that this was because of the soldiers. The next moment he thought that it was because Miranda had seen him coming out of her dead brother's room. The moment after he no longer knew why at all. He could not salute her as he had his hands full, and speech seemed impossible. So he nodded his head to her and turned hastily in the direction of his own tower. He wished she had not seen him. He wished she had not been there.

Chapter Six

THE big brightly lit stone-flagged kitchen was silent except for the click of dominoes and the perpetual purring of the Aga cooker. The shutters were closed and barred. The long rows of blue dishes on the dresser gleamed like so many approving Dutch cherubs. Hugh calculated that tomorrow he could decently tell Ann that he was leaving on Tuesday.

It was the evening of Saturday after supper. At the long deal table, its legs half clawed away by generations of cats, its surface blanched by years of scrubbing to the colour of light sand, Douglas Swann and Penn were playing dominoes. Miranda had gone to bed. Ann was sewing. Hugh was smoking his pipe and watching the others. Every now and then Ann looked up and smiled, at anyone who caught her eye, a pale encouraging smile.

Hugh reflected that it was a peaceful scene, a scene even of positive innocence: an innocence to which Penn youthfully, Swann professionally, and Ann with some more subtle resonance of the spirit, contributed each their note. Ann was certainly being bravely cheerful in a way which both exasperated Hugh and half compelled his admiration. He himself contributed nothing, he was the spectator. But then he was always the spectator, he reflected with a sad satisfaction which was a sign of returning vitality. He puffed his pipe and contemplated the happy little family group. Randall, it was true, was still brooding upstairs like an unexploded bomb. But even the thought of Randall seemed now less alarming. By a kind of inertia things were slowly subsiding back to normal; and from that point, he obscurely felt, his own new life would begin. The danger point was passed by now. Randall had been practically incommunicado for ten days, and if one were disposed to find things odd one might find this rather odd. But why be so disposed?

Ann, who was after all the person most affected, seemed to take it calmly enough; so calmly that Hugh, who had not discussed the matter with her, suspected that perhaps after all she had some subterranean mode of communication with her husband. Perhaps, contrary to appearances, she was seeing something of him. Perhaps she visited him when everyone else was in bed. In any case it was clear that there was nothing *he* could do about it. He had visited Randall once or twice since their conversation about 'the formal world', but had found his son remote and dreamy and more than usually evasive. Randall was drinking steadily. On the other hand he seemed peaceful, even cheerful, and had an air as of one positively meditating. The absurd siege could not last forever. The situation was too ridiculous for even Randall to sustain. He must soon return to some version of his normal condition wherein, unable to be in Ann's presence without irritation, he nevertheless followed her everywhere and could scarcely, while he was in the house at all, let her out of his sight. From this irritated and obsessive state his present isolation seemed like a disciplined abstention, from which some notable purging of the humours might be hoped to follow. It could even be that Hugh's departure would hasten the armistice.

So he reasoned. But, with a pleasantly complacent sense that he was justified in cherishing himself, he was clear that whatever the outcome of *that* argument he would stay no longer at Grayhallock. The big indifferent house, upon which the unhappiness of him and his had made so little impression, and where the phantoms of his sadness were without a resting place, seemed a device of punishment which was not designed for him. He had not made and deserved this cage and he could and would step out of it. He would exert himself later to help those that remained behind. Meanwhile he had had enough of Ann's worthiness, Randall's sulks, Swann's piety, Miranda's pranks, Penn's accent, and the gawky rows of dripping rose bushes. He thought of his cosy London flat and the glowing Tintoretto, and it seemed a shrine of refuge.

He wanted too to pass another stage in the distance that separated him from Fanny. He felt pain, he missed her; but part of missing her was knowing, with a cunning of the soul which he could but partly sanction, by what devices he could miss her less. He was able, he found already, to console himself; and he offered up to her, a melancholy wreath of homage, his consciousness of the inevitability of such consolation. The dead are the victims of the living, and he would live. Already he felt, from her death, obscurely more alive. She fed him. So it was, with misgivings yet relentlessly, that he wished to distance himself from her more accusing image, from the cat-hugging Fanny of the patience-cards and the swallows, the last really humanly-present Fanny that he had known. At the clinic she had been frightened with a fear which he could not contemplate; and then she had put on, or had had imposed upon her, the impersonality of the officially dying. With that, Hugh also wanted to escape from Ann, and from the way in which Ann's gentle, transparent, more reflective personality kept Fanny disconcertingly alive. Ann's consciousness of the matter seemed to leave no place for consolation, for that symbolic second slaying of the dead. But then Ann was unhappy and correspondingly unfair.

Laughter and the clatter of the dominoes being piled together on the table marked the end of another game. Ann was telling Penn that it was time for bed, and Penn was arguing that it was too early, and Douglas Swann was pleading for another round, and now Ann was smiling and giving way. Yes, it was an innocent little world. It was an innocent little world, except that Steve was dead and Randall was drunk upstairs and Emma Sands was at this moment existing somewhere in London.

After the violence of death, its unavoidable shock and horror, as his disturbed spirit began to compose into a fresh pattern, as the thoughts which came to him in the early morning began to take on form and structure again, he found that Emma Sands occupied a new and significant place. It was as if she had crept up on him, and he had turned to find her, large as life, sitting there. He was haunted by the image, the snapshot vision, which he had received in the cemetery, of Emma and the girl, black rainswept figures, clinging grotesquely together. He had reached indifference, he had passed into forgetfulness: he thought. But now Emma grew in his mind;

and the previous occasions of seeing her, so oddly spaced out through the past years, the bus occasion, the escalator occasion, the National Gallery occasion, fed retrospectively by the cemetery occasion, glowed and burgeoned in his memory.

He knew, of course, his own absurdity, knew even something of the mechanics of this tiny obsession, and how it had jerked into more evident life when Mildred had suggested the trip to India. Why could he not go to India? Because—yet why because?—of Emma. Emma still, magnetically, existed; and he had time too to reflect on how instinctively he classed her with the dark free things, with that other shapely world of the imagination into which he had failed, and he found himself using Randall's metaphor, to 'climb' at that crucial period of decision twenty-five years ago. But of course these ideas were without worth, cobwebs and mere childish haunt-ings which he needed only the time for drawing a deep breath to blow away altogether. He already knew, and he anticipated with pleasure the little struggle he would have with himself, that he would eventually decide to go to India with Mildred. That is what he would do. Ah, he would be free, he would show them all how much an old man could alter. In Vishnuland what avatar.

"Now, Penny, you really must be off!" said Ann. She put aside the blue-and-white check dress of feather-weight cotton which she was sewing for Miranda, pushed her loose loops of faded hair back behind her ears, and made a mock-stern face at Penn. He got up laughing and protesting.

"Well, well, my friends, I must go too," said Douglas Swann. "Penn shall set me an example! Weakness of will, that's our trouble, eh Penn? Up and away!" He rose too.

Swann was a good-looking man with a sallow face of great smoothness which seemed not to know of the razor. Into the smooth mask, the colour of honeysuckle, a pair of narrow dark eyes and a thin dry clearly outlined mouth had been let, as it were by an after-thought, so little were they, by any puckering or wrink-ling of the surface, worked into their surroundings. His very dark hair, lacquered with hair oil, was combed in a neat crust over his brow. He had, with his rather smart black suit and crisp dog-collar, a professional air of slightly self-conscious benevolence, a sort, as it were, of clinically compassionate stoop. Yet, and this too Hugh had had occasion to remark, although the context for thinking him an ass was almost completely there, the judgment could not quite be made: the elusive but indubitable light of intelligence flickering in that mild visage forbade any too casual dismissal of its owner.

Penn, tossing his dry mouse-locks, his small perky face animated with argument and affection, was still disputing with Ann, one foot on the coke bucket, one hand in the pocket of his dark grey English-purchased flannels, pushing back his blue school blazer to reveal, hanging from his belt by two metal chains, a leather sheath containing a dagger.

"That's a dangerous weapon!" said Douglas Swann, pointing to the dagger.

Penn blushed and removed his foot from the coke and pulled his blazer down.

Ann said, "Good heavens, that German dagger! Did you find it in Steve's room?"

"Yes," said Penn, distressed. "Is that all right?"

"Why, yes, of course," said Ann. "But how clever of you to find it. Felix Meecham gave it to Steve. Felix got it during the war sometime. And Miranda was very keen on it and kept asking Steve to give it to her, but he never would. Then when—we couldn't find it, though Miranda looked endlessly."

"Oh, I'll give it to Miranda!" said Penn. "Well, of course, it's hers anyway. I'm so sorry—" He was still blushing and trying to detach the dagger from his belt.

"No, no, certainly not!" said Ann. "You keep it! Miranda's forgotten all about it by now. It's more a boy's thing anyhow. Now off you go, Penny, this very instant!"

The door closed behind him, and Douglas Swann sat down again, having evidently changed his mind about going.

"I thought it was a horrible thing, that dagger," said Ann. "It's beautifully made of course, but it's got a swastika on the hilt. Felix said it belonged to a German officer. They used to wear daggers, some of them, to show off with. The whole idea is so repulsive. One never stops loathing Hitler, and the sight of that black object with the swastika on it—it's enough to make one feel quite sick!"

"The young are not touched by this," said Douglas Swann. He was sorting the dominoes into neat piles.

"No, I suppose not," said Ann. "It's a rather disconcerting aspect of their innocence. I never know whether one should teach them to hate Hitler or not."

"Of course one should," said Hugh.

"I'm not so sure," said Swann. "There's enough hatred in the world already. Only love has clear vision. Hatred has cloudy vision. When we hate we know not what we do."

"Are you suggesting that we should love Hitler?" said Hugh. He felt irritated with Swann and wished he would go.

"Not exactly," said Swann. "That would be, from the point of view of our generation, an impossible task, except perhaps for a saint. But there can be, even for Hitler, a sort of intelligent compassion. Involuntary hatred is a great misfortune, but cultivated hatred is a positive evil. The young have escaped the terrible compulsion to hate which has been our lot. They should be left uncorrupted and judged lucky."

"I can't agree," said Hugh. "It's a matter of practical politics. You speak as if we were in fact all saints. As the world runs, evil soon makes tools out of those who don't hate it. Hatred is our best protection."

"Would you like some coffee, Douglas, before you go?" said Ann.

Douglas Swann rose again, accepting his dismissal. "No thank you, Ann, I must run. Talk about weakness of will! Oh, I forgot to say, Clare wants to know if you're going in for the flower-arrangement competition this year. She said she hoped so much you would, as without you the women get no idea of the standard."

Ann laughed. "Perhaps, if I feel strong enough. Give my love to Clare. And thank her for the quince jelly."

PART ONE

Douglas Swann lingered, his arm on the back of Ann's chair, his smooth golden face bland and tender above the stiff dog-collar. The Aga cooker purred. The blue cherubs smiled. Hugh looked at his watch.

The kitchen door burst open and swung back to strike the wall with a noise like a pistol shot and Randall entered. Douglas Swann jumped away from Ann with as much alacrity as if he'd been caught kissing her. Ann half rose and then sat back again.

Randall, seeing Swann there, paused abruptly on the threshold and glared at him. Then he held the door open. Swann murmured that he must be off and shot past Randall through the doorway. The door banged behind him. It was not a dignified exit.

Randall was unshaven and in shirt sleeves. His shirt ballooned out over his trousers in the front, giving him a false paunch which made him look more than usually like an actor. His face was flushed. He advanced to the table and stared at Ann.

Hugh said, "Sit down, Randall, and stop looking like Banquo's ghost." At such a moment he feared his son.

Randall said to Ann, "Must we have that bloody priest infesting the house all the time?"

Ann sat well back in her chair, stretching her hands out on the arms as if to calm herself with deliberation. She gave him back his stare. "He's not a bloody priest, and he doesn't infest the house. He came over to see Penny."

"He came over to see you," said Randall, "as you bloody well know. Not that I care a fuck."

"Sit down, Randall," said Hugh, "and don't shout!"

"I'm not shouting," said Randall, "and I'm NOT DRUNK, in case it should occur to anyone to suggest it!"

"You are drunk," said Ann.

Hugh knew that Ann was capable of anger, but he was surprised by the readiness with which she produced it now. If Randall had prepared himself, by his own version of prayer and fasting, for this scene, so doubtless had she.

"Why did you give all Steve's things to Penn?" said Randall. He lowered his voice, but Hugh could see now that he was shivering with rage. His lips trembled and in a slower rhythm his hands opened and closed.

"I didn't give all Steve's things to Penn. I told him he could look through the cupboard to see if there was anything there that might amuse him." Ann was dead white and with her colourless hair swept back her face was naked and strong. She clutched the arms of the chair and kept her voice low.

"We mustn't call you a liar, must we?" said Randall. "Miranda saw Penn taking armfuls of stuff out of Steve's room this afternoon." He leaned forwards, his pendant shirt brushing the dominoes, his eyes bulging, his large hands spread out on the table.

"Well, why not?" said Ann. "Why shouldn't someone enjoy those things? Steve wouldn't have minded."

"It didn't occur to you that Miranda might mind, that I might mind?"

"If you'd been about I might have asked you," said Ann. "You weren't about." She was quiet, but quivering taut.

"You could have asked Miranda."

"Look here," said Ann, 'why ever should I? What I did was perfectly proper. God knows, we've given Penny a rotten enough time. I had no need to consult anyone."

"Randall," said Hugh, rising to his feet, "may I suggest—"

"*Perfectly proper*, Jesus Christ!" said Randall. "You just don't care how much you hurt Miranda. You've upset her dreadfully. You betray Miranda and you betray Steve. God, I hate you, Ann!"

"*Stop that!*" said Hugh. It was too late.

Ann got up, pushing her chair violently back. It screeched along the stone-flagged floor. "That's not true!" she said. "You don't give me an ounce of support. You hide upstairs for days and then you come rushing down to make a scene as soon as you think you've got something—"

"Don't you shout at me, you hysterical bitch. And you can tell that damn boy to put all that stuff back at once. And if you don't, I will!"

"Oh no you won't!" said Ann. She stood stiffly by her chair, her hands at her sides. "You leave Penny alone. And don't speak to me like that and don't look like that. You frighten me. I'm tired out and I can't stand it. I won't have you upsetting the boy. We have duties to the living as well as to the dead."

"I see—Penn's alive—and Steve is dead, so we don't have to bother about him any more—"

"Oh, don't be so hideously *cruel*!" said Ann, her voice rising at last. "How can you *use* Steve like that, you're *using* him—"

"You torture me, you torture me!" cried Randall, and he lifted up the end of the table and banged it savagely on the floor. "You take everything from me, you take even Steve from me!" His voice rose to a scream.

"Randall, *control yourself*!" Hugh gripped his son's violently trembling arm.

Without a glance Randall shook him off. "I've a bloody good mind to clear off to London!"

"Well, clear off!" cried Ann. "You expect me to wear myself out running the nursery single-handed to earn money for you to spend in London—"

"You've gone too far now!" roared Randall. As he moved half way round the table Ann moved quickly behind her chair; but he paused, and with a whirl of his hand which made Hugh flinch back he swept the dominoes off on to the floor. They clattered loudly away through the kitchen in all directions. "You make me miserable and take everything away from me and then you have the insolence to taunt me about money! I'm not going to stay in this house another bloody minute! And you can have your precious Penny and your precious priesty all to yourself!"

There was a moment's silence. Then Ann dropped her head. She said nothing. She stooped and began to pick up some of the dominoes.

"Stop putting on an act, Randall," said Hugh quietly. "Now may I suggest—"

"Did you hear me, damn you?"

"Yes," she said tonelessly, as she put the dominoes back on the table.

He stared at her for another moment and then went out banging the door.

Ann stood looking down at the table. Then she burst into violent sobbing. "Oh, I shouldn't have lost my temper, I shouldn't have said those things—"

"Don't grieve, Ann," said Hugh. He felt tired and disgusted and ashamed, yet he felt now too as if he had foreseen it all. He put an arm round her. "Don't you see it was a put-up job? You hadn't a chance. He was obviously determined to go away, and he just wanted a scene so that he could pretend to himself that it was your fault."

"No, no," said Ann, weeping. She wiped her eyes on Miranda's dress. "I'll go up and persuade him—"

"It'll be no use," said Hugh. He watched her gloomily. Now he would have to stay at least till Thursday.

PART TWO

Chapter Seven

RANDALL stretched his legs out comfortably on the big sofa and wriggled his back into the cunningly arranged pile of cushions behind him. He drew a little nearer to him the delicate table which held his cup of tea and a pink flowery plate with a diminutive sugar-cake upon it. He took a sip of the sweet Lapsang Suchong. "Come, come," he said. "Surely you knew I'd come back?"

Emma Sands and Lindsay Rimmer looked at each other. "What shall we say to him?" said Lindsay.

"We might say that we hadn't given the matter a thought," said Emma, "but he wouldn't believe that, would he?"

"If we say we were expecting him every day he'll begin to think he's important," said Lindsay.

"But he *is* important, isn't he?" said Emma. The two women laughed and Randall smiled with satisfaction. It was good to be back.

A golden afternoon sunlight, spread out now in a soft web upon the permanent mist of tobacco smoke, filled Emma's big drawing-room, which was crowded with slightly shabby, slightly dusty, beautiful things. It revealed the cleverly darned Turkey carpet and the cleverly mended porcelain and made its daily contribution to the further fading of the chintz curtains whose powdery haze of pink and blue birds was still just discernible against a threadbare tawny background. The room, which was on the ground floor, had windows on both sides, one looking through tall iron railings at the street, and the other looking on to a small lawn planted around with spherical bushes of veronica and laurestinus, whose dusty leaves and dry stems, dark and immobile in the cruel sunlight, made them seem now like grotesque indoor objects which had been temporarily put out of the room. It was a garden designed for winter and in the summer it looked sleepy and sulky. It was however no concern of Emma's, being maintained by the management of the flats wherein she lived, a large red-brick Edwardian block amid the early Victorian façades of creamy stucco in that part of Notting Hill.

The two women sat with their backs to the sun, which gave them each a halo, Emma's a jagged haze about her frizzy dark grey mop, and Lindsay's a thin smooth semicircle of brighter gold about the already bright gold of her neatly coiled hair. They were both doing *petit-point* embroidery on circular frames. Randall faced the light. He felt revealed, cornered, happy.

"Terrible as my lot is here," said Randall, "I assure you it was even more terrible there."

"I don't think his lot is so terrible, do you?" said Lindsay.

"Certainly not," said Emma, "Considering how bad he is, we let him off very easily on the whole."

"We hardly *ever* beat him," said Lindsay. She held the embroidery frame away from her, admiring the effect.

"Ah, but you don't understand my sufferings!" said Randall. "I won't always behave well, I warn you. One day I'll break out. You'll see!"

"He'll break out," said Lindsay. "What *fun*. More tea, Emma dear?"

Emma removed her glasses and set her embroidery aside. She caressed her closed eyes for a moment with long fingers. "A fag, sweetie."

Lindsay rose to light it for her. Their hands touched, golden in the sunshine as some complexity by Fabergé.

"But meanwhile, my dearest gaolers," said Randall, "I'm delighted to be here." He looked affectionately round the room, to which the puffing Gauloise was now adding a momentary intensification of the sunny haze and the old familiar tobacco smell. Emma, part of whose witchery it was to seem older than she could possibly be, had contrived to give the room an Edwardian look, and appeared in the midst of it, her voluminous nylon dress seeming like transparent muslin, her silver-topped walking-stick half lost in the folds, Edwardian herself. Even her tea-table was a tea-table in some now vanished sense. Only her tape-recorder, dog-like at her feet, recalled the present age.

He added, "It was hell at Grayhallock. Everyone was watching me to see what I'd do, to see which way I'd jump, to see how long I'd stay. I was slowly suffocating. I can't think how I stood it so long before."

After a pause Emma said, "I don't suppose people were all *that* much interested in your doings, except for Ann. In my experience people's real interest in each other is very small. Even the most delicious gossip dies quickly. Don't you think so, Lindsay?"

"Yes," said Lindsay. "Hardly anyone *really* notices either how good one is or how bad one is. Which I suppose is consoling, given that one is more often bad than good."

It was always like that. They never let him really complain. With an air of fastidious good taste they would turn his complaints away into general conversation. This sense of being petted, permitted, indulged and ultimately bullied exasperated Randall, yet gave him, too, a sort of agreeable shiver. He enjoyed the outbursts and the little feeling of guilt afterwards. Still, they led him on, they provoked him, in a way which satisfied their curiosity while leaving them guiltless. He idolised the serene quality of their egoism.

It was now over a year since Randall had fallen in love with Lindsay Rimmer. He had been, for nearly fifteen months, quite desperately in love. But the course of his love had been a strange one. He had come to see Emma, with whom he had previously had a slight party-going acquaintance, in order to ask her help and advice about getting his plays put on. He had also come to satisfy a persistent curiosity concerning his father's former mistress, about whose person in his imagination a certain lurid light had always played. He had, in that episode in the life of his slow orderly parent, an obsessive interest wherein resentment on his mother's behalf had no part; and his feelings had always veered between a sort of admiration and a sort of disappointment. The thought of it all certainly excited him and he wanted to see Emma. He came to observe her. He saw Lindsay and was instantly enslaved.

Lindsay Rimmer was not in the ordinary sense a particularly accomplished or a particularly distinguished girl. She was, to the very discerning nose, possibly even not a very *nice* girl. Her age, never divulged, was certainly a trifle over thirty. She came from Leicester, where she had been first a clerk, then a dental receptionist, and then a reporter on a local newspaper. Her general culture had startling *lacunae*, although, because she was also a clever girl, they rarely showed. She had come to London four years ago in search of adventure and in answer to an advertisement of Emma's for a secretary and companion. She was, whatever her other short-comings, undeniably beautiful, with a pale complexion, very rounded head, long golden braids of hair, large brow and great expressive light brown eyes. She resembled Diane de Poitiers, and had round small breasts which would have delighted Clouet, and with which Randall's acquaintance had been but brief and tentative; since Emma intervened.

Randall's love for Lindsay had come violently and suddenly, the entire transformation of the world in a second, a wild cry after long silence, the plunge of a still stream into a deep ravine. This falling in love was, he felt, the best thing he had ever done. It had that absolute authority which seems to put an act beyond the range of right and wrong. It had a splendour. Before it Randall had passed years of restlessness, weary of Ann, weary of the nursery, weary of himself, and yet not able to conceive of any other life. He had had two or three scrappy love affairs, but they had seemed to him, even at the time, senseless and ugly. He only half believed in his plays, only half believed that they represented a way of escape. There had been in his unhappiness no touch of fury or madness, only a dreary whining discontent. Steve had died; and after that there had been black lassitude and drink. And then he had met Lindsay.

Randall saw her, he was certain, with a clear eye. He was no longer a romantic boy; and this very fact made the sovereign violence of his love the more astonishing, the more worthy of complete and ruthless adhesion. He had never, he felt, really *seen* Ann when he loved her; and had indeed married her under certain complete misapprehensions about her character. But Lindsay, without illusion, he saw. He took her in, for what she was, her whole person: and her aroma of tough slightly ruthless even slightly vulgar vitality drove him mad. It even delighted him that she was the tiniest bit, but patently, 'on the make'. Some people, those ones with the discerning noses, might have called her calculating or sly; but with him she was honest, in a gorgeous and unpretentious way which made her little clevernesses all the more attractive. With him she was honest, she was open, and what was best of all about her, except perhaps for her resemblance to Diane de Poitiers, she was divinely indifferent to ordinary morality, she was, he felt, free. She was his angel of unrighteousness, so he often told her, and through her he enjoyed a most exhilarating holiday from morals. She was, he delighted to tell her, a demon, but an angel for him, heartless, but warm for him, a natural tyrant, but for him a liberator, evil, but for him good. She was indeed his good, that toward which his whole being magnetically swung. The madness, the fine fury, had come at last.

And Lindsay loved him: the miracle of that still retained its freshness. Taken by surprise, she had hesitated only a moment after his first cry. Then she had opened her arms. There had followed days of drunken beauty when they had wandered about half fainting hand in hand, and he had shown her things she had never seen and given her things she had never had, and watched the tall structure of her demonic self-assurance shiver and bow to the ground before him. That had been sweet indeed. He had only, and how often later he cursed himself for it, because of some lingering weakness caught in his years of frailty, because of some fear of her which persisted, because in a way he felt so certain and did not want to hurry, not possessed her; and then there had been Emma.

Emma had descended upon them with something which was not exactly anger, though it had seemed like anger in the first days; later it had seemed more like love. Whatever it was it had been like a storm. What exactly happened Randall did not know. But when the first whirl subsided he found himself confronted not with Lindsay, but with Lindsay and Emma. It was not that Lindsay's will had been subdued, for Lindsay was altogether unsubdued. It was as if she had moved smartly into another dimension, or on to a higher plane, and now looked down at him merrily with undiminished love through a barrier of glass. She was become suddenly as inaccessible as a Vestal Virgin. He was certainly still loved. Only now he was loved by both; and at times he wondered whether he were not coming, by some chemistry of the situation, or by some more positive influence of their wills, to be in love with both.

He now scarcely saw them except together; for they relentlessly chaperoned each other. He attended upon them, or more precisely he visited them, since Emma rarely stirred abroad, in a manner which would not have disgraced the most solemn of Jane Austen's beaux. When in their company alcohol never passed his lips. He was sober, quiet, serviceable, docile, and, alas, chaste. It was at times incomprehensible to him how he had come, to this extent, to kiss the rod. He desired Lindsay no less than before. He knelt trembling to her physical presence. The magnetism, the tension between them had not slackened, and he apprehended with continually renewed pleasure her half-concealed excitement at his arrival. Yet this totally inexplicit, never-discussed, 'temporary solution' had lasted now for nearly a year and all three parties seemed to have settled into it with zest. Randall was well aware of the deliberation with which they weakened him, with which they turned his love-relation .nto a play-relation. Yet he felt strangely little resentment. The strains and paradoxes were thrills and pleasures, and he came even to delight in the convention whereby his love for Lindsay was supposed to be still a secret; and the nearest he could come to his satisfaction was the guilty enjoyment of Lindsay's dry-lipped kisses while Emma's stick tapped slowly across the next room. It was, in fact, a pleasure so extreme that he could sometimes feel that a total possession could give him no more.

Emma, although he now saw so much of her, remained obscure
and still a little frightening. Emma was the centre-piece of the relationship, and it was here that the darkness was. Emma joined
with Randall in flattering Lindsay, and with Lindsay in teasing
Randall; but she was herself never either flattered or teased. She
would sit there, rather plump in her flowery old-fashioned dresses,
her short frizzy dark-grey hair standing out on either side of her
sharp-nosed intelligent face, which seemed like that of a clever dog,
and she would watch them with a morose benevolence, leaning
forward on her silver-topped cane. From the exact nature of the
relation between Lindsay and Emma Randall's imagination shied
away. But whenever they touched each other he felt the shock of
the contact within himself. That too was pleasurable.

Sipping his tea, Randall contemplated Lindsay now, as she bent
over her embroidery frame. She was wearing a green linen dress
with a low square neck. The plaits of hair, with the docility of gold
beaten into a close chain, coiled tightly about her head, empha-
sising its roundness. The pain of physical desire, which was sometimes so sharp, was deliciously diffused now in an aching of his
whole body. She raised her head and gave him a quiet solemn very
conscious look. Emma was lost in a haze of cigarette smoke. The
many clocks ticked in the quiet room. Randall was in heaven.

The situation often struck him in a strange way as an appeal to
his intelligence, and this pleased him. Only through intelligence
could such a structure remain rigid; and at times he felt the sheer
cleverness of Emma, Lindsay and himself, coiled like three great
muscular snakes at the very centre of the edifice. Yet also love was
its centre; and perhaps here cleverness *was* love. With the passion
of the artist which he now increasingly felt himself to be he adored
Lindsay's awareness, her exquisite sense of form, which was a sort
of dignity of wit, a sense as it were of the movement and timing of
life which made her like a great comedian. She was shapely and
complete; and like a kaleidoscope, like a complex rose, her poly-
chrome being fell into an authoritative pattern which proclaimed
her free. With exhilaration Randall felt himself become light, light,

able to rise at last into the airy world of the imagination, the world above the mess of morality, the world inhabited by those two angelic beings.

Yet there were weights. Randall could at times, in the midst of his curious enjoyment of his indulged frustration, feel a special gratitude to Emma for having so thoroughly 'swallowed' them. What, after all, could he have done, what *would* he have done? He could not have taken Lindsay away because, quite simply, he had not enough money. Some knowledge of her, which could not now be muted, told him that it would be idle to expect her to help him through some new beginning. The merits of his plays were still unrecognized; and he simply could not see himself starting again to build up, somewhere else in England, another rose nursery. He could not see Lindsay getting up at six and turning the earth herself. As Ann had done.

In any case, there was still Ann and perhaps there would always be Ann. Pity for unloved Ann haunted Randall like a demon, preventing him from rising, preventing him from being free. Yet he had advanced a little, had he not, he had gained some ground. During the years of quarrelling, the years of irritation in that indifferent house, when they had torn each other and then wretchedly sought each other out because in their solitude there was no other consolation, it had seemed to Randall that nothing could ever alter, it would always be so. Even his love for Lindsay had made at first no impression on the futility of his life with Ann. But after his mother's death something new had seemed possible, and something new had indeed seemed to emerge from the solitary vigil which he had imposed upon himself. The period of meditation in his room, the abstention from Ann, the long hours of whisky and roses, the walks in the misty dawn among the dew-laden rose bushes to a chorus of newly wakened birds, out of all this had come some fresh strength, some breaking of the spell. After the monastic dignity of this period of retreat, the final scene could not be dwelt upon with satisfaction. How unfair he had been to Ann, how cunningly he had awaited a pretext, how careful and deliberate his anger had been, all this was known to Randall; though he could not altogether suppress a sense of almost technical pleasure in the success of the operation. Only he was sorry his father had been there. He was sorry to have seen his father ineffectual, frightened, resigned. He was sorry to have exhibited to him that most sordid moment of his own mechanism of change. More obscurely he respected and at moments envied the presence in Hugh of workable principles. His father's life had had dignity, had not degenerated into chaos. But for himself, principles in that sense were out of the question. It remained to be seen whether out of his present chaos some higher form would yet emerge.

Of course he had been monstrously unfair to Ann; yet the unfairness was only something superficial and immediate, and in a more remote, more complex sense there had been justice. He could never have treated Ann rationally, he could never have explained to her what his grievances were. She would not have understood. She would have stood there, strong in her kind of honesty, that honest simplicity which destroyed the footholds of his imagination and which made her for him so deadeningly structureless, so utterly lacking in significance; and she would not have understood. As he pictured her thus he saw her indeed as the incarnate spirit of the Negative. The fact was that she was his destroyer, and some ultimate instinct of self-preservation initiated and justified his proceedings against her. Yet he pitied her; and he knew that he had not even now left Grayhallock for good. He was bound to the place, still by Ann, by the pilgrimage of the rose year which he could not yet do without, and by Miranda; by Miranda most of all, the heart of that mystery, the green central button of that rose: Miranda, whom he had seen asleep in the last moments before he left the house, the pointed strands of her blazing hair fallen across her cheek, and a doll open-eyed beside her on the pillow.

"Ah," he said to them at last to end the silence, although they were often thus happily silent together, "Whatever are you two like when I'm not here? How I should love to know that!"

"Whatever it is," said Lindsay, looking at one of the clocks, "we're going to be like it very soon, because we're going to throw you out. It's time for Emma's evening session, and I've got a pile of typing still. I don't want to be up all night."

"I shall be sleepless," said Randall, "so think about me if you are!"

"You'll be sleeping soundly, Randall, my son," said Emma. "And so will Lindsay, for I've no intention of letting her type after supper. Come here, little one, did you hear what I said?" She caught Lindsay's hand as the girl moved past her, and looked intently up into her face. "She's getting insubordinate and needs discipline!"

"Well, we'll fight it out when Randall's gone, shall we?" said Lindsay, looking down at her friend with a tender rapacious expression.

Randall got up. They were still holding hands.

"One of these days," he said, "I'll put Lindsay across my saddle and carry her away." He often said this.

Emma laughed. "No, no," she said. "I can't do without her, I can't do without my gaiety girl. And I saw her first, after all!" She pressed Lindsay's hand against her cheek and released it.

Randall picked up his hat. He said to Emma, "My father saw you at the funeral. He asked me about you."

Emma was leaning forward to take the lid off her tape-recorder. "Really?"

"Yes," said Randall. He added, "It wouldn't altogether surprise me if he were to turn up here one of these days."

"Well, well—" said Emma. She turned the switch and the tape began to purr backwards.

Chapter Eight

"I TOLD you Hugh said it was good of Felix to be so nice to Ann," said Mildred Finch.

Humphrey laughed. "Hugh is an ass," he said. "He has a quite remarkable capacity for not seeing what's under his nose."

Felix Meecham had been in love with Ann, in a gentle resigned gloomy way, for some years.

"Well, I think nobody has seen *that*," said Mildred. "Felix himself is like a clam. And you and I, dearest—"

"Are sufficiently oyster-like."

"When we want to be. I'm glad the poor things had a little moment together—while you so tactfully kept young Penn out of the way."

Humphrey smiled. He and his wife understood each other very well. Their relation was intimate yet abstract, a frictionless machine which generated little warmth, but which functioned excellently. "You're not worrying about young Penn, I hope?"

"Certainly not," said Mildred. "I don't think you're *quite* mad."

"You, after all, were tactfully keeping Hugh out of the way!"

"Ah, Hugh—" said Mildred. "Yes, he is an ass, dear slow old Hugh, but I love him. What's more, Humpo, I'm going to have him. Would you mind?"

Humphrey looked at his distinguished reflection in an oval gilt mirror and smoothed down his white hair. "Of course not, my dear."

"You often said you wished I had someone. And I've waited long enough for Hugh."

"But do you think you will positively get him?" Humphrey looked down at his wife, amused and coolly tender. It was evening at Seton Blaise and the big drawing-room was already obscure, the

79

lamps not yet turned on. But the garden was still full of light. A nearby thrush sang.

"I don't see what can stop me," said Mildred. "I mean to have him, what's more, deliciously all to myself! I've wanted him for years, and that gives me a sort of right, doesn't it? Only he was so infernally faithful to poor Fanny, except for that one business. Dear Hugh, he really thinks no one knew about his caper with Emma! Just as Randall imagines now that no one knows he's carrying on with the Rimmer girl, whereas everyone knows!"

"Ann doesn't know. You're a bit inclined to say 'everyone knows' when what you mean is that you know."

"Well, it's true I know plenty. I certainly mean business here. To flaming youth let virtue be as wax. You don't think I'm too old for such nonsense, do you, Piggy?"

"Too old? You?" Humphrey laughed. "I wonder what you really want, though."

"I want the impossible, Piggy. To be young again. I want a little miracle."

"Why not?" said Humphrey. "I'm not sure that I see Hugh as up to it, though."

"I'll bring him up to it!" She rose to her feet. "Now I'm going to interview Felix. Where is that boy? Is he still felling trees?"

"When I last saw him he was carrying logs the size of himself into the woodshed. I told him to leave them for Smeed and the boy, but he took no notice."

"He's trying to take his mind off things," said Mildred, "instead of using it *on* things. That's what I want to talk to him about. What are you going to do, Piggy?"

"I think I'll just drive over to Grayhallock."

"I know, dominoes and whisky. That's where Felix ought to be too, now that the cat's away, only the boy is so confoundedly honourable. I suppose there's no word of the cat coming back?"

"None at all, so far as I know."

"Well, enjoy yourself, only remember what I told you!"

"But you didn't tell me anything this time!"

"Well, remember what I would have told you if I hadn't thought you'd heard it so often before!"

Mildred drew a light shawl about her shoulders and issued from the house. She paused upon the step to survey the garden. Against a sky of intense blue the thrush sang upon the cedar tree, winding all the visible things into the endless thread of his song. The stream seemed motionless, a line of green enamel beneath the chestnut trees, but the bamboos moved ever so slightly, like the secret gestures of friends.

The garden, so long familiar that it seemed a part of her mind, rapt Mildred into a trance of recollection, so that for the moment she forgot about Felix. Who knows what may be the results of random and seemingly isolated actions? She herself had embraced men whose faces, even whose names, she had forgotten: gone, killed in two wars. So much of the past is annihilated and swept away. But other pieces live, and grow in the memory like powerful seeds. Perhaps some of her own forgotten actions were, in the minds of distant and unheeded persons, just such seeds. And Hugh, did he know, did he at all guess, what thing he planted, with what long consequences, when suddenly on that summer evening he had turned from looking at her reflection in the stream, and throwing his arm over her shoulder had kissed her, holding her tightly for a long moment before he let her go? They had not spoken, then or since. But that quite isolated moment had had, for her, results. She recalled it now with such clarity, saw it in such detail, that the relentless interval of time seemed itself a dream. She remembered. And after the citronella Hugh had certainly remembered too; she had tricked him into remembering, she had, with such joy, *seen* him remembering.

He had set her, then, upon a long path. And just as she had started, so secretly and happily, upon her task of loving him, he had fallen in love with Emma Sands. Mildred, in those early days of her transformed consciousness of Hugh, had suffered. Emma was an old acquaintance of Mlldred's, they had been at college together:

81

someone, even then, a little nervously and uneasily to be reckoned with, never quite a friend. And it was with much curiosity, some triumph, and a little sympathy that Mildred had invited Emma to stay with her at Seton Blaise after the catastrophe. In another clair-voyant crystal of memory Mildred saw Emma on the lawn in a short white tennis dress, being captivated and consoled by the boy Felix. But her dark eyes had rested thoughtfully upon Mildred and she had read Mildred's mind, and her sharp clever dog-face had closed and hardened. They had parted then, not to meet again.

She need not have hated me, thought Mildred, for I gained nothing by her loss. And for a moment she felt quite sentimental about herself and about the years which the locusts had eaten. Yet the next moment she told herself that in a way she had quite *enjoyed* it all, she had enjoyed making up her myth of being in love with Hugh, and embellishing it and adding to it, and having it as a secret when in a way it was hardly a *thing* at all. But now, she thought, now I shall make all those shadows into the shadows of something, I shall make that long road a road that shall have led, after all, somewhere.

As she now went down the steps she heard from the stables the sound of Humphrey starting up the Rover, and as she reached the lawn she saw Felix at the side of the house, his head deep inside the bonnet of the very dark blue Mercedes. She came towards him, and saw beyond him the Rover disappearing down the drive.

"Really, Felix," said Mildred, "I believe you love that car more than you love any of us!"

Felix lifted his head and smiled. He leaned on the side of the bonnet wiping his hands on a bit of newspaper. "It's the only thing I've got to look after!"

"And whose fault is that, pray?" said Mildred.

Felix was Mildred's half-brother, and fifteen years her junior. He was a very tall man in his early forties with a big face and very blue eyes and a lot of short receding colourless fair hair which stood up fluffily upon his head. His face was pleasantly weather-beaten and worn into an expression of non-commital professional superiority, and revealed little of what, if anything, he felt. There was no subtle play of light, no gradual dawning of awareness, but only the sudden gaiety of a very brilliant smile and then a return to routine solemnity. Felix treated his sister with an unvarying amused politeness and usually foiled her attempts to run him by ignoring them altogether. He did not reply to her last remark, but bent forward again to inspect the interior of the Mercedes.

"Felix, I want to talk to you seriously," said Mildred. "Close the bonnet of the car."

Felix obediently closed it and went on wiping his hands. He let Mildred draw him by the sleeve, and they began to pace together upon the lawn.

"Felix," said Mildred, "it's about Ann. Now what are you going to do about Ann?"

Felix was silent. He threw the piece of newspaper down in the corner of one of the rose-beds and waited while his sister picked it up and stuffed it into his pocket. He said, "Must we—have this—Mildred?" He had a way of pronouncing her name which made it sound like a monosyllable.

"Yes, we must," said Mildred. "I wish you weren't so infernally clammed up! I want to help you, but you won't give me a chance." She thrust her arm through his. He was so much taller than her that she could not see his face properly.

"I'd rather you didn't help me, actually," said Felix. They walked on slowly.

"Don't be silly," said Mildred. "Now you must simply give me some information. I'm not asking you to use your mind yet. That will come later. You must admit that I've been awfully delicate and tactful about Ann. I've never even questioned you before. So you must bear with me now."

"Mildred," said Felix, "I'm sorry to disappoint you, I mean to disappoint your curiosity and your interest, but there is nothing here."

"What do you mean, 'nothing here'? Must you talk like a telegram?"

"Nothing has happened and nothing is going to happen."

Mildred was silent for a moment. "Have it your own way. Let us talk about a related subject. You want to get married. Or, let me make things even easier for you, and simply say I want you to get married. I want the Meechams to go on, since the Finches obviously aren't going to. I want your children, Felix. I can't be a grandmother, but I shall be a quite formidable aunt."

"Sorry, Mildred, to disappoint you again."

"Come, come," said Mildred. She drew him along coaxingly. "What about that froggy girl, the one you met in Singapore? Come, unbend a little about her. Do that tiny thing for your aged sister."

"Marie-Laure," said Felix stiffly.

"That's right. What was her name?"

"Marie-Laure Auboyer."

"Well, what about her? Where is she now, anyway?"

"I'm sorry to keep saying the same things, but there's nothing there either. She's in Delhi, I think."

"Delhi!" cried Mildred. "And you want to persuade me there's nothing! With you going so conveniently to look after those Gurkhas! Not that I want you to marry a frog, but she sounded quite a nice girl, and at least she's a *girl*."

They reached the seat under the cedar tree and sat down. The thrush was silent. The garden, dissolved in granular points of colour by the intense evening light, seemed to quiver quietly before them.

"I'm not going to Delhi, as it happens," said Felix. He crossed his legs and thrust his hands into his pockets and looked away towards the bridge. "I'm going to take a job in England."

"Felix!" cried Mildred. "You might have told me! I'd quite counted on our going to India together. You are a pig."

"Sorry, Mildred—it's only just been decided. Well, it's not entirely fixed yet, but more or less."

"You mean you've only just decided it. What is it to be? Guarding Buck House?"

"No, I've done my stint. It's a thing in the War Office, in the Military Secretary's department, actually, dealing with postings and promotions and decorations. All that. Very dull."

"At least they'll promote you, dear boy, you'll be a brigadier?"

"Yes."

"But without a brigade?"

"Quite." It was a sore point.

"Ah well," said Mildred, "I always thought you were far too nice for the Army. I can't think now why you ever went into it. I never advised it. Not that you haven't done frightfully well. Anyhow, you'll be in England after all. And that brings us back to Ann."

"Mildred—will you—leave off?" said Felix. He cast her a frowning sidelong glance and made to rise. She detained him.

"Please, Felix, don't be cross with me because I see you think only of that. And don't try, this time round, to put me off with your 'nothing here' stuff. You must make some decision about Ann. You're fretting yourself to pieces and preventing yourself from thinking about other women that you might have. And you must be worrying Ann too."

Felix was very stiff now, sitting very upright and staring ahead of him. The colours in the garden had reached their peak and were now subsiding into twilight as one by one the nebulous grains turned to blue and purple. One huge bright star trembled above the darkening chestnut grove. He said, "You think I'm—acting improperly."

Mildred sighed. She knew from his more than usually strangulated utterance that she had his attention at last. She said carefully, "No, certainly not. What I mean is nothing to do with giving Ann up, but with *getting* her. She isn't young, but she's young enough to bear you a child. She was a child herself when Steve was born. And the point is that you love her. And she loves you. And Randall has gone."

"What makes you say *that?*" said Felix sharply.

"Which? About her loving you?"

85

"Yes." He shifted his legs, staring ahead intently as if he were watching something.

"Well, she does, doesn't she?" said Mildred. She had no idea.

Felix was silent. Then he said, "I don't know anything about what she thinks of the matter. Naturally."

"I like your 'naturally'!" said Mildred. "You wouldn't be here unless you thought she—didn't positively mind. At least she knows what *you* feel?"

Felix was silent again. He said, "I think she—understands." He tried to compress the last word into a single grunt.

"Of course she understands," said Mildred. "She's not a complete fool. And women always *know*. Forgive my being so crude, old thing, but have you ever kissed her?"

"Certainly not!" said Felix in a shocked tone. He added the next moment more softly, "Yes, of course she knows. But we've never —mentioned it, you know."

"You seem to me a proper pair of ninnies," said Mildred. "I wish I could put some stuffing into you, Felix. Well, let me repeat my last point. Randall has gone. Your move. Yes?"

"No," said Felix. He rose now and offered his sister his arm. "I wish you wouldn't—fuss about this, Mildred. Randall has gone, but he'll come back. He's only staying in London. Nothing has happened, nothing whatever. And as I told you, nothing is going to happen. You may be right that I'm making a perfect ass of myself. But that's another matter. Let's go in. You must be getting cold."

"I'm not letting you go just yet," said Mildred. She remained seated and Felix stood now as if at attention before her, his tall form blotting out the evening star. Other stars had come. "Felix," she said, "when you say nothing has happened you mean that Randall has not blatantly, publicly, taken up with someone else, he hasn't really 'gone off'. But if he did—go off—then you'd speak to Ann?"

"But he hasn't—gone off."

Mildred was tense. "And if he doesn't do anything public, if he just goes on, however shabbily, keeping up appearances with Ann, you won't ever feel justified in—saying anything?"

Felix breathed deeply. "No. Shall we go in, Mildred?"

"Ah, you are a fool," she murmured, taking his arm. "But I have confidence in Randall. Thank heavens one of you all has some courage!"

Chapter Nine

*"The sons of the Prophet
Are hardy and bold
And quite un-accustomed to FEAR!"*

sang Penn, as he leaned out of the window of his room, looking toward the light view, over the tops of the beech trees, over the hidden escarpment of roses, toward the grey and green plain of the Marsh, with its yellow lines of reedy dykes and its slowly flapping herons. There was a scattering of sheep in the near fields, seeming like pale spherical bundles. Where the horizon came it was not yet the sea, it was not quite yet mysterious Dungeness.

The sun was shining, but in a feeble unconvinced sort of way, making a lot of pale bright light. A brisk east wind was blowing. Call this a summer! thought Penn. It would scarcely pass muster as a winter at home. This was the sort of thing he would have liked to explain, in an aggrieved way, to someone; only no one wanted to hear. His mother had said as he was leaving, "They'll all ask you so many questions about Australia!" but his father had said, "Not they! They don't care a brass farthing about Australia!" Only he had used a rather more Australian expression than that. It looked as if his father was right. Of course he didn't really mind their lack of curiosity; but he did a little mind their assumption that he was not in as good a position to judge them as they were to judge him.

Today he was certainly feeling a little more touchy than usual, but perhaps that was simply on account of the charades. There had been charades last night at the Rectory, and he had not distinguished himself. Penn, who had never played this game before, had been amazed at the virtuosity of the others, who all dressed up so cleverly and invented the funniest things on the spur of the moment. Miranda had been especially funny, and had looked so pretty and grown-up in some of the costumes, and had dressed up so comically as a boy. The two young Swanns were very brilliant too; though they seemed to put on such airs, and to talk so extraordinary a language, that Penn could scarcely decide when they were acting and when they were not. They were back for a half-term week-end from their school, a place called Rugby which they seemed to think a lot of. They were friendly to Penn but without concealing that they regarded him as rather a joke. None of this diminished his awkwardness. Only Ann had kept him company by being patently unable to act, but she had laughed so much all the time at everyone else that it somehow didn't show.

He looked across at the other tower of Grayhallock. That other tower, which he had never entered, exercised a looking-glass fascination on his mind. Its shallow stairs and sweep of white-painted metal bannister, the replica of his own, seemed like the approach to Bluebeard's chamber. No one had ever suggested that he should mount the other tower, though equally of course no one had forbidden it; and although he had often, deceiving himself with casualness, wondered whether he might not just stroll up to Miranda's room, he could not confront the idea of passing Randall's door. Now that Randall was gone it seemed no easier. It was not just that he was constantly told that his uncle was expected back from one day to the next. The nature of that departure, the raised voices and banging doors which he had heard, so much appalled him, and in an obscure way so frightened him, that even Randall's empty room seemed a haunted place.

He turned back into his own familiar little room. He had made his bed neatly. The box of soldiers was still untouched under the bed. The veteran car book stood on the shelf next to his copy of *Such is Life*. The German dagger lay unsheathed on the counterpane. The privateness of this room was the best thing about being in England. At home he had to share a room with Bobby. Though now, with another Graham baby on the way, perhaps his father would build the annexe which was allowed for in the building plans.

He thought with satisfaction of the new baby. The Grahams, after all, were quite a clan.

"Young man," said Abdul,
"Has Life grown so dull
That you're anxious to end your CAREER?"

Bias, offensively Australian. Yes, the Grahams were a clan to be reckoned with. His grandfather had been a railway union organiser, his great-grandfather had been a drover in Queensland, his great-great-grandfather had been deported from England for persistent Trade Unionism, his great-great-great-grandfather had been a Chartist, his great-great-great-great-grandfather had been a Leveller. (The last three items, entered with little concern for chronology, were unfortunately speculative.) His great-great-great-great-great-grandfather—

The German dagger, at which he had been gazing unseeingly, suddenly took possession of his consciousness in a painful way. He thought at first that the pain was simply the realisation that he must shortly part with it to Miranda. Then he realised that it was a special pain compounded of this, and of a thrilling alarming consciousness that this would make an excellent pretext for mounting the other tower to her room.

"Foul infidel, know
You have trod on the toe
Of Abdul the Bulbul EMIR!"

He picked up the dagger and drew the beautiful thing lightly through his fingers. It was sharp, polished, dangerous, marvellously integrated and sweetly proportioned. He could not remember when he had loved an object so much. It was even better than the visionary revolver which he had once desired. He caressed its smooth black hilt and traced the enamelled swastika with his fingertip. He would never see its like. He sighed and went to the window and looked again at the other tower. The wind had dropped a little and from somewhere behind the house a cuckoo was calling its

hollow hesitating note. *Cu-cuckoo*. Of course there was no question
but that he must give it to Miranda. Ann had said no, but she had
only said it out of kindness to him, and he must do his duty in
spite of Ann's kindness. The idea of duty brought with it a sort
of dignity, and he decided he would do it, he would mount the
other tower.

As he thought this his glance strayed and he saw Miranda below
him, having just issued from the front porch. She was carrying a
shopping-bag and had now set off along the drive toward the front
gate. For a moment he wondered whether he should not take the
chance of running up now to her room and laying the dagger on
her bed. But he reflected that its sudden appearance there might
frighten her. The idea that he was sparing her a fright filled him
with a tender protective feeling. Then something about her slowly
disappearing form imparted a sense of urgency, and he slipped the
dagger into the pocket of his mackintosh and proceeded down the
stairs at a run.

When he got outside Miranda had disappeared, but he ran a little
way along the road which led to the village, and slowed down when
he saw her ahead. The road led downhill with the rose nursery
upon the left, and he could see Bowshott and one of the men working between the lines of bushes. The farther roses merged into a
multi-coloured blur. They were all in flower now. He wondered
where Miranda was going, and concluded that she was bound for
the village shop, which was odd since Miranda detested shopping.
At this point she turned round, saw him, and waited.

When Penn caught up with her he couldn't think quite what to
say. He was too shy to hand the dagger to her at once, so he said
the first thing that came into his head. "Have you found Hatfield
yet?"

"I'm not looking for Hatfield," said Miranda. They began to
walk on slowly together, she swinging the bag.

"Well, not *now* I suppose," said Penn, "but I thought you might
have found him, somewhere."

"I didn't look for him," said Miranda. "I don't like cats. I prefer hedgehogs." She said this in a judicious way which Penn found a little encouraging.

By way of making a joke Penn said, "I thought little girls always liked cats and ponies!"

"I'm not a little girl," said Miranda in a tone which left Penn's imagination reeling as to what indeed she *was*.

To recover he said with an even more ponderous air of jocularity, "And you don't like ponies either?"

"Oh, I like them all right," said Miranda, "but I got bored with riding. I get bored with anything as soon as I know how to do it. I only like doing things I can't do."

Penn considered this. "I think I only like doing things I *can* do." The conversation wasn't going too badly.

"What can you do?"

This disconcerted him. What, after all, *could* he do? He was a pretty good fast bowler; but he had not been able to display this accomplishment, since although a village cricket team existed, the Peronett family had no dealings with it, and Penn, unversed in the hierarchical intricacies of English village life, had not liked to suggest himself as a possible player. He was also, of course, clever with motor bikes, and used to get into the Adelaide stadium free as unpaid mechanic to Tommy Benson. But he didn't like to mention either of these talents to Miranda as it would sound like boasting, and they weren't very grand anyway. So he said, "I'm not much good at anything, really."

"In that case you don't like anything. Poor you!"

"Oh well, I do like things, of course," said Penn, irritated. They walked on in silence.

Then Miranda said, "Are you going to go to London with Humpo Finch?"

"Yes," said Penn. "I'm going up with him next Wednesday." He greatly looked forward to that. Humphrey Finch had called once or twice and found time to talk to him, for which he was grateful. Humphrey was indeed the only person here, except perhaps Ann, who seemed to have any serious desire to know what he was like.

Miranda laughed.

"Why do you laugh?"

"Never you mind." She turned suddenly in through a gateway and Penn found that they were in the churchyard. The church had a prettily shaped plump conical spire which he could see from his window. It was a large church, built in the great days of the wool industry on the Marsh, so he had been told, and the huge plain unstained windows let in the cold Kentish light to reveal a great pillared stone-flagged space in the midst of which huddled the few chairs which accommodated the present congregation. Penn had been in once or twice to look at it, but where everything was so old he could not readily distinguish one thing from another, and it looked to him just like a lot of other churches he had seen. He was on the whole inclined to agree with his father's judgment on English parish churches: "When you've seen one you've seen the lot."

Miranda, however, did not go into the church, but began to walk along the path that led through the old part of the churchyard between huge box-like stone tombs, yellow with lichen, adorned with crumbling angel-heads, sunk in ivy and brambles, and tilting crazily in all directions. Beyond them enormous yews, great fissured towers of darkness, flanked the churchyard wall.

Penn, trying to keep up with her and stumbling in the long grass, said, "I rather like churchyards, don't you?"

"How many dead people do you know?" said Miranda.

Penn was shocked at this question. He thought one should not speak of dead people in this manner as if they could constitute an acquaintance. He said, "I don't really know. Not many. Hardly any at all."

"I know more than twenty," said Miranda. She added, "Grandfather must know hundreds."

Penn had not had time to think of an answer to this when they turned the corner of the church and he saw a great lawn stretching away down the hill toward a line of more recently planted cypress trees which stood out, conscious and exotic, against a grove of pollarded chestnuts. On the nearer side of this lawn, which was mown and tended, unlike the wilderness through which they had just passed, there were a few rows of shiny modern grave-stones, and here and there a long mound of earth covered with withered flowers. Penn realised with a tremor that he was now in the presence of the dead, the real dead, not those who had died long ago. He could not think of those great crumbling tombs, riding upon the undulating grasses, as having ever covered a person who was wept for. But here there were the marks of real bereavement. People one might have known were asleep here.

People one might have known. He guessed where he was going just the moment before, as Miranda halted by it, he read upon a newly cut tomb-stone the name of Steven Peronett.

"Oh," said Penn, speaking out of an immediate shock and a sort of shame, "I didn't know he was here."

"He's not here," said Miranda.

Penn took a moment to understand her and then was silent. He felt ashamed at not having known where his cousin was buried and ashamed of having followed Miranda without knowing whether she wanted his company; and he felt a vast distress and incoherent pity at standing beside Steve's grave. He looked at the shining ugly surface of the stone. It was odd how stone that one saw nowhere else seemed to appear in cemeteries, as if it were indeed the portal of another world. *Steven Peronett. Beloved son of Ann and Randall Peronett. Aged fourteen years.* He was older than Steve now. It was a strange thought.

He said to Miranda. "I'm sorry, I didn't realise you were coming here. I'll go away at once."

But she said, "No, don't go. Stay and see the birds."

"The *birds?*" He turned to see that she had opened her bag and brought out another paper bag which was inside it. The paper bag was full of fragments of bread.

In front of the stone the grass was flat, mown over, and nothing marked the extent of the grave. Miranda began to strew the bread in a neat rectangle, of which she first marked out the sides with a trail of pieces, until she had covered with the white fragments an area upon which a boy might have lain down. Then she drew back a little across the grass.

Penn followed her in amazement at the strange rite. "What is this?"

"Steve loved birds," said Miranda. "He always used to feed them at Grayhallock. He would ring a bell every morning and the birds would come. And when he was dying he said to me, 'Don't bring flowers to my grave. But come sometimes and feed the birds there. I'd like to think that you might do that.' "

"Ah, gee—" said Penn. A confusion of emotions overwhelmed him. He felt a sudden grief which was like a kind of joy and for a moment he felt as though he might burst into tears.

Miranda sat down on a long recumbent tomb of plum-coloured marble a little bit away from the grave and Penn sat down beside her. He turned to look at her. An extraordinary dignity and solemnity had come to her from the performance of the rite. Her pale transparent slightly freckled face was serene under the jagged cap of red hair. She was serious, yet a strange smile was diffused upon her features, a light shining from within. She gazed away from him in the direction of the offering of bread, and he saw that she was beautiful. Then looking down he saw her knees.

She was wearing green stockings which were pulled up to just above the calf, and her short tartan skirt lay neatly across her legs, just above the knee. Her knees were revealed, bare, white and rounded, between the two garments. Penn stared at them and some stretched cord seemed to twang far away, something gave and broke. He had never thought that he could find a girl's knees exciting. But then Miranda was not a girl. Yet she was not a little girl either. What was she then? And what was happening to him? He stared down and felt quite clearly the urge to kneel before her and put his head upon her knees. The distant cuckoo cried out, hesitant, melancholy and hollow. He breathed deeply and raised his gaze. The birds were beginning to come for the bread.

Chapter Ten

"HUMPHREY is so disappointed," said Mildred. "It seems that young Penn has changed his mind and doesn't want to come to London after all. Do you think Ann is bothered? There's no need to be. Do you think I should speak to her?"

She was drinking sherry with Hugh at his flat in Brompton Square. It was raining a little and the great dome of Brompton Oratory could be seen standing out against a grey sky which intermittent sunshine made to glow with an unnerving radiance which brought the building into relief, making it suddenly delicate and Florentine, like something in an Italian coloured print. The room within was chilly and darkish, a momentary winter room in summer. The light had been turned on above the Tintoretto.

Since her remarks to Humphrey on the subject of Hugh, Mildred's imagination had been active. She was indeed surprised and almost alarmed at the intensity of its activity. It was true that she had for years 'adored' Hugh, and that if she had not had a gentle contempt for Fanny she would have been 'the tiniest bit jealous'. It was true that she had never forgotten the occasion of the kiss, and that she had, for a considerable time after that, suffered. She had certainly been ferociously jealous of Emma. She had often, somewhat vaguely, put it to herself that she 'wanted' Hugh, and had eventually taken it for granted that this was so. She coveted Hugh. And when it was known that poor Fanny was dying she had again vaguely, and a little guiltily, expected that, somehow or other, she would now 'inherit' Hugh.

But since she had, with a gay casualness which was not at the time quite misleading, summed up these ideas for the benefit of her husband, she had been startled by the growth of a much more positive need. It was as if *saying* these things had in itself set something off. She had, through the years, grown used to imperfect sympathies. Her intimacy with Humphrey lacked warmth, her intimacy with Felix, owing to his peculiar muteness, lacked detail. Her daughter, whom she secretly admired, was now almost a stranger. She had for long had, she reflected, no one to whom she could open her heart. And with surprise, fear and joy she noted now the extent to which, after all, she still *had* a heart. She, the clever, capable, sardonic Mildred Finch, the elderly philosophical Mildred, so very much the mistress of herself, the captain of her very private soul, was shaken. It was, she thought, almost as if she were falling in love. And then she thought, but I *am* falling in love!

When she had thus put it she felt so pleased with herself that it almost put her anxieties at rest. She had said to Humphrey that she wanted the impossible, to have her youth back. Yet in a sense these feelings were the very stuff of youth and their occurrence again, after so many years of quietness, seemed a sort of miracle. That she would, so inspired, be able, as she had put it to Humphrey, to 'bring Hugh up to it', she had little doubt, though she was cheerfully vague about what 'it' was toward which Hugh was so shortly to be elevated. For the present her own state of mental activity so much gratified her that she felt that if Hugh would only *acquiesce* she had love enough for both. All the same, she waited with increasing nervousness for his promised summons, and when it came, and when she stood at last outside his door, she found herself trembling like a young girl.

As she looked round Hugh's drawing-room, which she had not visited now for some time, she reflected how delicious it was to have him a bachelor once again. She had been used to come to these rooms to take tea with Fanny, sometimes glimpsing Hugh just as she was leaving. Now she was sitting behind closed doors with him and him alone, as the evening drew on, and hoping like a seventeen-year-old that perhaps he might invite her out to dinner. She laughed inwardly at these thoughts, with a laugh of exhilaration and triumph, and then guiltily, but only for a moment, remembered poor Fanny.

She felt delightfully at home in Hugh's drawing-room, and reflecting on this she felt how few places there now were where she did feel warmly and positively at home. Even her special boudoir at Seton Blaise, or the library at Cadogan Place, or Felix's rooms in Ebury Street, had not this quality of receiving her and soothing her spirit. She felt completely at ease. She felt as if, already, she a little bit owned the place. As she looked round at the familiar objects they looked at her with new obedient faces: the walnut writing-table, the oval card-table with the alabaster vase, the pair of Kazak rugs, the green glass shell from Murano which Fanny would never allow to be used for flowers, the set of Wedgwood jugs, the dappled Chinese fawns. It was as if from each thing some veil had fallen and they glowed at her: now we are yours. She noted already certain changes she wanted to make. Some things must be moved: and those big ormolu vases must, she was *almost* certain, go.

Most of all the Tintoretto glowed upon her with a jewelled beneficence. It lighted the room now, like a small sun. It was not a very large picture: it represented a naked woman and was almost certainly an earlier version of the figure of Susannah in the grea Susannah Bathing in Vienna. Only it was no sketch, but a great picture in its own right and justly of some fame: a notable segment in the vast seemingly endless honeycomb of the master's genius; and well might a spectator think of honey, looking upon that plump, bent, delicious, golden form, one leg gilding the green water into which it was plunged. A heavy twining complication of golden hair crowned a face of radiant spiritual vagueness which could only have been imagined by Tintoretto. Golden bracelets composed her apparel, and a pearl whose watery whiteness both reflected and resisted the soft surrounding honey-coloured shades. It was a picture which might well enslave a man, a picture round which crimes might be committed. Mildred regarded it now as it glowed in the darkening room and recalled with indignation that Fanny had wanted to sell it. Small Fanny had feared it perhaps: Hugh's golden dream of another world.

There was in Mildred's apprehension of the things about her nothing grossly predatory. They were like servants who run ahead of their master, symbols of a presence, almost sacraments. And still half amused at finding herself so elevated Mildred turned her gaze again to the worried preoccupied infinitely to-be-looked-after bald-headed Hugh. Slow old Hugh, she thought, and her heart dissolved in tenderness. Mine.

In answer to Mildred's question about Penn, Hugh replied vaguely, "Oh, I don't know. I don't think Ann is worried about Humphrey seeing Penn. I imagine the boy just decided, when it came to it, that he wanted to stay in the country. He seems to be having quite a good time now." He poured out some more sherry. It was raining harder and the hiss of the water was confused with the sound of traffic in the Brompton Road.

Mildred looked at Hugh affectionately and patted her fluffy pepper-coloured hair into place. Her mind reverted to Felix and his problem, a matter which had also considerably occupied her imagination. She had expressed to Felix a 'confidence' in Randall; but she had discovered nothing since to increase her hopes of Randall's positively 'going off'. It was obvious that Hugh really knew nothing about what Ann thought about Humphrey; and equally doubtless he knew nothing of Randall's intentions. But it was worth trying, so Mildred said casually, "Any news of Randall, by the way?"

"No," said Hugh. He seemed unable to keep his mind on these topics and answered in a distracted manner. "I haven't seen him."

"Do you think now he'll *stay* in London?" said Mildred. "I mean, he must have a girl friend here or something."

"A girl friend?" said Hugh. "I've no idea. I don't know what he does."

Mildred groaned to herself. Hugh was always the last person to hear the gossip which concerned him most. Yet she loved this in him, his inability to attract gossip. There was, in his obliviousness, in his utter failure to discover what was going on, a kind of positively beautiful stupidity.

The nervousness which Mildred had felt on the threshold was now quite gone. It was Hugh who seemed nervous, shy almost in a touching way and needing to be set at ease. She looked at his round wrinkled face, his round brown eyes and the bald globe above the thick tonsure of brown hair, and she wanted to take him in her arms: such a simple and yet it had seemed all her life such an impossible wish. Just the pleasure of looking at him so unrestrainedly was considerable. One cannot, in ordinary society, so rapaciously scrutinise one's friends; she enjoyed the liberty she was taking. At the same time she observed the shabby state of the loose covers, decided that all the chairs needed re-covering, decided where this should be done and approximately how much it ought to cost.

"Never mind about Randall," she said. "What about you? Felix probably isn't coming to India after all, so you absolutely *must* come. You will, won't you, Hugh?"

Hugh looked uneasy and picked at the braiding of the armchair. "I don't know whether I can, Mildred."

"What stops you?"

He made a rather weary gesture, seeming a little to avoid her eye.

"Come!" said Mildred. "Has it lost its magic? You *did* want to come, although you wouldn't say so. You can't have changed your mind."

Hugh was silent.

"Hugh dear, you're worrying about something," said Mildred. "Is it those ridiculous children? They'll be all right, you know."

"Mildred, you're so sympathetic," said Hugh.

Mildred moved her chair nearer his. She wanted very much to embrace him now but feared to do it clumsily. Their two large chairs were in the way and she could hardly pull him to his feet. So she contented herself with dealing him a light blow on the hand such as might more elegantly be dealt by a folded fan. "Now then, tell me all."

"It's not the children," he said. "It's just that I'm in a foolish state of mind."

So am I! thought Mildred. Ah, Hugh, if you only knew how foolish! She said nothing, but advanced her hand to the arm of his chair, ready to seize his hand in a friendly clasp when the next opportunity offered.

PART TWO

Hugh turned now and looked into her face and the shock of the straight gaze almost made her gasp. She had no expression ready for so direct a glance and with a sense of failure she fluttered and dropped her eyes. She wondered if she were blushing. She had forgotten what it felt like inside when one blushed.

"Mildred," said Hugh, "we have known each other a long time." He said it solemnly.

"Yes." Her nervousness returned. She had not expected such a sudden, such a wonderfully rapid, approach to seriousness between them.

"I hope that I may speak to you from my heart," said Hugh.

Mildred nodded mutely. She took his hand, pressed it, and laid it back on the arm of the chair.

"I hope too," said Hugh, "that you won't think I'm being terribly disloyal to poor Fanny."

Mildred didn't know whether or not to say no she wouldn't, so she simply approached her hand until, without grasping it, it was touching his. His big worried round face was close to hers. With very little movement she could have kissed him. Now it would come soon, the second kiss, to which the first kiss had so long looked forward. Lips parted, as she looked tenderly at him, she could feel her face moulded by the warm mobility of the feelings within.

"There's something strangely timeless about one's affection for people."

"I know—" said Mildred. She took his hand in a firm clasp and held it, stroking it a little with one of her fingers. "Dear Hugh—" she said. She felt happy, surprised, excited, very moved.

"I hope I won't upset or annoy you by speaking frankly," he said. "I didn't mean, when you came, to talk to you like this. But I'm surely old and foolish enough now to be able to talk when I want to and dispense with the dignity of silence."

"Talk, my dear, talk," breathed Mildred.

"I must have your advice, Mildred. It's about Emma Sands."

Mildred let go of his hand abruptly. Hugh, who had apparently not noticed either her affectionate grip or its cessation, got up and began to pace about the room. His head passed and re-passed in front of the honey-coloured Tintoretto.

"I don't know whether you knew," said Hugh, "but I was at one time very fond of Emma." He paused in the golden aura of the picture. "Well, I may as well be frank with you, Mildred. I was dreadfully in love with Emma."

"Quite," said Mildred. She had not meant it to sound so dry.

"Ah, did you know?" said Hugh. He looked at her eagerly, almost as if it would now give him pleasure to think that she had followed his adventures with interest.

"No, not really. I think I knew vaguely that you liked her."

Hugh seemed disappointed. "Well, I was," he said, in a tone which was both aggrieved and complacent. He set off pacing again and as he did so a look of serenity settled on his face and he seemed for a while oblivious of Mildred. She could see his face rounded out, softened by the thoughts within, very much as her own face had been a moment since. His head seemed to grow larger and more radiant, as he said again, "Yes, I was, I certainly was—"

He walked a little more and then stopped in front of her. "I've never spoken of this to anyone. Well, Fanny knew, but I never talked about it. It's wonderful, it's *remarkable*, to talk about it now, to talk out aloud to someone, to utter her name. Bless you, Mildred, bless you, dear!"

"You want to talk about—the past?" said Mildred hopefully.

"Well, no," said Hugh. He had turned away from her again and lifted his face to the gold of the picture. "I want to talk about—the present. Or rather—the future. Yes," he added with satisfaction, "the future. It's rather miraculous to find that, even at my age, one has one!"

Mildred felt that she had grown, in the big armchair, as dry and small as a nut. She said, "You are young at heart, Hugh."

The conventional words seemed to give him pleasure. What a perfect fool he is, she thought, and she yearned over him.

"Perhaps I am after all," he said. "But no one is more surprised than me. I told you Emma was at the funeral, didn't I?"

"Yes."

"Ever since I saw her there," said Hugh, and his words had the resonance of a song, "I have been able to think of nothing else. I've been in a haze of expectation like a boy, like a foolish boy. You would hardly credit it, would you, Mildred?" He seemed to address the Tintoretto, and leaned forward to touch it very gently with his finger in a way that Mildred suddenly remembered from long ago. She was afraid that if she tried to speak she might make some grotesque sound, so she remained silent.

"It's odd," he said, "to keep love for someone stored up so long and then to find it fresh and alive at the end. I thought I had quite sealed up that tomb, but no—no."

"It's hard for me to imagine," said Mildred, trying out her voice briskly. "But then I'm riddled with common sense. What are you going to do about it?"

"Ah, well," said Hugh, and the exaltation faded and the old worried look came back, "that's it. That's where I need your help, your advice. You know Emma. You know me. You must help me to be objective. I've really made myself thoroughly upset and anxious, worrying about this. I think it has even affected my health. I hope talking to you will have made a difference. Perhaps I shall find it has—and this absurd state of mind will simply fade away. I wish it would. I looked forward to—some peace, just, well, holiday, after—I'm too old for this nonsense really, don't you think? Why should one make trouble for oneself when one's old?"

"Heaven help us when we are too old to make trouble for ourselves," Mildred murmured.

"You must make up my mind for me, Mildred," said Hugh. "Your asking me to come to India puts me, in a way, up against it. Should I go and see Emma or should I not? I haven't really any idea how she lives now. Whether there is—anyone else. Do you happen to know?" He turned anxiously towards her.

"So far as I know there is—no one else." She retreated slowly back into the depths of the chair. The rain was beating down and it was quite dark in the room now except for the light from the picture which gilded half of Hugh's entreating face.

"But should I go," he said, "or am I just being foolish—romantic, meddlesome, or worse? Why open an old wound? Only pain and chaos would follow if I went to see her. She wouldn't want, after all those years, to see me, would she? I was exaggerating of course just now. I'm not in love, I can't be, one isn't at my age. I can overcome this—obsession—just be giving myself a good shake. You must help me, Mildred, you're so sensible. Why, you've no idea how much I rely on you! I think I feel better already. A long voyage would be just the thing, a long time away, travelling with you. Really, you must think me quite extraordinary, Mildred, a mild old fellow like me. You agree, don't you, it would be quite wrong to go and see her?"

Mildred was right back now against the back of the chair, her forearms stretched stiffly out on the two arms, as if she were pinned there. Once more in her mind's eye she saw dog-faced Emma, Emma in the short white tennis dress, defeated Emma talking to the boy Felix. She said, "You want to go and see her, Hugh. You want to, you're longing to, you're dying to. Why deny that you're sort of, almost, ready to be, in love?"

He let out a long sigh. He was silent a while. "Yes." Then again, "Yes. Yes."

Mildred relaxed slowly. "Go then," she said. "Go, go. Go and see her. You'll regret it forever if you don't."

"That's true," he said, nodding his head, "that's quite true. I would regret it." His face turned again toward the Tintoretto and seemed to fill out once more. His lips parted, his eyes widened, and he threw his tonsured head back as his gaze moved up toward the face of the golden Susannah.

"Then you must go, Hugh," said Mildred. "That's my advice.' She rose awkwardly and began to grope for her things.

"Oh, you're not leaving?" he said, coming to her and fumbling with her coat, crumpling it inconclusively in his hands and laying it back on the arm of the chair.

Standing now, Mildred was very close to him. She could have reached up and put her hands on his shoulders in a way she had often imagined. "Yes, I must be off."

"Please don't go," said Hugh, "please have dinner with me."

"I can't. I've got to be somewhere else."

"Oh dear," he said. "I've so much enjoyed talking to you, I've enjoyed every moment. I hope I haven't shocked or annoyed you, Mildred? I assure you I didn't intend all this to come out."

"That's all right, my dear," she said. She pulled her coat on. "It was very interesting."

"Well, at least let me get you a taxi."

"All right. Hugh, you will go and see Emma, won't you? You must have courage, you know."

"Bless you, Mildred," he said. "You've given it to me. Yes. I'll go. Bless you."

Mildred smiled at him. "You have quite a passionate nature, Hugh dear. I wouldn't have suspected it."

"Have I?" He seemed pleased, and pressed her hand with gratitude and cordiality.

PART THREE

Chapter Eleven

Hugh stood looking down the long corridor that led to Emma's door. He told himself, twenty-five years ago I was here. Only 'I' and 'here' refused to do their work. He put out one hand and touched the wall. The intermittent babble inside his head had this morning risen to a crescendo and he doubted his ability to hear anything that might be said. He also felt slightly giddy. He waited. He had, of course, arrived too early.

Hugh had been, he thought, when he saw Mildred, in two minds. His condition of trouble about Emma had increased steadily and alarmingly. It really had the air of being a disease. It was not like thinking and coming to conclusions, thinking further and coming to more conclusions. What indeed *it* was that was increasing so was something which his mind could not at all confront. It was sometimes like a great cloud emanating from him and surrounding him, a new form of his being, something almost physical. It was not regret for the past, it was not even exactly yearning for Emma: these were far too like thoughts. Whereas what was the case was opaque, it had no reflective qualities. What it was indeed was just— somehow—Emma, and nothing else; and this nonsensical way was the only way he could put it.

All the same, he kept his head, and beside, or within, this great balloon that tugged him off the ground a sort of monologue went on, though in a rather high-pitched tone, as if the Voice of Reason had become slightly hysterical. He knew perfectly well that conditions such as the one he was in—he did not give it a name—were temporary. He could weary out the inflated thing that so pulled him about, he could weary it out just by keeping his feet firmly planted and directing his attention elsewhere. He could be sane in a week, if he really wanted to be, he told himself; and he reflected that his condition undoubtedly had more than he had at first realised to do with his simply being tired and overwrought. He had so much looked forward, had quite childishly looked forward, to having a holiday when poor Fanny was dead. It sounded a very callous way to put it, but there it was, and it was perfectly natural. He had, since his retirement from the Civil Service, had no opportunities for self-indulgence, since Fanny's illness had followed so soon after. He had promised himself many things, reading, painting, travel, the untrammelled conversation of friends: these things, like toys put away in a cupboard, awaited him still. His freedom awaited him still.

It would indeed be an act of gratuitous folly to, as he had put it to Mildred, make trouble for himself at this stage. He knew nothing of Emma's present arrangements or state of mind and shrank from any attempt to 'make inquiries' about her. To try to re-establish any sort of 'relationship' however vague with Emma would be likely to cause pain and confusion and nothing else. And of course he would make himself ridiculous: though this thought in fact troubled him comparatively little, and he had been sincere in saying to Mildred that at his age one outgrows certain considerations of dignity. He was well aware that his selective memory retained for him, from that strange episode of the far past, only what was joyful and what was tragic. What it suppressed was that Emma was a tough and difficult customer and not by any means well adapted to get on with someone like himself. When, moreover, he reflected on the curious beauty which, after all, that memory retained, worked as it had been into a self-contained crystal sphere of intense experience, he felt at moments that it would be a pity to risk spoiling it: to risk spoiling it by a painful, embarrassing or irritating sequel, or worse still, by a boring one. For the most depressing thought was the thought that if he and Emma were to meet now the meeting might have no significance at all.

The trip to India was obviously a god-send. Two days out from Southampton and he would be in another universe: at times he thought, two hours out from Southampton. A long time away, packed with unforeseeable experiences which would compel thought and fancy, filling his mind with bright new images, would quite cleanse him of these weird cobwebs: he thus attempted to see his so improbably reviving feelings as the fabric of some dreadful re-animation, partaking of the unnatural, unnerving, almost evil. It was too soon after Fanny's death to be mad in this way. It was in any case, at any time, improper for an elderly man to be mad in this way. He would go, he thought, with Mildred, with solid, sensible, unemotional Mildred, to the ends of the earth: and there, at the ends of the earth, he would re-join his freedom. He set his mind upon this rendezvous, and relied upon Mildred to keep him to it. Only when Mildred had said, "You *want* to go and see her" all that structure had dissolved. It had been but a dream structure in any case, raised up to mask the determination, the rapacious need, which he had had all along to see Emma again.

He looked at his watch. He was still more than ten minutes too early. He had made the arrangement by telephone. He had not spoken to Emma directly, but to her secretary who had said yes, Miss Sands would see Mr Peronett, and would he kindly come at five o'clock, and that he was not to knock at the door but to come straight into the drawing-room.

As Hugh raised his head to look again at the distant green door he saw to his extreme dismay that it was opening. No votary surprised by the real presence of the goddess had a more potent urge to fall senseless to the ground or preferably to sink through it. Hugh took a step back, wondering if he had time to get away round the corner of the corridor without being seen. Then a sense of the stupid undignified nature of such a flight made him reverse his movement, and he began to walk very slowly toward the door, hoping that it was not evident that he had only been set in motion by seeing it open.

Two figures issued from the door and began to glide along the rather dark corridor towards him. As they grew larger he saw that one of them was a very handsome young woman and that the other was his son. The shock of seeing Randall in that context at that moment was considerable and Hugh's immediate feeling was one of sheer confusion, of having made some dreadful mistake. Of course he had not forgotten that Randall knew Emma. But in the picture of his own dealings with Emma, Randall had had no place, not deliberately excluded so much as automatically irrelevant and out of mind. Hugh was hurt by Randall's proximity to his own moment of truth. It was an intrusion.

Randall was now saying something to the girl, and they slightly quickened their pace as they approached him. It was plain that there was going to be no introduction, and for a moment it looked as if the advancing pair were simply going to sweep him out of the way. How they did get past each other was not, in Hugh's memory of it afterwards, very clear. He must have stood aside. Randall and the girl, as if sucked violently through a tube, held their course. He had a rapid picture of his son's face turned towards him, perfectly bland, saying Good-evening. He had an equally rapid but detailed picture of the girl's golden hair, and her also somewhat golden eyes regarding him with an expression of amused curiosity. Then they were gone and he was alone in the corridor some ten paces from Emma's door.

He stopped again and wondered if he ought now to wait till five o'clock. But upset and even angered by the meeting with Randall, he felt that he could not put up with the triviality of hanging around for another five minutes. He drew a breath, long enough to apprehend that he was about to step from one world into another, and that he had no conception at all what the new world would contain. He passed through the green door, which had been left ajar, went straight ahead into the drawing-room and found himself in Emma's presence.

Chapter Twelve

EMMA sat in an armchair facing the door. She was hunched up and looked small and round, almost humped. She was wearing a voluminous dark green dress which seemed to reach the ground, and a long slim cane was leaning against her knees. She was watching the door intently as he entered. She was smaller than he remembered. Hugh looked down at her in silence. The sense of being at last in her presence, the occurrence of something impossible, something contradictory, constituted a mystery so breath-taking that it forbade speech and almost with its intensity made him solitary again. Paralysed, he stared.

His imaginings beforehand of what this moment would be like had been hazy, yet they had seemed sufficiently lurid. He had pictured himself swept by irresistible emotion into her arms. He had imagined loss of consciousness. He had imagined tears and nervous laughter and every form of grotesque embarrassment. But this terrible silent confrontation had a quality of the real which stripped him. It was not Emma related to him but Emma *existing* which was the shock which so almost threw him back into a greater solitude. It was more like the snapping of a cord than like a reunion.

After a moment or two Emma uttered a sound which might have been 'Hugh', or perhaps it was 'you' or perhaps it was just a sigh. Hugh sat down. She was very much older. He had not, in the apparitions he had had of her, seen her ageing.

Emma drew herself back as if uncuinrlg a little. Then she said in a low voice, as if not to break a spell which kept him from being wafted back out of the door again, "Is your curiosity fed?"

"Not—curiosity—Emma," said Hugh. He now with relief felt the rush of warm emotion, the reassuring desire to kneel, the possibility of trembling.

Emma was silent, scrutinising him. She was neither smiling nor embarrassed nor solemn. She seemed distracted and morose. Then she said something.

"You'll have to speak up. I'm afraid," said Hugh. "I've become very deaf."

"So have I," said Emma. "I said you looked just the same, but of course you don't. It's just that I've got used to your face already."

"I hope it doesn't upset you, my coming like this."

"I don't see why it should *upset* me," said Emma slowly and irritably. "I could have said no. But I suppose I was curious too." She added, "It was a long time ago. Too long."

"Too long for what?"

She just repeated "Too long. Too long." Then, "Would you like some tea?"

"Yes, if it's no trouble."

"It is a trouble," said Emma, "and anyway I think I'd rather have a drink. Could you get the gin and stuff out of that cupboard?"

Hugh got up. It was odd to be moving about in this room. It was like moving about in a picture or beyond a looking glass and his body felt heavy with fatality. He looked around him at Emma's things. Generations of window-curtains must have come and gone since he was last here and he was vaguely aware of some notable improvements in Emma's taste; yet he thought he recognised a few objects, and he could scarcely believe that he was not visiting the past. He set the bottles and two glasses on the little table in front of her, beside her spectacles and an immense ash-tray and a blue packet of Gauloises; and as he came near to her he had an eerie apprehension of her whole body as older. It was as if her body and his sniffed each other like two old dogs while their owners looked on. Her hand rested on the arm of the chair like a wary lizard. The dry wrinkled skin, dark brown with nicotine, had fallen between the bones. He had the impression that she was holding her breath.

"It's odd," said Emma, when he had moved away from her. "I always thought I should faint if I were ever face to face with you again, but I seem not to have. I feel quite ordinary. It's just that we can't talk to each other. It's a meeting in Hades."

Hugh felt a humble gratitude to her for having at least expected to be moved. He said in a gentle voice, "We'll soon be able to talk. Just keep going."

Her face had sharpened with the years. It was more fierce and hungry than he remembered it, and the red-rimmed eyes showed luminous yet darker. Her hair seemed to have dried and stiffened into an iron-grey frizz. But already he was forgetting what she had looked like before, and the pale ghosts of familiar images fled like leaves before the wind.

"I'm not sure that I shall let you stay as long as that," said Emma. "I'm not sure that I want to talk to you. My curiosity is almost satisfied *now*. I don't want to discuss the past. I wonder why you came?"

Hugh paused. He could not find the right word. "Need," he said.

"What? Do speak up."

"*Need.*"

"Rubbish," said Emma. She sipped her drink and made a wry face.

"Why did you come to Fanny's funeral?" said Hugh.

"A final act of brutality."

"Rubbish."

Emma smiled briefly. She said, "Can't you see I'm an old dry object like a stuffed alligator? A voice comes out, but the thing is hollow really. It's no good looking for a soul inside me now."

Hugh was more pleased than otherwise at her expression of melancholy. He realised that he had dreaded to find her satisfied, to find her with some rounded perfection of her own, to find her *comblée*. He said, "Come, come, don't be so gloomy! There's plenty to do yet."

"You were always a sort of ninny, Hugh," said Emma. "I see you're as silly as ever. You still have no sense of humour. It's one of your charms, a sort of imitation innocence. Now tell me why you came."

"I told you. I couldn't stop thinking about you and it was necessary to see you."

"Well, you've seen me."

"I hope you will—permit this to be—the beginning of a friendship," said Hugh. He had said these words to himself before; now they sounded abstract and out of place.

"A *friendship?*" said Emma. She seemed to hold the word up between her finger and thumb. Then she said morosely, "You don't know what you're talking to." Then, "You must have run into Randall and Lindsay just outside."

"Yes," said Hugh. He had completely forgotten about his son and was not pleased to be reminded. "Yes. The girl is your secretary, Lindsay Rimmer?"

"Yes. That's her. And that." Emma pointed to two photographs propped up on her desk. "Isn't she perfectly gorgeous?"

Hugh recognised the thick plaits of hair, the wide-set eyes, and the amused expression which now struck him as a sort of complacent insolence. "Mmmm. Do you see much of Randall?"

"He practically lives here. Because of darling Lindsay of course. But you knew?"

"No," said Hugh. He was surprised and annoyed and chilled as if the temperature of the room were sinking steadily. "Why ever should I know?"

"I can think of a reason or two," said Emma. "Anyway, you must be the last person to hear. Yes, they're quite devoted." She said it with a sort of icy brutality, watching Hugh as if for signs of pain.

"I supposed he had—a mistress in London. I didn't know who it was."

"Oh, but their relations are entirely chaste!" said Emma. She said it with a viperous satisfaction, watching beady-eyed for its effect on Hugh.

Hugh's annoyance began to fix itself on Emma, and as he glared at her veiled sardonic face he felt with a certain zest more present to her, as if some more of him had arrived. "I'm shocked to hear it," he said. "That makes it worse."

"Why, pray?" said Emma. She was hunched, pleased, curled like a snake in a hole.

"I don't know," said Hugh. "Surely you understand what's involved? Randall's wife is made wretched—"

"And all for nothing? Oh, but it's not for nothing. It's for something beautiful."

"Is Lindsay in love with him?"

"She loves us both."

"But you know about Ann?"

"I've never permitted Randall to *discuss* his wife with us. That wouldn't have been right." She said it with an air of self-righteousness which was clearly designed as a provocation.

Hugh stared at her, bewildered and fascinated. He felt himself confronted with an entirely unfamiliar moral world, a world which seemed to have its own seriousness, even its own rules, while remaining entirely exotic and alien. Yet the experience itself, the puzzlement, the sense of danger, the shock, that was familiar; and it came to his mind how much of Emma's fascination had lain for him in her moral otherness. She had composed even the simplest scene quite differently. This had seemed to him her dangerousness, but also her originality, her freedom. And he had then been aware with a little thrill of excitement that this novelty of vision was related to something in her character which was dark, perhaps twisted. He had, in the interim, forgotten. He had withdrawn those darker colours from her image. As he now, hastily and imprecisely, began to restore them he felt something move within him. It was, surely the old love, the real one.

"Randall has behaved beautifully," said Emma. She gave a high-pitched laugh.

He had forgotten that laugh. "I don't understand you," he said, "and I certainly don't understand what Randall thinks he's up to. Are you fond of my son?"

"I love him," said Emma, with studied simplicity.

Hugh looked at her clever mysterious face. What was she thinking about him? He hardened his expression. She must not yet see his melting bewilderment, but only that he was still capable of fighting with her. He hated the idea of Randall's frequentation; and as he felt the old alarming thrill he measured with dismay the implications of Randall's being, so mysteriously but so authoritatively, around. He said, "Will you come over to my flat soon, tomorrow perhaps, and see my Tintoretto? You've never seen it, have you? I got it after we—parted. It's a very fine one." He wanted their speech with each other to become simple.

"See your Tintoretto forsooth," said Emma. "I shouldn't think so. I mean, I shouldn't think I'll come."

"Don't torment me, Emma," said Hugh. He said the words drily enough. He had said them before, and in wilder tones.

"How far you have come and how quickly!" she said with her shrill laugh. "You surprise me—and yet you don't. Do you realise we haven't talked to each other for twenty-five years? And you behave as if we were two people who were acquainted."

"But it doesn't matter, does it? It's impossible to believe it's so long. We patently *are* acquainted."

"Twenty-five years matters. I can hardly think of anything that matters more," she said sharply.

"Be simple with me, Emma," said Hugh. "Help me. Coming to see you like this I am put in the position of a fool. You must be merciful to me." He had often spoken to her like this in the old days.

She shook her head. "God put you in the position of a fool, my dear. And as for simplicity, I am being ever so simple. Honour satisfied. Curiosity satisfied. Time to go, Hugh."

"But you will come tomorrow?"

"Certainly not. Not tomorrow or the day after or ever."

"Emma!" Hugh rose. "You can't behave like this. If you weren't going to be kind to me you shouldn't have let me see you. I must see you again. I insist."

Emma looked up at him, toad-like, her shoulders humped. "Yes, I remember you," she said. "I remember those touching accents of the deprived child. The world has a strict obligation to be kind to Hugh Peronett. But I didn't particularly want to see you, it was your idea. I am happy here. I have all I want. I have my happy family. As for insisting, you know perfectly well that you are in no position to insist."

"I don't know what you mean by your happy family," said Hugh, "but I do know that you are being deliberately cruel to me."

"You were deliberately cruel to me."

He looked down at her cold face, and his hands moved weakly, gesturing the judgment away. He felt its injustice passionately. It was she who was the cruel one. And he felt that these words, these strugglings, had occurred before. "Ah, if you just want to punish me—but you can't—not after so long. Anyway you can, if you see more of me, do it much more beautifully."

Emma laughed. "You can still startle me with your moments of intelligence! Anyway, I didn't say I wouldn't see you, I only said I wouldn't come to your flat."

"So—you might see me—here, for instance?"

"Not for instance. Just here. But I'm not sure. I'll think about it. Now you must go."

"But I shall want to talk to you—properly. I shall want to talk to you—alone."

"Why don't you say what you mean? I had to adopt Randall, I had to let him in. It has worked beautifully."

"I'm not sure if I want to be—adopted—into your family," said Hugh. "It's—"

"You're not being asked," said Emma.

Yes, it was the old love and the old pain. He had forgotten the extent to which, before, he had quite simply been her slave. He said abjectly, "When can I come?"

"I'll think whether I want to see you again. I may decide there's no point in it."

"And you won't come to Brompton Square?"

"No." Then suddenly she said, "Would you take me to Grayhallock if I asked?"

Hugh was surprised, shocked, pleased. He said, "Certainly, I'd be delighted to." But the next moment he felt that his willingness was a betrayal of Ann. He ought not, surely, to display her abandoned condition to the cold curious gaze of Randall's protector. And it was almost as if he felt that if he allowed Emma to come there she might put a spell on them all. The people at Grayhallock, what was left of them, were after all *his* family.

"I'll think about that too," said Emma. "Now do go. I keep asking you to go and you pay no attention. Those children will be back any moment."

He approached her. He wished before leaving to startle her into a moment of warmth; for he had the impression, and he looked forward to reflecting on it, that she was concealing at least some pleasure at seeing him again.

She said, "I suppose I owe it to you after all that I turned to the consolations of art!" Her laugh, as she looked up at him, seemed more nervous.

She watched him with raised eyebrows as he knelt down slowly and awkwardly beside her chair. As he looked at her now in silence he felt again, as he had felt when he entered the room, that miraculous sense of her being which made a solitude; only this time it was a solitude where only she was. It was he who was absent. Surely this was love. Still looking he groped for her hand.

She drew in a long breath. After a moment she whispered, as if to conceal the words even from herself, "Ah, you should have been braver then. Shouldn't you? Shouldn't you?"

He said "Yes" with so full a heart that he could no longer face her. He lifted the dry, stained, bony hand towards his lips. It smelt so strongly of nicotine that he could not prevent himself from inhaling in an ecstasy of memory before he kissed it.

Chapter Thirteen

"SQUARE one," said Randall.

Lindsay laughed.

They were sitting side by side in a big Edwardian pub near the corner of Church Street. The door stood open to the dusty sunny road and the endless line of traffic. Their hands were clasped under the table.

"I wonder how my father is getting on with your—" said Randall. The final word presented insuperable difficulties.

"I hope excellently," said Lindsay. She had her big bland wide face turned towards him.

He did not look at her, but let his delighted attention wander about the pub, noting a pair of very young lovers, also holding hands, a Chelsea pensioner, two aged crones and a Teddy boy. About all these people a glory shone. Randall was experiencing somewhat the emotions of a dog suddenly presented with the Sunday joint; and indeed he looked, with his expression of rapturous doubt joined with apprehension of a higher and inconceivably beneficent yet also dangerous world, positively dog-like.

He said, "Do you really mean that?" Her tender, intent, ironical gaze gently toasted one side of his face.

"Of course I do," said Lindsay. She squeezed his hand with an increasing pressure, digging in her finger nails.

Randall winced. "She shouldn't have let us out, should she?" he said. "I mean, it puts ideas into our heads. We ought to have been sitting together on the sofa and being referred to as 'the young people'." He turned his wrist against Lindsay's hand until her grip relaxed.

"Ah, she trusts us!"

"But she's wrong to trust us, isn't she?" said Randall eagerly. He turned for a moment to face Lindsay. The big, intent, slightly mocking yellow eyes were very close to his own. He could not search their speckled depth for images of victory or flight. Joy and humility confused him utterly.

"That's up to you, boy," said Lindsay. She gave his hand another squeeze and withdrew hers. The pale eyes widened a moment with an intensified mockery and were withdrawn too. Randall now studied her profile. The lips and cheeks were moulded with a spiritual complacency which made him faint with delight. Just so arrogantly self-filled would an angel look in repose.

"Well, it's up to you too, my queen," said Randall. "You want to be—taken, don't you?"

"If you're brave enough to take me. Not otherwise. Otherwise, I'm very well off as I am, thank you." She spoke with a little-girlish satisfaction.

Randall sighed. This was the point they had got to the last time, just before Emma had so obligingly swallowed them up. "But you've got to *help* me to be brave. Don't let us have a vicious circle here."

"I'm afraid I'm not going to help you," said Lindsay. She spoke judiciously. "But I expect I shall watch your struggles with sympathy." She laughed.

"They *are* struggles, you know," said Randall. "I wonder how much you really imagine them? You know how I feel Ann now as a dead weight. Yet at the same time I'm terribly sorry for her. And I'm hideously—connected with her. It's odd how that *connection* survives any real relationship. And it seems to go out into everything. The roses. Even the bloody furniture!"

Randall spoke sincerely. He knew that there was a world of difference between a secret liaison and a public rupture, and he feared the latter in a dozen ways. Yet there was also in him, and it seemed at times to shiver through him like a shaft of light, a pure desire for destruction, to smash everything to bits. He worshipped the purity of that urge. He wished he could explain to Lindsay how important it was to him that she should let her wildness play, as it were, upon him. His tiny purity yearned to her immense purity as to the ground of its being, and he struggled with her wordlessly as a mystic struggles with his God.

"How you manage your wife is your affair," said Lindsay. "I don't want to hear about it."

"I don't see why I should do all the work!"

"Assuming your marriage *is* over," said Lindsay, ignoring his remark. "Is it?" She turned towards him again and gave him a hard look. Her face had at such moments a strength before which Randall foundered.

"Yes, of course it is."

"Well then, act accordingly."

"Ah, you are honest," he said. "You are so much honester than I am!" *So much stronger too*, it was on the tip of his tongue to say, but he refrained. He did not want positively to suggest to Lindsay that she was dominant. Lindsay bestriding him had better remain a private fantasy.

Lindsay smiled. The strength passed without remainder into the smile. The other side of a turning screw. "The world would not account either of us honest. I wonder how much you really fear the world, Randall?"

Randall did not know. He said, emulating her toughness, "Time will show." He added, "I suppose we are rather unprincipled, aren't we?"

"We don't live by abstract rules," said Lindsay. "But our acts have their places. They belong to us."

"Their places in a pattern," said Randall. "Yes. In a form. Our lives belong to us." But he thought at once, I am talking nonsense. My life has not belonged to me for years. And then he thought, but it *will* belong to me, and he felt the shaft of light go through him. To cover up his last remark he said, "Ann lives by rules and her acts don't have places, they don't belong anywhere. It's a very depressing thing to witness. I wonder why it's so depressing? It makes me so gloomy sometimes I want to die. Ann is *abstract*." He spoke with a sudden passion. What was it he so positively *hated* here?

"Morality is depressing," said Lindsay. She was smiling slightly and drawing her finger in and out of the wet rings on the table to make a complex rosiform pattern.

"*Your* morality is not," said Randall. "It invigorates, it inspires, it gives life. You have a marvellous moral toughness. You are so completely honest and genuine. You do me immense good."

"Get me another drink, Randall dear."

He rose and went to the bar. Simply drinking with her was paradise. He looked about him. A group of people had come in. A fat elderly woman joined them. She kissed each of them. They all began to chatter. Randall looked on them with amazement and affection. Wonderful ordinary people whose lives *worked*.

"You know," he said to Lindsay as he got back with the drink, "I long to spoil you! It's almost incredible to me, and somehow marvellous, that you've never been out of England. Think of the places there are to show you!"

"Ah, it is I who would spoil you," she said. "I would show you things you never dreamt of. If you turned out to deserve them."

There was in her cool stare a pinpoint of yearning which Randall perceived with joy, while at the same time he felt, at her so turning him away from her lack of experience, a pure compassion. Strength flowed into him. "We're pretty evenly matched, aren't we?"

She smiled now, and just touched him on the nose with her finger.

"Lindsay, Lindsay," he said, in an overflowing of tenderness. "This *is* the beginning of something? We will go away together, won't we?"

"I don't know," she said. "It's a matter of your deserts, isn't it? Don't for a moment forget that we're very well off as we are."

"We *are* well off, of course," said Randall cautiously. He was not sure how serious Lindsay was and he wanted to say nothing wrong. "All the same," he said, "I'm going quietly crazy."

"I'm not!" said Lindsay, with an affected little pout of complacency.

"But you *will* come?" said Randall. He desperately wanted to feel her spurs in him. "You do love me, Lindsay, for heaven's sake?"

She looked at him sombrely, and as he gazed in supplication he seemed to see another symbol taking shape in her eyes, as if her beloved initial, on which he had used to meditate as upon one of the names of God, had transformed itself into the relevant question.

"Money," he said. "Yes."

Lindsay nodded.

"Yes," he said. "We must have money. That's the trouble, isn't it?" He did not insult her by saying, "I can earn money, if you help me." That was not a thing to say to a girl such as Lindsay. The turn which the discussion had taken was a sobering one; but the cold touch of even a hostile reality, after the substanceless fantasy of the last year, thrilled his blood. He felt, blindly, almost hopeful.

With a coldness which matched her own, and which he felt as deliciously provocative as the tenderest *badinage* of love, he said, "Will you get her dough?"

Lindsay smiled faintly and respondingly and her hand sought his. "Not unless I stay till the end."

"And how near is the end?"

Lindsay shrugged her shoulders.

"She pretends to be old, doesn't she," said Randall, "and she isn't really so old at all. Do you think she's ill?"

"She's not ill. She'll live forever."

"Hmm," said Randall. "Then we must think of something else."

"*You* must think of something else."

"You're bloody helpful, aren't you." He squeezed her hand. "I tell you one thing. I must go to bed with you soon, my darling, or I'll die of unreality. The two of you have made me into a bloody dream object. I've got to have you Lindsay, or I shall just cease to be. So I suggest the programme is, first we go to bed, then I get hold of some money, then we think what to do next."

"No," said Lindsay, withdrawing her hand again. "The programme is, first you think, then you get the money, then we go to bed."

"Ah," he said, "you're going to put me to the question." He trembled, but he adored her for it. "Yes?"

She said impatiently, "Yes, if you will!"

He would, he would. He murmured submissively, "You are a tormentor—"

"Oh, don't be so feeble, Randall," Lindsay said with irritation. She looked at her watch. "It's time for us to go back now."

"Not *already*," said Randall. "God!" He regarded her, frowning. "Suppose I were just to take you away now, not to *let* you go back?"

"You couldn't," she said simply, rising.

It was so patently true that Randall did not even trouble to think in what sense it was true. He followed her dejectedly out of the pub.

"Don't look so hangdog," said Lindsay, thrusting her arm through his as they went up the hill. "After all, you *must* think, mustn't you? You must count the cost in detail. You may not really want me at all. Think of all that lovely furniture at Grayhallock!'

"You bitch," said Randall softly. "I count the cost day and night. Miranda. Everything. I've counted, and I want you, as you bloody well know."

"Miranda," said Lindsay. "*Yes.*" She sighed a long sigh and leaned more heavily upon his arm.

He knew that she feared this topic and he was at once in a flurry lest he should have discouraged her. He did not want to have thrown into her consciousness any hard thing round which hostility to him might quietly collect. He said, "That will be all right, you know. Miranda is nearly grown up and she's a very wise little person. You'll see. You'll like her and she'll like you."

"I doubt that," said Lindsay. "But never mind. There, there! Never mind."

They reached the door of the flats and paused in the dark vestibule. He took her two hands now, regarded her, and then took her slowly in a strong embrace. A moment later, as he almost groaned aloud with desire, he wondered why, in that sacred hour, he had accepted her idea of going to the pub, instead of taking her by taxi to his little room in Chelsea. But that was just another thing that, in that undefined way, he couldn't do. Then he felt in the sway of her body to his such an unambiguous answer to his fierceness that he became unaware of all else.

"Randall, Randall," she whispered, as if waking him from a long sleep, and gently undid his clasp. "Come," she said.

"No," said Randall. "I'm not coming in. You can go alone."

"She'll be disappointed if you don't come. Don't displease her. She's an old lady."

Randall hesitated. "No," he said again. He could feel himself swelling with strength. "I'll come tomorrow. But not now. I want to be quite alone now and think about you. I don't want this lovely piece of your presence to be spoiled before I quite make it over into my soul."

"Think, yes," she murmured. "But not about me. Think *practical* thoughts, will you, Randall darling, *practical* thoughts."

Subdued by her tenderness he said "Yes, yes, yes." And with a sort of triumph born of his recent abstention he watched her go down the long corridor. The green door opened and shut again and all was silence. He waited a minute of two. What in the world were they saying to each other now?

Chapter Fourteen

"THE Reverend Swann!" Miranda announced with a giggle, putting her head round the door. She never tired of this simple jest. She could then be heard pounding away down the stairs.

Ann was dusting Randall's room. She paused now with the duster in her hand. She did not want to see Douglas. She desired to stay quiet and melancholy, to be left alone. The melancholy itself was a sort of precious achievement. She came sometimes to Randall's room, though never without a pretext. She looked about her for a moment before going down. The sun shone brightly into the small bright room. Everything was neat. The little row of gold-rimmed Dresden cups stood in descending order on the mantelpiece. The bright blue bird-woven William Morris tiles glowed on either side of the grate. The two quartets of rose prints, with their dark red mounts, paraded upon the wall. The blue and white Welsh bedspread swept smoothly up the incline of the pillow. The only shabby things in the room were the two toy animals, Toby and Joey, who had their place on the bed, their limp threadbare paws intertwined. Toby was brown and Joey was white, and each had lost an eye and a good deal of fur in the course of the years. Ann felt an affinity with them, as if she too were an old dusty object off which from time to time pieces of vague woolly substance fell. She was glad they were still there. Randall had taken his big Redouté away with him when he left; she had noticed at once its absence from the white-painted bookshelves in the alcove. But where Toby and Joey were Randall would come back. She still had in keeping the innocent part of him. She paused again at the door. It was so oddly like a boy's room: the room of an aesthetic slightly feminine boy.

Ann had scarcely met Douglas Swann since the evening of Randall's departure, when the unfortunate priest had been made to retire with so little dignity, since Swann's mother had become very ill and he had had to depart almost at once to sit by her bedside. So that she had not yet had an opportunity to discuss her new situation, if it was a new situation, with her clerical friend. She was not sure if she was glad or sorry at the prospect of now receiving his consolation, perhaps his advice. Douglas Swann often seemed to her to take, perhaps for professional reasons, too rosily optimistic a view of Randall's character. The same could not be said of Clare, whose enthusiastic sympathy Ann had had in abundance, and whose picture of Randall tended rather to the lurid. Clare was not of course unaware of Douglas's chaste concern for Ann. As a counterpart to this, she maintained a somewhat morbid interest in Ann's husband, over whose excesses there was a certain licking of the lips. In some curious way, Ann had long felt, Randall played an important part in Clare's imagination; and when, after some Randallian outrage, Clare cried with particular vehemence "I wouldn't stand it from *my* husband. I'd leave!" Ann felt in her friend a positive yearning for violence: a yearning which could scarcely have been satisfied by the gentle and rational Swann.

Just lately, however, Ann suspected because of admonitory letters from Douglas, Clare's "Don't you stand it, dear!" had changed into "He'll come back, dear, you'll see." This doubtless would be the tone of Swann's own admonitions now that he was returned to offer them in person; and Ann felt, as she descended the stairs, a sense of guilty discouragement. The particular quality of her long battle with Randall had seemed progressively to empty the certainties by which she lived, as if the real world were being quietly taken away, grain by grain, and stored in some place of which she had no knowledge. This did not make her doubt the certainties. There would be for her no sudden switch of the light which would show a different scene. But there was a dreariness, a hollowness. She could not inhabit what she ought to be. She felt this, anticipating the things which Douglas would certainly say. Though as she approached the drawing-room she felt also a simple pleasure in the visit of a friend.

Douglas Swann turned from the window with an exclamation of welcome. As Ann greeted him she saw that Miranda had tiresomely taken up the whole centre of the room with what she called her 'Dolls' Durbar'. The whole gang of them was mustered, the 'little people', or the 'little princes', as Miranda sometimes called them, all sitting up in a wide-eyed semicircle. The effect was rich and rather startling, since the little people had exotic and barbarous tastes in clothes and jewellery.

"My dear Ann," said Douglas, skirting the dolls, "my dear—" He took her two hands and drew her with him toward one of the window-seats. He gave her an intense look of wordless sympathy.

Ann freed her hands and said briskly, "Well, Douglas, it's nice to see you back, and sweet of you to come over so soon." Then she remembered guiltily the cause of his absence and rebuked her own self-centred condition. "But how is your poor mother? I do hope she's a little better?"

Douglas shook his head. "I'm afraid not," he said. "There is little possibility of improvement. Indeed it must be faced that there is now *no* possibility of improvement. The end of her journey is in sight." He sighed deeply.

"I am so sorry!" said Ann. She pressed his hand and they both sat down.

"'Change and decay in all around we see'," said Douglas. "One must accept it. But it is terrible how one grieves over these partings. I'm afraid it shows a lack of faith."

A lack of faith, thought Ann. Had she got faith? Did she imagine that she would ever see Steve again? No. And yet she believed in God, she had to. "Poor Douglas."

"I always found my parents such a support," he said, "a support that never failed. I suppose I was lucky."

Ann looked out of the window. Miranda was capering across the lawn, swinging in her two hands like tambourines the white enamelled bowls in which each night she put out the milk for her hedgehogs. Did Miranda find her a 'support'? Her daughter had been exceptionally cold with her lately, and had stopped calling her 'mummy', attracting her attention when necessary by cries of 'Oh' and 'Ah'. Something had been wrong, indeed, with her relations with Miranda ever since Steve died. The same was true of her relations with Randall. It was as if everyone blamed her for Steve's death. Or as if, she sometimes a little resentfully thought, since the others wanted to blame someone and she did not, she made a vacuum into which their blame ran.

In the distance under the beech trees Ann made out a solitary figure. It was Penny. He watched Miranda cross the lawn, and then faded back into the shifting green shadows. He seemed like a poor faun watching human affairs. To distract Douglas from his grief, and also to put off the moment of talking about Randall, she said, "It was so kind of you to take such an interest in Penny before you went away. He's very fond of you, you know."

"He's a thoroughly decent boy," said Douglas. "I expect you'll miss him?"

"Yes," said Ann. It occurred to her that she would miss Penny dreadfully. She sighed, and then said, "Do you know, I think he's a bit in love with Miranda. Isn't it absurd? I believe he's positively suffering, poor child."

Douglas smiled. "How one suffers when one's young!" Then, as if thinking that this was tactless, he added. "You wait till Miranda's old enough to be in love. Then the sparks will fly!"

"That was probably why he decided not to go to London with Humphrey. He couldn't bear to leave Miranda. I couldn't understand it at all at the time."

"I imagined you'd thought otherwise of it because of Humphrey's er—"

"No, no, Humphrey has plenty of sense. And Penny can see no evil. But I'm sorry for him now."

They were silent, Ann twisting her hands and sighing again in spite of herself, and Douglas leaning forward with an air of gathering solicitude, his hands dangling at his knees in the attitude of one about to rise to make a pronouncement.

He did not rise, but said in a softened voice, not looking at her, "No news from Randall, I suppose?"

"Nothing," said Ann. "He hasn't written. I've written, of course, to Chelsea, but I don't even know if he's there." She stared at the dolls, whose ranks were drawn up facing her, little hostile presences. The fantasy occurred to her that Miranda had put the dolls there to keep an eye on her mother.

"We must have *good* hope, *good* hope," said Douglas.

"Of course," said Ann. She felt irritated. She added, "Don't let's exaggerate, Douglas dear. You know as well as I do that all sorts of catastrophes can happen inside a marriage without destroying it."

"I most heartily believe it," said Douglas, with the slightly self-conscious accent of the happily married man who knows about such things by hearsay. "Marriage is a sacrament. And we must believe, in such cases, a special grace assists our love."

"My love just exasperates Randall," said Ann. She wanted to bring the discussion down to earth. "But he'll come back, for hundreds of reasons of habit and convenience. Thank God marriages don't depend on love!"

Douglas seemed a little shocked. He said, "In a purely temporal sense, perhaps not. But the marriage service contains the word 'love'. It is the first thing that we promise to do. The continuation of love is a duty, and it is a matter much more genuinely subject to the will than is commonly supposed nowadays. Even if we leave divine grace out of the picture."

Ann felt tired and disinclined to consider the picture with or without divine grace. She could feel Swann's attention like a plucking of many strings. It was as if he wanted to break her down. Perhaps he did, even if unconsciously, want her to break down so that he could console her. There were a hundred things that she ought to be doing. She had promised Bowshott that she would help with the spraying. The proofs of the catalogue must be corrected. Miranda's clothes needed attention. She said, "Well, I doubt if Randall has any love left for me by now. It doesn't matter." But it did matter. What else mattered if this didn't?

PART THREE

"You must enclose him in a net of goodness and loving kindness," said Douglas.

The image of the enraged Randall so trammelled almost made Ann laugh, and with that an agonising protective tenderness towards her husband brimmed up in her heart, so that at the next moment she almost wept. She said, "I don't know about that! My love for Randall is terribly imperfect. I can't see it having any miraculous effect!"

"Most of our love is shabby stuff," said Douglas. "But there is always a thin line of gold, the bit of pure love on which all the rest depends—and which redeems all the rest."

Ann thought he was talking sense, but the slight tone of exaltation wrought terribly upon her nerves. "Perhaps," she said. "But one can't *see* things like that. All that one *sees* is shapeless and awkward."

As she uttered the words she felt, shapeless and awkward is what I am. She had been awkward at school, and had been told that it would pass. It had not passed, and she had learnt to live with it, and it had become no easier as she grew older. She had had, she must have had, some grace when Randall first loved her and when her hair was almost as red as Miranda's: some wild grace lent her by the very fact of the dazzling, the enchanting Randall's love. But that time was hard even to imagine now. What remained was awkwardness and effort, the endless effort of confronting people with none of whom she had any sense of fitting. Had she and Randall ever 'fitted'? Perhaps, in the days of their happiness, their personalities had been too hazy for the question to arise. Now the haze had cleared and they had hardened into incompatible shapes. Yet 'fitting' was still something that was possible. With Douglas, for instance, she felt almost perfectly at ease. And with Felix. Her thoughts touched this and took flight at once. That was a place where thoughts must not go. I am always saying no, said Ann to herself, all my strength has to go into saying no. I have no strength left for the positive. No wonder Randall finds me deadly, no wonder he says I kill all his gaiety. But why is it like this? And she recalled dimly and with puzzlement some quotation which said that the devil was the spirit which was always saying no.

"Shapeless and awkward," said Douglas. "Precisely. We must not expect our lives to have a visible shape. They are invisibly shaped by God. Goodness accepts the contingent. Love accepts the contingent. Nothing is more fatal to love than to want everything to have form."

"Randall wants everything to have form," said Ann. "But then he's an artist."

"He is a man before he is an artist," said Douglas with magisterial severity.

Ann felt she could not stand much more of this discussion. She hated this sense of their cornering Randall. She said, "I must get on with my work," and began to rise.

Douglas Swann detained her. He inclined his smooth face towards her, drawing his chin back over his clerical collar and opening a little wider his dark brown eyes which were let with such startling immediacy into the sweep of his cheek. He said, "Ann, you do pray, don't you?"

Ann said almost furiously, "Yes, of course. I pray every night that Randall will come back." Then she burst into wild tears.

"There, my child, my child," murmured Swann. They had both risen. He spoke with a sense of achievement, as of one who has brought a difficult piece of navigation to a successful conclusion. He began to draw the sobbing Ann to rest against his shoulder.

The drawing-room door opened abruptly to admit Mildred Finch. "Dear me!" said Mildred.

The next moment Ann was searching her pockets for a handkerchief and Douglas Swann was coughing and dusting down his coat.

"Oh, Mildred—" said Ann. She found the handkerchief. All her face, as she rubbed it, seemed to be wet with tears. It is astonishing how many tears can flow in an instant. The instant in any case was over and she dried her face and smoothed her hair back behind her ears.

Mildred came round the edge of the semicircle of dolls and said,

"There, my dear, don't take on." She cast a hostile glance at Swann who was standing a few paces away and looking anxiously at Ann.

Ann, who was fairly composed now, said, "I'm so glad to see you!" and blew her nose. "I don't know why I broke down so stupidly. I've been quite cheerful."

Mildred looked sceptical, and then set her feet apart in a patient yet stubborn pose which indicated with brutal clarity that she was waiting for Swann to go.

Swann said to Ann in a voice of significant tenderness, "Are you all right now?"

Mildred said, "Of course she's not all right!" Then she added conversationally, "I've just walked up from the village. It looks quite like rain now. Fortunately I've got my umbrella."

Swann looked at Ann for another moment. Ann said, "I'm fine. Thank you for being so kind, Douglas." Swann patted her lightly on the shoulder, smiled and nodded to Mildred, murmured something about having to get back, and left the room.

"Well, that's got rid of *him*," said Mildred.

Ann sat down. The outburst of tears had exhausted her. She was glad to see Mildred, yet she felt a strange alarm too at the sight of her, as if her old friend were becoming, in some inadmissible way, a rather too significant, rather too menacing object.

She said, "Do take your coat off and stop looking as if you were going directly. You'll stay to lunch?"

"That depends," said Mildred. "And I'll keep my coat on, I'm frozen. I can't think why you don't have a fire. There, I told you so, it's raining."

Ann looked out. The sun had gone in, and with one of those sudden tricks of the English summer the garden was windswept and the grass and trees darkened and dripping. Ann realised that she felt cold too. She said, instantly overcome by a sense of the meaninglessness of it all, "Oh God, I'm so tired—"

"You need a holiday," said Mildred. She stood there still, feet apart, umbrella under arm, hands in the pockets of her blue check tweed coat, her light sandy grey hair jumbled about her kindly face which had softened rather than wrinkled with the approach of age.

"A holiday!" Ann laughed a little harshly.

"Why not? This place could go on. Bowshott could run it."

"No he couldn't," said Ann. "Never mind. It doesn't matter." She seemed to be saying that all the time now.

"I suppose there's no news from the deplorable Randall?"

"No."

"I suppose he's going to settle down with the Rimmer girl?"

"With who?"

"Oh Lord!" said Mildred. "Have I put my foot in it? You didn't know he was having a terrific affair with Lindsay Rimmer, you know, Emma Sands' companion?"

Ann got up and pushed her handkerchief into the sleeve of her jersey. She had an immediate impression that Mildred knew very well what she was doing. She said abruptly, "I assumed he was having an affair with somebody. I didn't know who it was. And honestly I don't care much."

"Nonsense, child," said Mildred, after regarding her for a moment. "Of course you care. But I'm glad that you seem to have written Randall off."

"I haven't written him off. It's just that I'm not curious about the details. He'll come back." Ann spoke jerkily, her voice getting lower and hoarser like someone reciting a confession.

Mildred spoke more softly and lightly now, as if managing a transition from a spoken to a sung litany. "I don't think he'll come back, my dear."

"Yes, he will," said Ann. She didn't want to cry again. "Let's go to the kitchen. It's warmer, and we can have some coffee."

"And Randall is a brute," said Mildred. "Let us call things by their names. A brute and a cad."

"Stop it, Mildred, will you? Let's go to the kitchen. How did you get here, by the way? You said you walked from the village."

"Felix brought me," said Mildred. Her tone was bleak and provocative.

Ann said, "Oh."

When she said no more, Mildred pursued, "Yes, he's gone to Maidstone to pick up some new blades for the lawnmower. It's so useful having him at Seton Blaise. He's renovated all the machines. He's so mechanical."

"How will you get back?"

"Oh, he's coming back in an hour. I told him to look for me at the pub, or if he didn't see me there to come on up here. You might ask both of us to lunch. Or we might carry you over to Seton Blaise. Why not come and stay for a day or two and be looked after?"

Ann rubbed her mouth with her hand and pushed her hair back again. The front of her mind was composed, but in the far background there was a sense of foundering, of confused panic and flight. She said, "I'm so sorry. I think now that I really ought to go over to Clare's for lunch. I've kept putting her off. She wants to discuss the flower-arrangement competition."

"But you invited me to lunch!"

"Yes, but I'd forgotten Clare. I'm awfully sorry. It would be a bit difficult."

"Well, come to Seton Blaise tomorrow then? Felix could come and fetch you any time in the Mercedes."

"I can't," said Ann. "I'd love to, but I must keep things going here. It's an awfully important time of year. I must do the catalogue. There's a whole lot to be added to the proofs. We're putting some new things from Germany on the market and I've got to do descriptions and get photographs and so on. But thanks! Have some coffee before you go?"

Mildred just looked at her and said, "Ann, Ann, Ann, Ann!"

There was a silence between them, Mildred braced and staring, Ann with bowed head rubbing her brow and eyes slowly and methodically. Then Ann said in a weary voice, "Come on Mildred. I could do with some coffee myself."

Mildred stood her ground. She barred Ann's way and said very quietly, "You know that Felix is terribly in love with you?"

Ann was silent, and it seemed afterwards that she had passed a vast time in reflection. What she said and did now was crucial, not so much for Mildred as for herself. Mildred had led up to her moment of theatre, but she must be cheated of it and sent away empty. There must be no drama here, no possible foothold for the imagination. What Mildred was trying to conjure up must be made nonsense of, must be made somehow not to exist. The thing must be laughed off briskly, Mildred must be clapped on the shoulder and taken to her coffee. There must be no admission of knowledge or interest, no confused looks, nothing. Again it was no and nothing.

"Yes," said Ann.

A long silence ensued during which Ann lowered her head. She knew that she was blushing violently. Her head seemed like a heavy fruit about to fall from the bough.

Mildred was tactful and merciful. She could afford to be since she was not by any means being sent away empty-handed. She said, "Well, I won't torment you. I can see you're tired out. I won't stay for coffee, thanks. I'll improve the shining hour by buying one or two things in the village. Felix will pick me up there. Do think seriously about coming to Seton. We'd love to see you *any* time."

She turned to go, and nearly tripped over the dolls. "Isn't Miranda getting a little old for dolls?" She regarded the little figures. Then she began to knock them over gently one by one with her umbrella. As each one fell backward on the floor its waxen eyelids closed.

Chapter Fifteen

"I T's hard to believe she's not here," said Randall. He was standing in the drawing-room of Emma's flat, holding Lindsay by the hand. The tape-recorder was there, and the smell of tobacco, and the little table with the strewing of Gauloises, but the big armchair was empty. Emma Sands was at Grayhallock.

"If you'd like to make sure you can search the flat!" said Lindsay.

"I know it's absurd, but I think I will," said Randall. He made for the door. Then he said to Lindsay, "You lead the way."

Lindsay took his hand again and drew him through the hall. There was the kitchen, he knew that. Often enough he had carried tea-trays to and fro. There was the bathroom. He knew that of course. There was the dining-room, where he occasionally dined with them on treat days, such as Emma's birthday. On ordinary days Emma worked all the evening and had a sandwich supper. There was the spare bedroom, which was partially furnished and used as a box room. Emma never had guests. There was Emma's bedroom. Here Randall paused. It was a big Italianate room, airy, like something out of a painting by Carpaccio, and somehow attentive, significant. One expected to see out of the window a clear vista of a distant campanile, and not, through net curtains, the nearby railings. He had never seen this room before. A sweet herbal scent seemed to emanate from the old velvet hangings and from the double bed whose fringed red coverlet swept the floor.

"Perhaps you'd like to look under the bed?" said Lindsay jauntily.

Randall knelt down and lifted the coverlet. His heart was beating violently as if he really expected to see the form of Emma crouching in the darkness. There was nothing there except several pairs of shoes and a suitcase.

As he began to rise he received a sudden blow on the shoulder. He spun round on one heel and over-balanced backwards on the floor with an alarmed exclamation. The next moment Lindsay was lying full length on top of him. "It's only me!" she said.

"As the iceberg said to the Titanic!" He clasped his hands in the small of her back, breathing deeply.

"Why, Randall, I believe you really *are* frightened!" said Lindsay. "I imagined you were joking. You thought just now that Emma was stealing up on you with a blunt instrument."

"Yes," said Randall. "I'm afraid. And not only of Emma." He drew his hands now downward from her arched shoulders along her spine to her thighs. Her elbows were planted firmly on each side of his neck and her face hung over his, too close for him to see more than the hazy laughing glow of her expression. Her dress caressed the silk beneath as his hand gently moulded her and found the warm flesh at the top of her stocking. Randall groaned softly. Their feet were together under Emma's bed jumbled with the shoes.

"Don't be afraid," she murmured. Then she took her weight off her elbows and pressed heavily upon him while her hands fluttered about her head. The next moment something soft and cold descended and the light was blotted out. She had undone her hair.

Randall gasped at the sudden pressure and at the soft cascade. She propped herself up again, deliberately shaking her hair forward to hide her face and shaking it into Randall's eyes. There was a great deal of it. He raised his hands awkwardly and lifted the hair back over her brow, to reveal her bland and smiling beneath. He looked up at her for a moment, straining his neck, and then with a quick movement he shifted her off on to the floor. They both sat up, breathing deeply and staring at each other like two cats.

"Well, let's complete the search," said Randall abruptly. He got up and patted the side of Emma's bed into place.

Lindsay did not take his hand now, but led him into the last room, which was her bedroom. It was a smaller room which looked out on to the little evergreen garden. There was a narrow divan under the window, a table of light oak and a long shelf of brightly coloured paper-backs. The few objects which lay about Randall recognised as things he had given her: a paper-weight in the form of a hand, a miniature silver mirror, an Italian box with a lozenge pattern, a scratching dog of Derby china. It was as if she could not find things for herself. It was like a servant's room, simple, impoverished, and touching.

Randall looked carefully round it. Then he turned to look at Lindsay. Her golden hair, falling in disorder, reached well below her breasts. She looked younger, smaller, wilder. With deliberation Randall ran his two hands round the front of her dress and collected all the hair into a great bunch at the back. Then he drew her head right back with one hand and laid his other hand flat on her cheek. He saw with pleasure a momentary look of alarm. He said, "Since we've had this seductive routine am I to understand that you've changed the order of the programme you announced to me the other day?"

Lindsay's chin now pointed at the ceiling, her mouth gaped a little. But she kept her hands down loosely at her sides like a hanged girl. She said, "What will you do if I tell you that the programme is unchanged?"

"I shall probably beat you and certainly rape you," said Randall. He gradually released his grip on her hair.

She drew her hair forward again about her brow, massaging her scalp with her fingers. Then she said in a small voice, "Well, I shall have to change the programme, then, won't I?"

"Oh Lord!" said Randall. "Let's go back to the drawing-room. I want a drink."

When they reached the drawing-room Lindsay produced a decanter of whisky, two glasses and a jug of water which she had evidently had in readiness. Randall drank some of the whisky neat. Then he took to staring at Lindsay. She had somehow thrust all her hair down the back of her dress and looked demure and boyish. He would never understand her.

"Well," said Lindsay, "are you satisfied that she isn't here?"

It still seemed to Randall eerie and almost incredible that Emma was not in the flat. She hardly ever left it, and the only time he had seen her away from it was at his mother's funeral. He said, "I suppose I'm satisfied that she isn't here *now*."

"You mean you think she might have laid a trap for us?"

"Yes," said Randall. He thought: or you might both have laid a trap for me. Why, after all, had Lindsay so firmly refused to come to Chelsea? Now that he was passing, as he thought, out of fantasy into reality, the real world seemed a region even more fantastic than the dream palace he had inhabited before. He felt like a favourite slave who has been kept on cushions and fed on sherbet and who is suddenly put at the gate and told he is free. Such stories end with the sword.

Lindsay was very quiet. She stood with her hands behind her, head bent slightly forward. She wore a plain unbelted dress of brown linen which looked like some charming uniform, Her hair, still held in the neck of the dress, was beginning to fall forward in two heavy loops on either side of her face. She seemed some young exotic general planning the order of battle. She said, "Suppose we were to ring up Grayhallock. Would you be satisfied then?"

"Oh God!" said Randall. He began to pace up and down. He found the idea of Emma at Grayhallock very hard to tolerate. He had been surprised both at her wish to go and at the ease with which she had persuaded his father to take her. Randall, with an eye to his own interests, was of course by no means opposed to, though he was also irrationally disturbed by, a renewal of friendship between his father and Emma. But he was unnerved that the first rite to be celebrated in this revival should comprise a visit to his home. He could not think what it meant. He felt sure Emma was up to something, and, which he felt was indeed irrational, he resented goings-on between his father and Emma the significance of which he was not a party to. He felt himself unjustly robbed of the rôle of patron; and it was almost as if he were jealous, though quite of whom was not so clear. More simply and immediately he feared and detested the idea of Emma's visiting Grayhallock in his absence or indeed at all; and the thought of her presence there wrung from him a cry of: but those are *my* people!

It was important that Emma should be guaranteed to be far away. It was also important that Emma should not know of Randall's visit to the flat. Here he had had to rely on Lindsay. When it emerged that Emma was going to be away for a whole day, without Lindsay in attendance, Randall's mind had jumped at the obvious conclusion, only to fall away baffled. There was, to begin with, Lindsay's 'programme'. Randall was quite unsure how far this piece of blackmail would stand up, if they were given a glorious field of hours in which to disport themselves together alone. He knew, confidently, with satisfaction, how much he was desired. But there was another difficulty. He could not bear to go to bed with Lindsay with Emma's permission. To go to bed with Lindsay *without* Emma's permission was of course most hazardous and alarming, and the idea of it affected him with a guilty thrill. But to do it *with* her permission struck him as nauseating; and he had a fear, which increased within him now as he pondered the significance of Lindsay's abandonment of her 'programme', that they had decided between them that he was to be 'brought on'.

It had been essential that Emma should be deceived, and this he had impressed upon Lindsay. They had agreed that Emma should be told that Randall was out of London visiting a dangerously ill friend, how unfortunately, on the very day when Emma was to be at Grayhallock. When forming this plan it had seemed to Randall more than a little unlikely that Emma would believe him capable of putting even the last farewells of a close friend before the pleasure of a day with Lindsay; but Lindsay had apparently produced an extremely circumstantial account and Emma had seemed to be convinced. It occurred to Randall later that Emma's ingenious mind, professionally so used to devising stratagems within stratagems, might, even if she thought the story false, imagine that it covered up, not a day with Lindsay, but a day of snooping about Grayhallock spying on her own activities. Finally he decided there was no knowing whether she believed the story or not, but it was just enough for his purposes that she was not *certain* he was with Lindsay. With all this the terrible and humiliating suspicion remained that they were both in league against him.

Randall hated the idea of telephoning Grayhallock. He did not at that moment want to believe that Grayhallock existed. The mere notion that one could lift the telephone and conjure that whole world into being at the other end made him sweat and shiver as at some unsavoury piece of magic. Yet as soon as Lindsay had said it he saw that it was essential. It would remove from him the nightmare picture, which of all the gallery of spectres was the one which now most haunted him, of Emma quietly opening the door upon his embrace of Lindsay. He said, "How should we manage it?"

"Easily," she said. "You get through to the number and give me the phone. I'll ask for Emma. When she answers I'll give you the phone so that you can hear her voice. Then I'll have a little conversation with her. It can be perfectly natural and plausible."

"Do we have to have the conversation? Can't we just ring off without letting on who we are?"

"No. Then she *would* guess."

"All right," said Randall after a moment. He picked up the telephone. He said to the operator, "Can I have Netherden 28. It's near Ashford, in Kent." Uttering the familiar number in Lindsay's presence felt like betraying a precious secret. Yet there was a certain exhilaration in it too. In the silence that followed Randall felt his heart beating, painful blow after blow, as he stared at Lindsay with widened eyes. The phone began to ring. Then Ann's voice said, "Hello. This is Netherden 28."

Ann. The scene before him was blotted out and he stood paralysed in the presence of that voice. Of course he might have supposed that she would answer the phone. But Ann. Ann existed now, standing in the dining-room at Grayhallock this very moment holding the telephone and waiting for him to speak. Ann and all her thoughts. Then in a second it occurred to him that simply by saying "Ann" he could make his whole palace of dreams vanish away and end the days of his soft enslavement perhaps forever. If

he but spoke her name they would magically disappear, the
cushions and the sherbet, the tinkling bells and the gay-plumaged
birds, the golden collars and the curving blades. As if to remove a
terrible temptation he slowly let the telephone fall to his side.

Lindsay had taken it from him and was saying in her efficient
secretary voice, "I wonder if I could have a word with Miss Emma
Sands, if she's with you, please?"

There was a pause. Randall began to see the drawing-room
again. Lindsay had spoken to Ann. It was the sort of impossible
event which ought to bring the world automatically to an end.

Lindsay thrust the telephone urgently into his hand. After a
moment he heard, unmistakably, Emma's voice saying, "Hello.
This is Emma Sands." And after another moment, "Hello. Who is
that speaking?" He gave the instrument back to Lindsay.

"It's me, Emma dear, Lindsay."

Pause.

"Oh, quite as might be expected."

Pause.

"Yes, as it turned out. I hope you had a comfortable journey?"

Pause.

"Are you alone?"

Pause.

"I wonder if you know now what time you'll be back? That's
what I really rang about."

Pause.

"Yes, I'll do your sandwiches and milk as usual. Be well and
bless me."

Pause.

"Good-bye, darling."

Lindsay put the phone back and looked triumphantly at Randall.
"There!"

Randall stared at her, his big face wrinkled up in anxiety and
horror. This latest piece of sorcery had confused him utterly. He
was almost ready to believe that the sound of Emma's voice which
he had heard was an auditory hallucination induced by Lindsay.

And what was the significance of the telephone conversation? What had happened in the gaps? He felt obscurely that some outrage had been committed against Grayhallock and thus against himself. He said, "What were you talking about?"

"Well, you heard!"

"I heard your half of it!"

"She just asked how I was getting on without her and said she'd had a nice journey and that she'd be back about eight and would I do her sandwiches, and that was all."

"Was it?" said Randall. "Did she say she was alone?"

"She said she wasn't sure."

"Oh Christ!" said Randall. He supposed by now Ann *must* know all about him and Lindsay, somebody *must* have told her. Why did Ann have to intrude on this day of all days? He simply hadn't wanted to think about whether she knew or not. And she must have guessed it was Lindsay on the telephone, even if Emma didn't tell her.

"I feel sick," said Randall.

"Darling, have some sense, have some *backbone*!" said Lindsay. "At least you know now that Emma won't walk in on us. Hasn't ringing up made everything better?"

"No, it's made everything worse," said Randall. He went over to the window and looked out. The sun shone on the dusty twisted group of evergreens, huddling together like captives.

There was a silence. Lindsay said harshly, "Don't think I don't perfectly realise that you can drop me at any minute you please and go back to your snug cosy set-up at Grayhallock. Your dear dutiful wife is waiting for you. Why don't you go?"

"For Christ's sake," said Randall, "don't torture me. I love you to distraction. You know that perfectly well." He turned and came down the room towards her. She was leaning back in Emma's chair and had drawn out a long tress of hair and was pulling it through her fingers. The hem of the brown linen dress skirted her knees.

Randall dropped on the ground before her. He did not touch

her. He said, "Listen, Lindsay, I absolutely beseech you not to persecute me now. I've been under the most terrible strain."

"All right," she said. She looked at him coolly and began to loop the tress of hair round her wrist. "But you've so long been shouting, that you wanted me. And now when I positively offer myself you seem to be thinking better of it. I'm not sure how long the offer will remain open. So you'd better watch your step. That's all."

"I'm not thinking better of it!" said Randall frantically. "I'm—" How could he explain? He was terrified of making some dreadful irreparable blunder. "It's not that I believe that Emma really arranged all this—"

"What do you mean, that Emma really arranged all this? Are you mad?"

"I'm saying I don't believe it—"

"Well, why mention it then? Randall, you're beginning to rave." She pushed him aside as he now ineffectually clasped at her knees, and stood over him.

"Help me, Lindsay."

"You don't deserve it," she said. "For being so abject you deserve spurning, you deserve whipping. However, I'll do one more thing for you, one last thing. Get out of the way."

Randall removed himself on hands and knees and then got up.

Lindsay went on, "You said once you'd like to know what we were like when you weren't there. Well, now I'm going to show you."

Randall watched her open-mouthed, his hands hanging. He was prepared for anything, for a strange darkening of the room and the appearance in luminous effigy of a magical Emma and Lindsay.

Lindsay pulled the tape recorder out from where it was nestling under the frill of Emma's chair. Crouched above it she examined it and adjusted the tape. Then she set it going. With hypnotic slowness the two wheels began to revolve. She turned her eyes, sombre and stern, upon Randall. After a moment the silence of the attentive room was broken by Emma's voice.

"If you're going to do it its got to be now. There's no time for theory now, no time for ifs and buts. You're in the dark, and you must go forward in the dark."

"Look here—" said Randall.

"That's the novel, you fool," said Lindsay. "The real bit comes in a minute."

"God!" said Randall. He wiped his face all over with a handkerchief. "She didn't know you were recording it, the real bit?"

"Of course not. Otherwise what would have been the point? I fiddled with the machine and pretended to switch it off but didn't."

Emma's voice continued. "As he debated, his hand was already curling round the gun in his pocket. He who hesitates is lost and Marcus Boode had no intention of being that. Reason and hope of support lay behind him. Before him, somewhere in that uninviting labyrinth, was the murderer of Sebastian Leech. He shrugged, and glided on to the head of the downward-plunging stairs."

There was a pause during which the tape-recorder murmured quietly. Then in another tone Emma spoke again. "Lord, what stuff—"

Lindsay's voice said, "You're tired, my dear. Don't forget you're going to Kent tomorrow. Time to knock off, yes? Would you like some whisky in your hot milk? Lovely whisky, yes?"

"No, darling, no whisky. Well, perhaps a little. I hope you'll be all right here all alone."

"I hope *you'll* be all right. It's a long time since the old mole left its burrow. I shall be fine. Really, darling, you can't look after me all the time!"

"Mmm. Can't I? Ah well. It's hard luck on young Randall that he's got to be out of harm's way. He might have given you lunch and spoilt you a little. Or is it just as well, eh, little fox?"

"There you go! Yes, poor Randall was nearly in tears about it."

"We'll deal with Randall, we'll cheer him up when I get back. He'll be all right, oh yes, Randall will be all right."

Lindsay switched the tape off and rose to her feet. As if automatically overbalanced by her movement Randall sank into a chair. Hands on hips she looked down at him with an air of scornful triumph. "You see how well I look after you!"

"You could have faked that," said Randall.

"Oh, break it up, boy!" said Lindsay. She kicked his ankle hard.

"I don't know. I'm going crazy," said Randall. He supported his head in one hand and rubbed his ankle with the other. Once the possibility that Lindsay, even though through some kind of hideous tortuous benevolence, were deceiving him had been admitted to the extent of seeking proofs of her innocence, her innocence became so precisely unprovable that he was prepared to believe himself the victim of some unimaginably motivated hoax. Lindsay might have faked the tape, putting together remarks which belonged in other conversations. It was apparently quite easy to do this. Or she might really have had this conversation with Emma— and then told Emma afterwards that Randall was not in fact going away. Or they might cold-bloodedly have play-acted the scene together, laughing about it afterwards over their whisky. There were dozens of possibilities. After all, Lindsay had co-operated cheerfully for nearly a year in Emma's policy of making a lap-dog of him. But then after all so had he!

"Come. You'll have to start trusting me somewhere," said Lindsay more gently.

"I know," he said. "The trouble is if I don't trust you from the start I can't trust you at all."

"Well, trust me from the start then."

Randall got up slowly. Lindsay's hair had begun to escape from inside her dress and was lying on her shoulders in wide tangles and scatterings of gold. He was moved by how young she looked, how waif-like, a little waif out to make her fortune, a Dick Whittington of the passions.

"I will," he said humbly. It was a gesture of surrender.

Lindsay took him by the hand. She was all kindness now. "You know," she said, "I always thought this scene would be you seducing me—but it's turned out to be me seducing you! I've had to fight every inch of the way. Aren't you a perfect disgrace?"

"You've imagined this scene?" said Randall, gratified.

"A thousand times."

He was delighted and yet terrified, and as they reached the door of her bedroom he had a certain foreboding.

Lindsay pulled the curtain and turned the light on. She undid her bed. The room in the red glow from the reading-lamp seemed suddenly small and desperate. A line of strange daylight showed beyond through a chink in the curtain. Randall closed the door and leaned against it. He felt exhausted.

Lindsay turned to face him, twisting her hair together and throwing it back over her shoulder. With a half-shadowed face she looked like a figure on a playing card. She said in a cold murmur, "Just one last thing, Randall. I may have changed the order of the programme, but I haven't changed the items. Don't forget your practical thinking. No dough, no go." She began to take off her dress.

Christ, what a girl, thought Randall. He worshipped her. At the same time he felt paralysed with fear. He wondered now whether his crazy imaginings about Emma's complicity had not perhaps been devices designed by himself precisely to prevent his ever arriving at this moment. He watched her.

Lindsay pulled the brown dress over her head and shook her hair free of it. She was wearing a very brief petticoat underneath. She put the dress aside and stood now looking at him, gathering her hair once more with a hand that shook slightly.

"Oh God, Lindsay—" said Randall. She looked so strangely pathetic, yet why was he so strangely afraid? She looked like a poor condemned whore taken to execution in her shift. Yet his knees trembled.

"Come, come," she said very softly. "Come, Randall." She bent and began to take off her stockings.

Randall fumbled with his tie. He seemed to be tightening the knot rather than loosening it.

Lindsay had removed other undergarments but not yet the petti-coat. She came to him now and began to help him with the tie, murmuring "Dear, dear, dear." He felt the warmth of her arms. He got the tie off and took off his jacket and waistcoat and put them on the chair. He kicked off his shoes. Then he leaned back against the door panting for breath. By now he could hardly recognise Lind-say.

She regarded him with a tender irony. "Would you like to go home now?"

"Oh God, Lindsay," said Randall again, and he fell on his knees, grasping her about the legs. Her legs were infinitely warm and soft. As she began to pull the petticoat off he laid his head against her thigh. He could feel her trembling violently. He gave long sighs.

"Now, now, now—" said Lindsay. She was kneeling beside him and unbuttoning his shirt. He touched her breasts. He remembered her breasts. Then his searching hand was jerked upwards by Lind-say pulling his shirt and vest over his head. And now she was unbuttoning his trousers.

"All right, all right," said Randall. "I'll do it." He sat on the floor and took off the rest of his clothes.

Lindsay was lying full length on the undone bed. Randall knelt and looked. Then he looked into her face. It was as if their eyes had become huge and luminous so that when they gazed they were together in a great cavern. Slowly he pulled himself up to sit upon the edge of the bed. Then he turned away from her and hid his face in his hands.

"What is it, dear, dear?" murmured Lindsay. She caressed his back.

"I'm not going to be any good," said Randall. "God! I was afraid of this."

"It doesn't matter. Embrace me."

He stretched himself out almost stiffly and buried his face against her. His arms pinioned her with violence.

After a little while she said again, "There. Relax. It doesn't matter."

"It does. I wish I hadn't talked so much about Emma. I'm poisoned."

"Emma's not important here. She's not important any more."

"Ah—not important any more. You know, Lindsay, I don't think I really like Emma."

"I don't think I like her either. In fact I think I dislike her."

"I dislike her too."

"In fact I think I detest her."

"And I detest her. Oh Lindsay—"

It was a few minutes later that he said, "Do you know, I think it's going to be all right after all."

Chapter Sixteen

"SOME more coffee? Another biscuit?" said Ann.

"Thank you, my dear," said Emma.

It was nearly lunch-time, but she was still at it. She seemed to have been eating ever since she arrived, as if she had been starved before. Or as if, it occurred to Ann, she wanted to eat up the whole scene.

Ann had been surprised, even shocked, when Hugh had announced that he was going to bring Emma Sands to Grayhallock. It seemed a little soon after Fanny's death. However, her sense of the visit as improper soon merged into her sense of it as a perfect nuisance. Nancy Bowshott was ill, or pretending to be, and Miranda, in quarantine for German measles, was at home the whole week. It was as much as Ann could do to keep her outfit going at all, without having to cope with state visits. The house had become dusty and untidy and it had taken her several days of getting up half an hour earlier to put it into tolerable order. She refused Clare Swann's offer to do the flowers for her, and then regretted it. By the time her guests actually arrived she was in a state of irritated exhaustion.

Emma too had behaved in an odd and not very reassuring way. Instead of wandering about with Hugh, leaving Ann free to deal with the lunch, she had attached herself to Ann. She had installed herself in the drawing-room, beside the window, smoking innumerable Gauloises and eating cakes at the same time, and had there positively summoned for interview all the available inhabitants of Grayhallock, not even excluding Bowshott. She devoted particular time and attention to the children. During the actual interviews Ann had absented herself to put in some feverish work in the kitchen, only to be summoned from there by the outgoing interviewee. It was like having a government inspector in the house.

The only person banished from her presence was Hugh. This unfortunate was to be seen outside on the sunny lawn, walking up and down in front of the beech trees, biting his nails and casting aggrieved glances at the windows; while like personages in a play the other members of the household came and went at the double on errands connected with Emma. Miranda at this moment was crossing the lawn in a series of leaps, armed with secateurs, despatched to the rose slopes to cut a bunch of gallicas for the distinguished visitor. Penn ran along behind her like a starling after a blackbird.

Ann was walking up and down the room in the haze of Gauloise smoke. Emma affected her strangely, with a sort of easy restlessness. She had felt previously no particular hostility toward her father-in-law's mistress, merely a certain curiosity; and she had expected the day to be for herself a tiresome and un-noteworthy business of rushing about in the background. She was surprised to find that, on the contrary, she was to occupy the centre of the stage. She was even more surprised to find herself invigorated by, positively enjoying, the atmosphere of relaxed drama which surrounded Emma. It was as if Emma made her exist more, and cast upon her, out of her own more vivid personality, a certain light and colour.

The appearance of the well-known authoress had been at first sight disappointing. Ann had vaguely expected something more dashing; and there was at first something almost pathetic in this slow crumpled elderly person, with her air of a determined valetudinarian, seeming older than her years could possibly warrant. Yet the face was clever. The face was also in some curious way alarming. Ann had not shaken off the alarm; but she had not been long in company with Emma before she found herself cheered by her guest's intelligent friendly curiosity, and made to talk as she had not talked in years. She felt herself relax, as in a warm salty bath. She had an agreeable sense almost of being seduced.

Yet their talk had been random, disjointed, even trivial. Emma had questioned her about the children, about the nursery, about her friends in the village, about the Bowshotts' television, and about a recipe for quince jelly which Ann promised to get for her from Clare Swann. The only subject which had not arisen was Randall.

Since Mildred Finch's momentous visit Ann had been in a state of considerable wretchedness. Mildred had given her two shocks, one concerning Randall and one concerning Felix; and these two concerns worked in her mind somewhat absurdly jumbled together. Ann had been sincere in saying that she did not want to know what Randall was up to in London. She thought it better that her imagination should not entertain images of her husband's unfaithfulness: and in a way which was obviously incredible to Mildred she had not even felt curiosity about Randall's doings when he was away from home. How true her instinct had been she had occasion to know after Mildred had suddenly crystallised the situation by mentioning a name. The knowledge of a particular named rival made her whole situation seem different and at moments intolerable; and round the object named there flickered, casting upon it a vague but lurid light, intermittent flames of anger and jealousy which had been absent before. Ann suffered. She did not ask herself whether she was still in love with Randall. Her disillusionment about her husband had been, even before Lindsay, in a sense complete. Perhaps after so many years it hardly made sense to speak of love save as a blind yet powerful experience of their belonging irrevocably to each other. What had so grown together she had not yet in her imagination begun to set asunder.

Yet there was Felix. The extent to which there now indubitably *was* Felix she had also had occasion, since Mildred's visit, to observe. Ann had, and she admitted it to herself with some shame, averted her attention from what had certainly been for some time an increasing interest in Mildred's handsome brother. Ann had become aware, even years ago, that Felix was partial to her. She had accepted his exceedingly discreet homage, so discreet that it was, she was sure, invisible to all other eyes, with a warm and amused gratitude, as the sentimental foible of one who was by now a confirmed bachelor. She and Felix were, after all, dreadfully old.

But she had liked it; and when, during the last year, Felix had been, when alone with her, the smallest bit more frank, as if taking for granted a hazy and never actually mentioned *something* between them, she had liked that too. Then there was an occasion at Seton Blaise, when they had wandered away from the others along the shore of the lake, and in a moment of silence he had taken her hand. She had let him then look at her with eloquent eyes; and although she remembered the occasion with a certain alarm she remembered it too with a certain joy. There had been, she saw to it carefully, no development or recurrence of the scene: but Felix, both pleased and penitent, had drawn a step nearer. She knew of course that it would be insane of her to fall in love with Felix. But as soon as she had got as far on as to say these words to herself her heart began to flutter. She and Felix were, after all, dreadfully young.

Yet these imaginings had often seemed, when Randall was in the house, flimsy enough. They were a foolish solace, nothing dangerous. The reality of Randall was overwhelming, and with a total grasp of his existence which was perhaps, after all, love, Ann apprehended her husband, and was grateful for the extent to which, difficult as he was, he filled the scene. A Randall intermittently and still slightly apologetically in London had kept an unslackened hold upon Grayhallock and upon her. But a Randall gone to London in anger, a Randall quite generally known to be living with another woman, might be something of a different matter. Ann had, as yet vaguely, a sense of being abandoned, and with this a sense of a vacuum created into which something else might rush. More realistic now, she simply feared this. She decided for the present not to see Felix; and conjectured, half sadly, half with relief, that he had made some corresponding decision with regard to her. For she did not believe that Felix had authorised Mildred's recent invitation.

When Emma's visit had been announced Ann's first thought had been for Fanny, and her second for herself. The connection between Emma and Lindsay Rimmer made the presence of the former at Grayhallock particularly shocking; and for a while Ann was ready to feel herself insulted. Yet Emma herself, working hard, almost terrier-like, ever since her arrival had managed quite to dispel the suspicious stiffness with which Ann had greeted her.

Ann was still walking up and down as she talked, a thing which she rarely did, and the conversation continued to wander on fairly agreeably at random.

"What a delicious cake," said Emma. "May I have another? Have you got a cat?"

"We *had* a cat," said Ann, "a sweet cat, a big grey tabby called Hatfield. He was Fanny's cat, you know. But when she died he ran wild in the fields. I've seen him once or twice in the distance, but he won't come near the house."

"Oh," said Emma. And after a pause, "It's odd how animals *know*."

The subject had raised a little awkwardness. To send it away Ann said, "You so often introduce cats into your books. Are you fond of them?"

"I love the creatures. But I could hardly have one in my flat. It would mean too many open doors and windows, and I'm such a *malade imaginaire*."

"I do enjoy your books," said Ann. "I hope there'll be another one soon."

"I'm glad if they entertain you," said Emma, "but of course they are trivial. I wish I could have written a real book."

"I expect you will. I mean—but I *do* like what you write."

"There's no time now," said Emma sombrely.

The door opened and Miranda, in a purple-and-white striped dress, skipped in with the roses. Penn hovered in the doorway, uncertain whether to follow her in. Miranda brought the big jumbled bunch, which she was holding lightly together in her hands, up to Emma, curtsied and decanted it into her lap. Then before Emma could thank her she ran back out of the door, seized Penn by the arm and jerked him after her out of sight.

"What an amusing child," said Emma. "She seems almost capable of irony."

"Yes, she's a clever little girl," said Ann. "Brighter than poor Penny, I'm afraid."

"Isn't he in love with her?"

"How quick of you to notice! Yes, I'm afraid so. But she's too young to take anything like that seriously and she just teases him."

"I wouldn't have thought she was too young," said Emma. "I would guess that young lady was capable of anything. Though I can imagine young Penn is not her cup of tea." She began to examine the roses one by one. The thorns made them cling to her dress. "Now you shall tell me the names of these."

Ann spoke their names: Agatha Incarnata, Duc de Guiche, Tricolore de Flandre, Sancy de Parabère, Lauriol de Barny, Belle de Crécy, Vierge de Clery, Rosa Mundi.

"What lovely stripes," said Emma, "just like Miranda's dress. And what names! I really must write a murder story in a nursery garden. But there, how shocking! All I can think of when I find something beautiful is how to make it an occasion for violent death." The telephone rang.

"These old roses are more beautiful," said Ann. "But of course the nursery really depends on the hybrid teas. Excuse me while I answer the phone."

She went into the dining-room and lifted the phone. "Hello. This is Netherden 28."

After a moment a woman's voice at the other end said briskly, "I wonder if I could have a word with Miss Emma Sands, if she's with you, please?"

Ann felt confused, and then even before she knew the cause, angry. She said quickly, "Yes, could you hold on, please?" and put the receiver down on the sideboard. She felt herself blushing with a sudden mixture of anger and fear. It must be Lindsay Rimmer. With this there came back to her that sensation of being encompassed and plotted against with which she had first met the news of Emma's coming. The next moment she thought: is Randall with her? And she was near to tears.

PART THREE

She went back to the drawing-room. Emma was still examining the roses. "You're wanted on the phone."

Emma looked surprised and began to get up. Ann helped her, supporting one arm. The roses clung by their thorns to Emma's dress. Ann picked them off and pricked herself in the process. Emma followed her slowly to the dining-room.

"There it is," said Ann. She went out and shut the door. She intended to return to the drawing-room. But she found herself standing still where she was. Emma's conversation was audible through the door.

"Well, so I imagine. I don't know who else would ring me here. How are things at your end?"

Pause.

"I see. So was it really necessary to phone me?"

Pause.

"Very comfortable, thank you. Hugh drives beautifully."

Pause.

"More or less. I'm not sure."

Pause.

"Naturally. I expect about eight o'clock. Would you do my sandwiches and milk as usual?"

Pause.

"I bless you, my child. Good-bye."

Ann had been standing listening and looking with fascination at the little bead of blood which had appeared upon her finger. As she heard Emma replace the receiver she retreated hastily to the drawing-room door, from which she advanced again to take charge of her guest. They returned to the drawing-room in silence.

Emma resumed her seat. Ann picked up the jumbled pile of roses from the floor and dumped them on the table. A few petals fluttered down. She put the tea-cups noisily on to the tray. As the silence continued and something new now hovered between them, Ann thought, if she mentions Randall I shall burst into tears. Anger at the possibility of being so humiliated brought her yet nearer to tears. She said, "I must go and do the lunch. I'll return you to Hugh."

"Hugh can wait. He'll keep," said Emma. "And lunch can wait. Don't go yet." She looked up at Ann with a questioning, pleading look. She seemed to be trying to frame some important request.

"What do you want?" said Ann. She looked down at the older woman, standing one hand on hip with an air of hostility and authority.

The question, in its vagueness, was startling enough. "What do I want?" said Emma. "Ah—many things. To understand you, for instance. But you must forgive me—you *had* forgiven me—for having come. I did once love your absurd father-in-law very much indeed."

Ann was wondering how to reply to this when something else distracted her attention. She turned slightly to the window and saw that the very dark blue Mercedes had just swept in through the gates.

Everything left her mind except the proximity of Felix. No one else drove that car. A different blush now reddened her cheeks. She went over to the window.

The car stopped a little short of the house and Penn and Miranda came running towards it. Hugh also was hurrying across the lawn to greet the new arrivals. Mildred Finch got out and then Humphrey and Felix. When Ann saw Felix's tall figure beside the car she felt her heart turn over and fall like a stricken bird. That "yes" had done its work.

"What is it?" said Emma.

"It's Mildred Finch," said Ann. "She's just arrived with her brother."

"Felix Meecham!" said Emma. "Why, I was in love with him too, once upon a time."

"You in love with Felix!" said Ann, turning in amazement. "You too?" She realised too late her misunderstanding and the suggestion which her words carried.

Emma laughed. "Well, for about four days, you know. One *can* be in love for four days. It was long ago, when I stayed with them once, and he was a boy scarcely older than Penny. I was very sad about something at the time—well, about Hugh. And Felix consoled me. Quite unconsciously, you know. He just *was*, and that consoled me. He was an exquisite boy."

She got up and joined Ann at the window. The group was still by the car. Mildred was talking to Hugh and Humphrey was talking to Penn. Miranda had got hold of one of Felix's hands and was tugging him. He was laughing.

"You loved Felix," said Ann. She looked out at him laughing there with Miranda. Then he cast an anxious look at the house. Tears came up in Ann's eyes and began to pour down her cheeks. She turned away from the window with an exclamation and buried her face in her handkerchief.

"Ah," said Emma. And then, "*Tiens!*" She followed Ann and put an arm round her shoulder. "There, there, my child. You go and do the lunch. You have been patient with an inquisitive old reptile. I shall go out and greet my old friend Mildred Finch. Yes, I think I shall join them now. She *will* be pleased to see me!"

Chapter Seventeen

"BUT what was she *doing* there?" asked Mildred for the tenth time.

"Sort of sentimental journey, I suppose," said Felix. "Cheese, Mildred?"

They were sitting over lunch at Felix's flat in Ebury Street. Felix had prepared the meal. He prided himself on certain simple accomplishments. There had been *paté de foie gras*, a Spanish omelette with an excellent salad, and now a good selection of cheeses with celery and various biscuits in a big tin. A bottle of Lynch-Gibbon Nuits de Young 1955 had been almost finished.

"Sentimental journey pooh!" said Mildred. "Is the Camembert ripe? No, well I think I'll have some of the Cornish cream cheese."

Mildred helped herself to cheese and spent some time selecting a biscuit. As Felix was gloomily silent she went on, "She seems to have got poor old Hugh back into her clutches."

"I wouldn't exaggerate that, Mildred," said Felix. "You're such a schemer yourself, you're a bit too ready to attribute schemes to other people."

"Well, somebody's got to do some scheming," said Mildred. "Or let's call it planning, shall we? As you won't raise a finger to help yourself, dear boy, I have to try to help you. And then I'm accused of scheming!"

"I'm not *accusing* you of anything!" said Felix irritably, cutting himself a piece of Stilton. He had in fact been very displeased with Mildred when he had learnt that she had, without consulting him, visited Ann and invited her to Seton Blaise. He had, about her refusal to come, mixed feelings. He certainly had a horror of seeming in any way to press or pursue. He was satisfied that Ann perfectly understood his sentiments; and for the present he preferred to wait and see.

PART THREE

He was, concerning Emma Sands, not quite as untroubled as he pretended to his sister to be. Emma had always seemed to him an exotic and slightly dangerous figure. He well remembered her curious brief attachment to him, of which he had been, without showing it, perfectly aware at the time; and he recalled with a mixture of aversion and fascination how she had kissed him when she departed. He had scarcely seen her since then, but she was the sort of person one remains aware of. He had felt dismay at finding her, so unexpectedly, at Grayhallock; and he agreed with Mildred in thinking, however irrationally, that she was up to no good. *What* no good she was up to he could not conceive; but he saw her obscurely as a threat to Ann.

He was additionally distressed by a dreadful thing which had happened, and of which he had said nothing to Mildred. Mildred had persuaded him against his better judgment to accompany her and Humphrey on the visit to Grayhallock, and he cursed himself for not having had the sense to stay away. Emma had cornered him soon after his arrival there, before he had even caught a glimpse of Ann, and had made him accompany her down the hill as far as the roses. Then as they stood there, looking at the scraggy multi-coloured lines of hybrid teas, she had suddenly intimated to him that Ann had confided in her concerning a sentimental understanding between Ann and himself. Felix had been so taken aback that he had made no denial, and his behaviour must have served as a confirmation of what Emma could only have surmised; for he realised almost immediately afterwards that Ann could not possibly have confided in Emma. Felix saw that he had been fooled, and he felt with pain that something sacred had been profaned, something delicate had been prematurely named, and something precious and fragile made known in a dangerous quarter: for whatever Emma might think about Ann's feelings, his own must, in his confusion, have been made fairly evident. Emma had certainly had a field day. But to Mildred, from whom he would never have heard the end of it, he said nothing of this.

Felix was well aware of his foolishness in having made of his quiet love for Ann, during these last years, a sort of home; and he did not rate as high as Mildred did, indeed he did not *rate* at all, his chances of ever now having Ann. Ann, when he first met her, was already Randall's wife, and he had in the earlier time regarded her with an admiring affection which was in no way out of the ordinary. She had seemed to him, somehow, the ideal English woman, and he had been used to say vaguely to himself that he would like to marry someone like her. The years passed, and it became un-obtrusively evident that Ann was not happily married; and with an increasing interest in the situation Felix began to realise that what he wanted was not someone like Ann, but Ann. It was of course, he realised, a most improper ambition as well as a foolish one. The fact that a woman's husband is thoroughly unsatisfactory—and Felix regarded Randall as a four-letter man of the first order—does not justify others in paying their attentions to her. Ann was *married*, and Felix, from the depths of his conventional honourable soul, took the full measure of the great institution which con-fronted him. He could not, however, at any point quite make up his mind to sheer off. He was fairly certain that Ann in some undefined way cared for him, even perhaps, however vaguely, needed him. He watched with pity and with fascination, and at last with hope, the progressive *dégringolade* of Randall's relations with his wife. He asked no questions about the future. He waited. And he made of his strange friendship with Ann a place of security, a sort of permanent house, an English house for a wandering man, a place where his valued things could be stored in safety. He had come to depend on this.

Felix was not as innocent of sexual experience as his clever sister, with a rare naïvety which rather touched Felix, seemed to imagine. He had known, in various parts of the world, plenty of women. These relationships, with something of the brutality of the soldier and the complacency of the sahib, he made comparatively little of, though he was sometimes troubled by general pangs of conscience concerning fornication. Felix was a church-goer and a communi-cant, maintaining the unreflective unemotional traditional Christianity in which he had been brought up, and which was vaguely connected in his mind with the Brigade and the Queen. He felt he ought not to go to bed with women he was not married to; yet when he was seriously tempted he usually succumbed, especially in hot climates. But in some separate place in his mind he had kept his intention to marry, in the end, an English girl; an intention which gradually merged into his rather hopeless attachment to Ann.

But then of course there had been Marie-Laure Auboyer. Felix hoped he had succeeded in putting Mildred off the scent as far as Marie-Laure was concerned, for Mildred went on and on as soon as she got an idea into her head, and Felix was feeling rather sensitive and worried about Marie-Laure. He had met her in Singapore, where she was working in the French consulate and he was Intelligence adviser to the C.-in-C. Felix spoke fluent French, and when he was not away visiting Australia or India or Hongkong he had spent a lot of his time with the French colony. Marie-Laure had fallen in love with him instantly. Felix was used to impressing girls and did not at first notice her very much. He took her out occasionally, in a rather routine way, as he took out one or two other girls to dance at Prince's or to swim at the Tanglin or to drink at the Cockpit or to dine at the Raffles grill, and they were witty in French together about various subjects not excluding Marie-Laure's attachment, which he found she was able to treat with a satisfactory dryness. She was certainly an intelligent girl.

Then he began to want rather badly to go to bed with her. This was, just at that time, not easy, as she shared a flat with a SABENA airline typist of domestic habits, and he himself lived in the Senior Officers' Mess, a rather grim place presided over in effect by the Head Matron of the military hospital, who was herself a full Colonel. At length the typist went on leave and Felix got what he wanted. He was shaken by it. Once he had gained possession of Marie-Laure he saw her in a different light. Her very touching beauty and tenderness combined with the highly intelligent way in which she dealt with him, her developed sense of the strategy and tactics of love, impressed him and began to attach him. But then he began to feel afraid.

The period that followed, during which Felix's departure from Singapore became imminent, seemed in his memory to drip with colours almost too vivid to bear. There was something drugged about it, something over-rich. It seemed as if at that time it was always moonlight, the hot moonlight nights as bright as day, and that he was eternally in evening-dress wandering slightly drunk with Marie-Laure through endless gardens with lights hanging from the frangipani whose great lotus-like flowers gave out an overwhelming powdery fragrance, attracting white furry moths the size of sparrows. Or else he was lying endlessly with Marie-Laure upon her bed—the SABENA typist had inevitably by now been confided in—while the devastating rain beat down outside and the sweat poured quietly off their momentarily disjoined bodies. It was a time on which Felix looked back with an agitated fascination and many misgivings. He had never so entirely surrendered to a woman. He did not approve.

He had never, during this time, *said* anything to Marie-Laure which could lead her to regard this episode as more than ephemeral; and it was only her clever gentleness and tact which prevented him from feeling a cad. But he was aware of how far his behaviour must seem to commit him, and he knew that she hoped. When the time came for him to go he had not had the heart entirely to crush these hopes. They parted as people who would meet again; and when Felix asked himself whether he had, out of misplaced kindness, misled her, he found himself wondering whether his concern not to hurt her feelings did not rather mask from him some deep desire of his own somehow, somewhere, to be with Marie-Laure again. He shook his head over this and decided he must be firm with himself. He did not want to be seriously entangled with a French girl. He was not really in love with Marie-Laure, he thought, not quietly and deeply and with all his soul in love, as he could be with an English girl. There was a whole area of his being which could not communicate with Marie-Laure at all. And that brought him back to the problem of Ann, which he found, on his return to England, had moved several stages further on, and at once claimed all his attention.

When Felix had left Singapore it had been fairly certain that his next post would be in India. He was designated to be the Military Adviser to the U.K. High Commissioner in Delhi, liaison officer with the Indian Army, watching the interests of British Gurkhas in India, and Indian relations with Nepal. It was a job that attracted him. He had already, as Colonel of Intelligence, visited the Headquarters of British Gurkhas in India, in the old Barrackpore Cantonment at Calcutta, and as a soldier and as a man his imagination had been caught. He looked forward to India; and it had been with mixed feelings, of which irritation formed at first the major part, that he had learned soon after his return to England that Marie-Laure had got herself transferred to the French Embassy at Delhi. He soon forgave her; but by then he had become far more concerned about Ann and the image of Marie-Laure began to fade.

Briefed by Mildred, he had attempted to make a sober estimate of the possible outcome of the situation upon which his fate must depend. Would Randall go or wouldn't he? Would he, exasperatingly, go only partly, go, but not quite enough? If he went off openly, entirely, irrevocably, Felix would feel free to act. But short of that he must hesitate, he must hold his hand. Felix shied away from the thought of stealing another man's wife. That was an action he could not perform. If the man abandoned his wife, that was another matter. But would he?

Worked upon continually by his sister, poor Felix was by now in a state of considerable distress. He felt, since Randall's latest and more promising departure to London, unable either to see Ann or to keep away from her. He decided not to go to India. He felt he must stay, and keep an eye on things. He had an obscure but firm and wonderfully consoling sense that Ann needed him, that she did not want him, at this time, to be so far away. Some moment perhaps would come, some moment of cracking apart, some decisive moment, when he must be present in strength to press his advantage. He was not prepared, as things still were, grossly to address Ann. But he was prepared to offer her indirectly, by his continued presence upon the scene, a certain steady reminder.

The Whitehall job, through a highly placed friend, was made readily available. He had not yet said his definite yes, but he knew now what he would do. The Military Secretary's department was, of course, for him something of a dead end, and the job in question was a niche reserved for men of independent means and limited ambition. He was, in a way, sorry. Yet Felix, though he was still in love with the Army, was not now especially in love with his own career. He had commanded a company in Italy during the war, and had commanded a battalion before going on extra-regimental employment to Singapore. But he knew now that he would never command a brigade. He had been too long on the staff, and he had never, in any case, had the personality for it. He was not hearty with the right people. This disappointment, which had been bitter, he had digested some little time ago; and he told himself that since he could never have exactly what he wanted it didn't in a way matter what he had. In any case, his increasing devotion to Ann, appearing in the light of a duty, settled the matter.

It was at this juncture, indeed on the morning of the very day when he was entertaining his sister to lunch at Ebury Street, that he received a disturbing letter from Marie-Laure. He touched it now in his pocket as he finished off the Nuits de Young, and phrases from it were passing through his head as he talked to Mildred. Marie-Laure, as it turned out, was still in Singapore, not having yet taken up her Indian appointment. She was having second thoughts about going to India. Felix had written her a slightly sarcastic letter when he had heard of her *coup*, and although he had at once followed it up by an affectionate one, it was clear that he had hurt her. She did not, she said, want to pursue him if he found her a nuisance. It was still possible for her to stay in Singapore. So much had been unspoken between them and at the time it had not mattered. He had been thoroughly English, and though this was rather beautiful it was something for which she now had to pay. He must forgive her for asking for definitions. But she did not want to die of being quiet and reasonable. Did he want to see her again or not? He had said, when they parted, that he did, and he had said it with a fervour. On that fervour she had been living ever since. But had he spoken merely to smooth over a distressing parting? Now that he was back in England she would perhaps seem someone far off and unreal. There would be perhaps girls in England, a girl, indeed he had once hinted it, who would make him forget his Marie-Laure. Yet when she thought of their last time together she felt that there *must* be for them another time. She had never positively said it—but in case he had not understood, and for fear of perishing by a mistake, let her say it now: she loved him, she wanted to marry him, she wanted to be with him forever. All she asked of him now was some response, however vague, something quite non-committal: but which might help her to decide.

This letter disturbed Felix, and not only because it made him feel that he had behaved badly. It disturbed him for a deeper reason. He had left things unfinished between himself and Marie-Laure. And the devil of it was that he wanted them, for the present, to remain unfinished. The scent of her personality came strongly from the letter. He took stock of the extent to which she still existed for him. He did not want to tell her to forget him. Yet what else could he honestly tell her?

"Well, I don't know," Mildred was going on. "I'm sure she didn't go there for fun. Did you see how confused Hugh was? He hated our finding her there."

"That's perfectly natural," said Felix. *Je crois voir comment vous vous raidissez en lisant ceci.*

"Maybe," said Mildred. "Dear Hugh. Dog-faced Emma shan't have him, not if I can help it."

"How much do you think Hugh realises of your kind intentions?" *Vous préférez que les choses arrivent sans avoir besoin d'être décidées.*

"Oh, nothing, my dear! He's like a new-born babe, always was.

He thinks of me as a big solid sensible girl, a nice shaggy old friend, rather like Nana in Peter Pan!"

Felix laughed. "Will he get a surprise?" *Je ne veux pas que tout finisse entre nous à cause d'un malentendu.*

"If I succeed, you mean? I'm not sure. He *may* never know. Sometimes I think *that* would be the most beautiful. I should swallow him without his even noticing it."

"I think he'd realise *something* was up! Brandy, Mildred? or some Cointreau?" *Mon beau Félix, je ne veux pas mourir à force d'être raisonnable.*

"Thank you, yes, a little Cointreau. What a lovely meal, Felix. Ah, my dear, I wish I could screw your courage to the sticking point. I can inspire courage in quarters where it harms me. I can't inspire it in quarters where I want to see it. And I can't even use my own! I'm hamstrung."

"So am I," said Felix. "Do you mind if I smoke?" *Je vous aime de tout mon être, je désire vous épouser, être avec vous pour toujours.*

"Of course I don't mind if you smoke. Why do you go on asking me year after year? There's no need for *you* to be. You ought to approach Ann in a straightforward way."

"Let's not have this again, shall we?" said Felix. He added, "You know, I don't think Miranda likes me. It struck me again this time." *Félix, Félix, souhaitez-vous vraiment me revoir?*

"Stop making excuses," said Mildred. "Miranda doesn't like anybody except herself and possibly her papa. She'd put up with you. Really, it's difficult enough without having Miranda the measure of all things into the bargain. No, you should do as I say. If you're waiting for Randall to clear off properly, you may wait for ever."

"I wonder," said Felix, his attention caught. "I wonder."

"I'll tell you one good reason why Randall will never go off, not properly that is."

"I've thought of that one."

"Precisely. No dough. He just *can't* clear off."

Felix was gloomily silent a moment. "What's the answer?"

Mildred pondered. "I suppose we could *lend* him some."

Felix laughed. "Do you know, I think he'd take it?"

"Of course he'd take it. Anyway we could always make it anonymous. What do you think, Felix, seriously? I expect he'd need a great deal."

"Mildred, there are limits!"

"Are there? All's fair in love and war, they say. And you a soldier."

"Quite," said Felix. "All is *not* fair in war, thank God, and when it is I shall resign. Nor in love either."

"War is too terrible for fairness now," said Mildred, "and love has always been. Ann is probably dying for you to take her by storm."

"I don't think so," said Felix shortly.

"Well, he won't go," said Mildred. "He has no money. He won't go, he can't go. So there we are."

PART FOUR

Chapter Eighteen

"THEY'RE devoted, you know," said Randall.

It was late at night. The curtains were drawn in Hugh's flat in Brompton Square. It had been a breathlessly hot day, and now the purple airless dark trembled over London, opaque and very still.

Hugh and Randall had dined together, and dined well. They were returned and had been drinking brandy. It had been, rather to Hugh's surprise, an agreeable evening. When Randall had rung up to suggest such a meeting Hugh had feared that there would be some sort of unpleasantness. But in fact they had talked during dinner of indifferent matters and so revived the old comradeship between them that Hugh was ready to think it was just for that that Randall had come. Only now, very late, did the names of any of the women arise. Hugh looked at his watch.

Hugh had been doing nothing lately except think about Emma; and although many of the thoughts were painful the total activity was a joy and the degree of engrossment a miracle. He was still, of course, almost totally in the dark. He not only did not know what Emma was thinking, he did not even yet know exactly what he wanted, not *exactly* that is. But he knew relentlessly in which direction he must go, and in that direction he struggled on alone, under a banner on which were inscribed the words *Liberty* and *Starvation*.

For Hugh found himself somewhat in the position of one who has scarcely recovered from the first wild joy of release from prison when he discovers that though he is indeed free he is free only to starve. The extent to which he did now positively feel free struck him as amazing, since he had not thought himself, with Fanny, so especially tied. But the openness of the world now burst on him with dazzling power, and he felt faint with too much fresh air. Yet with this came other needs. As an elderly married man, surrounded by an accustomed and reasonably affectionate circle, he had been long settled in an emotional routine which was so much a routine that the emotions were indeed barely perceptible at all. But now, although the persons, all but one, who had cared for him were still in their places they no longer seemed to suffice. Hugh felt starved for human encounters and surprises, direct glances, wrestlings of soul with soul and wild unblunted affections.

His renewal of relations with Emma had been in many ways not what he expected. She was, he went on noticing, somehow older than he would have thought likely, and in some respects seemed older than himself. If he had imagined himself as it were waltzing away with Emma it was certainly not like that. Emma had changed, and there was something resigned and morose in her against which he blundered. Yet she was also the same Emma; and his sense of a certain compassion for her gave but a finer savour to his age-old acknowledgement of her superiority. What moved him most of all was the absolute directness of their communication which gave him just that salty taste of reality for which he craved.

But what did Emma want? He found her behaviour puzzling. She was glad to see him, more glad, he suspected, than she allowed officially to appear. Yet she kept him provocatively at arms' length. He had been delighted by her wish to go to Grayhallock, though a little, and ineffectually, ashamed of taking her. Her conduct when there had been most unaccountable. She had banished him from her company and spent hours, before and after lunch, talking to Ann, to the children, to anyone but him. Then there had been the exasperating arrival of Mildred and the others, Mildred's raised eyebrows and Emma's honeyed wit. The Finch contingent had tactfully not stayed to lunch, but they had appropriated the later part of the morning, and Hugh had had to attend to Mildred's chat about art exhibitions in London and other nonsense, while watching from the corner of his eye Emma disappearing through the beech trees on the arm of Felix Meecham. The only part of the day which had been satisfactory was the journey, during which Hugh had held Emma's hand on the dual carriageways and they had talked about old times.

She had refused to dine with him and he had delivered her back to the flat just after seven. There Lindsay Rimmer had greeted them with ebullient cheerfulness and embraced Emma as if she had been away for a twelvemonth. The immodest displays of affection on both sides made Hugh uneasy; but he observed Lindsay and thought her very beautiful. She was certainly all of a glow at Emma's return and the two of them laughed together a great deal. Since then Hugh had been allowed to see Emma only twice, when he was invited to tea, and on each occasion Lindsay had been present nearly the whole time. Hugh felt excited, restless and cross, and told himself afterwards that soon he must 'take a firm line'. But taking a firm line was likely to be difficult since he realised how far he was from understanding what it was that confronted him.

Now that Randall had positively named the two women Hugh felt rather relieved than otherwise. It was suitably late, there would be no time for protracted conversation, and it would have been too unnatural for them to part without some such reference. Also given the friendliness of the earlier part of the evening, some mention of these awkward topics might constitute, for the topics themselves, a civilising touch. Hugh hated to have unmentionable things about him.

So he now responded cheerfully enough to Randall, "Lindsay and Emma? Yes, they are devoted, aren't they. Lindsay was so pleased to see Emma back that day I took her to Kent."

"Was she?" said Randall. He laughed. He added, "Emma's very attached, anyway. She depends dreadfully on Lindsay."

"I dare say," said Hugh unenthusiastically. And then, "Lindsay is very beautiful, I must say."

"Yes!" said Randall, and sighed. "Emma must have been very beautiful too when she was young. She has a fine face."

Hugh did not want to take this turning of the conversation, so he said nothing, and went to stand in front of the Tintoretto, absorbed instantly into its honeyed being. He stared into it and then touched it with his finger. It was strange to think that it was simply made of paint.

"May I have some more brandy?" said Randall.

"Help yourself, help yourself."

There was a distant murmuring which increased to a drumming and filled the room with its noise. It was the rain.

"That's the end of the warm weather, I suppose," said Hugh. "Too bad." He reached behind the curtains to close the window and then gave himself some more brandy too. The rain was beating down, wrapping the room with its dim lamps and its glowing picture in a curtain of sound which made it solitary.

"But she was beautiful, wasn't she?"

Hugh was annoyed at Randall's repetition of the question. He glanced quickly at his son and decided that he was more than a little drunk. He remembered thinking when Randall first arrived that the boy must have had a few somewhere else before coming along. If Randall now wanted a maudlin conversation about 'women we have loved' it would be time to turn him out.

Hugh said in an unencouraging tone, "Oh yes, indeed, yes." He went to the window and jerked back the curtain. A flash of lightning suddenly revealed the gleaming dome of the Oratory and the car-encumbered square running with water. Then after some moments the thunder rumbled distantly. "I'd better order you a taxi to go home." He turned back to the room, leaving the curtains open.

Randall seemed not to hear him. He was slouched on the sofa, his head fallen back against the cushions, his eyes closed, the brandy glass tilting in his hand. His big large-nosed face was pale and slightly puffy, his curly dark hair, grown a little longish, fanned out above his head as he sank comfortably lower. He looked a harmless degenerate Dionysos with already the faintest touch of Silenus. Hugh looked at the plump cheeks. He wondered if his son had fallen into a drunken slumber.

When Randall spoke again however, although he did not open his eyes, his voice was clear and his tone positively careful, as of one who has for some time been thinking out what to say. What he did utter took Hugh's breath away. "Are you sorry that you didn't go away with Emma in the old days?"

PART FOUR

Hugh was deeply shocked and immediately angry. He turned away again to the window and stood with his back to the room. The rain fell steadily, noisily, out of a dark reddish-blue sky.

Hugh's first feeling was of the unutterable impropriety of discussing his former mistress with his son. The shade of Fanny rose before him and his anger mingled with a deep painful distress. All this was nothing to do with Randall. But then at once he thought: yet it was, it is, to do with Randall. He *knew* about it, it must have some significance for him, some effect on him, since after all I am his father.

Randall then spoke again. "Don't be angry. My imagination has worked on this matter. Inevitably. I couldn't not think about it."

This was true; and the word 'imagination' suddenly touched Hugh to a further vision. What Randall had suffered as a child from what he could discover about his father's conduct Hugh would never know. But Randall as a man would have seen the thing with other eyes. He would have asked himself more objective questions. Randall the child had suffered from his father's temporary unfaithfulness; Randall the man must have meditated on the significance of his father's ultimate faithfulness. And it came to Hugh in a moment: he stands now where I stood then.

This, together with the tone of Randall's last remark, steadied Hugh, and he thought: he deserves the truth. Then he wondered: what is the truth? And before he could ponder further something wild and almost delighted in him spoke. "Yes. On the whole I'm sorry." He turned back to the room.

Randall was sitting up now, open-eyed, and as he surveyed his father he gave a sort of relieved sigh, such as an interrogator might give who has extracted the vital admission, perhaps in a garbled form, almost without the victim realising it. There was another flash of lightning and the thunder nearer.

Hugh, his hands behind his back, looked at him for a moment with drooping head. As their eyes briefly met Hugh felt, almost shyly, the touch of an old deep attachment to his son. He felt too, as his gaze sought the Tintoretto, elderly and morose and sad.

Randall hitched himself up against the cushions, slopping his brandy, his legs stretched sideways on the sofa, his eyes fixed on his father. He said very softly, "Thank you." And then, "Shall I leave Ann?"

Hugh turned away again with a gesture of irritation. He should not have let this conversation happen. It was totally unfair, and his own better judgment seemed to be deserting him to a degree which made him unfit to think about his own affairs, let alone anyone else's. He felt he had had his moment of irresponsibility and should now be left alone.

However, some urge which might have been as simple as curiosity made him say, "You mean leave Ann—for Lindsay?"

"Yes," said Randall slowly, still with the air of one choosing his words or giving vital instructions. "Leave Ann completely and take Lindsay away, take her *right away*."

Something in the insistence struck Hugh and made him think; and there came to him a picture of the situation which he had already had in miniature, and which he had occasionally, as it were, popped out of his pocket to glance at guiltily. But now the picture presented itself to him blown up, huge, authoritative; and with its vast and as yet unclarified implications it frightened him. If Randall abducted Lindsay, what would be left behind? A sad lonely defenceless Emma.

Hugh shook himself. He must close down this conversation. He felt a sort of panic, but managed to say coldly enough, "Look, Randall, this is nothing to do with me. You really can't expect me to make comments or to encourage you. And now I think you'd better go."

Randall drew his legs towards him, curled gleaming-eyed in the corner of the sofa. He seemed powerful now, having got his foot through the door of his father's confidence. He said softly, "So you think I should stay in the cage?"

"I don't think anything about it one way or the other!" said Hugh, flaring with anger. "If the question is: ought you to leave Ann? the answer is no, and you know that as well as I do!"

PART FOUR

The rain drummed in the ensuing silence and the two men stared at each other.

Hugh was immensely affected by the way Randall had put it. Something in those words spoke so directly to him that he was immediately defensively angry as at a monstrously unfair appeal; though he could not at the moment see what had happened. Perhaps he was a little drunk too.

Randall said, holding his eyes, and with deliberation, "But that is not the question."

Hugh's mind, working slowly, formulated what it had obscurely sensed a moment ago. It suddenly seemed to him intolerable that Randall should imagine that his father grudged him the freedom which he himself had not had the courage to take: that Randall should see him as enviously blocking the road, as unwilling to let his son have what he himself had failed to get, and which he had confessed to regretting. With what cleverness, it now occurred to him, had not Randall precisely made him confess it at the start of the conversation! The sense grew upon him of being interrogated, manipulated, and he felt both anger and curiosity, but with it still an overwhelming desire not to appear to Randall as an envious old man.

The lightning flickered again, and the thunder, still not very near. The rain came down in thicker sheets, making the night darker. The reddish light was gone from the sky. Hugh said quietly, and giving conscious gaze for gaze, "You know perfectly well that I don't necessarily think you should stay in the cage, as you put it. But why put it like that?"

After a moment he turned away and went to the picture as to a shrine for refreshment. Randall's mention of a cage made him recall what he had only lately been thinking about his own astonishing sense of his freedom: and that in his heart which had replied so readily and so rashly to Randall's question about Emma now told him too that he wanted Randall to go. So far from grudging it to him, he wanted to see his son kick over the traces. And he wanted this, not for any possible advantage to himself: that existed too, but

181

that was quite another matter. He desired, for its own sake, Randall's will to take what he wanted and damn the consequences. These were mad thoughts, but they rose with authority, and he knew that, quietly, they had been with him a long time.

"So you think I should go, then?" said Randall behind him.

Hugh said impatiently, "No, of course not. I don't think that either. Why do you press me for advice? You know perfectly well I can't give it. I can't make up your mind for you!" He marched to the other end of the room. The lightning flashed more pale upon the dome, unnaturally close and clear, and lit up empty streets in other parts of London. It was very late. The rain seemed to be abating a little. Hugh pulled the window up and let in a rush of warm fragrant air. He had no wish now to end the conversation. With a curiosity which he felt to be depraved he wanted to hear what more his clever wicked son had to say.

"Can't you?" said Randall. As Hugh turned again, he swung his legs off the sofa and reached out to help himself to more brandy. He sat a moment with head bowed looking into his glass. Then he said, "I can't go, anyway." He drank some of the brandy and looked up at his father. "Can I?"

"What stops you?"

"Money. Lack of."

Hugh wondered if he had seen this coming. No, he had not seen it coming. He was obtuse. He shrugged his shoulders and avoided Randall's eye. He felt that he was running helplessly to and fro before his son. He said, "I can't discuss your plans, Randall."

"Ah, but you come into them," said Randall. He was rotating the brandy in his glass and looking up under his eyebrows with the cautious taut look of one who thinks that a quiet adversary may suddenly spring upon him.

Hugh replenished his own glass. He said, "You want a loan?"

Randall was now completely still and the silence in the room told that the rain had stopped. He said, "No, I don't want a loan, Father. I want a great deal of money, not on loan. Nothing else will do."

Hugh now looked at him steadily. He had rarely felt more strongly his connection with his son, his identification, almost, with his son. And with that he felt for Randall at that moment something akin to admiration. Yet he felt too, with all his more customary responses, profoundly shocked. The conflict of feelings brought about a strange moment of coolness. He said, "I'm sorry. I haven't got a great deal of money, Randall. And if I had I doubt if I should let you have it. You must have some sense of moderation."

"It's not a moment for moderation," said Randall. He rose and put his glass on the mantelpiece.

"It can hardly be a moment for anything else, since I haven't got the money that you say you need."

"No. But you have—assets."

"Assets?"

With a brief movement as of one perfunctorily acknowledging an altar, Randall turned for a moment toward the Tintoretto.

"Good God!" said Hugh.

The silence continued, and Randall, suddenly relaxing as after great exertion, went to sit on the arm of the sofa and rub his hand over his nose and back through his hair.

Hugh was made entirely speechless not only by the enormity of the proposal but by its unexpectedness. He saw now that this was the climax of the evening, this was the thing toward which Randall's carefully ordered conversation had been leading. He saw too that he was confronted by something so wide in its implications that he couldn't hope to take it in immediately. The twisted admiration of Randall which he had felt a moment since turned into a sort of gaping alarm as at one who has produced something monstrous and very large. But his main feeling was one of furious rejection, and he expressed it at once. "*No.* Never, Randall, never. There's no good reason why I should do anything for you at all, least of all that! Don't delude yourself."

"I don't see the objections," said Randall, now speaking in a tired casual sort of way, not looking at Hugh, and still ruffling his hair. He had shot his bolt and was now sitting back helplessly to take the consequences.

"If you don't see them you must be morally blind," said Hugh. Then he asked himself: what are the objections, exactly?

"I don't see *quite* how morality comes in," said Randall. "But I'm rather drunk, I think, and as morality seems to poke itself into most things I expect it's got in here too. I know you like the picture. But it isn't as if it would be a family heirloom. You know quite well I'd sell it before you were cold."

The ruthlessness of this chilled Hugh and dismayed him. He retorted, "What makes you so certain it would be yours to sell?"

Randall gave him a patient almost sleepy look. "You mean you might leave it to Sarah? Can you see Sarah and Jimmie hanging it on the wall of their tin shack? Sarah would sell it, and sell it foolishly, *pour nourrir les chères têtes blondes.*"

"And why should I esteem your little romance more highly than *les chères têtes blondes?*"

Randall withdrew his gaze and said nothing. The answer hung in the air as thick as cigar smoke. Hugh said "Well—" to close the gap into which if Randall had chosen to put a reply, Hugh would have felt ready to kill him.

Randall got up and began to pull on his coat. He said, "Never mind. I'm sorry. I've got a bit drunk. Think it over. Never mind. Don't bother to ring for a taxi. I'll pick one up. It's stopped raining. Thank you for dinner and all that. I'll let myself out. Good-night." He drifted out of the room.

Hugh sat down and covered his face. Without yet understanding entirely why, he felt appalled, degraded, defeated. The freshened warm night air blew into the room and the night had cleared to reveal a star. Like a poised angel, the golden Tintoretto beamed down upon the scene.

Chapter Nineteen

WHEN Hugh telephoned Mildred Finch and asked her in agitated tones to come round and see him at once she hardly knew what to expect. It was only ten o'clock in the morning, so she felt it must be something urgent. She could not help being pleased to be summoned, and she smoothed down her fluffy hair and put on her smartest hat as for some delicious outing.

It was a dark morning. The hot weather had broken with the thunderstorm of last night, and a light warm drizzle fell from an overcast sky. The stairs at Brompton Square were positively twilit, and when she reached Hugh's drawing-room she found it quite like a cavern, one lamp glowing and the light turned on above the picture. Hugh rushed forward at once and seized her hand.

"My dear Mildred," he said, "how frightfully good of you to come! I felt very foolish after I'd telephoned you, but I did feel I needed to see you."

"My dear Hugh," said Mildred. "I need to see you all the time. I'd like to have you on a slow boat to China!"

"Dear," said Hugh vaguely. "Now do sit down. Would you like a drink or something? Well, I suppose it's too early—"

"I'll have some whisky," said Mildred firmly. "Whisky and soda." One never knew what lay ahead.

Hugh got the whisky, absently, his face puckered up. He looked very tired and haggard. He put the siphon, decanter and glass beside her and stood back, looking down at her with his round brown eyes full of apologetic solicitude. He looked like a big podgy elderly faun. He said, "I know this is a monstrous imposition on you, Mildred. But one must *use* one's friends, mustn't one? When one's old and ridiculous anyway one may as well do as one pleases in this respect."

"But I'm dying precisely to be used!" said Mildred. "I refuse to say we're old. And I could never see you as ridiculous." How

185

adorably ridiculous he is, though, she thought. "What's it about? I'm all agog."

"Ah" said Hugh, shaking his head, in a tone which implied that their cheerful opening was sadly out of key with what must follow. He turned away from her and went to his customary place in front of the picture. Then he took to pacing. He said, "I've had a rotten night."

"I'm sorry," said Mildred when he failed to follow this up. "The thunder was something dreadful."

"Not the thunder," said Hugh. "I'm sorry. Perhaps I shouldn't have asked you to come. I feel feeble and stupid and mad."

He said this with such vehemence that Mildred felt an immediate alarm and concern, together with the thrill of being appealed to at such a level. She felt she must have her wits about her. She put her glass down. "What is it, Hugh?"

Hugh paced a while in silence, head hanging. He said, "I must sound off to somebody. It isn't that I want your advice. Or do I? No, I don't think so. I just must sound off."

"Sound away," said Mildred. She was tense with caution.

"It's about Randall."

"Ah—" said Mildred. She relaxed a little and suddenly with breaths of fresh air all sorts of green prospects hazily opened. Perhaps, after all, Randall was off.

"Randall has put to me—the—most—extraordinary—proposition."

"What?" said Mildred. She felt alert and brisk now.

"Well, wait a minute," said Hugh. He looked out of the window at the ragged drizzle and then started back. "Perhaps I'd better give you a bit of background."

"Perhaps you had."

"I don't know whether you know that Randall has been having an affair with a girl called Lindsay Rimmer, who is Emma Sands' companion. Perhaps it's common knowledge?"

"It's not common knowledge," said Mildred, "but I know. Go on."

"Well, to put it shortly, Randall has decided he wants to leave his wife and go off with this girl Lindsay."

Mildred let out her breath slowly. "I thought he *had* left his wife," she said. She wanted no *lacunae* in the conversation. She must have something very exact to report to Felix.

"Well, no," said Hugh. "I don't think at present he quite knows whether he has left her or not. I think he would regard himself as officially *not* having left her."

"And she?"

"She is—a faithful wife." He added, "She's a conventional person." He seemed dissatisfied with this and added, "She's a *good* person."

He seemed about to qualify this further, but Mildred said, "Anyhow, the point is that there's no question of her actually throwing Randall out, however bloody he is."

Hugh frowned a little, perhaps at the adjective, perhaps just at Mildred's directness. "She would never throw him out, never."

"So unless he very positively goes he counts for her as not gone?"

"Yes, you may say so."

Mildred did not want to seem too interested in Ann, so she said, "Well, Randall is more the point. What about him? Will he stay or will he go?"

Hugh still paced, looking at the carpet, his floppy brown tonsure falling forward on each side of his temples. Then he cast a keen look at Mildred and said, "He needs—a great deal of money—to go."

"Money," said Mildred. For a wild moment she wondered if Hugh was going to ask her to contribute. "But he hasn't any money, has he?"

"No."

"Not a bean, I suppose. Except for the nursery. Scarcely a bean. And of course Randall would want to do things in style."

Hugh looked at her sharply. She must mind her tongue. She

could not bear him to think that she mocked. So she murmured softly, "Dear Hugh, dear Hugh, go on."

"He'll go if, and only if, he gets the money."

"Well, will he get the money? Where from?"

Hugh turned and looked at the Tintoretto. For a moment Mildred thought he was waiting to speak. Then she realised that he had spoken; and she cried out of an immediate scandalised shock, "No, no! Certainly not!"

"That's what I said," said Hugh. He spoke in a soft tired way. He sat down opposite to her on the sofa.

"It would be utterly wicked," said Mildred. She spoke without calculation, with a sense of the monstrousness of the thing. "No, Hugh, no."

In the silence that followed Mildred drew out some of the implications of the matter and gasped at them.

"Yet—it's complicated," said Hugh, in the same small voice. He added, "Perhaps I'll have some whisky too."

It was indeed complicated. No money, no departure. No departure, no Ann for Felix.

Mildred pulled herself together. The strain of being objective here was like a physical pain. But she said firmly, "Hugh, have some common sense. You can't sell your beloved Tintoretto so that Randall can have a caper with a girl which may last six months. It would be totally wrong. Tell Randall to pull his socks up. If he wants to leave Ann he can get half the value of the nursery and start himself up again. And can't the Rimmer girl work? By not treating them as ordinary mortals you'll do them nothing but harm."

"I've thought of all this," said Hugh. "I've thought of Ann. I've thought of Sarah. I've thought that if I sell the painting I ought to give the proceeds to Famine Relief. Everything."

"Well, if you've thought of it, why aren't you convinced by it?"

"It's complicated," he repeated. He poured himself out some whisky. "Randall's thing is very serious. He's really in love—the way it only happens once or twice in a lifetime. And with someone like him the mature love is the one to trust." He sighed. "I think it *will* last. She's awfully beautiful, by the way."

"Hugh, don't be frivolous."

"And without the money he won't go."

"Well, let him not go!" said Mildred, exasperated. She grieved for Felix, but she saw nothing here which was in the least unclear.

"Well, you see," said Hugh. He paused as if wondering whether to go on. "There's another—aspect to the matter."

At that moment, with a sudden switch in her vision, Mildred saw the other aspect: and if the first picture had made her gasp, this second *gestalt* left her positively winded. Before she had time to recover, Hugh was going on.

"There's no way of saying this," he said, "which doesn't sound monstrous. And of course it *is* monstrous, and not anything which could possibly form part of a serious intention. It's a sort of nightmare, the waking nightmare that I've been having all night. And when I rang you up I was possessed by an urge to confess it to someone, to confess it to you. Just to get rid of it. Yes, to get rid of it. You'll think me mad when I tell you. And what you've been saying is quite right. And of course I can't possibly sell the picture." He stopped as if he had said everything.

"But you haven't told me," said Mildred, when he was silent still. "This—other thing. Is it to do with Emma?"

"Mildred—" said Hugh. Then he suddenly covered his face with one hand, the fingers spread wide upon his bald forehead, while he gave a groaning sigh into the palm.

"It's as bad as that, is it?"

"You're so quick and so sympathetic," said Hugh, removing his hand. "You understand everything before I say it. You remember I asked you something a little while ago, about going to see her? Well, I did as you advised, I went to see her. I thought I might calm down then. But I didn't calm down. I haven't calmed down."

"And you remember that I said you were ready to fall in love? You have fallen in love." Her voice trembled.

"I have fallen in love." he repeated solemnly, absorbed in the majesty of his own fate.

Mildred was so confused by the demands of her new insight and by the pure piercing pain of jealousy which had just passed through her like a spear, that she could think of nothing to say.

Oblivious, Hugh went on in a moment, "To someone as clever as you I needn't explain what my nightmare was. Emma and I— well, there are possibilities. But the fact is that Emma isn't alone. She's—entangled—somehow—with that Rimmer girl. Well, no, that's a misleading way to put it. They're very fond of each other, and terribly sort of domestic together. And with Lindsay there there's no place for me. And, well, there it is." He added, "And that's that," in case she should misunderstand him.

"But," said Mildred, "if Randall could be enabled to buy Lindsay, you could move into the vacant place at the hearth." She instantly cursed herself for this bitter speech. She felt tears of vexation and defeat waiting behind her eyes.

Hugh's face wrinkled at her sharp words and he bowed his head with an air of vexed humility. He said, "Of course, you must understand that I've just been raving to you in order to clear my head of poisonous fumes. Now I expect I've shocked you. You're so honest and simple yourself, you probably don't realise what fantasies, and what duplicities, can reside in the bosoms of—quite ordinary people. Perhaps I oughtn't to have troubled you." He closed his lips, biting them into a hard line. She had hurt him.

While Mildred gained control of herself by taking some deep breaths and a mouthful of whisky he went on in a more conciliatory tone, "You speak to me, as you always do, with the voice of reality. That's why I summoned you, I suppose. Of course, I never seriously thought I would sell the picture. It would be wickedly unfair to Ann and Sarah. And it would be very bad for Randall. That's the main point really. It would deprave Randall."

Mildred got up and went to the window. She blinked at the pale hazy light and the lines of the rain. If only she could *think*. She said, "Wait a minute, wait a minute."

Before her own interests had come with such violence upon the scene she had seen things clearly. Now all was stirred up and confused. Almost laboriously she worked it out. If Hugh sold the picture Felix would get Ann. If Hugh did not sell the picture she would get Hugh. That was what it came to.

Mildred was not the first to feel doubts of a good cause when she saw that it was also to her advantage. Or rather, when she saw this, she began to think more passionately about the advantages of others. And she was acutely and increasingly conscious of her power to influence Hugh and of Hugh's wish to be influenced. It was clear that what had racked Hugh all night was an overwhelming desire to sell the picture. Yet at the same time he saw the moral obstacles as insuperable. And he saw justly.

Mildred knew that whatever she said she must say it quickly and it had better be to the point. But where was the point? She did not want to make up Hugh's mind for him now. She wanted to keep it in the balance, to keep it wavering, to give her time to reflect further. But she seemed already to have helped him to his decision. What was there, more subtly, to be said on the other side? She tried desperately to see the thing as Hugh saw it, to see Randall as Hugh saw him. She said, "And yet as you said—it's complicated. I can well understand your desire to set Randall free, to give him suddenly perfect freedom."

"Well, yes," said Hugh with alacrity, getting up from where he had been hunched in an attitude of rather sulky gloom. "Yes. There's that in it too, I suppose."

"And to do it with no ungenerous hand," said Mildred, "to do it with a reckless hand."

"Reckless," he said. "Yes," He joined her by the window and looked up at the misty dome which hung before them like some southern cupola in a painting by Turner. His eye glowed at a hidden thought.

I have touched the right place, thought Mildred. Let me think of a few more epithets. She felt by now a little reckless herself. "I can see," she said, "that, in a way, you want to do something extravagant and foolish for Randall. You want to help Randall to do something extravagant and foolish."

"Yes," said Hugh. "In a way." He added, "I was never myself—extravagant and foolish."

That's it, is it, thought Mildred. I should have seen it sooner. She meditated. And as she estimated the complex strength of Hugh's motives she thought with a passing wail of despair for herself: he will surely sell the picture.

"You see," said Hugh, now, assisted by the wind which Mildred had puffed so heartily into his sails, getting going on the other tack, "if one *were* to look at it from that side, it isn't as if the girls would be at all hardly done by, Ann and Sarah I mean. They'll get quite a lot anyway."

"And Ann might always marry again, I suppose," said Mildred. Then she thought this was incautious. She did not want to confuse Hugh's simple mind with hints of further complications.

She need not have worried. Hugh said, shaking his head, "Oh, I doubt it. Who would want to marry poor Ann?"

Mildred felt that by now she had had enough. She was confident that she had set the balance level. She was confident too that whatever she might decide as a result of her further reflections she could make Hugh decide too. She wanted to get away and reflect. She said abruptly, "I must go."

She went back to pick up her gloves and bag which she had laid on the mantelpiece underneath the Tintoretto. She looked up at the gorgeous valuable trouble-making object. Hugh followed her saying, "Mildred, I can't tell you how grateful—"

"But I haven't decided anything yet," said Mildred. "I mean, you haven't decided anything. There are too many factors, Hugh. I saw the thing too simply at first. You were quite right to hesitate. It's a big decision. You don't have to make it in a hurry. You really must reflect further, don't you think?"

"Reflect further, well, yes, perhaps," said Hugh eagerly. "But you'll help me reflect, won't you? You don't feel imposed upon, do you, Mildred? You've understood it all so quickly and so well. You help me marvellously to know what I think."

"I'll help you if you want it," said Mildred. "I'll always help you if you want it." She took her things.

"Ah, my dear Mildred," said Hugh, suddenly rapt into a soft dream and taking hold of the mantelpiece. "If you only knew! To be at my age so foolishly in love!"

Mildred felt her tears coming now. There was no resisting them. She turned half about and saw that the rain had stopped and it was a little brighter outside. To conceal her filling eyes she reached up and switched out the light above the picture.

Chapter Twenty

" A ND what will Hugh decide?"
"He'll decide what I tell him to decide."

Felix was exceedingly upset by Mildred's story, and was upset too by her manner of telling it. Yet he could not help pausing, as he so often did at moments when he most apprehended her difference from himself, to admire his sister. She had presented the issues with a ruthless frankness which he respected though it made him shrink. She was, in the more delicate affairs of life, positively military.

They were in the drawing-room at Seton Blaise. The weather had re-established itself and out of a sky sparsely scattered with small white clouds a fairly determined sun shone upon the midsummer garden which, refreshed by recent rains and now dried by sunshine and a gentle west wind, combined a clean matutinal freshness with the luxuriance of a tropical forest.

"Of course," said Felix, "none of your predictions is certain." They had already been over the ground a number of times.

"You want to know the future in detail," said Mildred. "Perhaps soldiers always do. But the future isn't like that." She spoke in a tired way and sat down on the window-seat in the bow-window. The sunlight found the faded yellow in her untidy fluff of grey hair. Although it was evening she was still wearing the tweeds in which she had arrived post haste from London.

"It is when it comes to it," said Felix gloomily. "That's the trouble."

"Don't be metaphysical. One can only go by probabilities." She pulled a white foxglove out of the vase on the table and began switching it nervously about.

Felix, who had been wandering about the room, paused by the window. Outside, Humphrey could be seen, remote on the far side of the stream, motionless, as if he had been put there by a painter, facing the house with head thrown back in the attitude of one

194

expecting to be addressed at any moment by a cry or a shot. His white hair made a vivid highlight in the unbroken greenness of the scene.

"What a trio we are!" said Mildred, following his glance. "All of us in love! And poor Humphrey always wanting not only the unmentionable but the unattainable! But at least Humpo tries. He deploys his resources."

"Anyway the probabilities are not the point," said Felix. He set off again, receding into the dimmer part of the room which was rich and hazy with summer light.

"What else is the point, for heaven's sake?" said Mildred. "Haven't we agreed that you have more chance of Ann if Randall goes than I have of Hugh if Randall stays?" She began to dismember the foxglove.

Felix did not like this way of putting it. He did not like this degree of explicitness at all. And he was appalled as well as impressed by Mildred's grasp of the present issue simply as a conflict between her interests and his.

"I mean," he said, "we are not thinking about it in the right way. Isn't the main question one about Hugh and Randall? And isn't it plain that what Hugh proposes to do is something impossible, simply not done?"

"It'll be done if Hugh does it," said Mildred impatiently. "And in a way he's dying to. The thing has caught his imagination. You neglect the sense in which the act would be a good act. It's not just a matter of our ends and means. For Hugh it would be something splendid in itself, whatever its results: a vicarious violence, a symbolic redemption of the past."

"I'm precisely objecting to your regarding it as just a matter of our ends and means!" said Felix. "And I don't see why we should take Hugh's romanticism as our standard either. The past is dear at sixty thousand pounds, and money won't buy spiritual goods anyway. But apart from that, what about Randall? It could hardly be other than bad for *him*."

"You leave me gasping," said Mildred. She had pulled all the flowers off the foxglove and was arranging them on the table. "Money *will* buy spiritual goods, as a moment's reflection would show you. And is this really a moment for worrying about the moral character of your rival? Randall's character can surely look after itself by now." She added, "I must say, I can't help rather admiring Randall. To be a cad on quite such a scale has something sublime about it."

Felix's feelings about Randall were by now mixed up to the point of explosion. He could not help feeling guilty before Ann's husband. His sense of the purely proprietory rights of marriage was very strong; and although he had not even been tempted to break the seventh commandment, he had certainly broken the tenth. Jealousy, envy, contempt, anger, guilt, and a kind of pure amazement which was analogous to, though not exactly akin to, admiration strove confusedly together in his bosom.

"So you see," Mildred went on, "the pattern does emerge pretty clearly. This talk with you has helped enormously. I can *see* it all now. And Hugh must be allowed his crime. Don't you think?" She began to crush the foxglove flowers one by one between her fingers.

"Nothing is clear to me," said Felix. He put his hand into his pocket, where it came into contact with Marie-Laure's unanswered letter. "I hate anything of this importance being done by *money*."

"It will be done, however it is done, by violence. And money is only one kind of violence. It's simply a matter of taste that one likes it less than screaming and shedding blood."

"Don't try to confuse me, Mildred," said Felix. "I just hate juxtaposing anything like this with—Ann. Whatever will Ann think of it?"

"Ann won't know," said Mildred composedly.

"Oh, yes she will! I shall tell her, if no one else does."

"You won't be in a position to tell her, dear, until after the deed is done."

Felix knelt on the window-seat, looking out. The boards

groaned under his weight. Humphrey could be seen sauntering away now, his hands in his pockets. He had the look of an idle discontented boy. Felix restrained himself from cursing aloud. He did not want things to happen in this way. Yet, as Mildred said, whatever way they happened would be an ugly way. Perhaps what he was so much disliking was being made to see the ugliness and to be, however remotely, a party to it. What was right here?

Felix had grown used to his rôle of waiting, to his sense of everyone being active except himself. There had been, in this attitude, he realised, a certain consoling fatalism. Events would proceed without his assistance upon their due course, and either he would quietly and inevitably get Ann—or he would not, in which case at least he would have nothing to reproach himself with. He would have much preferred whatever happened to happen under its own laws, far away from him, and for him to be able to stroll in when all had been completed. He had been all along, he realised, alarmed and repelled by the idea of anything approaching a public showdown between himself and Randall. He had been at every moment afraid of not being secretive enough, fearful of somehow entangling himself to a point where something public would be unavoidable; and he could not help caring how he would look.

He wished heartily that Mildred had not consulted him. She had now given him, against his will, a glimpse of the machinery; and the pattern which was emerging, with what she wished him to think of as necessity, was the more alarming since it was also so attractive. It was an involvement indeed, but an involvement which precluded any confrontation of himself and Randall. With a Randall spectacularly, scandalously and definitively withdrawn, a Randall bought, branded and gone, he might at last approach Ann in a straightforward fashion. By the extraordinary device, invented after all by Randall himself, of which his sister had told him, it could be quickly and cleanly done, what might otherwise drag out hideously, what was in any case surely in the end inevitable. It was just that he would have preferred not to know; and in a way that was almost superstitious he felt that by thus forcing the pace he might lose what by a slower course of nature might more securely have been his.

Mildred was watching him, leaning back in the other corner of the window. She said slowly, "Look, Felix. I might have let you off this. I might have advised Hugh as I pleased without telling you. But why should I let you off? Why shouldn't you take your share in this like the rest of us? Randall wants it. Hugh wants it. The result of it will be good. Neither you nor Ann are getting any younger. As for its having a nasty look, anything to do with Randall will have a nasty look. As far as I can see, all you object to is having to put even your little finger into the pie that you propose to eat."

Felix frowned at her and got off the window-seat. He found a cigarette, crumpling Marie-Laure's letter in the process. His consolation of honour, which Mildred saw as cowardice, seemed indeed a little tarnished. To be involved or not to be involved now seemed equally unsound, and he had a disconcerting vision of new shades of shabbiness in his behaviour. Lighting the cigarette, he lifted his head and saw outside upon the gravel the very dark blue Mercedes, waiting.

He wondered if it was only an effect of Mildred's cleverness that it now seemed to him all one to be involved or not to be involved. For if it was indeed all one then he might as well do what he wanted; and with this thought there came suddenly a vision of himself as active, as able at last to *do* something without secrecy, without indirectness, without dishonour. Then, dissolving all else, came the image of Ann: Ann, near, Ann attainable, Ann his. Darling, darling, darling Ann.

He threw his cigarette into the fireplace and said to Mildred "All right."

"What does 'all right' mean?"

"It means advise Hugh as you think fit and count me in."

Mildred let out a sigh and got up. "Thank you, Felix." She swept the *debris* of white flowers into the waste-paper basket.

Something in her now strangely dejected acceptance of his surrender reminded him of its significance for her. He had, for a moment, rather lost sight of their conflict of interests. He said, "I'm being selfish, of course."

"Ah yes," she murmured, "be selfish, be selfish, dear boy. It's your privilege after all, being younger and a man. It's still in front of you, the whole goddam business."

He said, "God knows what is for the best."

"Doubtless. But now at least something will *happen*." Her head thrown back to look up at her tall brother, she stroked her fluffy hair and caressed the soft skin beneath her eyes. She seemed now after the excitement of the argument, tired and flat, a frail old person cherishing herself.

He felt sorry for her. But he was already breathing a larger air. Tonight he would say farewell to Marie-Laure. He said as drily as he could so as not to offend her, "Sorry, Mildred."

"I shall take my chance. Who knows?"

"Quite," he said, as he drew her to sit down again and sat himself close beside her. With his new resolution, Mildred seemed suddenly eclipsed and the leadership of the conversation passed naturally to him. "To begin with, Hugh may not take your advice."

"He will."

"And even if Hugh does take your advice, he may get nowhere with Emma."

"He'll have an open field. And Hugh tries!"

"Randall may not clear off. And even if Randall does clear off, Ann may still not want to marry me."

"Here we go again!"

"And even if Ann does want to marry me, she may feel she oughtn't to, on religious grounds for instance."

"And even if—?"

"And even if she doesn't feel she oughtn't to on religious grounds, she may feel she oughtn't to because of—Miranda."

"To the Devil with Miranda," said Mildred. "You're getting neurotic about that child. You must take the brat in your stride."

"She alarms me," said Felix. "Who knows what is locked up

inside a child, especially a child like that? She *could* oppose it passionately. She *could* refuse to let her father go."

Mildred looked at him wearily. She said, "If you want Ann enough, you'll get her. You will have justice, Felix, you will have justice. And don't then complain of your lot. I think this is my last piece of advice to you before you go over the top. And now I must go and deal with Humphrey."

She went out into the darkening garden; and a little later Felix saw them arm in arm upon the lawn walking slowly up and down, an elderly pair of married people. As he smoked in the unlighted room cigarette after cigarette he heard the distant murmur of their voices. The sound went on without interruption through the long twilight and into the darkness.

Chapter Twenty-one

RANDALL pushed the cheque across the counter. The cashier, who was well trained, betrayed no interest or surprise. After all, most of their clients were men of substance. Randall, less well trained, could not control his face, which burst intermittently into nervous beaming as at the jerk of a string.

The Tintoretto, sent promptly to Sotheby's, had been purchased by the National Gallery, who outbid several American dealers, to the satisfaction of the cultivated public. It had reached a suitably high figure. Randall received Hugh's cheque on the following day.

Out in the street now, Randall walked along in a daze, fingering the paying-in slip in his pocket. He had a sense of liberation so total that he almost staggered. It was as if he had grown to some enormous size and at the same time everything solid, every resistance, had been removed. He floated in the air like a huge undirected balloon. He wanted nothing.

He did not even want to see Lindsay. He had a luxurious, positively Oriental, sense of having Lindsay *stored away*; but he did not want to see her. She had in any case, with a sort of *pudeur*, arranged to be out of London at the moment of the crime, like a great lady who delicately and fastidiously absents herself from a scene of violence which she has ordered. Violence it was, and Randall loved every moment of it.

Looking back on his interview with his father, it seemed as if he had gone through it in a dream, as if he had inclined the scales in a moment of unconsciousness; and a certain fatalism, a sense of being carried by larger forces, had also prevented him from worrying about how his suggestion would be received and whether it would be adopted. The good news was conveyed laconically, and the cheque with the briefest note in Hugh's neat writing, *Dear Randall, please find enclosed*— But what his father's emotions and opinions about the matter really were Randall no longer cared. He felt as if he had killed his father. The sensation was not unsatisfactory. He was himself the more increased.

He jumped into a taxi and told the driver to take him to Jermyn Street. It was still early in the day. Arrived there, he went into a shop and ordered six shirts of very fine striped flannel. The assistants treated him with a special deference, almost with a special love. It was as if they *knew*. Everything is going to be different now, thought Randall, from now to the end of my life, everything is going to be quite different. He left the shop in a state of ecstasy verging on coma. Even the image of Lindsay was dissolved in a big golden consciousness, vast and annihilating as the beatific vision.

He entered a pub, smiling uncontrollably, and absorbed two double whiskies into his nebulous floating being with as little consciousness of what was going on as an amoeba swallowing its prey. He began at last to wonder where he would have lunch, and gained sufficient contact with his surroundings to enable the names of Prunier and Boulestin to flicker attractively before him. He decided on Boulestin, and found himself without apparent transition sitting in the murky and distinguished gloom of that establishment eating a magnificent piece of steak. The claret, which had appeared magically with the steak, was château-bottled. The waiters murmured about him like cherubim about the risen Lord.

It was after lunch when he had been somehow transported to a Renoir landscape which was a heavenly version of Hyde Park that the curious idea came to him of going to call on Emma Sands. This idea brought him rocketing back to earth. But he stood thereupon like a giant. He would go and see Emma, he would go and triumph over Emma: and it would be the lifting of a burden, the breaking of a chain. The perfection of his condition lacked only this.

Since Randall had set in train the events which were to bring to such a spectacular outcome the practical thinking recommended by Lindsay, a curious silence had fallen between the lovers. It was as if they were, during the count down, holding their breath. And when Lindsay had announced to him that she was going to Leicester to pay her annual visit to her mother, no significant looks had been exchanged although they both knew perfectly well that they were entering a sacred and dangerous time. Randall had told her nothing of his plans, though he was well aware that his prophetic bearing, a certain glorious stricken look in the eyes, must sufficiently have proclaimed that he *had* plans. He had not heard from her since she left, except for a postcard, and he did not know whether she had seen the news about the Tintoretto in the paper, and whether if she had seen it she had understood it. Above all, he did not know if she had spoken to Emma.

This doubt, once it came to him, was sobering and painful. He had, in the last days, during his symbolic assassination of his father, during his trance-like pursuit of the golden grail, rather lost sight of Emma. He had in the end lost sight even of Lindsay. Like the mystic who pursues the great Other only to find at the last that there is only Himself, Randall, through the very labouring of his spirit, had entered a region of beautiful solitude. All the same Emma existed, and with what authority, with what horrible contingent power, he suddenly felt as he neared the raucous whirlpool of Hyde Park Corner. He felt himself in the mood for another assassination.

There was a flower stall outside St George's hospital, and he paused there. Roses. The long-stemmed neatly rolled and elongated buds affected him sadly. They were more like City umbrellas than flowers. They were scarcely roses, those skinny degenerate objects, meanly and hastily produced by a coerced and cynical Nature for a quickly turning market, and made to perish unnoticed by bedsides or to be twisted in the nervous hands of girls in long dresses. And Randall was for a second blind to the outer scene as he saw the hillside at Grayhallock turning purple and lilac and pink with an abundance of plump formal Centifolia and Damask. All the same, with a sort of gloomy relish, he bought a bunch of the poor unscented London roses; and then thought after all that they were like little girls' breasts, small and pointed. But that made him remember Miranda. He hailed a taxi.

It was almost his usual tea-time, his usual time of going to see Emma and Lindsay. His usual time, that is, in the old days. He was staggered, as one in the first days of a war, to feel how far off already those old days were. The old days were gone forever, and never again would he enter that drawing-room to find the two together, busy with their embroidery, and the tea-trolly thrusting its side into Emma's voluminous skirt. He thought of this with awe, with a certain curious sadness, and with ecstasy. Now it was war.

As he rang Emma's bell he thought: but she will have to answer the door herself. And for a moment he felt a thrill of compassion which almost made his errand seem improper. But the next moment, when Emma stood before him, there was nothing but the old fear, attraction, puzzlement and hostility, which had once together composed a sort of enchantment, but which now rose up, grim, separate and unadorned.

Emma did not seem especially surprised to see him. She said, "Oh it's you, Randall, good," and shuffled back to the drawing-room, leaving a trail of Gauloise smoke behind her.

Randall followed. Without Lindsay the room was empty, weird, and he realised as if for the first time that he had never seen Emma without Lindsay. He had never seen Emma alone.

He laid the roses down on the little table with a gesture of donation.

Emma had sat down in her usual chair and was regarding him with a lively yet sombre expression. She said, "How very sweet of you, my dear. And how especially sweet of you to pity my abandoned state. Would you like some whisky? With my gaiety girl away I haven't the heart for tea."

Randall was penetrated again by a demoralising sense of pity. He wondered whether he should drink her whisky or not. He decided that a murderer need not boggle at an error of taste, and set out two glasses. He thought, does she realise that it's the end?

Emma went on chattily, "I'm a dreadful old *malade imaginaire*, but I do feel really helpless without someone to look after me. I've been spoilt, of course."

Randall poured out the whisky and brought it to her. As she was just taking another cigarette he produced his lighter and offered her the flame. Their hands touched, and he felt her eyes upon him, dark and inquisitive. Seeing her without Lindsay was somehow obscene, it was seeing her as bare and terrible: pitiable too but terrible. And he thought, she has brought me here, she has drawn me here, witch-like, out of London, it is she who has summoned me.

Emma was watching him. Her frizzy hair had a tangled unkempt appearance as if she were becoming already a neglected old woman. Her skirt was covered with cigarette ash, and an overflowing ashtray strewed cigarette ends at her feet. But her ferret nose pointed at Randall like a dagger and her mouth narrowed slowly with an irony and humour which were a menacing prelude to a smile.

"I had such a charming postcard this morning, from her I mean," Emma continued. But she uttered the words absently, as one whose attention is elsewhere.

Randall sat staring at her. He had just realised that he had not spoken since he arrived when Emma said, "Well, Randall, has the cat got your tongue?"

Randall had intended to say to her at once: Lindsay is mine. But he found now that he had no words ready with which to make the disclosure. What had happened was not so easily named. He stammered a moment, and then said thickly, "I had a postcard too." This was pathetic.

Emma, who had been leaning forward to study him, relaxed back in her chair and said, "Perhaps you'd put those flowers in water that you so kindly brought. It makes me nervous to see flowers out of water. Doesn't it you?"

Randall got up quickly, seized the flowers and went into the kitchen. He sat down on a chair and covered his face. He decided that he was still drunk. It could not be just the effect of Emma, this tongue-tied state of confusion. His recent exercises in violence had evidently not trained him in the technique of destruction required on this occasion. He drank a lot of water and looked at his face in the mirror. He looked stupid. He found a vase and filled it and jammed the roses in. The miserable things were dying already. They were never intended to be more than buds. They probably *had* no insides. Then he saw Lindsay's coat hanging behind the door.

This gave him a dreadful shock. He stared at it, guessing at meanings before his mind could formulate them. Would Lindsay have gone away without her coat? Yet he *had* had a postcard. But had she really gone away? In this warm weather she might have gone away without her coat, she might have taken her light mackintosh. Then the nightmarish idea occurred to him that Lindsay was somewhere in the flat, hiding. She was somewhere in the flat, waiting to be produced gaily by Emma, like a girl whom an enchanter has changed into a doll. Or waiting, not to be produced. He put the flowers down.

He emerged into the hall and looked about him. The drawing-room was closed. He looked quickly into the dining-room, and then cautiously opened the door of Lindsay's bedroom. The room was empty. But there was a clock ticking, and with it a sense of presence. Randall shivered and retreated. He took two paces to Emma's bedroom door and opened it. The big fatal room with the red expanse of the double bed and the Italian light was quiet as before. There was no Lindsay, no angel poised in the corner. He was taking in its attentive emptiness when he realised that Emma was watching him from the open door of the drawing-room.

Randall returned Emma's look, closed the door, and went to fetch the roses. When he came back to the drawing-room she was settled again in her chair.

"She *isn't* here, you know," said Emma softly.

Randall could hardly bear it, that she should have witnessed his doubt. He felt at last a blind rage coming to his aid. He said clumsily, "Of course I know!"

"Then why were you looking into my bedroom?"

"Look, Emma," said Randall. "I've come to say that it's the end for you and Lindsay, I'm taking Lindsay away with me." He was not quite conscious of the words he used and wondered afterwards if he had really composed a sentence.

"Yes?" said Emma, as if expecting more.

Had he made sense? He began to say it again "I've come to say—" but Emma interrupted him.

"But didn't Lindsay tell you?"

"Tell me what?" said Randall, spluttering.

"About our agreement."

"What agreement?"

"About you."

"Good Christ!" said Randall. He got up and stood by his chair. He felt baffled and at bay and vaguely conscious that his scene was being taken from him. He said, "There can't be any agreement. I mean, it's Lindsay and I who arrange things now, not Lindsay and you. That's certain."

Emma looked at him coolly. "You don't seem very certain of anything just now. But don't worry, Randall. It'll be all right."

"*You*'re telling *me* not to worry?" His voice rose.

"You see, when I saw how things were at Grayhallock—"

"What has that got to do with it? God, if you mean you went there to make a survey of my marriage—"

"Oh, I wouldn't put it like *that*," said Emma cosily. "Now do sit down, dear boy, and stop making me nervous. You haven't touched your drink."

Randall stood before her open-mouthed. He thought, this woman has talked to Ann, has talked to Ann about me. She has been all over Grayhallock leaving her snail's traces. She has even got hold of Ann, she has stolen even Grayhallock from me. He said half shouting, "Look, what *are* you saying? Are you mad or what?"

"Never mind, Randall," said Emma, "and *please* don't shout. Never mind. One must not play the god in other people's destiny. In any case, one can never do it properly." She spoke in a tone of rather casual disappointment.

"Emma," said Randall, pulling the chair back and banging its two front feet on the ground, "don't pretend that it's you who have done this. It is I who have done it."

"Yes, yes," said Emma soothingly. "Don't let's quarrel about it, anyway. Do sit down, my child, and stop being unpleasant to me and spoiling the afternoon."

Randall felt frantic. There was something of which he must convince her, of which he must convince himself. There was something which he must not in these moments let her forever steal. He said, "You're going to lose your gaiety girl. You won't like that!"

Emma just murmured, "Why, Randall, Randall, I believe you're drunk! Whatever will Lindsay think when I tell her?"

Randall lifted his glass and for a moment intended to hurl it on the ground. The word 'agreement' flashed luridly before him like a neon sign. Then he put the glass down with a crash and turned and ran out of the door. He ran out of the flat and into the road and didn't stop running until he reached the corner.

He walked on breathless and found that he was talking to himself aloud and cursing. He was still unsure what had happened, but he knew that he had been defeated. Emma had made it appear that even this had been decided, had been arranged, by her and Lindsay. Even here he was excluded, even here his action was stolen from him. He knew of course that it was only an appearance, a cheap magician's trick. It was not really so. Or was it? How deftly, how cleverly, had not Emma sowed the seeds of doubt in his mind! He would never understand, he would never know the truth, he would never be at peace.

The curious calm which he had felt this morning concerning Lindsay was completely destroyed. Frantic doubts and anxieties about her flooded and overwhelmed him. He must telephone her at once, he must see her, somehow, that very day. She must never be allowed to go back to Emma's flat. Would he ever, in the end, really get her at all? As the spur of this terror drew his blood he revolved a whirl of instant schemes for driving at breakneck speed to Leicester.

Yet, by some devilish chemistry, even in the midst of this he felt as he walked on more slowly now, a quite new and different pain. Emma had destroyed his peace not only concerning Lindsay but concerning Ann. It was as if he were now being made to face *that* horror squarely for the first time; and he recalled with a groan something from which he had averted his eyes, something which he had been putting off till this time, till the time of his criminal freedom. The question of Miranda.

Chapter Twenty-two

MIRANDA was already there when he arrived. The hayloft was full of a half light, a shadowy light impregnated with scattered grains of gold, and by the open door, through which the swallows darted softly to and fro, a square of sunlight fell upon the worm-eaten floor.

Miranda was sitting at the far end of the loft, perched on a beam. Two of her dolls sat beside her. Randall strode towards her and leaned his head against her side in a sudden abandonment. "My little bird!"

The beam reached to his breast, so that Miranda was seated a little above him. She put her two hands over his shoulders and laid her head down upon his, holding him close for a moment. Then she gently pushed him away.

After his defeat at the hands of Emma, Randall had remained for some time in a state of frenzy. He had telephoned Lindsay's Leicester number in vain and had been beginning to believe the most terrible and fantastic things when at the third attempt he got hold of her. Lindsay by telephone was perfection itself. She had been rational, masterly and loving. The last, especially, he by now voraciously required. When he had suggested that she should not return again to Emma's flat she had replied reasonably enough that after all she must go back some time to fetch her things. So it had been agreed that she should for the moment, go back to Notting Hill. But the way in which she now assumed that things were moving into their last phase was tacit and beautiful. It was she who had, with a clairvoyant perception and with the firmness of an able general settling outstanding problems in a due order, raised the question of Miranda. And Randall had agreed that he must, now at last, speak to his daughter. He said nothing to Lindsay about the money. But he knew she knew.

The rendezvous with Miranda had been arranged in conditions

of secrecy with the help of Nancy Bowshott. Randall had walked from the station across the fields and through the hops, reaching the stable block, which stood on the edge of the wood, without misadventure. He was terrified of an encounter with Ann; and as he came distantly within sight of the house, terror, pity, and a dreadful old indestructible tenderness devoured his heart. But the prospect of Miranda, the sight of Miranda, drove these things away.

"You've grown!" said Randall. It was true. She had changed. She was dressed in a light jersey and trousers, her long legs swinging. He saw, on a level with his eyes, the slight lift of her breasts under the jersey. He stood leaning against the beam beside her.

"You've been ages away!" said Miranda.

He was glad to find her completely composed, as self-contained as she always was. He feared her emotions, he relied hopefully upon her reason.

"I'm sorry," said Randall. "I've been going through a bad time." The presence of his daughter made him feel suddenly very sorry for himself.

"Poor Daddy!"

"Look, Miranda," said Randall. He felt he must talk quickly, although they ran little risk of interruption in the abandoned loft. "Look, girlie. I must talk to you seriously about what I'm going to do. You're almost grown-up now, and I'm going to talk to you as if you were grown-up. And you must help me."

"Is it about going away?" said Miranda. She swung her legs. Swift as a racing shadow a swallow passed behind her head to its nest with a soft flurry of wings. There was a distant jargoning.

"Yes," said Randall. "I'm afraid so." He did not look at her. He leaned on the beam like a prisoner in the dock. He said, "Listen, Miranda. I don't know how much you know about this—but I've fallen in love with somebody, somebody else, somebody in London, and I want to leave your mother and marry this person." It was very hard to say. It sounded, in this place, beside Miranda, suddenly unreal.

"I know."

"How did you know?" said Randall. He lifted his eyes to his daughter's. Her pale freckled face, under its tousled cap of autumn reds, was poised above him. She was beginning to resemble Ann, as Ann had been when he married her. Only this was a thought to be shunned.

"Oh well," said Miranda, "one does know these things." She added, "Mummy knows, of course."

"Yes," said Randall. Had they, could they have, discussed it? "And you're not angry with me?"

"Of course not, silly. These things happen." She was wonderfully, almost appallingly, grown-up.

"You see," said Randall, "I wouldn't go if you—didn't want me to." He felt, after her last words, safe in saying this; and it was something he would wish to have said.

"Are you—asking my permission?" It was almost cruel in its deliberate clarity.

"Well, yes," said Randall, suddenly afraid again.

"But of course you must go!"

They had certainly got quickly to the point. Randall gave a long sigh and took her hand and pressed it against his brow.

"You don't think I've enjoyed it," Miranda went on, "this quarrel-feeling between you and Mummy all the time, the scenes I've been made the witness of? A broken home is better than an atmosphere of violence." It sounded like a statement made in a police court.

"Oh God," said Randall, "I'm sorry, Miranda." I've been a rotten father, he thought; but the thought was as artificial as Miranda's words. Poor Ann, he thought. But these words too were dead. They did not dare to go out and touch their object. At last with conviction he thought, poor me.

"Don't be sorry," she said. "I'm saying I'd be relieved, relieved if you went, if it were all settled somehow."

Randall had a curious sense of being positively seen off. He said, "Of course I'd never lose touch with you, you know that. You could come and live with me and Lindsay if you wanted to. You'll love Lindsay, she's a dear person. We'd share you with—here. We'd all manage." Would we? he wondered.

Miranda was so cool now, but what really went on in that little head? When he had gone, positively gone, what grief perhaps would follow? From the idea of Miranda's suffering he turned away as from an object both too sacred and too terrible to contemplate. And it occurred to him how much she had always in fact spared him the sight of it. When Steve died, when the end came suddenly, when he had told her, how she had twisted from his embrace, running to her room and locking the door. And there had been a silence within more terrifying than any wail. Now too she would suffer in private. She'll survive, he thought, children just do survive, they get on. It was shabby, all the same.

"Will you live abroad?" said Miranda. "I should like to visit you abroad." She swung her legs. It sounded gay, like the prospect of a holiday.

"Perhaps," said Randall. "We shall be abroad a lot, I expect." Would they live abroad? He had scarcely thought about it. The barriers between himself and Lindsay had seemed so vast that his imagination had never properly overshot them. What *would* it be like? He lifted his head and saw close above them, glued to a rafter, a swallow's nest from which the young swallows were looking out, a group of strange little faces. They reminded him of Miranda's dolls.

"Don't worry about me, Daddy," said Miranda. "And don't worry about Mummy either. She'll be all right."

"God! I hope so," said Randall. It sounded so weak. He looked up at her. Yes, she was changed. She was already a separate being, a possible judge.

"You know, Mummy will be relieved too," said Miranda. "It's better to *have* a horrid thing than to have it hanging over you. And Mummy will manage. She's awfully tough really. She hums all the time. I thought at first she was crying, but it was only humming."

God, I can't bear this, thought Randall. "I'm glad you think she'll manage. I hope she'll be happier. I know you'll look after her." I am a swine, he thought; but this thought too was resolved into, poor me; and he felt near to tears.

"Mummy won't be happy, it's not her thing," said Miranda. "But she's brave, and I *think* she's good." She spoke judiciously.

This must stop, thought Randall. He said, "How are you in other ways, Miranda? How's school getting on?"

"Very well, thank you, Daddy."

I'm a bloody travesty of a father, thought Randall. There was a sudden sound behind him, and he turned with a sick jump of the heart; but it was only a pigeon which had alighted at the sunny loft door. Miranda laughed. A swallow passed, and another almost above their heads began its long jumbled song. "I suppose no one's likely to come here, are they?" said Randall. "No one saw you on the way?"

"No," said Miranda. "The only person who *might* come is Penn, but I told him I was going to the churchyard to feed Steve's birds and he wasn't to come, so he'll be mooching around at the gate waiting for me to come back. He's got quite soppy about me, it's so funny!" She laughed again.

"Really? I hope you keep him in order!" Impertinent little puppy, he thought. And at the juxtaposition, so carelessly made by Miranda, of Penn's name with Steve's, his heart swelled. Life had been unjust to him, terribly unjust.

"Oh, don't worry!" said Miranda. "I just twist his tail. You will write to me a lot, won't you?"

"Of course, my bird. I'll write ever so much. And you must write too. But you'll be *with* me half the time, anyway."

"I suppose Mummy will be my legal guardian," said Miranda. "But of course she wouldn't prevent me from seeing you."

She seemed to have thought of everything: and in his gratitude for her calmness Randall had occasion to think too that she was, almost, making too little of his predicament. "We shall see each other a lot. We can't do without each other, can we?"

"Don't write to me at the Bowshotts'," said Miranda. "You shouldn't have done that. It's so undignified. You surely don't think that Mummy would open a letter addressed to me?"

"Well, no," said Randall. "It was just *that* letter—"

"You must write quite frankly. You know that no one will see your letters except me. And I'll burn them if you like."

In her remarkable grasp of the situation, her expert reassurance of him, Randall felt again the curious sense of being bundled off. He said, "You're wonderful, Miranda. I can't tell you how grateful I am." He put his arm round her knees and looked up into the pale steady face of his child.

Again, as if she did not want to be moved or softened, she pushed him off. "When you go away now, will you never come back?"

Randall took a deep breath. He was certainly being put through it. Never was a long time. He said, evading it in his thought, "I suppose that's it."

"Never after today?"

There was no avoiding it. "Never after today."

"I can pack up your papers and stuff, you know," said Miranda.

She had thought of that too. "Thank you. But we can see about all those things later."

"I've brought you something to take away now," she said. She took up a parcel which had been lying on the other side of her on the beam, next to her dolls, and put it into his hand.

Randall took it with surprise. It was soft and light. "Is it a present?"

"No—it's something of your own. Look and see!" She seemed pleased with herself.

Randall undid the string and began to pull the paper apart. The parcel contained the toy animals Toby and Joey. He turned and leaned against the beam burying his face in his hands. The toys fell to the floor.

Miranda jumped down. She picked them up and dusted them and put them beside her dolls. "There, Daddy, there. Don't take on so! Don't be upset! You've got to help me not to be upset, haven't you? Don't, Daddy, don't!"

"Christ in heaven," said Randall. He laid his cheek against the rough wood. A whole world of innocence was broken and gone forever. His world. Miranda's world. "I'm sorry."

"Don't keep saying you're sorry, Daddy. Everything will be all right. Now do stop or I shall cry."

He straightened himself and picked up the toys again. Miranda was standing close beside him, so slender, older, taller. He said, "I should like you to keep one of them for me. There, I'll give you Joey. That will make sure that we meet often. Because Joey must come and visit Toby, mustn't he?"

"Of course! And now, Daddy, I think I'd better go back, in case Mummy's wondering where I am."

Randall looked at her as she stood there, Joey under one arm, the dolls a-swing from her other hand, and he saw her, almost objectively, as a beautiful young girl. Her face seemed to have changed so much, even since he last saw her, to have formed, to have hardened. It was as if she had already had, in some indefinable but crucial form, experience. And where could experience have come to her, he half proudly wondered, but somehow from himself? He had, somehow, touched her consciousness and made her, beautifully, older. Soon she would be ready for love: and as he thought prophetically of the suffering which she would inflict, and how she would doubtless suffer herself at the hands of the god, he shook his head over her, sadly, but still with pride.

"Come along, my dear," she said. She had never used such words before. He wanted to embrace her, but could not. He kissed her hand. It was a strange gesture.

From the open loft door, as they moved toward the stairs, he saw, across the vegetable garden, the back façade of Grayhallock, flat and formal, its windows like so many eyes. The shadow of one of the towers stretched almost to his feet. He looked at the house, and the house looked back, cold, distant and preoccupied. It had never cared for him and Ann. A swallow rushed past his head, startling him into motion again; and as he descended the stairs he remembered his mother and her endlessly repeated questions about the swallows in the days when she was dying. That had been this spring and these swallows. But it seemed already that she had been dead for years.

"Don't be afraid of meeting Mummy," said Miranda. "She's inside trying out a new flower arrangement. She's decided to enter the flower arrangement competition after all. Clare Swann is furious!"

The flower arrangement competition! How he had hated and despised it all. Yet now he felt an agonising sense of exclusion. Never is a long time.

"That's good. Thank you, Miranda, thank you from my heart. You're sure you're all right yourself? I've been talking about me all the time."

"I'm fine. Oh, I didn't tell you, I met Emma Sands when she was down here. I had such a good talk with her. I think she's an awfully interesting person."

Emma again. Randall heard the name with nausea. The bloody woman cropped up everywhere. Emma talking to Miranda, Emma seducing Miranda: the idea was intolerable. Even here Emma had pushed in. Would he never be allowed to forget her? "Yes, she is, isn't she? But you must run along. I'll write to you very soon, Miranda. I'll write tomorrow. Don't worry about me."

"And don't worry about me either. Good-bye, Daddy. Good luck."

He took her hand again, looking into her face. Her lip trembled now. She looked away from him, shook her head, and then jerked from him and ran off toward the house.

Randall stood watching her until she disappeared. Then he turned back toward the hops. But when he had got under cover, in the shade of the heavy green festoons, he paused again. He would go and take a last look at the roses.

The great hop field, passing behind the stables, reached as far as the road, and he walked in concealment through the quiet loaded colonnades. The ripe papery hops smelt sweet-sour and beery. He crossed the road quickly and came among the roses. The empty expanse of the Marsh opened in front of him, greyish-green in the bright light. No one was in sight, and everything was exceedingly quiet in the midday heat.

He stood for a while looking down the hill. He could hardly believe that this was the end and that he had struggled for so many years to arrive simply at this moment of annihilation. He felt like a sorcerer who has created a vast palace and adorned it with gold and peopled it with negroes and dwarfs and dancing girls and peacocks and marmosets, and then with a snap of his fingers makes it all vanish into nothing. Now when he turned his back upon it the Peronett Rose Nurseries would cease to be as completely as if they had been sunk in the Marsh. Here was the slope where he had first planted his roses, against much wise advice, in the face of the sea winds from Dungeness. Here he had created Randall Peronett and Ann Peronett, names to keep company with Ena Harkness and Sam McGredy, and also his darling the white rose Miranda. They would live on, these purer distillations of his being, when their namesakes were only so much manure. He wondered, will I ever do all this, somewhere else, again, making roses with different names? Will I live through this whole cycle of creation again? And as some ambiguous voice in his heart answered no, and that he would now never breed a blue rose, or win the Gold Medal at the Paris Concours, or send Lindsay's name round the world in a catalogue, he told himself that he was tired of it all anyway: tired of the endless feverish race to market new floribundas and new hybrid teas, the endless tormenting of nature to produce new forms and colours far inferior to the old and having to recommend them only the brief charm of novelty. What was it all for, the expulsion of the red, the expulsion of the blue, the pursuit of the lurid, the metallic, the startling and the new? It was after all a vulgar pursuit. The true rose, the miracle of nature, owed nothing to the hand of man.

There was still no one to be seen. He walked a little way down the hill, drawn by his favourite corner where gallica and bourbon, moss and damask, made with their more luscious and ferny foliage a welcome haze of green beyond the gawky stems of younger breeds. He passed a toolshed and impulsively entered and picked up a pair of secateurs. All was in order in the shed. He noticed, half with disappointment, that the place did not seem to be deteriorating.

The old roses were at the height or their season, and Randall stood still among them, completely absorbed into a heaven of vision. There were moments when he knew that he loved nothing in the world so much as he loved these roses; and that he loved them with a love of such transcendent purity that they made him, for the moment, like to themselves. He could have knelt before these flowers, wept before them, knowing them to be not only the most beautiful things in existence but the most beautiful things conceivable. God in his dreams did not see anything lovelier. Indeed the roses were God, and Randall worshipped.

Moving slightly in the breeze the intense little heads surrounded him and drowned him in their odour. Lifting a few towards him he looked with his ever new amazement at the close packed patterns of petals, those formulae that Nature never forgot, those forms that were the most desirable of all things and so exquisite that it was impossible to carry them in belief and memory through the winter; so that every year one saw them as if for the first time, and as they must have looked in the Garden of Eden when in a felicitous moment God said: let there be roses. So Randall moved on, deeper into the rose forest, between the tall thickets with their crossing and interlacing boughs, and as he went he picked them, snipping off here a faintly blushing alba and here a golden-stamened wine-dark rose of Provence.

A woman started up suddenly, appearing on the grass path between the bushes with the sudden illuminated presence of a Pre-Raphaelite angel. He turned with a gasp of fear. But it was Nancy Bowshott.

She came up to him breathless, her dress billowing, her eyes wide, her chestnut hair wild and bushy after running fast down the hill. "Are you going away, Mr Peronett? I had to see you."

He contemplated her: pretty buxom Nancy, a rose of a different sort. No one could have been farther from his thoughts. She had indeed never really occupied his thoughts at all, and he resented her intrusion now upon the rite of farewell.

"Yes, Nancy, going away."

"For good, is that, Mr Peronett?"

"For good, Nancy."

"Ah—" she said, and turned from him, her eyes filling with tears.

Randall was shocked. The roses had put him into a trance-like state, and Nancy's red face, her heaving bosom, her moist and spilling eyes were suddenly too real, too close. He said, "Come, come, Nancy. You mustn't be upset. It had to be, you know."

"I can't stay here without you," she said. "The place will be horrible without you."

The thought that he would leave at least this aching heart behind him at Grayhallock did not altogether displease Randall. He said, "Now don't be tiresome, Nancy. Don't be so emotional. You'll get on perfectly well without me."

"No, I won't," she said. "I shall die here without you. Please let me come too. You'll want a servant or something. Let me come with you, Mr Peronett. I'd work for you, I'd be no trouble, I promise I'd be no trouble!"

"What nonsense!" said Randall. But he was touched. "Your place is here, Nancy. You must help Mrs Peronett. You know how much she relies on you. And after all, there's Bowshott. You can't leave him, can you?"

"If you can leave her I can leave him." She looked at him fiercely, her tears mastered, suddenly his equal.

"What you ask is impossible," said Randall. "I'm sorry. You'll soon settle down again. Now stop being so foolish."

They stared at each other. He saw her, but only for a second, as a separate being with troubles and desires of her own. Then the silence between them took on a new quality. She seemed to him with her flushed face and her fierce brow and her disordered hair suddenly beautiful. The wind from Dungeness drew her dress tight about her.

They stood for another moment, close together, perfectly still. Then Randall took her in his arms and as her body yielded to him, faint and sighing, he began to kiss her savagely. The roses fell to the ground.

PART FIVE

Chapter Twenty-three

THE news that Randall Peronett was off, that he had left his wife and gone away, positively and definitively gone away with Lindsay Rimmer, was greeted with almost universal satisfaction. There are few persons, even among those most apparently strait-laced, who are not pleased by the flouting of a convention, and glad deep inside themselves to think that their society contains deplorable elements. Randall indeed, when it came to it, did his job properly. He did practically everything except announce it to the press. His timing was careful. Nothing was said to anyone until the day when the plane was due to leave for Rome. Then Randall fired off a number of decisive letters. He had even with demonic efficiency arranged that Ann should receive the letter from his solicitor about the divorce arrangements by the same post as his own letter announcing his final and irrevocable departure from her life. His thoroughness amazed and impressed his father; and Hugh felt, at the spectacle of his son's ability so ruthlessly to kick things to pieces, admiration, revulsion, distress, disapproval and envy.

The whole world now converged upon Ann. She had never been, to persons who had throughout years neglected her, almost forgotten her, a more interesting object. She was besieged by inquisitive and sympathetic visitors and received by every post letters of condolence in which scandalised exclamations and offers of help mingled with the triumphant satisfaction of the virtuous in what had occurred. She was simultaneously invited to ten different houses: she should come and rest, be looked after, stay as long as she liked. Randall and Ann were become, overnight, universal favourites.

Hugh learnt the news from Ann, who rang him up half an hour after the receipt of Randall's letter. Ann asked him to come to Grayhallock at once. Hugh answered vaguely. He *would* come. But he had, for the moment, urgent business in town. She was to ring him up whenever she liked, and of course if there was anything he could do for her without actually coming to Kent. He would ring her up in any case at least once a day. She was to look after herself and keep cheerful. Why not have Mildred or Clare Swann to stay with her in the house? What a blessing Miranda was at home. He thought about her constantly and would come down at the earliest possible.

Since the sale of the picture Hugh had been in a curious frame of mind. He felt like someone who had lit a long fuse to a barrel of gunpowder. He had done his task and now had only to wait for the explosion. But how odd the waiting was; and when it occurred to him sometimes that perhaps nothing would happen at all he did not know whether he was glad or sorry. Since the moment when Hugh had indicated to Randall that he would get the money, communication between father and son had ceased by tacit mutual consent.

It was still not very clear to him what he had done, what sort of crime he had committed and whether he had committed a crime at all. His curious son had, he realised, a certain power to confuse him morally. He had been, however, much set on his way by Mildred who showed, suddenly, a remarkable firmness about his doing the bold thing, the brave thing, the beautiful thing, without regard for a structure of convention which, as she now pictured the matter to him, was too gross to have any relevance to an action so unusual and somehow great. She did not altogether convince him, but he let her words comfort him all the same.

His conscience continued to be busy with the matter. Was he depraving Randall? Was he depriving Ann? But Randall was depraved and Ann deprived already. The new situation would have at least a clarity and an honesty. Nothing, he felt, could be worse for all concerned than Grayhallock with Randall *there*. He shuddered whenever he recalled the last days, with Randall sequestered in his room brooding and drinking. So bad for Miranda. And at the end of this frequently repeated argument he could sometimes achieve a moment when he felt himself to be a fairy godfather. But then he would start off again with picturing the loneliness of Ann, the despair perhaps of Ann. Yet Ann had had, for long already, her solitude and her despair. Ann was tough, Ann would manage, Ann would survive. And then with a strange vicarious thrill which silenced his officious conscience for the time he envisaged the lovers in flight. And with that his thought returned to his own affairs and to Emma.

Hugh had felt, during the interim between his action and its results, unable to see Emma. Too much depended upon the issue and he did not want, as it were, to spoil the effect of his reappearance in a new situation of which he would be the acknowledged author. Also, he did not want to be chaperoned by Lindsay and that this would be, if he went sooner, with impish cruelty insisted on by Emma he was fairly sure. He had, about his ultimate reception by the abandoned Emma, oddly few fears or misgivings. He knew her well enough to think that she would greet his *coup* with admiration rather than resentment. He had not been to see her; but he had sent, every day, and with a luxurious pleasure, letters, chocolates, and flowers. She had not replied. And now, an hour and a half after Ann's telephone call, he stood upon Emma's doorstep. He had rung up to ask if he could come and she had briefly said yes.

*   *   *   *

"I miss my pretty one," said Emma. "You'll find me dull."

She had not responded to the gentle drama of Hugh's arrival. He had imagined the scene far otherwise. She made no secret of her bereft state. But her remarks about it had a peevish and casual air, and she had spent the first ten minutes of their encounter complaining about her charwoman. There was a depressing lack of intensity. Hugh was at a loss.

The flat looked odd too. It had a sort of stripped appearance, like Aladdin's palace in a state of partial demolition. When Hugh commented on this, Emma replied, "She took her things and a lot of mine as well. You just wouldn't recognise the bedroom."

"Why didn't you stop her?"

"Ah well," said Emma vaguely, "I wanted her to have them really. I told her she could take a few mementoes."

"You parted—in anger?"

Emma laughed. "Lord, no! How could you think it? Surely you know what an old matchmaker I am."

"You mean you—"

"I invented it, after all, Randall and Lindsay."

Now when she said it it seemed true. Yet Hugh did not know whether to believe her. His imagination drew a blank. He had never been able to, would never be able to, picture that friendship. He was disconcerted too to find Emma claiming to have done what he thought he had done. He said, "I wonder what Randall will make of it."

Emma was grave for a moment. "Randall may be saved in the end because at least he loves *something*. Though I'm afraid Lindsay may be only the symbol of it. Now you can give me some whisky. Did I tell you? I've decided to take to drink."

He poured out two glasses and then stood before her frowning and biting his nails. He pawed absently at his ear where a large ball of steel wool seemed to be grinding to and fro. He said, "You're not angry with me, are you?"

"You keep attributing anger to me. I can certainly be ill-humoured. But neither lust nor rage dance attendance upon my old age. There is no citadel any more upon which the flags can wave defiantly. Why ought I to be angry, though?"

"I didn't say you *ought* to," said Hugh. "I meant—" He hesitated. He did not want to lay claim to an act which had harmed her, if there was any way of getting out of it, and she had already shown him a way. Yet he did want the credit of an act performed for her sake. Yet again, he did not want, in disputing her own picture of the matter, to seem even for a second to pity her. And yet he had indubitably done something and he wanted at least to be noticed for it. A subdued noise like a distant pistol shot went off in his head and the grinding stopped.

Emma watched him with some amusement. "If you want me to chastise you because you gave Randall a dowry, you will be disappointed. It was a beautiful idea. I wish I had thought of it myself.

Have you any spare cigarettes, by the way? I seem to be running out. Oh, those horrid healthy ones. Well, I'll have one all the same."

"I didn't exactly do it for Randall," said Hugh. He kept his eyes upon her pointed face which was veiled with fugitive lights of frivolity and humour.

"Ah, but you loved it," said Emma. "Confess you loved it. What a wild reckless streak you have in your nature after all! *And* a light please, if you don't mind."

"You know I did it for you."

"Sweet of you to say so. I'm flattered of *course*. So bad for my character. But all our characters seem to have taken quite a beating lately, don't they? I think I'll have a little more whisky. This malt stuff is rather good. I much prefer an unblended whisky, don't you?"

"Listen," said Hugh, sitting down beside her. He did not want his passionate intention, his entreaty, to be lost in her badinage. He did not want to be cheated of his scene. "I am a selfish man, and when I say I did it for you I mean I did it for myself. Be sincere with me, Emma, and don't mock me. Is it not a miracle that we are together again, and if it is a miracle is it not a destiny? Do not make my words seem foolish. You know they are truthful. I love you and I need you and you belong to me in the end."

"Good heavens, are you proposing to me?" said Emma with a little shriek. "I haven't had a proposal in twenty years!"

"Stop it!" He seized one of her hands.

"But wait—*are* you proposing?" said Emma, her eyes humorous and intent.

He let go of her. "I hadn't got as far as that."

They were silent for a moment and then both burst out laughing.

"I must say, I do rather love you, Hugh. There is something sublime about you. But I don't know if anything follows. Perhaps there is nothing but this."

"But—what?"

"Well, just this, this understanding, this talk, this laughter, perhaps just this moment."

"If there is this much there must be more," said Hugh. "When I said I hadn't got as far as proposing I didn't mean the proposal came later in the speech, but just that we couldn't yet know what we wanted, exactly."

"Well, what do you want, roughly?"

"Roughly, everything."

She laughed again. "That is a lot, Hugh. Or is it? Aren't we perhaps dried up now, all hollow inside like shrivelled gourds, dry and rattling? Belonging to each other 'in the end' is a rather metaphysical sort of belonging. The trouble is, it is the end already."

"No, no, no!" He could not help being elated by the directness of their exchanges and by his sense of the continuity of the old love with the new. It was the same love, the same girl.

"Ah, you're pleased with yourself, really!"

"Emma," he said, "just don't say no to this in your heart. And let our good fates do the rest."

"My dear, I don't say anything in my heart. I'm a perfect phenomenalist. Or if anything is said it is something like 'whisky' or 'tea-time'. Can I have another of those horrible cigarettes?"

"You know perfectly well we aren't old. People don't grow old. Old age in that sense is an illusion of the young."

"I am old," said Emma. "Or rather I lack an attribute of youth which you have got: a sense of the future, a sense of time. I am just a bundle of perceptions, most of them unpleasant. As for other people, either they're with me or they don't exist."

"Well, let me be with you!"

"Oh, you're so *tiring*, Hugh," she said, looking at her watch. "You must go out and get me some Gauloises before the shops shut."

"Don't be so complicated about it," he said. He was holding his breath, fearing now to press her too much in case she should say some words of rejection. "You are lonely with Lindsay gone. Let me look after you a little. I'm sorry if I went too far today. Let us be simple and slow."

" 'Simple and slow'," she murmured. "How adorable you are. I'm really quite fond of you."

"You said a little while ago you loved me. Fondness is less."

"I have told you I am not a continuous being. My words cannot be used as evidence against me."

"But you'll let me come again?"

"Perhaps."

"We'll see what happens, shall we?"

She gave a deep sigh and turned upon him her dark luminous eyes of a nocturnal animal. "We'll see *that* in any case."

Chapter Twenty-four

"WELL, old thing, he's gone," said Mildred to Felix. "Now to work!"

Felix had been camping uneasily at Seton Blaise, waiting, as Mildred put it, for the balloon to go up. That it *had* gone up Mildred discovered from Clare Swann in a matter of less than an hour after Ann had received Randall's letter. Ann had telephoned the rectory and Douglas had set off immediately for Grayhallock, followed by Clare, who paused only long enough to make ten telephone calls.

Mildred at once summoned Felix. "Quick," she said. "Get out the Merc. We're off to Grayhallock."

Felix hesitated. "Is it quite proper," he said, "to go over at once? I mean, won't it look bad? Won't we be just a nuisance?"

"I despair of you," said Mildred. "You should be wearing a smock and chewing a straw. That's your uniform."

"I don't want to intrude on a grief that I can't altogether either sympathise with or understand," said Felix stiffly.

All the same, five minutes later the Mercedes was at the door.

The scene at Grayhallock resembled a curious sort of fête. Work in the nursery had been suspended. Bowshott and one of the men were conversing on the gravel outside, and Nancy Bowshott and Clare Swann were having an animated discussion in the hall. There was an atmosphere of suppressed excitement.

Felix still felt that there was something highly improper in his presence there so soon after news of what must be felt as a bereavement. But his appetite to see Ann, after more than a fortnight of inactivity and sheer waiting at Seton Blaise, was intense. He had felt, and Mildred had agreed, that during the interval between what Mildred referred to as Hugh's crime and the longed-for departure of Randall he should make no attempt to see Ann. That Randall *would* go he now felt curiously certain; and he had made no plans, envisaged no possibilities, in the event of Randall's not going. He waited. During the interval he had made several attempts to write the letter to Marie-Laure, but without success; and he had heard again from her two days ago saying that although he had not written she had decided to go to Delhi. Her beautiful French seemed to him dry and unreal as a language of substanceless birds.

Clare Swann, delighted to see them, ran up to Mildred. "She's in the kitchen with Douglas. I thought I'd leave them together. Of course, she can't be *surprised*. She must have seen it coming a mile off. And it wasn't exactly a happy situation, was it? But it's a shock all the same, like when someone actually dies after they've been ages dying."

She fastened on to Mildred. Felix averted his eyes from their gay avid faces. Now Clare was drawing Mildred confidentially aside. "My dear, I must ask your advice. It's so hard to know what will cause offence . . ."

Nancy had joined her husband outside, and Felix was left standing uneasily in the middle of the hall. The hall at Grayhallock was a cheerless place at the best, like the entrance to a seaside boarding-house. One expected to find notices saying what time breakfast was. Felix wondered if he should sit down somewhere; but it seemed so meaningless to sit down. He did not know whether to go to the kitchen or not. He was in a physical agony at the nearness of Ann.

The boy Penn passed him by, mumbled something and made for the stairs. His face had a stricken appalled look. He bounded up as far as the first landing and stopped as if deprived of purpose. Then he went more slowly on up.

Felix had just decided to take refuge in the still-room among the Wellington boots when he turned to find that Miranda was standing beside him and regarding him with a hostile look.

Conversation with Miranda was the last thing which Felix felt able at this juncture to sustain. What after all did one say to a child whose father has just publicly gone off with his mistress? How much did Miranda understand about the matter? How much did she know of the Facts of Life? How old was she, anyway? Utter paralysis gripped Felix.

As she showed no signs of going away but still stood provocatively beside him, he muttered, "Bad business, Miranda. Sorry to hear about it."

"Sorry to hear about what?" said Miranda in a clear voice.

"Well, about your father—going away—well, all that."

"You know all about it too, do you?" said Miranda. "It looks as if everybody knows. I think everybody knew before Mummy did."

Felix could make nothing of this. But at least the child was composed.

"Do you think it will be better in the long run?" said Miranda.

Felix was taken aback. "I don't know, Miranda, I can't say really. I believe your mother is in the kitchen with Mr Swann. I think I won't disturb them. I'll just wait a minute." He looked for somewhere to escape to. He could hardly go to the still-room now.

"Mummy got a letter from the lawyer about the divorce," said Miranda.

"Oh, did she?" This was appalling.

"Yes," said Miranda. "He said there should be no difficulty as it was a simple case of adultery. Mummy will have to appear in court, but Daddy won't have to."

Felix stared about him in desperation. He could not stand any more of this. A quick glance at the bright faces of Clare and Mildred made him shudder. He mumbled an apology to Miranda and fled in the direction of the kitchen.

He knocked on the kitchen door and entered at once. Ann was sitting at the far end of the table in close converse with Douglas Swann. Swann looked up with annoyance at the interruptor. It was not every day that he had a chance of holding Ann's hand.

Ann rose when she saw him with an exclamation of surprise, brushing the clinging Swann aside. "Why, Felix! How good of you to come. I didn't know you were in the country."

Of course, she doesn't know, thought Felix, she doesn't know anything. She did not know that he had been sitting at Seton Blaise waiting for exactly this to happen, she did not know about Hugh's crime. A mind like Ann's would not have seen any special meaning in the sale of the picture. Ignorant and innocent, there she was surrounded by schemers. He felt, before her, confused and ashamed. He stammered out, "Old friend . . . just thought I'd call . . ."

"I'm so glad" said Ann, and she sounded very glad. She had obviously been crying, but seemed calm now. "I'd better make some coffee," she added. "There's quite a rout!"

"You'll do no such thing," said Douglas Swann. "Coffee indeed!" He was standing close behind her and lightly resting his hand on her shoulder.

"Douglas, dear, would you just go and see what's going on outside? Did Mildred come with you, Felix? Douglas, would you go and ask Mildred to sit in the drawing-room? And thank you for being so sweet and helpful and for coming so soon. I'll just talk a bit with Felix now, I think."

Douglas Swann murmured obediently and retired. Ann flopped back into her chair. "Oh, Felix—"

"My dear," he said. "My dear." He took the chair, drawn close to hers, which Swann had vacated, and took her hand. He felt her grief as something small and precious in the midst of his own joy. He wanted to embrace her and cry out with emotion. He was so far on in his thoughts, it was strange to think that she was not yet with him.

Ann pushed her hair back behind her ears. "I didn't know you were at Seton Blaise. I suppose Clare told you. I feel such a fool. I rang up Douglas at once, and now Clare has told everyone and it seems as if I'm making a sort of public fuss."

"Well, you have something to make a fuss about, I should think!" said Felix. He squeezed her hand rhythmically.

"It was such a shock, the letter," said Ann. She released herself and put both hands to her brow. "And it was such a horrid letter. I suppose I'd been half expecting something like that for ages. But when it comes it's different. Randall did write sometimes and ask me to send things, books and things. Quite nice letters. But my heart always turned over when I saw his writing."

Felix could not trust himself to speak in case his feelings about Ann's husband should come pouring out in a vitriolic flood. He contented himself with touching her arm in a timid way.

"You see, he always came back for Christmas and for Miranda's birthday and was here a lot of the time really. I liked to feel it was his base, that he needed it. This last time he was home was terrible, of course. But it wasn't usually so bad. It's extraordinary what one can survive in a marriage. And I kept thinking things might get better. They did get better when Fanny was ill. Oh, Felix, all that long road, all those hopes and struggles, to lead us *here*——"

"Well, it's not your fault," said Felix.

"It is, it is," she said with a groan. "These things are never unjust!"

"I can't agree," he said. "But did you not—somehow expect it now?"

"Why now more than another time? No. But I might have known, as he came secretly last week to see Miranda. Nancy Bowshott told me."

"Didn't Miranda tell you?"

"No. And I didn't say anything to her. God, how painful!" She put one hand to her side. "He took his toys away," she added. "I should have known then that it was the end!"

"His toys?"

"Yes, it sounds so silly, but he had them beside his bed, things he'd had as a child, a toy dog and a——" She became silent, breathing hard. Then great copious tears rolled down her cheeks and she hid her face with a cry.

Felix was overwhelmed. He put his arms right round Ann and and drew her close against his shoulder. With a sigh he lowered his face into her cold pale hair. He had waited years for this.

Miranda came into the room and shut the door sharply behind her. Felix quietly released the sobbing Ann. Ann found a handkerchief, blew her nose and said "Sorry". Miranda approached, and after looking for some time at her mother's red damp face, leaned against her shoulder and transferred her gaze to Felix. He moved his chair back and got up.

"Felix," said Ann, putting her arm round Miranda, "would you mind going to tell Douglas to tell everyone to go away?"

"All right. Is Douglas to go away too?"

"Yes. Tell him I'll ring him."

"Am I to go away too?"

"Yes, please. I'll ring you later."

Felix moved reluctantly towards the door. He would have liked to have held Ann's hand again before he left. As he reached the door he heard a curious sound and turned about. Miranda had started to cry hysterically, her head buried in her mother's shoulder. He left them locked together.

Chapter Twenty-five

ANN looked, for the twentieth time, out of the window, and her heart staggered as she saw, at last, the very dark blue Mercedes coming through the gate.

Randall had now been gone a week, rather more than a week. It seemed to her a century of experience. She had been amazed, frightened, at the intensity of her pain. Envisaging beforehand the situation she was now in, Ann had thought that at least whatever else there was there would be an element of relief. But there was no relief: only a blank misery of loss shot through with the most terrible jealousy. She was astonished at her sudden capacity to be jealous; she had somehow, and she saw stupidly, imagined herself to be above jealousy. But now she was positively brought to the ground by it. Randall, for all his tiresomeness and badness, had always been *her* Randall, and she had thought of him as such even when she half knew, even when she knew, that he was going to another woman. He was hers as a mild chronic illness might be hers, when one knows all its strange ways and it has become a part of the personality. He belonged to her and in her, this was loving him, for better or worse she *was* Randall. And she had really believed that however broken down and odd things became, at least they would continue. But Randall absolutely gone, Randall referring her to his solicitor, this was fearful and dreadful, and she was not prepared for bearing it.

She missed him hideously, and yearned for him with a violent fruitless yearning which was a kind of maimed falling in love. His absence had not so much mattered, had not so much been felt, before. It had not been real absence. But now the house gaped and rattled with it. She began to be afraid of the house, especially at night. It was as if its old indifference, now that Randall's protection was removed, had begun to reveal itself as something more sinister. She felt, upon dark stairways and in quiet empty rooms, a brooding hostility. She wished she could leave it.

Mildred Finch, who with a rather shame-faced Felix had in fact still been waiting around when Ann had emerged after comforting Miranda on that first day, had most cordially invited her to stay at Seton Blaise. The idea of the comfortable friendliness, of the sheer beautiful orderliness, of the other house, the idea of being taken charge of and looked after, tempted Ann extremely; but she said no. She had her reasons for not wanting to go to Seton Blaise at present. Mildred had then offered to have the children to stay, but Ann had refused that too. She did not want to be separated from Miranda, and it seemed cruel to send Penny away at a time when, rightly or wrongly, he might feel that he could be of some service to his cousin. Miranda, after her early hysterics, had retired into a moody taciturnity, and Ann could only conjecture what she thought and suffered. Hugh had been down twice, each time for the inside of a day, but had seemed restless and self-absorbed and could not be persuaded to stay.

Ann had written to Randall at Chelsea saying that she did not want to divorce him. She wrote this coldly, as the situation seemed to leave her no other way of writing it. It would have been inconceivable to wail or entreat. But the coldness chilled her all through and she felt herself already in the grip of some machine-like necessity. She had never in the past, however violent and unpleasant Randall had been, met him with coldness, and only rarely with anger. Even now she did not feel resentment against Randall. Perhaps she would yet have to learn it in order to survive. She had written to the solicitor saying she had no wish to discuss divorce proceedings at present. She did not exactly expect Randall back, and she certainly did not intend to go on refusing him a divorce. But she could not suddenly, and however great the shock of his departure, give up all her old hopes.

She was sorry that, on the first day, she had made that distracted telephone call to Douglas. He meant well, but his sentimental sympathy had been irritating, unwelcome, almost degrading. And then the arrival of all those inquisitive people had made such a rowdy undignified scene. She ought, at that time, to have made sure that she had her grief to herself. A fuss and a drama had been made, and Miranda, who at breakfast time had been fairly calm, had become quite hysterical later in the morning. She was rather sorry too that Felix had come.

Ann was surprised to discover that even in the midst of the acute pain she was suffering she did continue to think about Felix. His image was present constantly in the background of her preoccupations, like a picture in a busy room, not regarded yet somehow affecting the consciousness. She was obscurely aware too of the possibility of recent events having altered her relation with Felix; but she was not sure whether the effect was simply to make him more remote or whether it was something else. While Randall's protection, however unwillingly given, had formally remained to her, there had been as it were a separate compartment in which Felix could be stored. Now she would have to make, for him, some other arrangement. She had not thought this out, and occupied with her maimed and obsessive passion for Randall, she had let the image of Felix recede a little and grow dim. Yet it still remained like a distant light and though she did not look at it she was glad it was there.

She had told him that she would ring him, but she had not done so. When it came to it, the action seemed a little too significant, and she had put it off. It was better to leave things. Then she had received a rather formal little note from Felix saying that he was going back to London, but that he would be returning to Seton Blaise, after dining early, on a certain evening, and might he drop in briefly on the way to take a cup of coffee and inquire how she was? Ann had said yes to this, as it seemed too unkind to say no— and because she suddenly felt she wanted to see him. Oh, as the day went on, she wanted very much to see him. And she trembled now, seeing the Mercedes.

It was late evening and the sky was an intense blue from which the radiance had been gradually withdrawn. The colours in the garden had risen to their last peak of shimmering brightness and now faded quietly like a descending hand. Murky purples and browns thickened in the distance. It was a very quiet evening. The church bells had been ringing for a practice, a sad sound, but they were silent now. As she went to the door Ann switched on the lamps in the drawing-room, and as she did so she glimpsed herself for a moment in the big mirror. She had put on a summer dress instead of her usual blouse and skirt, and the unexpected image startled her. She seemed another person.

"Come in, Felix, come into the drawing-room. How very nice to see you. Would you like the electric fire? It's getting rather chilly now. I've got some brandy for you, I hope it's the right kind. You have dined, haven't you?"

Felix came stooping through the doorway. He looked, she thought, terribly *respectable* in his dark suit and outrageously immaculate shirt and narrow tie. Ann, even in her best cotton dress, felt shabby and tousled beside him. She smiled at the thought.

Felix accepted the electric fire and the brandy, said he had dined, and answered questions about Mildred's welfare. Then silence fell between them.

They were sitting in armchairs on either side of the fireplace. The electric fire sat a little forlornly in the big grate. Ann could feel him looking at her and tried quickly to think of something to say. It struck her suddenly as extraordinary that she should be sitting here so late at night alone with Felix: extraordinary and pleasant and alarming. Then she was amazed to find herself feeling tearful. She said quickly the first thing that came into her head. "Oh, everything is such a *mess* here. I do wish I could catch up. I just get into more and more of a muddle. I still haven't sent out those catalogues."

Felix said, "I wish you'd let me help you. Couldn't I do the catalogues?"

"No, of course not! It's only a few hours' work really. It's just that I've got so terribly tired."

"You certainly look tired," said Felix. "You ought to have a holiday. Let me drive you to Greece."

Ann was startled. Instantly she had a clear almost magical vision of herself flying southward with Felix in the very dark blue Mercedes. With this there came a very odd and unfamiliar feeling, and she said with frightened vehemence, "No, that's quite impossible I'm afraid."

"Ah well," said Felix. He inhaled his brandy. He said, "Have you heard anything from Randall? I hope you don't mind my asking."

"No." She looked blankly at the electric fire. For some reason Felix's presence was making her feel dreadfully sorry for herself.

"I'm sorry I came rushing over last week," said Felix. "I realised afterwards that it was impertinent and tiresome to intrude at such a time. But I was getting rather tired of cooling my heels at Seton Blaise."

"I didn't even know you were there," said Ann. "You should have come over sooner."

Felix bowed his head, looked intently into his brandy, and muttered something about "didn't know if you wanted to see me".

"You know I'm always glad to see you," said Ann. The words, although true, had a casual lying ring. It was not like that. She was speaking as if she did not know things which she did know. She was talking to him as if he were just an old friend. But was he then not? Ann felt confused. She found herself thinking that through sheer tiredness and blankness she might kill something in the conversation, and she recalled Randall's taunts: she killed gaiety and spontaneity, she banished life. The spirit that says no. But why did it matter so much now?

"Ann, forgive me," said Felix, straightening up, "but will you give Randall a divorce if he wants one?"

Ann took a quick breath. She was not ready for this directness. But she felt immediately more alert. "He does want one, and if he goes on wanting it long enough I suppose I'll give it to him. But I'm not going to do anything about it at the moment."

"Do you think Randall will come back?"

Ann felt the touch of something deadly. She wanted to cry out with wild tears, "I don't know, I don't care!" Catching herself she said coldly, "I really can't say, Felix, I've no idea." She added, in spite of herself, in a tone of bitter bad-tempered weariness, "I've no idea. I've no idea. I've no idea."

"Well, quite. I'm sorry," said Felix. He seemed discouraged.

"I do apologise," said Ann. "I'm in a rotten state of mind to-night. I'm not fit for human company. I think perhaps you'd better go now, Felix." She could not think why she felt so wretchedly nervous and cross. She didn't really want him to go.

"Let me stay a little longer," he said gently.

Ann replied with a weary gesture and went on staring at the fire. Her body felt strange.

"I hope I didn't—offend you last week," he said suddenly.

"No, when?"

"When I—" he fell silent.

She looked at him quickly. "No, no, of course not." Ann thought, I must gather my wits. Something is going to happen. Something is happening.

"Oh, Ann—" he said. He put the brandy down on the floor. It was a declaration of love.

Ann sat quite rigid for a moment. Then she turned her face full to his and they looked steadily into each other's eyes. Such gazing is crucial; and Ann did not even see the barrier until she had sped far beyond it. Nothing now, between them, could ever be the same again.

"Well—" she said, and looked away. Her cheeks were burning, her throat was painfully constricted and she shivered with something which was like terror.

Felix leaned back in his chair, stretching out his long legs, rotating his brandy and looking at the ceiling. He said "Mmm." It was scarcely an eloquent scene, but much happened in those minutes.

"I'm sorry," he said at last. "I really didn't mean to spring this on you tonight. It's damned unfair. Though I suppose you've known it in a way for some time."

"Yes," said Ann. "I've known, in a way." But knowing in a way was very unlike knowing like this. She felt a little sick and concentrated on the electric fire while Felix continued to look at the ceiling.

Felix went on, "You needn't pay any attention, of course. I mean, I don't want you to worry about this for a second. I'll have to ask your help over just one thing, and even that's not urgent. I'm still not quite fixed about my next job. If you feel later on—I'm not asking you anything now—that you'd prefer me off the scene I can clear off to India. But if you don't say that, I'm sure you know that I wouldn't ever be a trouble to you. I'm in love with you, and there's no point in saying I'm not. But I'm good at being kind and reasonable and quiet. If you thought even that I could be of any help to you, practical help, or as a friend, I'd be very glad, I'd be very very happy to be allowed to stay around. And of course I wouldn't *expect* anything. It will be months, years, before you get over what's just happened here. Whatever happens in the end. All I'm asking is to be allowed to see you a little and help you. I can't tell you, Ann, what joy that would be to me. I'm glad, after all, that I've come out with this thing. And I can't help saying, please don't send me away. I assure you I expect nothing."

He spoke with more feeling than she had ever heard him display. After his normal muteness, it was almost terrible to her to see him so moved, although he spoke quietly and with averted eyes. Yet the next moment she was wondering: why does he expect nothing?

"I hardly know what to say, Felix," she said, wanting to slow things down while she got her thoughts in order. It was very important what she said to him.

Felix, interpreting these words as some kind of negative, said hastily, "Forgive me, forgive me. Let us drop the subject if you will. I should not have troubled you. And of course I can perfectly well go to India. Yes, really, it would be more sensible."

"Felix!" said Ann. "Stop it! You really exasperate me!"

He gave her his eyes again, his wide blue puzzled scrupulous soldier's eyes. He did not know what to make of her reaction. She hardly knew herself.

"I'm sorry," she said, ready for nervous laughter or tears, "but you are so *foolish*! Of course we must talk about it now that it's come up. And of course I don't want to send you to India. But I must see what I'm doing. Could you be quiet for a moment instead of bounding around like a frightened horse?"

Felix looked at her gratefully, entreatingly, and opened his hands towards her.

"You put me in a difficult situation," she said. "You know I'm very fond of you. What more can I say? I can't tell you either to stay or to go. Don't you see? Oh dear—" she floundered. She must not let him see what she really felt. So there was something which she really felt? She added suddenly and as if irrelevantly, "Randall might come back tomorrow." It had a cold dreadful sound. She felt her face harden in response to Felix's changing look.

"And if he came back tomorrow you'd take him back?"

"Of course."

"And if he came back next year or the year after you'd take him back?"

Ann looked away from him and out of the window. She saw outside in the last light the figure of Penn examining the dashboard of the Mercedes. She must be very very careful what she said. "Yes, yes, I expect so." That was the right answer, wasn't it?

Ann went on hastily, "I'm sorry to sound unsympathetic, Felix, but we mustn't be a pair of fools about this. I mean, you mustn't be a fool. This—about me—is a sort of nonsense. You must—attach yourself—to someone younger, to someone—free." She almost choked on the word. "There was a girl, wasn't there, a French girl? Mildred said something about a girl."

"There *was* a girl," said Felix. He hated this bit. "There was a girl I was fond of in Singapore. But that's over and it wasn't important. Ann, please, I don't want to trouble you at all, but don't just thrust me aside like this. I've been in love with you for years, and it's not a sort of nonsense. I don't want to have to roar at you to convince you, but I'm prepared to roar if necessary."

"What's her name?"

"The Singapore girl? Marie-Laure. Marie-Laure Auboyer. But really, Ann—"

"Have you got a picture of her?"

"Yes, but look here—"

"Could I see it?"

"I haven't got it with me!" said Felix, his voice rising. "But I tell you that's all over!" Then he murmured "Sorry."

What am I saying? thought Ann. Does he realise I'm jealous? She put her hand to her head. She had momentarily lost her balance. She said as calmly as she could, "Felix, you really had better go now. I'm so tired and you startled me and I'm probably being stupid. We are old friends, and I certainly don't want to send you away, but I don't exactly want to 'keep' you either if that means any sort of encouragement. Forgive me."

"I startled you—" he said. "I'm a brute. I think I *will* stay in England, if you don't mind. Perhaps I ought just to have waited without telling you I was waiting. But I assure you I'm not at all encouraged. I hope nothing and I expect nothing. I only ask you to let me see you a little and help you a little. I *want* the joy of serving you, even if it only lasts for a while. I *want* it, and I feel that because I love you I have a kind of right to it."

They both got up and stood rather stiffly beside their chairs. It was the moment of departure. Ann felt a strange heaviness of the limbs. It was as if for a little time she had been separated from her body and had rejoined it to find that it had lived, it had changed, in the interim. Perhaps it had been inhabited by an angel. She shivered again as at the light touch of some image, some thought. What was it? Then she realised that it was, absent from her for so long, the idea of happiness. No wonder she had not recognised it.

Felix moved after her towards the door. Then they stopped and stared at each other. Ann said to herself, and the thoughts came quite clearly, Felix assumes it may be years before I get over Randall, years before I am ready to fall in love again. But I am ready to fall in love again now.

It was not that she had suddenly ceased to love Randall. But she was certainly able now, if she relaxed her grip for a moment, to fall in love with Felix. She felt a terrible weakness at the knees. Did love really come upon one like this? Yet this love had been long enough in preparation. Was this falling in love? It was certainly falling. Falling. Falling. She held on to the back of a chair.

As Felix inclined his head and began to move on in the direction of the door she realised with anguish that he was going to go without kissing her.

Chapter Twenty-six

PENN GRAHAM found the behaviour of his English relations absolutely incomprehensible. His uncle Randall had gone off publicly with another woman. Yet everyone was behaving quite calmly and cheerfully as if nothing had happened. Even Miranda, though restless and rather sulky, was scarcely more so than usual. Penn knew that if his own parents had parted he would have run mad.

They were over at Seton Blaise. Humphrey, Mildred and Felix were all in evidence, and Ann had come over with Miranda and himself. They had had a bonzer lunch with a butler waiting, and now they were walking in the chestnut grove which lay between the loop of the river and the little lake. Penn, who was walking by himself, could see the pale blue water between the trunks of the trees. It was a beautiful day, and a shifting yellowish green fell in elliptical coins of light through the gently moving branches. Penn was miserable.

His first feeling on realising that he was in love with Miranda was a certain sense of achievement. He too, Penn Graham, was suffering from that famous ailment; and it did not take him long to realise that he had it in a very acute and probably quite exceptional form. Since then he had, he felt, lived through the whole history of love, and the dialectic of his suffering seemed to have spanned, in a few weeks, the whole of human experience. He began with a sense of exhilaration and with a pure unquestioning delight in the sheer existence of the beloved object. That Miranda should *be*: that was enough of joy. He contemplated, lying in bed that night, her marvellous beauty, her grace, her cleverness, her wit, her impish sharpness, and that sweet childishness which still hung like a veil upon her qualities of a lovely girl. Turning over and burying his face in the pillow he groaned with ecstasy and fell into a sleep of happiness.

The next morning, to which he woke with an undifferentiated
sense of bliss, produced however, as it wore on, a state of mind somewhat less solipsistic. Penn strayed forth into the world on that
morning as into the Garden of Eden. He was a new man. A first
man. A man. And since he had been made new it seemed to him
somehow deeply evident that Miranda had been made new as well,
and he wandered towards her through a rose-entangled forest full
of sweet airs that gave delight and hurt not. He felt positively mag-
netic with the power of love, and did not doubt that since he loved
Miranda so much he would be able irresistibly to draw her to him.

What this conjunction would, exactly, consist in was less clear to
him nor did he give it thought. He did not avert his attention from
the problem of sexual desire, the problem simply did not exist for
him. His image of Miranda rose like a column of flame from the
pure re-created form of his new life, and he and she existed in a
golden haze of love and worship and diffused desire. And in so far
as he precisely pictured himself at all as keeping company with the
new Miranda, he saw them wandering eternally hand in hand in
some flower-scattered field of bliss.

He absented himself from breakfast that morning, partly because
he felt that if he ate anything he would be sick, and partly because
he wanted to see Miranda in a more spiritual atmosphere than that
induced by questions about eggs and cornflakes. He wandered
instead upon the lawn, waiting for her to come out, as she always
did after breakfast, to see if her hedgehogs had eaten up their bread
and milk in the night. When she did appear he approached her,
spoke to her, followed her. She was, as usual, detached and impish,
full of the rather malicious gaiety which had confounded Penn from
the first; and in the midst of the acute sensations occasioned by her
presence Penn was forced to suspect that she was still the un-
regenerate old Miranda.

Penn shook himself at this point and reproached himself. He had
learnt, he told himself, an important lesson. The lover readily
imagines that he and his mistress are one. He feels he has love
enough for both and that his loving will can swathe the two of

them together like twin nuts in a shell. But what one loves is, after all, another human being, a person with other interests, other pains, in whose world one is oneself an object among others. While Penn glided after her in tune with the music of the spheres, Miranda was more concerned about the hedgehogs and about whether Hatfield had perhaps come to steal their milk, a question upon which she condescended to ask Penn's opinion. That she so consulted him disconcerted him at first but later delighted him. He must learn, he realised, to live in the real world with Miranda.

The real world however was a thorny place. Penn at this stage pictured himself somewhat as a disciple of Courtly Love. He imagined himself Miranda's slave, devoted to her service, running errands for her or, preferably, rescuing her from terrible dangers. And he envisaged this too, though less clearly, as a process which would transform Miranda, which would, in short, make her love him. His desert, he felt, was infinite and must in time be evident and then compelling. Service would call forth love and the new Miranda would arise, an apotheosis of the sweetness and power which he so powerfully divined as hidden within the puckish *gamine* who, alas, sometimes enjoyed teasing and tormenting him.

But the process did not work out quite like that. At least, as Penn told himself, the *early* stages did not. Miranda very quickly guessed what was the matter with him. It would have been difficult not to. And when she had guessed, the tormenting and the teasing got worse. And the more she teased him the more owlish and donkey-like he felt himself becoming. He could not toss back witty remarks. he could not fence with her, he could only, with patient stupid smiles, endure the continual piercing of her wit. The injustice of the situation tortured Penn. There was within him so much that was marvellous. If he could, even for a short while, have made Miranda *quiet*, he could have unfolded a seriousnesss and an eloquence that must have impressed her. He could have talked *deeply* to her. But at the superficial level at which she continually disported herself he was tongue-tied. ·

He was made very miserable by this situation, yet one inestimable blessing kept him from despair, and that was the almost continual company of his beloved. The blessed German measles quarantine turned up just at the right moment, and he could now see her every day and indeed most of the day if he dared to brave her annoyance by pursuing her. He did not cease to hope that he would make her love him; and he noted with a recurrent joy that if ever, wounded by some particularly malicious or irritable sally, he wandered away from her by himself, she would after a little time come to find him. She came, it seemed, merely to torment him more, but she came: and he could sometimes persuade himself that he loved the torment.

During all this time Penn had not of course *said* anything about love to Miranda. It was not only that he was not able to find, in the sparkling play of her conversation, any place for his more solemn words: he was also restrained by certain scruples. She was, after all, very young. It was easy to forget this most of the time, so ready and so sophisticated was her mastery of him. He never for a second questioned that she was far cleverer than he was. But she was younger. And even apart from this, a sort of shame possessed him at the thought of uttering words about love. The hidden eloquence which he felt himself so marvellously to possess was not exactly about *that*. He felt able to tell Miranda the wonders of the universe and the secrets of the seas but not exactly to say in words that he was in love with her.

Miranda was often out of temper; and at these times Penn suffered most. It was as if, almost absent-mindedly, she were taking it out of him because of pains and troubles of her own of which she would tell him nothing. Penn told himself that he must make allowances. He knew that Miranda was devoted to her father; and he conjectured that it must have been torture to her to see Randall gradually withdrawing from Grayhallock. All the same, it was difficult sometimes to be patient with her, and he wondered if perhaps his whole approach was wrong. It was the first time that he had thought explicitly about strategy, and he felt, at the first touch of the idea, ashamed, as if he were profaning something innocent.

Miranda gave him no peace, however, and began at this time liter-
ally to pinch him. She would come suddenly up behind him, seize
the skin of his arm or some other part of him between her little
pincer-like fingers, and squeeze as hard as she could. Penn became
covered with bruises. At first he was pleased and excited by this
treatment. But Miranda put so much malice into the pinches and
was so unpleasant if he touched her in response even so far as to
push her off, that this new policy soon reduced him to a state of
black almost revengeful agitation. He began to see her as a demon;
and deep within him there was some darkness that gave answer.

He had not so far thought very much about touching her; at
least he had not thought about it with any kind of precision. He
had been content to touch her hand and her shoulder in a way
which was natural, but had an added sweetness and excitement: and
the thrill of her presence had affected his whole being like a warm
breeze which soothed rather than disturbed. Now however it began
to be different. It was as if Miranda's savage pinches were designed
to awaken in him something far more primitive, and he felt, sometimes with wretchedness and sometimes with a sort of dark zest,
more depraved. The thoughts of strategy found here their context.
Penn found himself wondering if it wouldn't be a good plan, if it
would not perhaps further his cause, if he were to give Miranda a
hard slap one of these days. Perhaps this indeed was what her treatment of him was designed to produce, perhaps she *wanted* him to be
brutal? Before this conjecture Penn paused, first with amazement
and then with a sort of pride. He was in deep waters. But he was
shocked to find, now that it was suddenly released, how much sheer
animosity he had in him against his young mistress. With this
release, terrible, black, new, came sexual desire. Penn had imagined
earlier that he was suffering. But those had been pure flames. Now
he lay tossing sleepless in bed and imagined her body. Guilt now
blackened his vision and complicated his pain. His desires grew
hideously precise; and in the dark stream of his new yearning it
was as if he were back at the beginning again and the real Miranda
had disappeared. Only that had been heaven whereas this was hell.

The first Miranda had been a heavenly vision. The last Miranda
was a doll of flesh.

On the day of the expedition to Seton Blaise Penn's gloom had
been a little alleviated at first because Miranda had been nice to him
in the morning. She had been particularly unpleasant to him on the
previous day; and although Penn believed that he filled a certain
need for her, during the time after her father's departure, her malice
was hard to bear all the same and he was glad, the next morning, of
a kind word. Lunch had been all right. He had felt a little reconciled
with Miranda, and he couldn't help enjoying the food; but after
lunch, in the garden wanderings, she had avoided him. He had
hurried away, he hoped not too rudely, from the kindly Humphrey
who had seemed disposed to talk to him, and pursued her a little
through the trees; but each time as he came near she had run on,
and he could see her now ahead, following close behind Ann and
Felix, going in the direction of the lake. Mildred, who had detached
herself from that group, had joined her husband beside the water,
and they seemed to be discussing a possible new landing-stage.
Penn was alone with his trouble.

They all converged upon a place where the trees ended and
there was a little gently sloping shingly beach. The sunshine was
bright and large after the scattered light of the grove. The lake
stretched away into flat expanses of reddish and yellowish reed
beds, in front of which a few coots and tufted ducks swam lazily
about. The open fields, scarcely visible on the other side, were
fringed with ragged lines of elm and hawthorn. Penn edged near
to Miranda, but she was holding on to her mother's arm in a
little-girlish sort of way and paid him no attention.

Mildred and Humphrey had joined them. "We *must* get that
boat, don't you think?" said Mildred. "A boat is what this scene
needs. It would look so romantic nestling among the reeds."

"It wouldn't be so romantic having to paint it every winter and
stop up the holes. Eh, Penn?" said Humphrey.

Penn laughed.

"Felix would do all that," said Mildred. "Wouldn't you, Felix?

It's so nice that you're going to stay in England. You're so *useful.*"

Felix smiled, but did not seem disposed to pursue the question of the boat. He was looking, Penn thought, very fine today, huge and brown in a sagging open-necked white shirt.

Ann picked up a pebble from the shingly beach and threw it into the water. She stared at the ripples. She was looking rather nice in a pretty flowery dress, but sad. She had her hair sleeked back as usual, but Penn thought she must have put on some make-up or something. Her face looked different.

Felix picked up another pebble and threw it after Ann's. It fell dead into the centre of her circle of ripples. They looked at each other smiling.

Almost automatically Penn selected a rather larger stone and threw it far out over the water. It fell near the coots, who beat a hasty retreat into the reeds on the other side.

"That was a mighty throw," said Humphrey. "But you're a cricketing man, aren't you, Penn?"

Penn was pleased. He picked up another stone.

"I bet you couldn't throw as far as that, Felix," said Mildred.

"I'm sure I couldn't!" said Felix. He found himself a stone and mounting a little up the beach discharged it high into the air. It fell with a loud splash a good few yards beyond Penn's.

"Oh, well done!" said Ann.

Miranda had detached herself from Ann and mounted to the top of the bank behind Felix. She was watching with interest.

"I don't think Penn was really trying," said Humphrey. "The competition hadn't begun, so it wasn't fair."

Penn mounted a little too, getting a good foothold in the shingle. He was conscious of Miranda behind him like a pale cloud. He threw his stone with an easy strength and outstripped Felix's throw by a yard.

Everyone cried "Splendid!" and began to egg Felix on to try again.

"Let each of them have three throws," said Humphrey, "not

counting Penn's first throw. I will undertake to give a first prize and a booby prize."

Felix prepared to throw again. As his great shoulders moved for the throw he seemed to Penn giant-like, yet of an extreme grace. His shirt billowed and his sleeves flapped and he was perspiring freely. Penn, who was wearing a tie and a blazer, felt dapper and neat by comparison. But he was glad to be throwing the stones in front of Miranda and he felt suddenly happy.

Felix's next stone fell a little way beyond Penn's last one.

Penn was now determined to excel. He took a little time, as when he was about to bowl, trampling about and weighing the stone, pleased to have all eyes upon him. Then with an easy turn of his body he sent it flying. It fell, amid applause, well beyond the last mark.

"It's incredible," said Mildred. "I can't think how a human being can send a stone so far. Penn must be a superman!"

Felix, with a look of comical determination, took his stance, and without preliminaries, while the others were still exclaiming, hurled his pebble. It out-distanced Penn's last throw by several yards, landing almost among the reeds on the other side of the lake. There were admiring cries.

Penn thought, I can beat that. It was almost as if his will alone could carry the stone bird-like and drop it out of sight in the middle of the reed bed. He loosened his shoulders and drooped his arms for a moment as his coach had told him to do. He moved into action. But just as his hand was coming forward he saw Miranda, who had advanced to the edge of the beach a little beyond the group, and with apparent unconcern was taking her shoes and socks off. Penn's stone fell a little short of his second throw and well behind Felix's. There were groans of commiseration.

"Never mind," said Mildred. "We think you're both wonderful. Now let's go in and have some tea, I'm getting cold."

"You shall both have a prize," said Humphrey. "What would you like for yours, young Penn? I've got a fine Swedish knife. I'll show it to you when we get back."

"Miranda, do be careful," said Ann. "You may cut your feet on those sharp pebbles."

They began to trail back through the trees. Penn wanted to wait for Miranda who had walked out knee-deep into the lake, but Humphrey was still making conversation. Penn, who felt a little guilty at having refused Humphrey's invitation to London, thought he had better not run away from him again, so with frequent backward glances he answered as best he could.

They moved on slowly. Back in the grove it was dark at first until they got used to the greenish half light. Patches of sunshine high up, moving in the leafy space like miraculous fishes, illumined sudden vistas of thick boughs and canopied galleries. Penn looked upward as they walked between the huge trees and it seemed as if there were a silence spread above them, a brooding green silence beneath which their voices ran to and fro. He wished Humphrey would stop chattering and leave him in the quietness of the wood to wait for Miranda.

"Ha-a-a-ay!"

There was a loud cry from behind and everyone stopped. It sounded at first like a cry of fear, and Penn felt an immediate sickness of alarm before he realised that it was a cry of triumph. It came from somewhere high up.

"Hey, everyone, come and see where I am!" Miranda sang out.

"Good heavens!" said Ann. She began to run back and Penn and everyone else ran too.

They reached a slight clearing where a great tree spread its arms over a circle of grass. There, near to the top, half hidden in the leaves, was Miranda. They had to strain their necks back to see her as she edged out on to what seemed a perilously thin branch.

"Miranda, come down at once!" cried Ann. "Are you mad? Come back off that branch."

"Ho, ho, ho! Come and fetch me!" called Miranda. She began to swing on the branch.

Ann turned away, hiding her face.

"Miranda, don't be a bloody little ass," said Mildred. "We think you're very clever to have got up there. Now come down and stop frightening us, or by heaven you shall have no tea."

"I'm going farther up," Miranda announced. She edged back off the thin branch and began testing higher footholds.

Penn felt giddy at the sight of her so high up. He wondered crazily if he ought not to climb the tree after her. But he had a horror of high places and felt so sick he almost had to sit on the ground.

"Miranda," said Felix in a voice of authority. "Don't go any further up. Come down now and come down *slowly*." He had a hand on Ann's shoulder.

"Do you really want me to come down?" said Miranda. She had stopped and was half visible, her legs pale among the dark leaves.

"Yes, I certainly do," said Felix. "Come down at once."

There was a moment's pause. "All right," said Miranda. "Watch out. I'm going to jump."

"Don't—" cried Ann.

But the next moment Miranda had jumped. Someone screamed. Penn rushed madly forward. He had a strange instantaneous glimpse of her leaving the branch, her skirts flying up. The next moment something struck him on the shoulder so violently that he was hurled stumbling to his knees several yards away. It was Felix, who arriving first, caught the falling Miranda in his arms and the two of them whirled to the ground in a spinning hurly-burly of arms and legs.

There was, after the tumbling heap came to a stand-still, a moment of immobility. Then Ann rushed with a cry to where Miranda lay. But already Miranda was picking herself up. She got as far as a sitting position and began to rub her leg. Felix was getting up slowly.

"Are you all right?" said Ann, kneeling beside her.

Miranda didn't answer at once. She breathed deeply. She said then, "I'm all right except for my ankle. That hurts a lot." She began to cry.

"Don't try to get up," said Ann. "Move yourself about a bit. No bones broken?"

"Needs whipping if you ask me," said Mildred.

"I'm all right really," said Miranda through her sobs, one hand on her leg and the other in her eye. "It's just the ankle. It hurts so much."

It took a little while for everyone to be satisfied that nothing was indeed broken except perhaps the ankle. Then it was decided that she should be moved back to the house. After consulting with Ann, Felix knelt beside the child and gathered her carefully in his arms. He rose bearing her, she still weeping, and the others formed a procession behind and set out toward the bridge.

Penn had picked himself up. He was still aching dreadfully from the collision with Felix. But no one asked how *he* was. He and Humphrey brought up the tail of the procession. As they passed slowly over the bridge Penn found that he was crying quietly. Humphrey put an arm round his shoulder.

Chapter Twenty-seven

IT was of course Mildred's idea that Miranda should stay on at Seton Blaise: and once suggested the notion seemed to please everybody. It pleased Miranda because it represented a holiday, it pleased Felix because it represented a chance to get to know the child and because Ann must be constantly at the house, it pleased Ann (he hoped) for the same reasons, it pleased Humphrey because it left Penn in need of consolation, and it pleased Mildred because she had thought of it. Only Penn was cross.

The doctor, summoned at once, had declared the damaged ankle to be severely sprained and had prescribed rest and quiet; more danger was to be apprehended from shock than from anything else, he privately explained to them. Miranda herself, cheerful at first, was established upon the big settee in the library, and from there lorded it over the household, consuming during the day fantastic quantities of coffee, biscuits, chocolate, cakes and ice cream, as well as her usual meals.

Felix was in a strange state of mind. He was by now very much in love. He observed with mingled feelings of delight and dismay the terrifyingly rapid alteration of his (as it now seemed in retrospect) gentle and sensible love for Ann into a passion which shook him with stormy gusts and left him trembling. By declaring his love he had completely changed the world. He was a different man, she a different Ann, and the place they inhabited was not the same. Yet in the midst of the new landscape they constantly apprehended, in ways which seemed to puzzle them both, their old knowledge of each other; and upon this, when their steps faltered, they laid a steadying hand.

On the whole, for Felix, joy predominated over fear. Falling in love is a rejuvenating process, and he surrendered himself to it as to a delightful course of treatment. He had, too, the reassuring sense of an interval during which forces were working on his side. He had cast a stone and now watched the ripples. He had, at moments, gaped at his audacity. Yet his haste, which seemed like a sort of violence, also seemed to him to merit, to compel, its reward. He had a sense of acting upon Ann at a distance; and his powerful love, making him feel a giant, filled him with confidence in his cause.

Chronologically speaking, Felix was completely disoriented. He had told Ann, which now seemed a positive and also an absurd lie, that he expected nothing. He had said that he did not want to rush her, and had implied that he would wait for years if necessary. He did indeed at times try to picture himself as patient, and as settling down for a long siege. But his forces were constantly demoralised by the idea of an immediate capture, and he caught himself more than once with the expectation that the whole thing could be settled in months or even weeks. He tried not to think too much about what Ann was thinking. Tacitly, for the present, they avoided intense conversations and were indeed not often alone together. But Felix could not help watching her for signs of love, and at moments when their eyes met he felt he could not be mistaken about the message. He felt, could almost see, powers within her working for him. He waited; and as a result of his dislocated time scheme could do nothing, could plan nothing. He prolonged his leave and procrastinated about his job. He did not write to Marie-Laure; and decided after a while that his silence, functioning instead of a letter, was the right answer.

After a day or two of Mildred's bright idea the arrangement began to seem a little less inspired and to afflict Felix, in the midst of his hopes, with a certain immediate nervous melancholy. The weather changed, became colder. Rain battered the garden and a gloomy yellowish light lurked at the windows. Lamps were turned on within. A fire was lit in the library and Miranda shivered and called for rugs. Ann came over regularly, driving the Vauxhall through the spitting downpour. She would not let Felix fetch her. She came, and she sat with Miranda in the library, sometimes with Felix there, sometimes not. She seemed exceptionally absorbed in her child and Felix had an unnerving sense, even when he was sub-

sequently alone with Ann, of being somehow chaperoned by that
mysterious little nymph. Ann was depressed and jumpy; yet she
gave him, by wordless looks, by pressures of the hand, and by an
increasing helplessness and reliance upon him in various practical
matters, enough encouragement.

Mildred seemed thoroughly depressed and moody too. Having
suggested the retention of Miranda, she would have nothing to do
with looking after the child, of whom she privately professed dislike, and left the task entirely to the embarrassed Felix. It was as if
Mildred had suddenly given up hope and consented to become
older. She looked older, frailer, less interested in life. There was
only, through Ann, the most perfunctory news of Hugh, who
could now spare no time at all from his London activities, and
limited his evident concern with his granddaughter's accident to
the despatch from Hatchards of a complete set of the novels of Jane
Austen in a modern leather-bound edition. Mildred seemed to have
no spirit left even to be curious about Felix's progress, and they
now talked rarely. She had been prepared to launch him with a
brave face, but not to follow his subsequent vicissitudes. Her
excitement about his match seemed to have faded, and she left him,
after so much encouragement, to paddle his own canoe. She withdrew, and he missed her.

Humphrey was also depressed. Felix had always, from the very
beginning of his sister's marriage, found it a trifle difficult to believe
in Humphrey. He found his brother-in-law mysterious, in some
ways substanceless, in some ways too good to be true. There was
something in him he admired and to which he found it hard to give
a name: perhaps it was Humphrey's courage, or an artistic aloofness
from conventional life. His brother-in-law had particularly taken
his breath away at the time of the catastrophe, which Humphrey
had weathered with a calmness and irony which made him seem a
man truly superior to fortune. Yet Humphrey was also, for Felix, a
nothing. It was partly that Felix could not really believe in homo-
sexual love. Mildred had many a time, defending her husband out
of the curious deep attachment which bound them together, tried

to make him see the seriousness of the matter; and that Humphrey often *suffered* Felix was prepared to believe and could even see. But he could not envisage Humphrey's bizarre relationships as having any possible connection with the human heart; and there was, in his picture of Mildred's husband, a chilling void at the centre.

That Humphrey was suffering now was indeed evident enough; and Felix took Mildred's word for it that it was because of young Penn; though his imagination, when it occasionally had time to spare for Humphrey's troubles, could do little with the almost ludicrous idea. Humphrey visited Grayhallock several times during Miranda's sojourn at Seton Blaise, and returned each time with a long face. He and Mildred drew together in a private sombre communion which excluded Felix. They were often to be discovered, almost like lovers, holding hands and having conversations which terminated abruptly on Felix's arrival. He could not conjecture the nature of their complicity and when he wondered what they were talking about he found himself shuddering. Eventually Humphrey took himself off to London and Mildred retired morosely to her room.

Miranda, after a day or two of rather feverish elation, joined herself to the general gloom. She seemed incapable of reading anything except the newspaper, and after remarking upon the extreme pliancy of their covers, took no further interest in Hugh's Jane Austens. She lay for hours huddled upon the settee with a rug over her, staring out at the rain, and consoling herself with snacks. Someone, usually Felix, had to come and make conversation with her. She seemed to him ill in some indefinable way, and, in consultation with Ann, he asked the doctor to call again. Ann thought she might be sickening for German measles, but the doctor could find no symptoms, spoke again of shock, and departed cheerfully after accepting a glass of sherry.

Felix found the conversation hard going, but he kept at it. He was not used to children, and as he sometimes listened to himself talking he found his tone of a jovial uncle horribly unnatural and patronising. He could not imagine that he was making a very good impression, and their relations remained embarrassingly formal. Yet he was at the same time troubled by a continual sense of her exigence and his deficiency. He was still rather vague about her age, and simply could not bring himself, at this point, to reveal so shocking an ignorance to Ann. But although he now felt that the whole idea was a depressing mistake, he took it as his duty to get to know the child a little better. The trouble was, there were so many forbidden topics: everything, in fact, to do with her father and mother. This left Felix, as far as he could see, with books, school, animals, the countryside, and such few mutual acquaintances as could be mentioned with impunity. He soon ran through these subjects and had to start again at the beginning, trying in vain to interest Miranda in the contents of the library, which were in fact mainly historical volumes which had belonged to Felix's, also military, father. But Miranda, unmoved by *Pride and Prejudice*, was not likely to become absorbed by Motley's *Rise of the Dutch Republic*.

In despair Felix decided he must supply her with *some* reading matter, if only in order to give himself some time off, and he drove to Canterbury with that end in view. But the bookshops provided no inspiration. He finally went to a newsagent's and bought a great pile of periodicals and women's magazines which he hoped would placate the child and keep her quiet. Then he had, before he left the town, another happy conjecture. He thought he would buy her a doll. Whatever age Miranda was, she was certainly still interested in dolls, and had had a large number of her 'little princes' brought over from Grayhallock to keep her company. Of course, for such a discriminating child, it must be no ordinary doll, and he wondered if he should not drive to London and see what Harrods could do. But a Canterbury shop in fact provided him straightaway with a distinguished little toy which seemed to him just right. It was a rag doll attired in the dress uniform of the Brigade of Guards, prettily turned out and complete with a sword and a very convincing bear-skin. Felix congratulated himself. Even if he could not entertain Miranda he might at least give her some pleasure. He was, after all, more or less wooing her, and a wooer ought to bring gifts. For Felix never stopped being conscious of the influence which a hostile Miranda might have upon his suit with Ann.

After a windy overcast morning it was raining again when he got back to Seton Blaise. He had missed Ann's visit, but arranged by telephone that he would go to see her later that evening at Grayhallock. He hoped that his thought for Miranda would please her. With the doll in his overcoat pocket he went to the library.

The lit lamps and the blazing fire gave the room a winter appearance which contrasted uncannily with the greenish yellowish light at the window and the lush wet garden outside. Gusts of rain crossed the lawn and lashed the house. Felix shivered, aware of a pain in his shoulder which might be rheumatism or perhaps just the bruise which he had received when, in catching Miranda, he had cannoned into Penn.

Miranda was lying as usual, stretched out and doing nothing. She was propped up on cushions and a rug covered her legs. Several dolls, dislodged no doubt by the child's restless tossing, had fallen down between her and the back of the settee so that she was half sitting on them. A row of protesting heads rose above her thigh.

"I'm so glad someone's come at last," said Miranda. "I was getting so bored."

Someone's come, not *you've* come, thought Felix, discouraged. But he was glad he had got the doll.

"Have some tea with me," said Miranda, indicating the trolley. "I asked for a spare cup in case anyone turned up."

"No, thanks. But you go on having yours, don't mind me."

"I've finished ages ago," she said, and pushed the trolley irritably away.

Felix took a chair and sat down near her. He felt the familiar constraint, the fatal mask of brightness. "And how's Miranda today?"

"Terrible!"

Felix laughed. "Oh, I'm sure it's not as bad as that."

She was staring at him again in the disconcerting way children have. She lay back against the cushions with an air of languor, pale and yet with a thin warmth in her cheeks which made Felix think again of the German measles. He supposed he ought to take her temperature, but he shrank from any close-quarters looking-after of her as from something obscene. And now with a slight distaste, almost disgust, he apprehended her immature girl's body spread out beside him, soft, formless, white, like a helpless larva. She was wearing a tartan dress with a neat little collar which made her look childish, yet her face was not exactly that of a child: it was not a woman's face either, but like the smooth ruthlessly innocent visage of some mythological creature, some little demi-goddess of the woods. Ah, he thought, I shall never win her.

"I've been to Canterbury," he said conversationally.

"I know. You said you were going."

"Did I? Ah well. How's the ankle feeling now? Any better?"

"Dreadful, Felix."

Her rare use of his name always unnerved him a little. He glanced at her, met the stare, and looked away again. Her face certainly had something of Ann: the pale colouring, the delicacy of nose and mouth, the impression of a slightly strained nobility. Only Ann's worried look was absent, that look which summed up for Felix so much of her concern for others. Miranda's face, with its frequent expression of triumphant mockery, and now in repose a certain stony aggressiveness, suggested rather the insolence of her father; and as Felix for a second sensed what was almost like the proximity of Randall's soul, he nearly started back from her.

Feeling guilty at this thought he said jovially, "Better rescue those dolls, you know, before you squash them completely." He reached across her thigh and tried to pull the dolls out of their uncomfortable situation.

"*Don't!*" said Miranda. She pushed his hand away, and began to lift the dolls out herself. She shook each one crossly as she did so as if to punish it.

How clumsy I am with children, thought Felix ruefully. I expect I simply annoy her, and am doing myself no good at all. He touched the doll in his pocket. He felt a little shy about giving it to her.

She sat now looking at the dolls with an expression of apathy.

Felix said, "I'm going to Grayhallock tonight. Can I fetch you anything? Any more of the—er—little princes?"

"No, thank you." She added fiercely, still looking at the dolls, "I wish beastly Grayhallock didn't exist."

"Come, come!" said Felix, surprised and a little shocked by this outburst. "Why have you got it in for poor old Grayhallock?"

"Nothing ever happens there," said Miranda.

Felix thought this was an odd judgment, considering recent events. "I should have thought where *you* were things would always be happening." In that, you take after your father, he continued to himself. God help the young men who love you. And those you love.

She just shook her head and posed the dolls upon the rug, spreading out their skirts.

"Whatever possessed you anyway to jump out of that tree?" said Felix. He felt a sudden irritation with the hostile young person, an embryonic desire to spank her. He had not liked her remark about her home.

Miranda looked at him, and he saw in her face some strange reassembling of inner elements, like the moving of stage scenery behind a gauze curtain. She looked alert, wary, older.

She said after a moment, "I felt, just then, entirely indifferent to life. Does that surprise you?"

Felix was irritated still further by the complacent formality of her tone. "Not particularly," he said. "Very young people often think they feel something of the sort. Though I doubt if you were *really* indifferent." All the same, he thought, she did risk her life.

"Was it very naughty of me?" she said, with an affected childishness which seemed to invite reproof.

"Yes, I think it was," said Felix. "You might have seriously damaged yourself or someone else, and you scared your mother out of her wits."

"Yes, I was very bad," said Miranda with satisfaction. "Don't you think my mother is an awfully sweet person?"

Felix restrained a desire to slap her. "Yes, charming," he said. Then, in case she should make some further insufferable remark, he said, "Why all this indifference to life, anyway? In lots of ways you're a very lucky little girl." Annoyance is making me stupid, he thought. No daughter of Randall's could be a very lucky little girl.

Miranda stared at him, her big hazel eyes glistening and the new liveliness working in her face. Then she looked away and said, "Sometimes I see no point in going on. We're all going to be blown up soon anyway. I'd rather die young in my own way than die slowly of radiation sickness."

Although she still spoke with a certain complacency, her words shook Felix. He was indeed being stupid with her. He only hoped she was not noticing it. "I think," he said, "that one should take life as a job. Just like the Army. Go where it sends one and take whatever comes next."

"But *you* don't do that," said Miranda, her gaze returning to him mischievously. "You can choose your job, choose whether you go to India or stay in England."

How smart and well-informed the brat is. "Well, I'm lucky this time," said Felix. "It's not usually like that."

"I want to be lucky—or nothing."

"You're very young," he said, beginning to weary a little of the discussion. "Other people are what matter about life, and that's the best reason why one can't just contract out of it. We are members one of another, as the service says. But perhaps a child can't be expected to understand."

"Am I a *child*?" said Miranda. Hugging the dolls now she held his gaze. Her eyes were stonily provocative.

Felix hesitated. "Damn it, of course you are, Miranda!"

They both laughed.

"Which reminds me," said Felix a little awkwardly, "I've got a present for you."

He took the doll out of his pocket and set it on Miranda's knee.

It was unexpected. Dropping the others she looked at it for a moment, her mouth slightly open. Then she looked back at Felix and there was in her eyes a dark violence which he could not decipher. She turned back to the doll and reached out a slow hand to pick it up. She drew it towards her as if to hug it, and then let it fall in her lap. She gave a little whimper and covered her face and then laid her brow against the back of the settee. A series of little cries followed, her shoulders jerking. Then she straightened up, wiped her eyes in which there had been but few tears, and said drily, "Thank you, Felix."

Felix watched the curious, almost contrived, little storm with amazement. He would never never understand her. He looked surreptitiously at his watch.

Chapter Twenty-eight

Ann walked slowly up the hill along the grass path between the gallicas. Behind her the thick white tower of smoke from the bonfire rose straight up into the air. It was a still day, not raining, but overcast and heavy, under a yellow sky. Ann had been lighting the bonfire, taking from the stables one of the buckets of torn paper kept for this purpose. Nothing was wasted at Grayhallock, and Nancy Bowshott was well trained in the segregation of the contents of waste-paper baskets. Now as Ann mounted she looked on either side of her under the red prickly arching stems to see if she could catch sight of Hatfield. Bowshott had reported seeing him earlier that morning, in the field just below the nursery, devouring a young rabbit.

There was, of course, no word from Randall. A friend of Clare Swann's had reported seeing him in Rome lunching in an expensive open-air restaurant with Lindsay, and Clare had passed this on, with scandalised exclamations, to Ann. The absurd intelligence had hurt her terribly. Of course, if Randall was in Rome with Lindsay, obviously he would be lunching with her at expensive open-air restaurants. But the vague words had stirred her imagination, and she saw the trailing canopy of vines, the cloudless radiant sky, and beneath in a dappled shade the lovers leaning together.

Ann's mind was out of her control. She had never had this sensation before and it afflicted her with a sort of sea-sickness. She was racing somewhere so fast that she could no longer focus her eyes. Her images of those she loved, her image of herself, seemed lurid, inflated and blurred. Everything was getting monstrously larger and hazier at the same time. She wished that she could rest; but the machine only whirled the faster, dazzling her and inducing a continual nausea.

Ann was by now dreadfully in love with Felix. From the moment when, after his own declaration, she had realised with a shocked surprise that she was *ready* to fall in love, the descent of her mind into love had taken place with the power of an avalanche. There was nothing between her and a total love of Felix, no barrier, no resting place. Once she had seen the possibility, the whole thing had been there, and with such an authority and completeness that she could now convince herself that she had loved Felix for years. Certainly the thing had been long preparing; and for all the madness of the present moment, she knew that it existed not as something crazy or trivial, but as a deep belonging of her whole personality. She fully laid claim to, she fully inhabited, her love of Felix.

That she was in this extremity she had so far concealed from him, by an avoidance of long or intimate talks, and by a partly simulated concentration upon Miranda. She had even managed, in Miranda's absence, to keep her daughter with her as a topic of conversation, and in this rôle as a sort of chaperone. She feared some terrible breakdown with Felix, some hurling of herself into his arms or at his feet; and her efforts to preserve an erect posture made her positively stiff. For she knew very well that great as was the sum of her love and of his love at this moment, any such scene would increase it a hundredfold. And she still did not, in the most fundamental terms, know what she was up to.

For the fact was that, keeping pace demonically with her love for Felix, there had developed in her a dark new passion for Randall. It was as if one were the infernal mirror image of the other; and at times when she woke from a troubled sleep, not sure which of the two she had been dreaming of, she almost felt the loves to be interdependent. Being in love with Randall in this way was something entirely painful and with a brutality of its own, as if such a love could not but hurt its object. It was quite unlike her old romantic love for the young Randall, or her steady married love for her husband. She was not sure indeed how she recognised it as love at all. It was a kind of mutual haunting. It made her frightened; and because she suspected at times that it was simply her resentment and her jealousy run mad, she tried not to indulge it. She began to need help.

Felix had attempted to give her, and she had attempted to give herself, the sense of there being plenty of time. But she knew that this was just a reassuring fiction. There was, really, very little time. It was not just that at her age, at Felix's age, it was senseless to talk of waiting for years. There was something in the situation itself which demanded a quick solution. She did not doubt either Felix's love or her own, nor had she in general any sense that she ought to send him off to a younger woman. Her own appetite for Felix, with a rejuvenating sharpness and authority, made her feel herself a proper enough object. Soberly, she did not think it likely that Randall would return. She had been for years unwilling to see that Randall hated her, she had been unwilling to use that word even to herself. But lately she had been compelled to see it, to see the strength and a little to understand the nature of that hatred. Randall saw her as the destroyer, as the devil.

These considerations, however, were very far from adding up to an answer. There were, she felt at times, insuperable barriers between herself and Felix. There was Miranda. The child worshipped her father. Would she tolerate a step-father? Ann had had experience of Miranda's will. Even if this difficulty were overcome there was another, vaster, harder: the Christian view of marriage. Ann had always been a member of the Church of England, zealous, serious, on the whole undoubting, but a little vague about dogma. She had never reflected before upon this particular question. She did not know how to find out what she thought about it and she was afraid of finding out. She thought that she had it in her to defy authority; but defying her own conscience would be another matter. As yet her conscience, lost somewhere in the uproar of her feelings, had made no pronouncement.

Ann was troubled too by the existence of Marie-Laure Auboyer. She wished that she had not asked Felix for her name; pale and silent now behind the name, like a funeral effigy, stood the figure, both pathetic and menacing, of the French girl, whom Ann found herself thinking of both as a rival and as a victim. She had learnt of her existence some time ago from Mildred and had gathered, and felt some quiet pain at the news, that Felix was greatly in love. Mildred had mentioned this in some context of deploring foreigners; and had obviously at once regretted her indiscretion. She had been at Grayhallock twice in the last week, on each occasion in a state of listlessness out of which she only roused herself in an effort to efface the impression she had then made. In the course of those attempts she let it slip out, perhaps imagining that Ann knew already, that Marie-Laure had gone to Delhi. It was another reason for haste. Felix must if necessary be despatched to India before it became too late.

Ann began to be tormented by a terrible sense of urgency. She tried to think clearly, especially about the matter of Christian marriage. But whenever she tried to order her thoughts there rose huge and scarlet before her the Randall-demon, her new and terrible relation to her husband; and she knew that before she could move towards a decision that ghost must be somehow laid. She wondered at moments if she should not talk to Felix about the whole thing; but she realised that to do this would be to prejudge an issue about which she would wish to have decided coolly and rationally. As the situation was at the moment balanced, any move she made would be likely to have decisive weight. If she took another step now in the direction of Felix she was lost. Ann decided to talk to Douglas Swann.

Douglas was really the only person she *could* talk to. He was not impeccably wise, but he was discreet and the scrupulousness of his attachment to her could serve instead of, could even induce, wisdom. So she had summoned him. And as she now emerged from the nursery and crossed the road she caught sight of him further down the hill entering the main gate of Grayhallock. When she arrived he was already waiting in the drawing-room.

"My dear Ann," said Douglas Swann, bowing and swaying over her hand, "how are you, my dear? You wanted to see me? I was coming anyway, you know."

Ann had not at all thought out what she wanted to say to him, but she felt relief as at an imminent confession. He was, after all, a priest.

She said, "Douglas, I want an exorcism."

"An exorcism?"

"I think I'm going mad."

Swann looked at her anxiously, not sure how to take her words, and smoothed his black bird's plume of hair. "*You* couldn't go mad if you tried, my dear. Now do let's sit down and smoke a cigarette Shall I make you some coffee?"

"No thanks," said Ann. She sat down heavily in one of the arm-chairs and Swann pulled his chair up beside her. She said, "It's just that I'm somehow obsessed with Randall. He stops me from think-ing. I feel that he's got inside me. I feel that he'll be with me, like a cancer inside me, for the rest of my life." The violence of her own words startled her.

"That is just the reverse side of your love for him," said Swann. "You must purify that love. You *will* purify it."

"I'm not sure that it *is* love any more," said Ann. "Not proper love." She stared at the dead electric fire. Was her long love for Randall over? It was possible.

"Oh yes it is," said Swann. "One doesn't stop loving a person just like that, whatever they do. We spoke of this once before. Marriage is a sacrament. Here especially God's grace can lift and enlighten our poor human loves."

"Marriage," said Ann. "Do you really think Randall will come back?" It seemed a hundred years since she had talked of married love with Douglas and he had advised her to hold Randall in her loving net.

"I don't know," said Swann. "But whether he does or not it will matter how you love him. And whether he does or not you will still be married to him."

There was a hardness in the words which bruised Ann. "You think that I should keep a light burning for Randall?"

"Yes, of course," said Swann. "And humanly speaking, as it were, as well as ecclesiastically speaking. But surely you think this too?"

Ann got up and stared out of the window. Out of a dirty golden

273

sky a few drops of rain were falling. Penn in mackintosh and wellingtons was tramping across the lawn. He waved to her and she waved back. She said, "I shall give Randall a divorce if he wants one."

"I don't think you should be in any hurry to do so," said Swann. "But in any case that won't alter your own position. We know, don't we, what we think about the permanence of marriage."

"So I should devote the rest of my life to purifying my image of the absent Randall?"

"This isn't like you, Ann."

"I don't know what I'm like any more. I feel now I've lived all the time in unconsciousness."

"Being good is a state of unconsciousness."

"Then perhaps I shall stop being good. It looks as if it's going to be too difficult from now on anyway." She sat down again and pushed her hair back.

"You're tired out. Can't you manage a holiday?"

"Someone offered to drive me to Greece."

"Well, why don't you go? Do go. Clare and I can keep an eye on things here."

She felt again that unfamiliar sensation and she saw herself on the road south in the very dark blue Mercedes. "Ah, I've been dead all these years."

"You are precisely mistaken," said Swann. "You have been alive all these years. You are momentarily dead now."

Ann was silent. What did she want from Douglas? She wanted him to support her own view of the matter. And since he was not doing so she might as well end the conversation. So she had a view of her own which was different from Douglas's?

"You're doing me a lot of good," she said.

Swann smiled and patted her knee. "Is the exorcism working?"

Was it? She lifted her head and it was as if the great scarlet cloud were gone, the whirling images were gone, and there was only a great space and a great light. "Yes, it's working."

"I'm so glad," he said. "I know we think alike really. Prayer, if

I may say so, is so important here. I have known constant prayer to remove the most rooted resentment."

"Ah, but I don't feel resentment," said Ann. "I don't, I don't." It was true.

"If you can love him *now* and keep him in your heart that will be a joy that is better than happiness."

"Better than happiness." She rose to her feet. She wanted to be alone now.

"The marriage bond is an indissoluble mystical union of souls. Who knows what good your love may not do him, even if you never meet again."

"How true," said Ann. "You know, I think I'll take that Greek holiday after all."

"Well done!" said Swann. He was being led towards the door. "On no account miss Delphi. Clare and I were in Greece ten years ago. I think we've still got all our guide-books. We'll lend them to you."

"You are very kind. Thank Clare for the bottled apricots, will you?"

The door shut behind him at last. Ann returned to the drawing-room. She lay down on the floor and buried her face in the hearth rug. She felt exhausted, purged. Yet it was a strange purging. Perhaps Douglas had been right to say that goodness was a state of unconsciousness. But what she had to do with now was consciousness, and she was profoundly and terribly aware of a change in the structure of her world, as if the crystals were forming with a difference. It was not that her image of Douglas himself as good had in any way altered. It was that he could no longer, in the mirror of her being now so alarmingly brightened, properly reflect himself. His words, which in him were good words, were at her side of the picture temptation, almost corruption. Whatever she could do for Randall she could not do *that*. A saint might do it, but she could not. She could not thus hold him; and as she imagined this 'holding' she saw it almost as vindictive, revengeful, something to do with death. No, she must let Randall go, she must let him go *properly*, she must cut the painter. This idea of cutting him free shed for her a certain light, wherein she glimpsed for a moment, like a figure seen in a flash of lightning, what she herself must look like to Randall, what she must, in these last years, have looked like, have *been*. She saw the deadness of it; and Randall's words came back with a force which she could almost echo. "You weigh upon me. You imprison me." She must set Randall free.

But was that not also setting herself free? She had never thought about freedom, it had never been a value to her. Now suddenly, as she felt it to be so vividly desirable, she looked back over her thoughts, trying to doubt them. Where did the corruption lie? Yet, as she reflected, this question seemed less important, consumed, dimmed by a sort of realism which she still hesitated to dignify with the name of truth. The world *had* changed and there was no going back. She must live as best she could in the new world. She rolled over on her back and looked at the high white ceiling of the drawing-room, now dusky and yellowish in the rainy afternoon light, and it seemed to her like a lofty Southern sky, infinitely far and blue and hazy with brilliance. She lay there stunned and dazzled.

The telephone rang and she pulled herself to her feet at last. It was Mildred ringing up from Seton Blaise to say that she and Felix would be bringing Miranda back tomorrow morning. Miranda.

PART SIX

Chapter Twenty-nine

MIRANDA was back at Grayhallock and Penn was in torment. He had been, at the idea of her staying on at Seton Blaise, very cast down at first; but in fact her absence had been for him a time of welcome respite wherein he could spend the day dreaming of her without those sharp and painful disturbances of his private image which the actual presence of his darling so often occasioned. He had also enjoyed looking forward to her return. But the return itself had had a terrible quality.

It was as if the house feared Miranda. The darkness, the coldness, the dampness of the still rainy weather seemed to gain, from her return, an extra shadow. The house groaned and huddled. Miranda herself was in an evident state of extreme depression and was very short with anyone who came near her. Ann was jumpy and nervous and more than usually awkward with her daughter, though she was also at times merry in a way which unnerved Penn more than her accustomed soberness. One morning he heard what he had never heard before, Ann singing; and this sound, echoing through the darkened arches of the brooding and prophetic house, made Penn shiver with a sense of ills to come.

He was now tossing on his bed. He had already got up several times and looked across at the light which was still burning in Miranda's bedroom in the opposite tower. It was not in fact very late. After Miranda retired Penn had gone to bed in a mood of mingled boredom and desperation, and had been trying to cheer himself up by reading *Such is Life*. But even Tom Collins could not speak to his condition. For the time the myth of his past seemed dead, the great image of the new free man in the appallingly ancient land. They were far off now, the drooping myalls and the lordly kurrajongs and the crimson quondongs and the spotted leopard trees. The huge coloured country might have been a dream; and Penn apprehended with alarm a sort of failure within him for the first time of his sense of nationality. It was no use, in the crisis which faced him, being, even, an Australian.

He could not get comfortable. His body ached through and through with desire, producing a sort of perpetual tiredness which was half pleasurable and half painful. He got up again and went to the window. The light was still on in Miranda's room. He put on his dressing-gown and began to wander about his own room. He looked gloomily at the wrecked bed, and at his few books on the white shelf. On the table in a blue vase were roses Ann had brought up that morning. Beside them lay the Swedish knife which Humphrey had given him. He snapped it open and tried the blade. Humphrey was kind to him. He was the only person who had really wanted to be told about Australia. And now he had asked Penn to London again and Penn had again said no. It was a good knife; but of course it was nothing like the German dagger.

Penn opened the drawer and took out the dagger. He drew it silkily out of its sheath and balanced it in his hand. It made him feel dangerous. He was very sorry to think that he would have to part with it. He had put off telling Miranda about it; and in any case, since the occasion in the churchyard when he had nearly given it to her he had had other matters on his mind. He went to the window again and gazed at her light, scratching the palm of his left hand gently with the point of the dagger.

Penn felt sorry at the thought of losing it, but he also felt pleased to be able to delight Miranda and to make, for her, some evident little sacrifice. He did not want to waste the scene of returning the dagger, and he began to wonder, when shall I give it to her? He opened his window a little wider. The night was very dark but warmer and there was a flowery smell, the smell of thousands of roses. The idea came up to Penn out of the darkness, I shall give it to her now.

Why not? His heart accelerated and he turned back from the window blushing with excitement. He had never entered Miranda's room. She had never asked him up there, and indeed the whole of the other tower had a perilous taboo quality. He was exceedingly frightened by the idea which he had just received. Could he mount the other tower? The notion that he might thereby frighten Miranda made him even more frightened himself. But it was also fearfully attractive; and the next moment he had a vision of himself running up the stairs and seizing Miranda in his arms.

Things are getting out of hand, Penn said to himself. I'd better get back into bed. But he didn't, and stood there tense and frowning. Where had he, with Miranda, really got to? He felt convinced that she needed him and that she really liked him far more than she pretended to. Why otherwise did she so often, even though to tease him, seek his company? He was convinced too, though this more irrationally, that the leap from the tree had been aimed at impressing him. When he thought of his failure *there* he groaned aloud. If only he had got there first, and, preferably, broken a leg or something in the attempt! He was not managing to cut much of a figure. Perhaps he was being altogether too gentle with her?

He could at least try. Anything was better than the torment of inactivity and helplessness. He would, for once, stretch his limbs. She herself was violent, wild, extreme; he would try to deserve her. He put the unsheathed dagger into one pocket and the sheath in the other and softly opened the door.

He listened. The house was silent except for his own heart beats. He wondered if Ann was in bed. He did not want to meet her on the way. He began to descend the stairs barefoot in the dim light from his open door. He reached the gallery. Here it was dark, but it was as if he saw and he glided along it confidently until he reached the foot of the opposite spiral. Here he hesitated.

He did not want to pass the door of Randall's room, which seemed to him, far more than the room his grandmother had been dying in, inhabited by death. Perhaps it was very foolish to disturb Miranda now, perhaps she would simply hate him for it? Could he indeed prevent himself, finding her there warm, reclining, undressed, from crushing her like a nut? An image of her suddenly accessible, defenceless, near, rose before him and he nearly fell on his knees on the stairs. Then his yearning body decided the issue and he ran on up to her door.

Breathless he knocked. There was a silence and then her voice. He entered.

Miranda was lying opposite to him tucked up in her divan bed. She was propped on pillows and had been reading. She looked towards him now, raising a pale startled face. Her hair was tousled and the collar of her striped pyjamas stood on end about her neck.

As soon as Penn found himself in Miranda's presence his violence was blunted and his purposes dimmed. Her small imperious being confronted him and he felt confusion. He said hastily, "Hello, Miranda, I hope you don't mind my butting in. I saw your light was still on and I thought I'd just come and say hello."

Miranda had recovered herself at once. She adjusted the pillows, sitting up a bit more, and buttoned up the neck of her pyjamas. She gave him a fastidious look which made him feel like Caliban. "This is a bit unusual, isn't it?" The remark had a little conventional grown-up sound.

He took in her room a little. It was a replica of his own, but a de luxe replica. Here, after his monochrome, all was coloured. All was vivid, figured, flowered, spotted, striped. He had an impression or a clutter of small things, making of the room a little treasure trove, a miniature queen's boudoir. There were a lot of little square rugs end to end, several bowls of roses, and a shelled arched built-in bookcase, dotted with objects, two shelves of which were occupied by dolls sitting in jumbled rows with their feet protruding. Their wide blue eyes stared out censoriously. Rich furry curtains were half drawn to reveal upon the long windowsill a row of round glass paper-weights. A single lamp cast an ivory light upon the white sheets and upon Miranda's multi-coloured head.

Penn took a little chair, he swung it by the back like a small animal. He felt very large in the room, Gulliverian, both powerful and clumsy. He feared to hear the sound of something he was crushing with his feet. He felt he might crack anything in the room like an egg shell. He put the chair near Miranda's bed and sat down.

Behind her, where the curtains revealed the black window pane, he could see moths with pale bodies and red eyes hurling themselves against the glass. Miranda waited.

Penn felt the silent empty night all round him, as vast and as sterile as if he and Miranda were afloat in a space ship. He began to feel the yearning, he rang with it like a filling vessel. He crossed his legs and said, "Your room's nicer than mine."

Miranda said nothing. She watched him, curled like a small cat, with a feline face almost vacant, yet with a vacancy that could precede some sort of spring; and Penn felt he could scarcely be surprised to see her suddenly run up the curtains. He desired her.

"What are you reading?" he said.

Miranda frowned and tossed the big coloured book on to the counterpane. Penn picked it up and saw that it was a sort of comic strip; and as he looked back to Miranda he guessed that she was annoyed that he had not found her reading something more grown-up. Then he saw that it was in French. *Les Aventures de Tintin. On a Marché sur La Lune.* He glanced at a few of the pictures.

"That looks good. Perhaps I could borrow it when you've finished? I don't think I'd understand much though. My French is hopeless. But I expect I could follow the pictures."

"It's no use without the text," said Miranda, retrieving the book and pushing it under her pillow. "The words are the point. They're so witty."

'Text' and 'witty' rather disconcerted Penn and he got up again and began to pace about, squaring his shoulders. Then some of the ebullience of his body gave him strength and he felt a sort of almost impersonal exhilaration, as if he had leapt at a bound into an adult world where the tempo of life was altogether slower and more confident, where glances could be significantly held and relinquished and where words had a new weight and splendour.

"Everyone thinks you're being awfully rude to Humphrey," said the pale curled Miranda.

"But I don't want to go to London."

"Why not?"

"I think you know why not." He sat down abruptly on the end of her bed. She drew her feet away and half sat up, bracing herself against the pillows. He sensed with ecstasy that she was a little frightened. He felt like a god, like a man in a film. The warm silence was full of the smell of roses.

Miranda stared at him and he stared back, she held his gaze as never before, and he rocked in it like a light plane in a gale. "I haven't the faintest idea," she said, her voice slightly high.

"I love you, Miranda."

"Oh *that*. I thought you meant something about Humphrey. Could you get off my bed please? You're crumpling the counterpane."

Penn leapt up. Now that he had uttered the words he felt frenzied. The bright room rotated about him like a whirlpool whose vortex was Miranda. Only somehow he must keep himself from sinking, from whirling, into the centre. He receded to the book shelves and hung on to them for support. He saw, fragmentarily, the black square of glass and the red eyes of the beating moths.

She had spoken with a raised note of excitement. She was, as he looked down at her, tense, moist-lipped, her face, as it seemed to him, radiant with a delighted dread. He whirled to the door and held on to the handle. "Oh Miranda, Miranda, I love you so dreadfully!"

"Don't be so *silly*," she said. But she stared steadily at him and her hand grasped the neck of her pyjamas in an expectant way.

Penn clutched at the table. His need to touch her was agonising. He reeled with it. They were silent a moment, and as he gasped for breath he saw her hand rising and falling at her breast. He could think of no words with which to express: may I touch you. He lurched forward.

"Go away," said Miranda.

"No," he said, standing over her.

He was at the innermost circle, slipping, slipping into the very centre. He sank one knee on to her bed. The silence of the house surrounded them attentively, fascinatedly, coldly.

"Horrible!" said Miranda. She uttered the word softly yet with a force of venom which for a moment held him. Then almost like a blind man, spreading his hands, he began to descend upon her.

What happened next happened very quickly. Miranda reached behind her to the window sill, took one of the glass paper-weights, and brought it down with violence across the knuckles of Penn's hand as it travelled across the sheet. The paper-weight, flying from her grasp, shot across the room and shattered into a hundred pieces. Penn recoiled with a cry of pain, clasped his wounded hand with the other, half fell from the bed and lay collapsed beside it on the floor. The German dagger, emerging from his pocket, slid across the rug and came to rest against the leg of the table. Miranda shot out of bed, put on her dressing-gown and slippers and retired to the door. There was silence again. The cold watchful house had relished the little scene.

Penn lay with his face down, clasping his hand against his chest. He saw under the bed three pairs of Miranda's sandals, a wooden box, and small pieces of the paper-weight scattered like gleaming eyes or tiny coloured flowers. He rolled over and sat up, leaning against the side of the bed. He looked at his hand. The skin was slightly broken on the knuckles. Then he looked at Miranda.

Her face was quite transformed. The nervous excited look had gone and it was as if a white light from within had composed her countenance into an indistinct yet authoritative form. So it might be to see an angel. She glowed upon him, her head poised above him, and a warm bright ray fell upon him and held him breathless. With astonishment and abject gratitude he realised that he had not displeased her.

"Ah, you fool," said Miranda. Her voice was deep now. She leaned back against the door, regarding him with a sort of gentle triumph, and he felt as if she were, for the first time, really seeing him.

"I'm sorry," he said, rubbing his hand and stretching out his legs as he leaned back against the bed. The sharpness of desire had gone, or had spread rather into a haze of enslaved delight, a luminous atmosphere in which he floated, held and guided in the beam of Miranda's gaze.

"You surprised me," she said. "But I like to be surprised."

"I'm afraid it wasn't a pleasant surprise," said Penn. He felt an agonising lack of proper words, but the great light supported him. He began to rise slowly.

"Did I hurt you much?" The sheer rich satisfaction of her tone, so unlike her old petulant teasing, nearly brought him again to the floor.

He said humbly, "No. Anyway I deserved to be hurt."

"You deserved it, yes. But let me see."

He advanced to her, and his body as he came felt limp and broken as if his flesh were beaten into rags. He lifted his hand before her as if presenting it for a severance. She took it at the wrist and held it, examining it. Then she took a handkerchief from her pocket and with her other hand clasped it gently over his knuckles. Penn groaned and fell on his knees before her. She released his hand and he knelt before her swaying, not touching her.

"Penn," she said softly. The silence that followed began to coil and accumulate into a great white shell of eloquence and understanding. Penn lifted his eyes at last to her face.

But all was changed again. She was looking over his shoulder at something with fascination, with twisted anxiety, almost with fear. As Penn moved and rose to his feet, towering over her now again, turning to see what she saw, she said sharply "What's that?"

Penn followed her gaze to the German dagger. He stepped quickly back and picked it up. "I brought this for you. I found it. I hope you don't mind. I think you wanted it and I brought it." He held out the hilt with the enamelled swastika towards her.

Miranda took it. "But that's Steve's dagger. His special dagger. The one that Felix Meecham gave him."

"Yes. I brought it to you. I hope you don't mind."

"But where did you get it? Why did you have it?" She moved away from the door, putting the table between them, glaring at him and clasping the dagger to her breast. Its bright point pierced the blue woollen stuff of the dressing-gown.

"I found it in Steve's room. I'm sorry. I hope you don't mind. I brought it—"

"Oh, shut up!" said Miranda. She gave a little cry and her face grew suddenly red and her eyes filled with tears. She stamped her foot and gave a wailing cry. "Go away! Get out of here!"

"I'm terribly sorry," said Penn. "I just wanted to please you by bringing it because Ann said you liked it."

"You stupid, horrible fool," said Miranda, and the tears were coming so fast now she could hardly speak, "I hate you. I'd like to kill you. Putting your horrible hands on me. Stupid Australian fool. Everyone knows you're stupid, with your beastly common accent. Nobody likes you here, they just put up with you because they have to. You're boring and ugly and stupid and we all want you to go away. Go back to beastly boring Australia. Go back to your low common father and your vulgar home. Go away. Get out of my room. Steve would have killed you with one hand. Go away, you horrible thing, go away, go away!" Her voice rose and she drew the dagger back in her hand as if she would have flown at him.

Penn had a last vision of her, the dagger raised, her face crimson and wet with tears and saliva and twisted with spitting fury. He got himself out of the door and half fell down the spiral staircase. He heard the door bang behind him. He ran along the black gallery and gained his own staircase where the light from his room showed him the white metal steps. He got into his room and shut himself in.

He leaned back against the door panting. Pain and fear made his breath come in long shrieking gasps for several minutes. He felt ready to be overwhelmed by a storm of hysteria. He braced himself back against the door, digging in his heels, trying to quiet himself. The room heaved before him.

A little while later his breathing became less violent and his body went limp and he sank on to the bed. He looked about. All was quiet, orderly, waiting for him. All was as it had been—how long ago?—before he went to see Miranda. The Swedish knife, the veteran car book, his battered copy of *Such is Life*, said to him: hello. But it was like the voices of thoughtless children to a ruined man. Between imagined violence and real violence there is a dimension of difference. Some innocent thing was broken forever, frightened and killed. A blackness in the heart of his world was even now spreading outward. He fell on his knees beside the bed with a groan.

He looked dully at his hand. It was aching and some blood was congealed on the knuckles. His dressing-gown was covered with little bits of coloured glass. As he shook it out he touched something under the bed. He turned to look and saw that it was Steve's box of soldiers. He stared at it and then pulled it close to him. After a moment he opened it and looked at the red and blue jumble of innumerable lead figures. Scarcely able to focus his eyes, he took one out and stood it upon the floor. Then he took out another and another. As the file lengthened his wild tears came at last.

Chapter Thirty

"BE nicer to poor Penny when he comes back," said Ann.
Penn had now been in London with Humphrey for nearly a week.

"He won't come back," said Miranda. She was sitting up in bed. The uncurtained window was wide open to the hot summer night. Miranda had been unwell for two days and had retired to her room. The doctor said there was nothing wrong with her, but Ann was sure it was the German measles coming on at last.

"Why ever not?" said Ann.

"He won't come back," said Miranda. "He'll stay in London till the last moment and then ask you to send his things."

"But he *said* he'd come back. He must come back to say a proper good-bye."

Miranda shrugged her shoulders. "He's a rude boy," she said. "What can you expect, considering what his father is?"

"Miranda!"

Ann frowned at her daughter across the table littered with dolls, comics, Tintins, women's magazines, chocolate, newspapers, tins of orange juice, and the remains of a cherry cake. Then she resumed her restless pacing. She was very sorry that Penn had gone. She had not, till his departure, realised the extent to which he had, as it were, blessedly kept Miranda off her. She was frightened and a little shocked to find herself thinking in this way. But since she had been alone in the house with Miranda there had been a tension, an excessive mutual consciousness, a hostile magnetism. They were continually watching each other and seeking each other out, and making each other's activities seem pointless. The situation had been only partially resolved by Miranda's becoming ill.

Ann was still undecided about Felix. At least she *told* herself that she was undecided, although the comparative steadiness with which she endured the interval which she had imposed upon them both sometimes suggested to her that she must have decided in his favour, that she must by now, without noticing it, have crossed the line. Yet she went on from moment to moment without doing or saying anything decisive. The great dazzling void which had, at the end of her talk with Douglas Swann, so authoritatively contained her, was shrunken now and darkened and crossed with the old cares. She felt, about Randall, a little less mad. But she did not really feel free or like a person who decides things. She was, after all, the same timid conscientious worrying Ann. She had not achieved, after all, a new personality.

Ann had never really had the conception of doing what she wanted. The idea of doing what she ought, early and deeply implanted in her soul, and sedulously ever since cultivated, had by now almost removed from her the possibility, even as something *prima facie*, of a pure self-regarding movement of will. She felt, at the moment, the lack of this strong uncomplicated machinery. The clamorous needs which devoured her were hideously unpractical, and she envied those for whom the want and the grasping movement were one and the same thing. She was prepared, moreover, and especially when she considered the wreck of her marriage with Randall and what she had somehow done *to* Randall, to see in her absence of straightforward operative desires something corrupting, something deadening. There was, in her open formless life, some dreadful lack of vigour, some lack of any hard surface to grasp or to brace oneself against; and as she thus accused herself, ready almost to call her good an evil, she found herself again echoing some of Randall's words. She had not got a new personality. But the old one was certainly cracked.

She had not succeeded, either, with Miranda; and it sometimes seemed to her that both Randall and Miranda shrank away from her for the same reason. They needed about them the invigorating presence of shapely human wills; and they could not but see Ann's absence, in this sense, of personality as something mean and spiritless and almost insincere. The idea had sometimes occurred to Ann, and she hated it, that quite involuntarily and unreasonably she made them both feel guilty. But now it seemed to her more likely that their reaction to her was a sort of aesthetic one. They found something messy, something depressing, in her mode of existence. And now it was she who felt the guilt.

It was by this time desperately necessary for her to talk to Miranda about Felix. It was not that she expected Miranda to have much to say about this, and she did not really expect anything in the way of an argument. She would put the matter to her, she thought, rather vaguely. But it was necessary simply to have *said* these things, to have at least mentioned his name; and Ann was surprised to find how hard it was to bring herself to do so. The sudden growth of her relation with Felix might seem to any observer odd and even improper. Whatever would Miranda, who loved her father so much, make of these hints? With this reluctance to speak came a nervous anxiety which was now almost unbearable. There seemed a taboo on speaking of Felix to her daughter; and Ann knew that until she had broken this she would not be able to think further about what she was going to do. At moments she suspected that once she *had* spoken of the matter, however remotely, with Miranda she would be awakened to the fact that she had indeed crossed the line; and then she saw Miranda in a benevolent light, as a helper, as someone who would bring her to a bright new consciousness of herself.

Meanwhile there was the task of deceiving Felix; for that was what it came to. Though she longed for his company, she was afraid to see too much of him in case there should be some revelation of her need which, if he were but to glimpse it, would whirl them blindly farther on. She did not want too much to enslave him when she was still not certain that she would keep him; and she did not want to be herself driven mad by his loss, if it should come to that. She wanted to see what she was doing; but this was what, with Miranda watchful, curious, morose, terribly present and officially unenlightened, she was not able to do. Her ideas remained separate and refused to crystallise into a policy. She wondered if having failed in one marriage she should hastily contract another. She wondered if she would make a soldier's wife. She wondered if Randall would ever come back. She wondered about marriage, and Miranda, and Marie-Laure. She doubted everything except that she and Felix were in love. If only she could, quite simply, see that as the solution. She craved for that simplicity as for some unattainable degree of asceticism.

"Do stop walking about the room," said Miranda. "You make me quite tired. Do stop or sit down. If you're going to stay."

"Sorry, dear," said Ann. She stopped again behind the table. Miranda must think she was behaving oddly. She *was* behaving oddly. But the great dark void of the house gaped behind her and she could not bring herself to leave her daughter's room. She must speak to her now.

"What are you so nervous about?" said Miranda. "You're making me nervous."

They stared at each other in the silence of the house, and it was as if they were listening for distant footsteps. If there were other listeners they were hostile ones. Ann shivered. A big white furry moth entered through the window and began to circle the lamp. Beneath them was Randall's empty room.

"I'm sorry."

"Don't keep saying you're sorry. Tell me what's the matter."

"Nothing's the *matter*," said Ann. She started pacing again. The room about her seemed tattered, shabby, dusty, untidy, as if she and Miranda had been jumbled together in an old bag. Nancy Bowshott was supposed to clean it. Ann took some faded roses off the mantelpiece and dropped them into the waste-paper basket.

"Miranda," she said, "would you mind if I married again?"

There was a silence in which the fluttering of the moth could be heard. It was beating on the inside of the lamp shade. Ann knew that these were the wrong words. Yet what ought she to have said? She turned towards her daughter.

Miranda's face was a wooden mask. She plumped up her pillows and sat up straighter. "But there's no question of that, is there?"

"Oh well, there might be," said Ann. She added, "It's only a very vague possibility, you know, nothing immediate." She was sounding guilty already. A scroll of coloured glass, like a misshapen marble, was lying in the fireplace. She picked it up.

The silence continued until she had to look back again, when Miranda said, "But you *are* married. To Daddy."

"Yes, but I suppose I won't go on being."

"I thought marriages were for always," said Miranda. She was tense, pinning Ann with her gaze.

Ann felt within herself the blissful stir of a selfish will. She welcomed it as a mother might welcome the first movement of her unborn child. She said, and then regretted it, "Your father doesn't think so." Then she added, "You know that he wants a divorce. He wants to marry someone else."

Miranda said after a moment, "That's what he says *now*."

"Do you think he'll—stop wanting that?"

"Well, he might, mightn't he?"

Ann tossed the piece of coloured glass in her hand. The room constrained her, closing in upon her, soft and flabby. She wanted to shake it away with her shoulders. She said, "You saw Daddy, didn't you, when he came that time—a little before he—wrote to me."

"Yes."

"Did he say anything then which—well, about going away for good? He must have let you know that he was." Ann was breathless. She felt she was asking the wrong questions. She could feel Miranda's will controlling her from the bed. She walked to and fro like an animal upon a short string. She could feel the cord jerking.

"I can't remember exactly what he said," said Miranda, "but he seemed to think he might want to come back. He didn't seem at all sure. You know what Daddy is."

"But you must remember!" said Ann. "What did he say exactly? Please try to remember."

"How can I?" said Miranda. "I was so miserable. I *am* so miserable." Her voice was tearful.

"Dear, I'm so sorry!" said Ann. She looked at the screwed up hostile little face and felt pangs of guilt and pity. She had not worked enough at measuring Miranda's suffering.

The white moth, who had been silent for some minutes, fell out of the lamp with singed wings. It writhed on the floor.

Miranda leaned over to look at it. "Better kill it," she said. "It won't fly again. What won't fly is better killed. Better dead than crawling. It's burnt its wings off."

Ann trod on the moth. It was a plump moth. She returned her attention to Miranda, who seemed revived by the incident and was looking singularly like her father.

Colder herself, Ann said, "But you thought he seemed to think it at least conceivable that he might come back?"

"Oh, certainly," said Miranda. "He talked about coming back." She began to rearrange her bed with an air of casualness and tossed two dolls off on to the floor.

Ann walked to the window. The night was suffocating. She looked out into the darkness. A distant owl hooted throwing successive rings of sound out over the roosting birds of the Marsh. Outside a silent world waited for the conclusion of their interview. No lights could be seen, and even the stars seemed to be stifled in the dark velvety air. She looked out into the close black emptiness and her heart seemed like a bird ready to break from her breast and fly over the quiet Marsh, to Dungeness, to the sea.

She turned back to the little crumpled room and Miranda watching her. The cord twitched her back. She said, "But if he doesn't come back and we do get divorced. Well, then I might think of another marriage. And I felt I should just say this to you, though it's something so vague and really unlikely." These were blundering incompetent words.

"Do be clear," said Miranda. "Do you mean that you're thinking *now* of marrying someone in particular?"

"Yes."

"Who?"

"Felix Meecham."

"I see," said Miranda. She showed no surprise. She reached down for one of the dolls she had dislodged. "Why are you suddenly so keen on Felix?"

"It's not sudden," said Ann. "Felix and I have been fond of each other for years." She felt a failure of control before the judging eyes.

"Did Daddy know about it?"

"There was nothing *to* know!" said Ann, exasperated with herself. She had dreadfully mismanaged the scene.

Miranda was silent, pursing her lips and jogging the doll before her.

Does she believe me? thought Ann. I can't ask her. It suddenly seemed a new and horrible pain that Miranda, here, should have any misconceptions.

After a moment Miranda said, "Of course you must please yourself. It's your life."

"I just wanted to speak to you," said Ann. "I don't want to surprise you or upset you." It sounded cold and awkward. She added, "After all, you know Felix and you like him, and that's all to the good. But of course this is just a very vague possibility."

"I don't know him particularly," said Miranda. "I've hardly ever spoken to him. And I'm not sure that I like him."

"Oh, come!"

"Daddy doesn't like him either," said Miranda. "Perhaps he guessed."

"I've told you, there was nothing *to* guess!"

Miranda raised her eyebrows to the doll.

Ann felt she must get out of the room or suffocate. The owl was hooting again. The wide open window seemed a menace, as if at any moment Randall might fly in through it like a bat, with a great spreading and folding of leathery wings.

As if catching her thought Miranda said, "You know Daddy could come home at *any* time. Any minute now we might hear a car . . ."

They both listened, holding each other's eyes. The great silence seemed pregnant with sound as if the other listeners were holding their breath.

Ann felt herself near to panic. She went to the door. "Well, let's see, shall we? We won't talk about it again. I've made too much of it, really. We'll see what Daddy wants. It was just something vaguely possible."

As her hand strayed to the door handle something on the white shelves beside the door caught her eye. It was one of Miranda's dolls which had been transfixed through the middle by the German dagger and pinned to the shelf. Ann looked at the sinister little portent. "Why have you murdered that poor creature?"

"I was punishing it," said Miranda. "It's an Assyrian torture." She pushed the bedclothes aside and began to get out of bed.

"A rather savage punishment. Don't get cold, dear. I'll say good-night now. Don't be bothered by anything I said."

"Wait a minute," said Miranda. Boyish in her pyjamas, head thrown back, she faced her mother across the table. They were almost of a height.

"*Whatever* Daddy does it would make no difference."

"What do you mean?"

"You can't get divorced in a church."

"Opinions differ about those things," said Ann. She felt fear, but with it a little anger and the stirring of will which was like a kind of joy.

"So you'd still be married to him," said Miranda, "and he'd still be married to you. Suppose he wanted to come back later on? If you'd run off with someone else he wouldn't be able to. He might come back crying for you and looking for you and you wouldn't be there. But if you waited for him it would be all right. He would always have somewhere to come back to. This would always be his home really and if he were unhappy he could come back to it." She spoke vehemently and a thin speckled flush covered her face.

Ann was shaken. She said, turning the handle, "Well, we'll see." She wanted to run.

"No, we *won't* see!" said Miranda, her voice vibrating. "Daddy *will* be unhappy, he *will* want to come back, I *know* it, we *must* wait for him!" Her eyes filled with tears.

She reached out to the table and pulled something out of the heap and held it to her face. She began to shake with convulsive sobs. "I love Daddy. No one must have his place. I don't want to be a step-daughter."

Ann moved towards her; as she moved she saw what it was that Miranda was holding. It was the white rabbit Joey, Randall's old toy. So Randall had not taken the animals after all. Miranda had simply moved them up to her own room. Randall had not taken them away. Ann's arms encircled Miranda and Joey; and as her own tears began to flow and as the bright multi-coloured head came to rest against her shoulder she felt herself with despair suddenly weakened, loosened, unbolted by her old love for Randall.

Chapter Thirty-one

FELIX brought the very dark blue Mercedes screeching to a halt. Its front wheels seemed to have got on to some sort of flower bed. He did not pause to investigate, but jumped out and looked up at the dark front of the house. There was no light in Ann's room, there was no light to be seen. Of course it was after midnight and Ann, whose ambiguous telegram he had received in London only two hours before, would doubtless be expecting him in the morning. He wondered what to do. He entered the glass porch, tried the front door and found it open.

He fumbled in the dark hall for the light switch and then stood looking about him in the rather dim illumination. The shabby hall, full of crouching furniture, looked sinister, a place through which a midnight agent might glide to make an arrest. Felix felt a sort of fright which was really fright of himself, fear of the fear he might, by his sudden silent entry, cause. Yet perhaps it was he himself who was the victim. He had not understood Ann's wire.

He went into the drawing-room, stepping softly, and turned on the lights. The room looked desolate as if it had not been occupied for weeks. It smelt musty. He turned an electric fire on. Sparks flew out of it and one bar seemed to be out of order. There was a smell of burning. He took off his coat. Of course he would not go and wake Ann. He would compose himself somehow, somewhere, until the morning. He looked gloomily at the sofa which was long, but not long enough for him. Then he thought, what lunatic conventionality now bids me lie down and sleep when what I want to do is to seize Ann in my arms? He knew he would not sleep, he would lie in agony. His heart beat fiercely at the nearness of Ann, at the nearness of his fate. He stood there, his hands at his sides, a big quiet man, waiting and wondering.

Ann entered with a soft flurry, and they both, at seeing each other, gave a little cry. She was wearing a very long dark green dressing-gown. She raised a hand to Felix and then sped to the windows and pulled the curtains. When she was at the third window he advanced as if to put his arms around her, but her gesture as she turned arrested him, and for a moment they stood there rigid a few feet apart, like people suddenly frozen by a spell.

"I didn't expect you tonight. I'm sorry. It was an absurd time to send a wire. I thought it wouldn't reach you till the morning."

"Ann, Ann," he said, "I want you now. Forgive me. I want you now. Ann, what is it to be?" The late hour, the half darkened room and Ann so close, pale and slim in the long robe, filled him with a frenzied certainty of desire.

"Ah no," she said. "It's no use. That's what I called you to say."

He had somehow known this. It had come to him on the drive down, streaming like fog against the windscreen. But he said, "No, I can't accept this, Ann. You don't mean what you say. You love me. Recognise it, have the courage of it, I beseech you." He spoke softly, abruptly.

"It's no use," she said again, turning from him and smoothing her hair.

"Is it—Miranda?"

"No, no. It's Randall."

"Keeping the light burning—all that stuff?"

"Well, yes."

"You perfect fool," he said, and he really wanted to shake her, "Randall will never come back. That's all over, done for, for ever. And if he ever hears you're sitting waiting for him he'll think you're doing it just to spite him. And you probably *will* be doing it just to spite him. Let him go, Ann, for God's sake let the poor devil go."

She fluttered away from him across the dead room and stood by the mantelpiece with her back to him. He saw her twisted face in the mirror before she covered it with her hand. "It's hard to explain.

299

It isn't exactly that I expect anything. I just can't stand the *idea* of Randall coming back to look for me and my not being there."

"Do you imagine Randall has any grain of love or affection left for you?"

She said in a low voice after a moment's silence, "Evidently."

It seemed dark in the room and the sense of midnight violence was still with them. Cold as he was at Ann's words, Felix still trembled with desire. The hour, his strength, the nearness of their bodies, made him feel that he could, he must, make her assent. He said, "You're wrong. But never mind. Wait a while, and see what you think then. I've told you I'm .n no hurry."

"If I can't say yes now I can't say yes at all," she said in a monotonous voice. "How could I expect you to wait around? Randall *could* come back. I half thought tonight when I heard the car that it was him and not you. He *could* come back. That's the truth, and it's the decisive truth." She spoke heavily, mechanically, without looking at him.

Did she mean it, Felix wondered, was she perhaps trying him, wanting him to force her? He felt almost grim enough to push her struggling into the Mercedes. He said, to gain time, "You really think he might come back? Aren't you being naïve?"

"I think he *might*. Miranda thinks so, much more. And she knows him."

"Oh, to hell with Miranda."

"You must go away, Felix," she intoned again.

He bit his lip and worked his jaw and realised from her expression as she now turned to him that he must be scowling. He said, "I admire and love you, Ann, but there are moments when I wonder whether you aren't just a muddled sentimental ass."

She looked at him with an austere sadness. "Forgive me, Felix. I can't explain properly, but I'm quite sure. Oh, my darling, let us do this thing quickly." Her voice trembled.

Felix faltered. He knew very well how to deal with some women.

But he did not know how to deal with her. His very apprehension of the difference paralysed him. He wished he could force her now with a look or a gesture. "I won't let you," he said.

Ann was staring at him desperately, her eyes full of pain and fright. She said, after a moment of seeming to wait for him, "I must, you see, give Randall the benefit of any doubt."

"Why is it Randall, Randall? Why don't you do what *you* want for once? Or have you forgotten how?"

"Perhaps I have forgotten how," she said slowly. "I don't in a way see myself. I see him. It's not that I'm being unselfish. He just too much *is*."

"Don't you see me?"

"Ah," she said. "You. That's the trouble."

"You mean," he tried to read her face rather than her words, "that I've become—with you—invisible? You can't see me—because I'm—simply something that you want?" He feared to put it too clearly. But that he should be so almost mechanically renounced with the renunciation of her own will seemed to him too cruel. He was to be destroyed, with her, by the sheer overbrimming existence of the absent Randall.

"How do I know what I want?" she said almost impatiently. "It's *not* wanting things, it's denying things, that makes me so bad for people, that made me so bad for Randall, that would make me so bad for you."

"I don't understand you," he said, approaching her now. "*You* couldn't be bad for anyone. You are good, and good cannot be bad. You speak so abstractly. Be natural with me, Ann. Let go, give way. And don't talk any more damn nonsense to me for Christ's sake." He towered over her.

"*Don't*," she said looking up at him, and her voice was timid, almost querulous. "I do what I have to do. Don't make it hard, Felix. I am bound to Randall, I am *bound*, don't you see?"

He spread his hands as if to take her, but dropped them again. He wanted to seize her, to shake her to and fro. He wanted to hurl himself before her and bury his head with cries against her knees. He said quietly, "Stop it, Ann."

"You must go away, Felix," she said in the same inert trembling tone. "What will you do?"

Felix felt pain and anger. He could not believe her. For a moment he almost wanted to hurt her. He said, "Well, if I were to let you turn me off like this I suppose I should make some other arrangements. I certainly wouldn't mope. I should go to India. I suppose I should marry someone. I must get married soon or I shall dry up completely. But I intend to marry you, damn it."

"What about—Marie-Laure?" said Ann. She receded from him now step by step toward the window.

"Well, what about Marie-Laure?"

"You once said you'd show me a picture of her," said Ann. She was strained and white and small.

Why does she torment us both, thought Felix. "Yes," he said with irritation. "I've got one here. Would you like to see it?" He fumbled in his pocket. Marie-Laure's letter was still there, and with it the photograph which he had slipped into the envelope some time ago. With a slight shock he glanced at the photo: the clever long-nosed girl with the narrow dark eyes and the great cascade of almost black hair. Marie-Laure. *Mon beau Félix, souhaitez-vous vraiment me revoir?* He handed it to Ann.

Ann took one look and began to cry.

"Oh, my God!" said Felix. He started to walk up and down the room.

"I'm sorry," she said, controlling herself and laying the photo down on the table. "I didn't mean to inflict this on you."

"Look, Ann," said Felix, "to the devil with Randall and Marie-Laure. They've got no business here. We're both tired and over-strained and it was lunatic of me to come so late at night. Go to bed now and in the morning we can talk again."

"No, no," said Ann, all tearful now, "I couldn't bear it, Felix."

"You're not sending me away *now?*"

She nodded mutely, gazing into her raised handkerchief, the tears still slowly falling.

"Ann," said Felix, "do you love me?"

She was silent, and then still staring at the handkerchief said in a dull hoarse voice, "Yes. But not enough I suppose. Or not in the right way."

Felix went cold and rigid. He said stiffly, "Well, why didn't you say so at once? This makes everything much simpler. Of course I shall go. But you should have told me sooner."

"Ah, I don't mean that!" she said, raising her head, and her face was wild with some appeal. "I don't mean *that*. I do love you. God knows I love you. But I can't see my way out. I'm still too involved with Randall. He's too real. I don't understand it myself. But I do love you. Oh Felix, I'm wretched, help me, help me!" Her voice ended in a high-pitched wail. She sobbed for a moment and then was quite still, her hands hanging at her sides, the tears coming.

Felix looked at her miserably. "There's no need to be kind to me," he said. "There's no need to be evasive with me. Naturally I won't press you or bother you. Don't worry about me. I'll go to India. I won't trouble you any more. I think you're wrong about Randall. But I suppose you have a right to love him and not me. I suppose you have a right to think as you please—about your husband."

The word fell dully between them and Ann moaned. She said again, scarcely articulately, "I love you, Felix, I love you."

He said, "I know. It's all right. You don't have to be kind." He picked up his coat. He pocketed the photograph of Marie-Laure.

For a moment they stared at each other. "Don't go," said Ann, almost in a whisper, her tears suddenly checked.

Felix shook his head. "You're right," he said. "It's better to do it quickly. I have no taste for suffering. Forgive me for having troubled you." He made for the door.

He dragged savagely at the wheel of the very dark blue Mercedes and drove it half across the lawn toward the gates. A strange cry seemed to linger in the air behind him. He pressed his foot down and down on the accelerator until the car screamed under him. He was paying the penalty, he knew it even then, for being an officer and a gentleman.

Chapter Thirty-two

MIRANDA, curled upon the window-sill, watched the lights of the very dark blue Mercedes disappearing down the drive. She watched the bright illumination move, with sudden glimpses of green trees, at an increasing pace down the hill until it vanished. The sound of the engine remained with her, at first growing louder as the car gathered speed, and then quickly diminishing. At last there was complete silence. Miranda listened to the silence. Then she moved with a kind of lassitude back into the bedroom. A world had ended. An enterprise was complete.

She knew what had happened in the drawing-room. She had listened long enough at the door. She stood now as if at a loss, without employment, not knowing what to do. Then she pulled the curtains, locked her door and knelt down to rummage under her bed. She dragged out a large wooden box, a box designed for books with a strong lock on it. She searched the table drawer for the key and opened the box. She tilted it over until its contents streamed on to the rug. She began listlessly to sort them.

There were a few letters and a lot of cuttings and photographs. There was that photo of Felix in tennis kit as a boy of fifteen which she had stolen from Mildred's album. There were several photos of Felix at Grayhallock, pictures taken years ago at some party: Felix talking to Ann and Clare Swann, Felix talking to Ann and Nancy Bowshott, Felix talking to Ann. There was an old picture of Felix with Hugh, with herself, a little white-frilled and bowed creature, in the foreground. There were pictures too of Felix and Mildred which Ann had acquired sometime and which Miranda had filched from her desk; and one or two treasured pictures, similarly acquired, of Felix in dress uniform. But the ones she liked best were the ones of Felix in ordinary uniform, Felix during the war, Felix shaggy, Felix armed, Felix in the desert, Felix examining a map in some desolate unknown piece of country. Then there were the wartime cuttings, including the account of how Felix won his M.C. at Anzio. And the peacetime cuttings, including the ones from the *Tatler* with pictures of Felix dancing with Lady Mary Hunwicke and drinking champagne with Miss Penelope Fanshawe. And "Colonel Felix (Yoyo) Meecham and friend at Ascot." More precious even than these were the letters, the letter he wrote to her when she had mumps, the letter he wrote to her when she had chicken pox, a postcard he once sent her from New York. Alas, their correspondence had come to an end when she was seven.

Miranda had loved Felix Meecham with all her heart ever since she could remember. She could not trace the moment at which her childish adoration of that tall gentle-spoken demi-god had changed into the possessive jealous agony with which she now lived day and night. It sometimes seemed that her love had always been the same, always equally great in sum, only at a certain time it had been set on fire. And in those flames she writhed. It was not, as a child, that she had not suffered, that she had not missed him, yearned for him, and felt wild joy on his occasions of return. She had suffered bitterly because of his interest in Steven, who also idolised him, and his comparative lack of interest in herself. But at least as a child she had not conceived of possessing him. The terrible pain began when, at some half-noticed turning of the way, she found herself in the same world as Felix. For now that nothing separated them everything separated them.

Miranda was of course aware of a certain something, a trembling of interest and sympathy, between Felix and her mother. This too, she felt, she had always known about; but when her love burst into flames she was driven to a sharper curiosity and a more exact observation. There was in truth little to observe, nor did Miranda conjecture more than she saw. But what she saw was enough, and she watched and suffered.

Miranda was sure that no one knew about her condition. Asked at the age of five whom she wanted to marry, she had answered without hesitation "Felix". Everyone had laughed, but no one had remembered. That her love was in secret became the more important as she observed, sharp-eyed and prophetic, the breakdown of her parents' marriage; and as she saw the pattern of events develop in an ever more menacing way her hopeless will to have Felix produced, as a secondary growth, a more viable will at least to prevent her mother from having him. Miranda had been fond of her mother, she supposed, in earlier years; but the mother of her childhood was an anonymous faceless figure. All the colour of that early world had belonged to her father. Her mother first gained individuality and personality as her rival; and to the prosecution of that rivalry Miranda dedicated herself with ferocious efficiency.

She could not, of course, confide in anybody, not even, or especially not, in her father, to whom she had always been so close. Her attachment to him was something warm and organic and formless and infinitely comforting, though at moments too it caused her a sort of shame, almost a sort of disgust. He was the sole recipient of her tenderness, the only one for whom she was still a soft and nestling creature; and with this softness she combined, as she grew older, a fierce loyalty and a desire to protect him whenever, as it increasingly seemed to occur, he was any way 'in danger'. That her love for Felix was a sort of danger to him she early apprehended. He would be hurt by it if he knew. And from this knowledge also she protected him. She did not conceive her two loves as rivals. They were as different in nature as were their objects. Randall seemed to her infinitely frail compared with Felix, but through frailty infinitely dear.

When it became abundantly clear, and it was clear very early to Miranda, not only because of her almost scientific observation, but also because of hints her father dropped, that her parents were going to be parted for good, she felt that she could scarcely endure what was to come. She felt it as very likely that Felix would court her mother, that her mother would hesitate and procrastinate, but that Felix would get her in the end. Miranda told herself that she would not survive that moment. If Felix married Ann she would kill herself; and indeed the terrible interim, the new situation, with its promise of such interesting developments, which had been initiated by her father's departure seemed equally likely to torture her into desperation. The indifference to life which she had expressed to Felix at Seton Blaise seemed to her genuine, and she had leapt from the tree with, she felt, a real preparedness for death, though also with the hope of impressing Felix and landing in his arms. The days that followed, during which she received a demonstration of what she more than half knew, that Felix saw her as a child and noticed her only because of Ann, brought her private anguish to a climax.

In general, and from the point of view of her troubles, Miranda was in fact far from seeing her father's departure as an unmitigated disaster. In a curious way, even apart from Felix, she had often wanted him to go, wanted him to take off, like a bird sent from her hand to guide her into a better country. Miranda loved the violence latent in her father, she longed for an assertion of his strength, and the spectacle of his at last bursting out made her lick her lips and open her eyes. Randall would go ahead of her, her envoy, her ambassador, into the land of colour and shape, the country of her embezzled delights, and she would follow him there. It had the air of a rescue; and there was a place too for this romance in the economy of her nature. But as far as the matter of Randall's flight had repercussions on the matter of Felix, Miranda's feelings were at least mixed. Randall left a place for Felix and produced a state of affairs more immediately tormenting and menacing to her. But his disappearance, by making things more acute, brought them also, one way or another, nearer to their end; and Miranda told herself that anything was better than the indefinite, year after year, continuance of Felix's mute passion. Now, he would have either to succeed or to fail, and if thus explicitly he failed he would have to go away altogether. Miranda made it her business to see that he would either succeed or fail soon.

The strategy, when it came to it, was almost a consolation. There was her father to be seen off, to be encouraged not to hesitate to go. Now that she had at last decided to pull everything down, for better or worse, on top of her, Miranda felt a frantic impatience for his departure, and hoped indeed that she had not too evidently bundled him off. She could not have borne, now, hesitations, heart-searchings, partial reconciliations. She wanted Randall well cleared off the scene. About how to handle her mother she had had before-hand little idea. But when she began to try she was amazed at how easy it was. She felt, and this too was consolation, the beginning of a sense of her own strength. Her mother by comparison was a shapeless directionless mass, full of guilt and confused attachments, still hopelessly married. Miranda saw enough for her purposes and saw it with surprise and a little shuddering.

She sat moodily turning over the photos. They had little effect on her now. She felt as if Felix were dead, and she felt in a way that was not totally disagreeable that she was, for the present, dead too. She felt dull and listless, like after an examination. She looked at the photographs with unfocussed eyes. Then she began slowly to tear them up. She tore them as they came, not troubling to turn them over or notice them as she did so, and then she tore up the letters and cuttings without reading them. She reduced everything to small pieces. Then she put the fragments into a big envelope and sealed it. Then she sat there on the floor pursing her lips and scratching her ankle and humming a little tune.

She looked back over the country she had traversed, but already it seemed covered with mists and she could not see it as a whole. She was too tired to peer, and anyway it didn't matter any more. She speculated a little blankly about her mother and Felix. It didn't matter. She would never know, but she was indifferent to knowing and she would survive. People survive, and she would devote if necessary the whole of her life to a programme of survival. Coldly she surveyed its elements. In a year or two she would run away to her father. He would have left that other woman by then; or if he had not yet left her Miranda would soon persuade him to. He would be living in some gay Southern town. She saw him there, brown, exotic, vivacious, free, speaking foreign tongues. There she would arrive, thin, pale, mysterious and sad; and though greatly courted she would remain with her father. That is how it would be; and until then she would live as one dead.

She got up stiffly and walked to the shelves. She looked dully at the German dagger on which was still impaled the doll which Felix had given her. She pulled the dagger out and threw the remains of the doll into the waste-paper basket. Tomorrow she would drown the dagger in the Marsh. She stared at the quiet rows of dolls and picked one up mechanically and held it to her breast. It was a thing she had done a thousand times. But now suddenly it felt as if she were hugging a dead puppy. It came to her eerily that the dolls were all dead. The life with which she had endowed them was withdrawn. They were nothing now. She looked at them with widened eyes and touched her lips with her tongue. They were rows of dead semblances, mocking her solitude. She held the doll dangling at arm's length; then she took hold of its head and body and pulled. The china head came off and she threw it on the floor and it broke. She took the next doll and hurled it by its legs against the wall. Gradually the room filled with sawdust and fragments of pink china. What she could not smash she slashed to pieces with the German dagger. Poussette was last. She looked into the inane familiar face, and tore Poussette's head and limbs off. Now they were all gone, the little princes.

Chapter Thirty-three

A BIRD was singing somewhere out in the beech trees, somewhere in the great still light of the summer morning. The Marsh would be pale green beneath the sun, mixing its own strange light with the gold, and stretching away to end in a blue haze. Already upon the slope the ten thousand roses would be opened, uncovering their exquisite hearts and making of the hillside a great unfolding fan. Up above him Miranda would be still asleep, but Ann would be up already, at work in the kitchen. Nancy Bowshott would be arriving with the milk. Lazily he listened for the sounds of the early morning household. Randall Peronett was waking up.

He turned over and came into contact with something. He opened his eyes. With a rush which made him start up now on to his elbow it all came back to him. He was in Rome, in a hotel in the Piazza Minerva, in a big bed with Lindsay. The great summer light was there, but muted by Venetian blinds to a hot twilight, the singing bird was there, but it was a canary in a cage that hung outside a nearby house. And here was Lindsay lying beside him on her back fast asleep. The sheet was thrust down from her nakedness to make of her a sort of recumbent Aphrodite Anadyomene, an Aphrodite of the world of sleep. Her pale metallic golden hair, flattened into shining strips, spread over the pillow and down onto her breasts. Lifting himself a little, Randall detached some tresses from the side of his sweating body. It had been a hot night.

He looked at his watch. It was not yet seven o'clock. He decided not to wake Lindsay yet. They had been late to bed. He studied her face. Her head was thrust back and her chin pointed at the ceiling in an attitude of decisiveness which she retained even in sleep. Her lips, so much more beautiful he thought in their untouched pallor, were a little parted and there was a gleam of teeth between. The

311

thin veined eyelids were as smooth as the skin of some miraculous fruit. Her breathing could be heard in a soft repeated sigh, gentle, insistent, suggestive. The wide serene oval of the face, the big rounded forehead, slightly domed, pale and even for such a scrutiny quite unlined, lay before him like a lovely domain seen from a mountain. Here sleep seemed a miracle of beauty, warmth and life strangely arrested and made into a thing of contemplation. So in miraculous castles great princesses might slumber out the centuries. Randall gazed and worshipped and felt again the thrill of achievement and possession.

Yet these awakenings were always the same. He woke always thinking himself at Grayhallock, as if the fact of his new condition had not yet been broken to his unconscious mind. His unconscious mind had indeed, and luridly enough, other concerns. He had never dreamed so much in his life. Every night in dreams he saw Ann, a wild Ann running past and not hearing him call, an Ann passing strangely in a boat as he watched from a window, an Ann receding down an avenue of trees and becoming, by the time he had followed her, a glimmering statue. Once he saw her in a dream weeping and holding Joey in her arms; and the next night he was trying to reach her through a hedge of roses. He dreamt too, and disturbingly, of a youthful figure who was both Ann and Miranda, and who in one dream of hallucinatory power seemed to rise like a goddess, with her dazzling crown of hair, at the very foot of the bed. At other times he dreamt of Steve, simple realistic dreams: Steve playing with his soldiers or his trains, Steve throwing the German dagger at the stable door. He dreamt a little of his mother. He dreamt twice of Emma Sands, but forgot the dream. He did not dream of Lindsay.

Randall had never dreamed so much, and he had rarely eaten and drunk so much. They were drunk every afternoon and every night, and what with the drink and the dreams and the curious gaps in his memory and the dazed excitement and exhaustion induced by perpetual love-making Randall was at times at a loss to know where reality lay. For reality he made do with a vague shimmering apprehension of Lindsay's continual presence. She was indeed the Aphrodite of the world of sleep.

They made love continually. Randall made of Rome a sort of map of love, a series of love-pilgrimages where places were identified by embraces and ecstasy as if they only came into existence when they rose into the heightened consciousness of the lovers. He took Lindsay to the Appian Way and made love to her behind the Tomb of Caecilia Metella. He took her to the Palatine and made love to her in the Temple of Cybele. He took her to the Borghese Gardens and made love to her near the Fontana dei Cavalli Marini. He took her to Ostia Antica and made love to her in the back of a wine shop. He took her to the Catacombs. He took her to the English Cemetery and would have made love to her on Keats's grave only some American ladies arrived. And it was as if at these places the map had smouldered leaving a round hole, a blankness which was at the same time an opening into another world.

What, through these openings, Randall *saw*, in so far as at this dazed time he either saw or expected to see anything, was another matter. He had not neglected to take Lindsay, in a more ordinary sense, on tour, and he had, in this city which he knew and loved, shown her a great deal. Her ignorance of Italian art and indeed of anything pertaining to the past staggered him, and he was a little pained, not so much by the ignorance itself as by a tendency on Lindsay's part to conceal it where possible. What he had in England cheerfully and robustly thought of as her vulgarity appeared in this context as an uneasiness which detracted the tiniest bit from her grace. But these were details.

Settled back on his raised-up pillows now above the sleeping girl, Randall lit a cigarette and contemplated the hot blurred rectangle of the window, the doors open to a balcony behind the long Venetian blind, the white curtains, soft and translucent as a dream, falling unstirred by any breath of air. The canary continued its song. There was something unfocussed, something a little unnervingly fragmentary, in his present apprehension of Lindsay. A number of things, seemingly unrelated, contributed to there being, in his attempted pattern, significant gaps. Talking casually about her childhood Lindsay had given him a quite different account of certain matters from the one she had given at first. Yet what did it matter to him if she was a liar? He was a liar himself. One evening in a restaurant when he had tried to buy her some roses she had said absently that she did not really like roses, as if she had forgotten who she was talking to. But what did it matter to him if at moments she hardly knew who he was? There were moments, particularly late at night, when he hardly knew who she was. Then again she had said to him, only the previous day, "It wasn't true what we said about Emma Sands. We *did* like her, didn't we? We did *love* her."

Randall had figured his flight in the perfect image of freedom. To be alone with Lindsay in Rome and to be rich seemed to constitute the very peak and essence of unimpeded activity. He had a little reckoned without his mind; and although he told himself that he would change, that he would soon don a new personality, the personality which he had slipped on, as for a tailor's fitting, the day he lunched at Boulestin's and saw the waiters bowing to the ground, he had not yet, he had to admit, quite put off the bad old self. He worried. He could not help reflecting still about Lindsay and Emma, though he told himself it was ridiculous to speculate about that now. Even if his more bizarre images of their relationship, even if his more nightmarish suppositions concerning their collusion about *him* should have some part of truth, why should he trouble about that *now*, why should it matter *now* what Lindsay was *then*? He shrugged his shoulders but he could not get Emma out of his mind.

This unfortunate obsession had another aspect. It was as if Emma had *produced* the situation in which he had desired Lindsay. Emma had been, as it were, the impresario of his passion. He had loved Lindsay as the enticing but untouchable *princesse lointaine* which Emma had (how deliberately and with what end?) made of her; and in now possessing Lindsay Randall experienced, though very rarely and for a second at a time, the touch of a disappointment analogous to that of the girl who desires the priest in his *soutane*, but wants him no more when he has broken his vows to become, less ceremoniously, available.

It was not that Lindsay, possessed, brought with her anything of the sober commonplace. The region they jointly inhabited was mad and exotic enough. But Randall felt curious stirrings of another freedom, as if this degree of hurling himself about still did not satisfy his awakened energy. It was not, either, that Lindsay was below her destiny. She was, on the whole, magnificent. Her moments of faltering were few compared with her great serenities and certainties. She dressed exquisitely in the array of flowered marvels, soft or crisp, flowing or sleek, which Randall had bought for her by the armful. She wore her jewels like a duchess, and everywhere she went, leaning upon his arm, admiring heads were turned. Whatever her occasional blanks where the *quattrocento* was concerned, Lindsay could sufficiently impersonate a great lady. She had, in the void of their new existence, both style and form, and moved in its boundlessness with a boldly spread and finely articulated wing.

Randall wished that he was sure that he could say the same of himself. He had said once to Lindsay that they were, in strength, an equal match. He had in the last weeks quietly become aware, in the nebulous inexplicit way in which one realises such things, that this was not so. He noted in her a barbaric strength which her present finery made subtly more apparent. Lindsay was the stronger, Lindsay was the boss: and even if she herself had not yet realised it, it could not be long before she did. Randall sometimes wondered whether this discovery were not the real source of his discontents. He attempted in any case to survey it with a cool eye. In spite of his anxieties about the present and the past, he had gained, for a further future about which he remained totally agnostic, a little self-confidence. As for the past, he would never know; but people survived. *He* would certainly survive.

He could not help being disappointed in his performance. He

remembered how much he had admired Lindsay and Emma, and wished to emulate the serene quality of their egoism. He had thought of them as living high up in a region of perfect freedom, in a sort of paradise of the imagination. He had thought of this as some quite different mode of being to which he was prepared to attain even by committing crimes, to which perhaps he was likely to attain especially by committing crimes. But he had not, or had not yet, been able to live up to the promise of those dreams and those early moments. Something in his slovenly darkened self prevented his attaining the immaculate condition which he had pictured, and for which he had conceived Lindsay as the perfect consort.

What here impeded him was, he was fairly sure, not the demon of morality. It was more like some restless rapacity, a rapacity such as is the mark of mediocrity in art. The great artist is not rapacious. Randall felt restless, he wanted, now more than ever, to have everything; and he could not but picture his life with Lindsay as a perpetual flight, from Rome to Paris, from Paris to Madrid, from Madrid to New York, from New York to . . . And as he imagined them thus covering the globe he also put it to himself: the world is large and there are other women in it besides Lindsay.

Randall stubbed out his cigarette. On the table beside the bed was a glass of water, a little pile of aspirins, a detective story, and a toy dog which Lindsay had bought him two days ago at a street market. They had not named it yet. Toby was still packed away in his suitcase. He caressed the other dog and fancied he heard from the cupboard Toby's disapproving barks. He smiled a little and ate an aspirin. Would he, in the end, ditch Lindsay?

What was he going to do, in the big airy spacious future, anyway? He knew in his heart, and he knew that Lindsay assumed, that he would never be a playwright. Distanced now by so much more of experience and suffering from his plays he realised clearly that they were no good. They were pretentious, muddled and insipid. Perhaps he would try his hand once more; but it would be merely an amateurish game. There was only one thing in the world that he was really good at, and that he would never do again. He saw in a vision the sunny hillside at Grayhallock with its slight haze of green and its myriad little coloured forms and he sighed. Ann.

Through some mechanics of reality the figure of Ann remained steady. But its power was broken. It was this breaking of the power which enabled him to entertain, half laughingly, a sort of nostalgia. Ann's tyranny was broken, her dead hand was gone. Why had he fretted so in the old days when freedom was, after all, so easy? Perhaps this, and only this, was what Lindsay was for, to free him from Ann; and if it were so it would be justification enough. Whereas Emma's awareness of him still seemed to hover over him like a cloud, Ann's awareness of him had vanished, it was nothing. By passing through extremity, by committing the final crimes, he had freed himself forever of any concern about what Ann thought. And sometimes he imagined weirdly that this put them into a new and innocent relationship, as if they could set up house together like Christie and Old Mahon; and he would be the boss then. Or more vividly at other times he pictured himself based on Ann and the roses and having as many other women as he pleased without troubling. Perhaps after all it was there where the new world lay, in some almost impossible fusion whereby he could eat his cake and have it. He knew that these were only wild fancies. But it gave him pleasure all the same to think, almost with a perverted tenderness, that now he did not care a fig about what went on in Ann's mind.

The great thing was that there was no hurry. He turned on his side to look at Lindsay and saw that she was stirring and would soon be awake. He looked upon her with love, with a possessive positive love which made nothing of his moments of disloyalty. He prepared his presence, his smile, for her like a table arrayed. In a moment she would open her eyes and draw him instantly to her with a beaming laziness. She always knew deeply and at once where she was and with whom. He waited tenderly for her to awaken. Had he made a terrible mistake? The wonderful thing now was that no mistake was terrible. There was plenty of time, and time would show him what he really wanted to do. He would survive. He could always, and after his own beautiful fashion, return to Ann. Ann would always be waiting.

Chapter Thirty-four

"WELL, Emma", said Hugh, "what about it?"
"Oh *that*", she said. "Was I supposed to be thinking it over?"

For some weeks now she had managed by a combination of procrastination, feigned illness and sheer vagueness to see him only infrequently, while the idea was kept up of a continual communication. Much time was spent on the telephone making and unmaking arrangements which rarely matured: which was all mysterious to Hugh, since it seemed that, especially since Emma was not working, she should have nothing in the world to do except to see him. However she patently did not want him to go away and appeared to put considerable energy into tormenting him, and he had to be content with that.

For Hugh the interim had had a sad and haunted character. He shunned society and seemed to wander in a void where tall shadowy figures with ghostly heads loomed over him and vanished. He heard a babble of voices and was at a loss to know whether they were the product of a deranged ear or a wandering mind. He visited his ear specialist and departed from him with his usual contempt. Yet he had his own grip on life and took the time almost after a religious fashion as a suspense to be endured. He took out his old painting equipment, looked at it, and put it away again. He went often to the National Gallery and gloomily visited the Tintoretto which still drew its knot of admirers at lunch-time. Once he stroked it absently, as he had done when it was his, and was savaged by an attendant. He called on Humphrey at Cadogan Place and drank sherry with him and with Penn. Penn was looking better, altogether gayer and more attractive, quite the young man. He had let Humphrey buy him a new suit as a retrospective birthday present. He met them again by accident when they were on their way to the Tower, and saw them distantly another time lunching at Pruniers.

He was sorry not to see anything of Mildred, who was the only person he could have talked to, but she was still in the country.

This occasion of visiting Emma he was resolved to make into something of a crisis. He had a sense of a due time, perhaps a significant testing time, having passed: and he feared to fail with her simply through timidity. He had by now sufficiently also a sense of grievance. His need for her did not diminish; and very sweetly now the notion of her as a strange forbidden fruit mingled with the old passion which had so risen from the depths, encrusted and yet the same. She filled his mind, she was his occupation. Though *what* solution, bringing them together, would crown this time he did not know or trouble too closely to enquire.

It was tea-time. It seemed to be always tea-time at Emma's. The weather had changed and it was a bleak windy day, and tugged-at leaves and whirling branches knew that summer was defeated and departing. Outside the window the little evergreen garden tossed itself about in a tumultuous undulating mass of dark shapes. The wind came in sudden roars and whines. In the room a fan heater purred, mingling its faint rattle with the now perpetual noises inside Hugh's head. He had just made the tea and brought it in.

Emma was sitting in her usual chair. She had a new dress on, or at any rate one which Hugh had not seen before, and looked singularly handsome. The dress was of a dark fine very light tweed with a thin green stripe, cut wide and long in the skirt like all her dresses. Leaning back, the silver-topped cane in its place, her frizzy grey hair more orderly than usual like a contrived and generous wig, she seemed something remote, something French, something vastly clever and timeless out of some courtly world of ceremony and sophistication. Tender, admiring, covetous, and unreasoningly pleased with himself, he took her good looks as an omen and as a tribute.

She looked at him with the air of resolute vagueness which he had come to know, and said, "Would you pour out the tea, dear? I just don't feel strong enough. I'm sure you've made it beautifully."

Hugh poured out. "Now don't put me off this time, Emma.

Don't treat me as if I scarcely existed. Talk to me properly. I deserve some real speech."

"Real speech?" she said. "You're bullying me."

"Me bullying you, for God's sake, when you haven't seen me in weeks? And you know how much I want from you."

"Oh yes. You were the one who wanted, roughly, everything. The second time round." She laughed her shrill little laugh.

He edged his chair closer. "Well, what about it, Emma?"

She turned to stare at him, her eyes heavy with some sad extinguished light. "I could never decide in the old days whether you were divinely simple or just stupid."

"What do you think now?"

"I don't know. Perhaps that you are divinely stupid and God loves fools. Perhaps God is a fool. Could you fetch me those tablets, please, from the desk."

He fetched them and stood fidgeting, aware of himself as stout and shambling before her. He was vaguely conscious of the room as looking different. "Why must we always fight? Why can't we be at peace together at last? Why do you always try to confuse me?"

"*This* isn't fighting, Hugh. I've been very gentle with you. I haven't struck you once, really to hurt. Though I *could*. As for the other, you are so adorably confusable. *C'est plus fort que moi.*" She swallowed a tablet with a gulp of tea.

"Talk to me properly!" He let his voice now entreat her shamelessly.

Emma was still looking up at him sadly. Then as if shaking herself into an effort, she said, "You want some real speech, do you? All right, I'll see what I can arrange. Do you notice anything different in this room?"

He looked about him. There were many new things. The but too symbolically stripped look which the room had worn as a result of Lindsay's depredations had quite gone. There were new rugs, a new bookcase, a new writing-desk in the window, cushions, miniatures, Chinese vases, which had not been there before, and on every level surface were scattered little specks of treasure in gilt and silver and glass. The room had put on its attire again, it was adorned like a bride.

"Good heavens!" said Hugh.

"You *are* an unobservant chap, you know."

"Is it—for me?" he said. He was moved, and also sad that he had not thought himself to bring her armfuls of expensive nick-nacks to fill those empty spaces.

"No, it's not for you," said Emma. "It's for Jocelyn."

"For *who?*"

"For Jocelyn. Jocelyn Gaster. She's my new companion. Lindsay's successor."

"*What?*" said Hugh. He glared down at her with anxiety and suspicion.

"Well, really," said Emma, "your inability to think about anyone but yourself is absolutely colossal. How do you think I can manage without a companion?"

"But the whole point was—"

"That you were to have the job? But that would never have done. I need so much attention. And you're so unpractical, you know. Would you like to see a picture of her?" She pointed to a thick envelope on a nearby table. Hugh brought it to her and she drew out a large photograph and put it in his hand.

Hugh saw a dark tousled boyish-looking girl with an arrogant ironical face. He laid the photo down. "Well, I think you might—"

"I wanted to be sure she'd come," said Emma, speaking quickly. "I always ask them to send photos. She's handsome, isn't she? Such a clever face. And her dossier is good too. Second in Mods and a third in Greats. That seems all right, doesn't it? Somerville, of course. I like them to be well educated. I took Lindsay *plutôt pour ses beaux yeux*. But Jocelyn is really cultivated as well, and awfully nice. She starts work next week."

Hugh stood before her looking down at the dog-mask of her face in which the eyes burned so sadly and anxiously. Did he see there pity or cruelty? He felt with a gloomy foreboding that he was near the truth with her. "Emma, why did you come to Gray-hallock?"

"Oh, *that*," she said, with the same emphasis as if he were always mentioning the irrelevant. "I had my reasons."

"What were your reasons?"

"Is this real speech? All right, let us go on. I wanted to see Randall's wife."

"Why?"

"I just wanted to make sure it was all all right."

"What was all all right?"

"What was going to happen."

"And *is* it all all right?"

"You mean Ann?"

"I mean myself."

"Oh, *you*. I don't know. But Ann—I did develop a little plan for Ann that *would* have been nice—"

"A little plan?"

"Yes. Did you have no *ideas* yourself, for Ann, no *ideas* at all?"

Hugh stared at her in complete puzzlement. "Ideas? What sort of ideas?"

"Never mind. They came to nothing. The girl is a goose. She's not the only one. And of course I was just curious."

"Look," said Hugh, "I don't understand. You speak as if you arranged everything yourself. You're confusing me again. Please—"

"Arranged? How crude you are. No, no. But I had another reason. I wanted to decide about the money."

"About what money?"

"My money."

"Decide what?"

"Who's to have it."

"But—why now? And why there?"

"You see," she said, "I had the beautiful idea of swindling my way into your family via your descendants! I thought it would be marvellously confusing. Perhaps confusing you is a way of loving you."

"I don't understand," he said, humbly now and encouraged by the gentleness of her teasing manner.

"I have selected my heir. Your grandchild."

"Miranda!"

"No, not Miranda. I didn't like her. Young Penn. He's the lucky one. Isn't it a happy idea?"

Hugh sat down heavily on a delicate *petit-point* stool which creaked violently under him. The wind moved and the bushes hurled themselves about outside like puppets and the fan heater clattered and the voices that argued inside his head continued their yapping polemic. He said, "But why, why?"

"Well, someone's got to have it!" said Emma impatiently. "And I have no family except for two cousins I detest, and I don't like my old college, so what can I do? And there's no point in leaving it to you."

"Anyway I'll be the first to go. But you astonish me."

"You won't be the first to go," said Emma. "That's rather the point." She looked at him still with the holding gaze, sharper now and more anxious, as if trying to retain him in a difficult argument.

"You mean—?"

"I'm ill, really ill. I've never told anyone, and I've let people think I just make an absurd fuss. But I've got a heart thing that could take me off at any time. Or of course I might live for years too. But that was why I hurried you about Grayhallock. One never knows how much time one has."

"Oh, my darling—" said Hugh. He put his hands to his face.

"Now, now!" she said. "Don't be emotional. You make me soft, and that's bad for me. That's another thing I've got against you. Anyway, I've made the will, so if I die soon Penn will get the lot. Unless perhaps I get awfully fond of Jocelyn and give her some. But there's plenty. Poor old Lindsay!"

"My darling one—" Hugh had got hold of her hand which she

324

gave him now with an air of relief and abandon. "Oh, my dear—"
He felt a desperate scandalised pain. "Lindsay didn't know?"

"Certainly not. I wanted to be loved a little longer for myself
alone and not my lovely dough."

"She would have—had it all?"

"She would have had it all. If she'd stayed. Then she would have
been free, and she needn't have taken Randall. I would have set her
free. Like Prospero and Ariel. I often thought of it."

"You think she took Randall—for the money?"

"Well—for the freedom. I'm not blaming her."

"But then—will *they* be all right, I wonder?"

"You are still so romantic, Hugh! Why shouldn't they, whatever Lindsay's motives were? Doubtless we shall never know. But
people survive. Still, it may not be next week that Lindsay will be
kicking herself. I *may* live for ages! I'd like to live for ages to spite
Mildred Finch. And if I die soon I'll spite Lindsay. So I'll be content
either way."

"Don't," said Hugh. "Oh don't, Emma! Why do you want to
spite Mildred?"

"Oh, for her heartless curiosity that time when I stayed with her
after you left me. And—well, for that."

"I didn't know you stayed with her then."

"What a lot you don't know, my dear! She only asked me out of
curiosity. I scarcely saw her after that. She interrogated me for ten
days while I adored Felix. She didn't like that either. Of course I
told her nothing. But I quite fell in love with Felix. *He* didn't know
of course, he lived in a world of knives and ropes and things. Ah,
he was enchanting at fourteen. That particular faun-like grace
which fades later. Penn has it now. And some girls have it. Lindsay
has it. She's very boy-like. And Jocelyn has it. Something slim and
piratical. Yes, I think I'm really made to love boys of fourteen. It
sounds awfully immoral, doesn't it? But then I am immoral. That's
why I was so much at home with Randall and Lindsay." She
squeezed his hand and withdrew from his clasp, smiling now and
calm.

"Why did you love me, I wonder? I was never particularly faun-like!"

"Heaven knows. Perhaps I only really woke up to myself later. Perhaps Felix woke me. Yet I did love you; yes, you were the great thing. Wasn't I unlucky?"

"Emma," said Hugh, "let me look after you properly. I wouldn't bother you. You could have your Jocelyn. But please let me *somehow* take you over. I know I don't deserve it, but I do love you. Only I must have some sort of status and security. I can't go on like in these last weeks. Just say in principle yes and we'll find a way to be together." He leaned forward, touching her skirt.

"Ah, my dear," she said, "wouldn't we be ridiculous, two old people shouting endearments at each other?"

"Emma, let us be together, let us have some *reality* together at last."

"It is too late for reality," she said. "It is better that you should dream about me. Why spoil your dream? Keep it intact till the end. I'm terribly ill-natured really and not to be lived with or even near. I gave poor Lindsay a bad time, words and blows. Yes, I used to beat her. Now she's beating Randall! Could I have some more tea, if it's not too cold?"

"I don't understand. Do you—want me to remain as I am—in love?" He still clawed her dress.

"Yes, if you can. I'd adore it! If we must ape something in the past let it not be the marriage you were too cowardly and I not clever enough to get. Let it be some innocent dream love, a courtly love, something never realised, all dreams. And Penn shall be our symbolic child. And you can telephone me and send me flowers. It will be quite like being seventeen again. Won't that be youth enough, restoration enough, redemption enough?"

"You cheat me," he said in a voice of anguish, "you deny me."

"Hugh, stop believing in magic. You are just like poor Randall after all, who thinks he can conjure up pleasure domes and caves of ice just by boarding a plane and sending off a few letters."

"But—how will you manage?"

"I shall manage. I shall be happy. I shall be beating Jocelyn."

"But at least," he said, "you will talk to me more. We shall have real speech, you will tell me about yourself?"

Emma laughed. "I doubt if such tales would be suitable for young Jocelyn's ears."

"You mean," he took it in, "that you won't see me alone?"

"Well, young Jocelyn will be here, won't she?" said Emma. "I shall keep her a prisoner as I did Lindsay. Only more so!" She gently extricated the fabric of her dress and drew it down about her knees.

Hugh leaned forward and took her chin in one hand and turned her face towards him. With his other hand he grasped her shoulder. The gesture had an effect of violence.

She let him hold her so for a minute, and then shrugged him off. "You see how much I need a chaperone!"

"So I'm to take Randall's place?"

"How prettily you put it. You're to take Randall's place."

He let out a long sigh and stood up. "I wonder if I shall be able to stand it."

"If you can stand it, come. And if not, not."

"But you look so sad—"

"Ah, I'm not sad for now, my sweet, I'm sad for *then*."

PART SEVEN

Chapter Thirty-five

THE wind took one of the dust-bin lids and rolled it clattering across the yard. Ann pursued. The little paved area behind the kitchen, bright with dandelions, was damp from the recent shower. Some washing which Ann had hung out and forgotten jerked and dripped. She retrieved the lid and returned to the waste-paper bin out of which she was filling her bucket as usual to restart the soaked bonfire. She packed the paper firmly into the bottom of the bucket and held it there while she scrabbled with the other hand to pick up some flat stones to weigh the paper down. Already several white fragments were dancing about the yard, joining some dead leaves which the trees, despairing already in their summer fulness, had surrendered to the confident wind. The sky was a thick grey suffused with points of gold from the hidden sun. There would be a rainbow somewhere. Ann crossed the road and started down the hill.

Miranda was away staying with a school friend. She seemed to have escaped the measles. Penn had behaved as Miranda predicted. He had waited till the last moment before the date of his plane, and had then written to ask Ann to send his things. He was very grateful and apologetic, but simply could not manage to get down to Grayhallock to say good-bye. Ann had packed his belongings with a heavy heart. She included the veteran car book, which was still in his room. He had himself, apparently, taken the box of soldiers back to Steve's room. She could not find the German dagger anywhere, though she spent a long time searching for it. Miranda said she had mislaid it.

The Swanns had departed on holiday with their caravan. She had waved them off, a boisterous business-like family party, organised and conducted laughingly away by the purposeful vigour of the Swann boys, who behaved like junior officers on a combined operation. She had been asked to join them but had refused, and not only because Clare's invitation had been less than irresistibly pressing.

She feared to see, at present, too much of Douglas in case her own blank need for affection, for the most elementary consolation, should make him positively fall in love. She had hoped that Hugh might come to keep her company, but though he often rather guiltily telephoned he still did not seem able to leave town. So she remained solitary at Grayhallock except for the now frequent company of Nancy Bowshott, with whom she picked and preserved the soft fruit and helped Bowshott with the endless spraying. Drawing close to Nancy, she guessed one day, hardly now with surprise, that Nancy was grieving for Randall.

Ann tired herself out each day with physical work. She lived in exhaustion, unhappiness and muddle as in a now accustomed medium, flopping in it like some creature in the mud. She was still stunned by her own action, stunned partly by the fact of having acted at all. It seemed to her that she had not done such a thing in years. She had become quite unaccustomed to action and utterly unaccustomed to reflection upon action; and when she attempted the latter she found herself dreadfully unable to determine what she had done and why. She *ought*, she felt, to know this. Yet looking with desperate glances back over the expanse of her conduct she could not discern where the actions lay at all or what, amid the general drift, they positively were. She *had* acted, she *had* altered the world; but how, why, even when?

Looking back on her last interview with Felix, Ann felt that it had simply been a muddle. Yet deep in the muddle there was, there must have been, some decisive form. What had most struck her, before seeing him, as essential had been her image of Randall returning, Randall searching for her, Randall crying for her, and not finding her. She had been, at this, overwhelmed by a tide of pity and compassion for Randall, a tide she could only in the end say of love for Randall. This feeling, which was in its way blinding and suffocating, seemed to make it impossible for her to say yes to Felix: made it impossible for her to say yes then, and if not then, then not at all, as Felix must not be made to spoil his life by perhaps fruitless waiting.

That much, before he came, had seemed if not 'clear' at least irresistible. Yet Ann had summoned him. She had not, as she might have done, told him her decision by letter. What could this mean but that there had really been, as yet, no decision? She had perhaps however vaguely relied upon him for a certain hardness, a certain grimness, something that would lend, to the other side, a sense of fatality. She had perhaps half hoped for an exorcism, for the removal, somehow, of that overwhelming image of Randall: to have her view unravelled and shown to be wrong. The interview had seemed to her, she now sometimes thought, while it was going on, like a trial run, like something incomplete, something symbolic, a symbolic sacrifice. She was suffering for Randall; but when she had suffered enough, when both she and Felix had suffered enough, the suffering would end. She would go the whole circle of suffering and at its close she would be able to take Felix in her arms. That was what had driven her on through Marie-Laure, even to her ultimate words of denial.

The utterance of the words of denial had seemed to wake her from a trance, and she had lifted her face to Felix's stricken and stiffened countenance. She had reached the end and had then been ready to begin the scene again with every difference. Only it was too late. She had not meant the words as Felix had taken them. She had only meant to say everything, to show him everything, the ultimate difficulties, the ultimate problem—and then ask him at one step to solve it all. But the picture, as she had too truthfully revealed it, was too much for him. If he had only seized her when he came in, if he had kissed her, if he had as much as touched her, or if he had at the end simply shouted her down, she felt she must have submitted. If she had only not for that instant tried him with the words of denial everything might have been different. Yet had she not merely and exactly done as she had decided beforehand she would do? And had he not acted as she must have known he would act? It was scarcely a matter of 'motives'. She had had no motives. Her whole life had compelled her. They had each of them their destiny.

333

It was as if what she had done was plotted on different and incongruous maps, which made it seem to her sometimes that different lines or levels of conduct must have co-existed, and sometimes that what she had really done was some yet other indiscernible thing. She *had* worked it out, or partly worked it out, that it was her duty to hold to Randall; yet the reasoning of this and the idea of this, though persistently present, lacked clarity. She did not really believe that Randall would come back; nor did she believe that her actions, one way or the other, would affect him any more at all. He would not be oppressed by her faithfulness or released by her lack of it. The 'cutting of the painter' had been an idea that concerned only herself: it was her own freedom only which had been in question. Randall, without further reference to her, was in possession of his. Why then had she not cut the painter? The intoxication of freedom had even come to her, like a helpful attendant spirit, at the due moment. But she had dismissed it.

Here she was bound to reflect upon the notion of the sacrament of marriage which had so authoritatively come up for her in her talk with Douglas. The notion was constantly present to her mind now, but in an utterly inert way. It was like a great lump which she kept turning over but in which she could discern no significant shape. *That* was something which she had simply not thought out to the end, and she had not done so because she must somehow have realised that it was not essential to her decision. It was not that she had from this derived some decisive command of duty which she now saw, because her poor heart was elsewhere, as an empty form. She could have born this comprehensible pain more easily. She suspected she had not been moved by the command of duty at all.

Yet when she tried to see her conduct as determined by emotion, by desire, by a will seeking, however deviously, its own felicity, she could not on those suppositions either make sense of her actions. She had let go of the exceedingly dear and precious Felix whom she loved and needed with all her heart, almost, it seemed to her, because of a naked meaningless incapacity to take what she wanted. Or was it that some other, stronger, emotion had really moved her, some completely mad, even almost corrupt, emotion of sentimental sympathy for Randall? At a certain moment perhaps she had not been able to bear the break with Randall, ignoring the dreadful fact that it had already taken place; and the flood of feeling which had perhaps been fatal to Felix seemed to her indubitably more like some unrealistic haze of sentiment than like the heavenly love desiderated by Douglas Swann. *That*, unless it was very heavily disguised, she did not feel to be in the situation at all.

Miranda was perhaps the key to the matter; yet had she acted persuaded by Miranda, for the sake of Miranda? Her daughter had, in some simple terms, reminded her of her duty; yet Ann could only remember having felt, at this reminder, a sort of irritation. But Miranda had certainly shaken her. There had been some terrible accuracy of aim in Miranda's words. And Miranda had helped to set loose that fatal pity for Randall. Perhaps even her cry of "I don't want to be a step-daughter!" had worked with Ann more deeply than she realised. There was no denying that the child herself was very disturbed at present. Ann had been shocked, and indeed frightened, to hear from Nancy Bowshott that Miranda had broken all her dolls. Her own failure, after their momentous discussion, to communicate at all with her daughter left this massacre as something barbarous, fearful and unexplained. Ann yearned to help her child but could not. She grieved to find herself regarding Miranda's presence in the house as almost menacing, a source of strange rays; and if her own decision had indeed been 'because of' Miranda she still could not in the end see quite why.

She could not see her actions. But the pain of their results, the pain of loss, was overwhelming and with a dreadful separate quality of its own. It was as if she were perpetually haunted and mocked by a music of happiness which came from some inaccessible elsewhere. It was the sheer beauty of love which at such times she apprehended and at such times felt herself to have criminally betrayed; and what she had denied would not let her rest, coming to her as a sort of golden aura about her memories of Felix. She felt herself here sometimes as the victim of a sheer wilful vagueness, one who had made, in the calculations of life, simply an unnecessary howler. She had not been trained for this, she told herself. Yet ought she not to have been? And with this she came back to the fruitless task of asking herself whether after all she had done the right thing.

Felix had written. He had written such a quiet kindly gentlemanly letter that Ann had wondered for a moment whether he were not perhaps relieved. Perhaps he was glad really to have tried and failed and to be able to turn with a clear heart elsewhere. Yet she could not credit this. The gentleness was a part of Felix, a part that made her love him, perhaps also a part that made her lose him. She recalled his cry, "I've become, with you, invisible." He too, alas, was one of the invisible ones. She had opened his letter trembling with a scarcely rational hope that he would, on reflection, not accept her refusal, that he would again press her. She had read through his resigned considerate message and burnt it at once. She could not now remember its exact wording and did not try. How much had Felix really wanted her? She would never know. But Felix would certainly survive.

Ann pressed along the path between the gallicas, her Wellingtons deep in the wet grass which needed its next mowing. She noted with an expert eye which buds would be ready, in three days' time, for her flower-arrangement at the Women's Institute. Perhaps it was just as well that Clare would miss the competition this year; she never became resigned to not winning. Ann reached the bonfire and set the bucket down. The big mound of foliage and grass cuttings occupied the corner of the nursery site, and beyond the wire fence the fields sloped down towards the Marsh. There was a distant sound of folded sheep. The near sky was paling to a watery grey and there was a segment of rainbow with its foot on Brenzett church tower. Further off, toward Dungeness, were dark clouds and a shadowy curtain of rain. But the nursery slope lightened.

The bonfire was wet, but Ann hollowed out its ashy centre as she had done a hundred times before and began to stuff her waste paper in, taking it in cautious handfuls from under the weighty stones so that it should not blow about in the brisk wind. When she had packed in enough she rearranged the foliage on top of it, poured on a little paraffin, and tried to strike a match. It took her some time to get one alight, and she cupped it down to the fringe of the paper. When the paper was well afire she gave the structure an adjusting kick with her Wellington.

Something seemed to burst, and a stream of smaller torn-up papery fragments descended from one side of the bonfire. Absently Ann began to boot them back in again. Then she saw that they were fragments of photographs and she stooped to pick one up. It was a piece of a photograph of Felix. She stared at the little image of his face, upset and startled by the coincidence. Then she picked up another fragment. It was also a piece of a photograph of Felix. She picked up another. The fire was blazing up. Ann kicked back the flaming paper and the already smouldering branches and tried to pull out whatever was not already alight. She burnt her hands, but rescued and threw clear a half-charred envelope and the heap of pieces which seemed to have been coming out of it; and as the wind seized and began to scatter them she threw herself on top of them on the grass. Half sitting half lying on her discovery she began to turn the fragments over, trying to shield them from the wind at the same time.

There was a lot of stuff, some photographs, some newspaper cuttings, some letters, and as far as she could see, as with a kind of horror she turned them over, they all related to Felix. She wondered if she were dreaming or the victim of some devil's trick. She recognised bits of two snapshots which she had bitterly missed from her album. She deciphered yellow fragments of wartime newspapers. With trembling hands she held them together, the jagged dismembered pieces of ghostly occasions, the vanished moments, the dear looks and smiles and caught familiar glances. The pieces of manuscript too were all in his writing. They seemed to be letters. Then, as she began clumsily to assemble them, she realised what letters they were. And with that she realised everything. *My dear Miranda—*

Ann stood up. Her shoulder and side were soaked by the wet grass. Automatically she brushed herself down. The wind, coming in a sudden rainy gust, took the heap of fragments and tossed it into the air and began to scatter it up the hillside among the roses. The pale scraps chased away in every direction, racing along the grass, somersaulting across the flower beds, flying even as far as the road, and coming to rest in muddy pools and against heaps of manure and among thorny branches or being carried off upon the wheels of passing cars. Ann made an ineffectual gesture to stop them and then let them go. The image of Felix was dispersed and scattered.

Ann put the paraffin tin into the empty bucket and began slowly to ascend the hill. It was drizzling a little now and the rainbow had gone. She turned up the collar of her coat and smoothed back the damp hair. About half-way up the hill she noticed something stirring under a big arching bush of Stanwell Perpetual. There was an animal under the bush. She put down the bucket and peered and saw that it was Hatfield, a thin and rather bedraggled and wild-looking Hatfield. She began to entice him. He cowered and then retreated a little between the bushes. Ann followed, her coat dragging on the thorns. She crouched down and called to him. After staring suspiciously he approached a little and she was able to pounce on him before he again took flight. She stumbled out from among the roses with the cat struggling and growling in her arms.

By the time she reached the kitchen the rain was heavier and her hair was plastered to her head. She shut the kitchen door behind her with her foot and released Hatfield who shook himself and then sat down looking damp and puzzled in his old place in front of the Aga. Ann rubbed her hair with a towel. So Miranda had loved Felix. Why had she not seen it? But she could not have seen what she could not have conceived of. And yet why was it so inconceivable? Miranda had loved him and had, Ann could now work it out in detail, acted accordingly. Ann felt no resentment; she felt infinitely sorry for her daughter and in a strange way impressed. And she blamed herself for being insensitive and blind.

She fetched out some cold meat and a bowl of milk for Hatfield, which he sniffed over and then delicately consumed. He stretched himself out on the flag-stones. Ann sat down with the cat at her feet. So the act had been Miranda's, it had indeed all happened 'on another plane'. She had had no act at all of her own, she had been part of someone else's scheme, a thought, almost, in someone else's mind. And yet surely this was not right either. She shook her head. Had she acted, or had her act been stolen from her? Can our acts be stolen from us? She was certainly not good at thinking about such matters, she had lived in unconsciousness too long. Then she recalled how Douglas Swann had said to her that "being good is a state of unconsciousness", and she shook her head again.

She leaned down and stroked the cat. She had lived in unconsciousness and doubtless she would again, for it was her nature. She was not framed for recognising, let alone for grasping, her own felicity. In the end perhaps, for her, not knowing was better than knowing. Felix would never understand either. But to be understood is not a human right. Even to understand oneself is not a human right. She would leave the vain pursuit of the elusive act. What had happened had happened; and even if it were indeed the case that some obscure degenerate love for Randall had moved her, had it almost seemed frightened her away from what was rational and beautiful and free, she could not feel any clear remorse or regret. Felix would be well, Felix would be very well, without her. Still less did she feel any inclination to call her obsession by any grander name. Not to know was best, to forget was best. But it would not be Randall or Felix that she would forget but only herself, only what she had done and what it meant.

As she looked down at the big stripey cat purring and beginning to wash itself she remembered Fanny, and saw Fanny communing with Hatfield in a special way that she had, lifting him high up in front of her face with his feet and tail dangling. He would dangle patiently there, staring intently into her eyes. How little she had known Fanny. Yet she supposed she had loved her. She thought too of Steve, hidden and lost now in the mystery of his arrested boyhood. And from these two stilled centres, as between two pale and clouded stars, there arched for her a great silent dome of resignation. She had not known them. She did not know herself. It was not possible, it was not necessary, it was perhaps not even proper. Real compassion is agnosticism; and we must be compassionate to ourselves too. Tasks lay ahead, one after one after one, and the gradual return to an old simplicity. She would never know, and that would be her way of surviving.

Nancy Bowshott came in carrying a big tray covered with pots of raspberry jam. Ann jumped up almost guiltily. "Oh, Nancy, look who's here, in front of the stove!"

"There now, there now! Didn't I always tell you he'd come home again?"

Chapter Thirty-six

DEAREST DAD, I hope you got the cable all right to say that Penny was back safely. He enjoyed his trip and arrived in the pink and has been full of beans ever since! He would send his love I know only he's off at the Stadium at the moment servicing Tommy Benson's bike. Jimmie says he can have one of his own next year, and you can imagine he's starry-eyed! But I'm rambling on as usual and haven't properly said from all of us thanks *awfully* for giving Penny such a stunning time. We're madly grateful to you for making it possible, and he obviously enjoyed every moment. We've been positively *grilling* him you can imagine since he got back, poor boy! You know how inarticulate he is, but he's obviously had the time of his life. He's awfully improved too in lots of ways, so much more confident and grown-up. And *tidier*! You've all been an education and an eye-opener for him. Jimmie even accuses him of having an English accent!

Dear Dad, I've thought of you all so much this summer and wished I could see you. (I quite understand you can't visit us—it *is* so expensive.) I've thought and *thought* about Randall and I do feel sure, don't you, that he'll just turn up like a bad penny one of these days and expect everyone to embrace him and kill the fatted calf and so forth and what's more they will?! Jimmie says people like Randall can get away with murder and it's but too true. It's a case of to him that hath shall be given and so on and Randall's always known he can do whatever he likes and still be loved. I'm sure he'll come back. (Jimmie isn't so sure actually.) But poor *poor* Ann. I expect you have been with her a lot. I do wish I could be. I've written her reams of letters of course.

I mustn't go on about these sad things. There are so many nice things too. Jimmie has had another promotion and has ordered the annexe to be built! (Just as well, as our dear shack is about busting at the seams.) Jeanie has won a prize for geography. (I think she's quite the intellectual of this family!) And the baby's due in less than a month! Everyone is so impatient, they practically crowd round me shouting! We've decided, after *endless* argument, to call it Andrew if it's a boy and Margaret if it's a girl. I do hope you approve! Penny wants it to be a boy and Bobby wants it to be a girl and the rest of us will be delighted with whatever's sent along, so long as it's the proper shape and in its right mind! I'll cable you, of course, as usual.

I'm so terribly grateful to you all for Penny's holiday. His time in England had such a sad beginning—but young creatures recover quickly and so they should. I wish I could have seen the times you all had! Miranda must be a sweet little thing now—it's a pity she's a bit too young to have been a playmate for Penny. But he seems to have found a real playmate in Humphrey Finch! What a charming old fellow he must be to give so much of his valuable time to a young boy. They seem to have had a great spree in London, though Penny was a bit vague about what they actually *did* together. (I believe he's still mixing up the Tower and Buckingham Palace!) Wouldn't it be too heavenly if Humphrey came and saw us all out here as he said he might?

Forgive this dreadfully short letter. I'm as round as a barrel and terribly tired these last few days though *madly* cheerful! Try not to worry about Randall. Jimmie says maybe after all he'll come back where the money is! And I say (less cynically!) that he'll surely come back where he knows he belongs.

With lots of love from us both, and from Penny and Jeanie and Timmie and Bobby—and Maggy-Andy!

ever your loving

Sally

Hugh folded up the letter. He had not had time, in the flurry of embarkation, to read it properly before. He was now on the ship and some hours out from Southampton. He was going to India with Mildred and Felix.

They were sitting together in the bar, after having had an excellent dinner. The bar was at the stern of the ship, and behind them the white wake boiled and curled away into the darkness. Hugh felt at ease. He smiled across at Mildred.

Mildred was radiant. The slight illness which she had complained of earlier in the summer seemed to have left her completely. She was wearing a smart blue dress of some silky-lineny stuff which brought out the extreme blueness of her eyes, as blue as scyllas, Hugh poetically thought. Her petticoat was *not* in evidence and a discreet touch of rouge upon her cheeks gave her face a youthful definition. She was wearing just enough lipstick and her soft peppery hair which had, it was clear, lately received the attentions of an expert hairdresser, was cut short in a neat yet raffish style about her beaming countenance. Her hair seemed less grey, in fact hardly grey at all, Hugh noticed; he must have mis-remembered its colour. He had never seen her looking so nice, and he was tempted to pay her some compliment, only refrained because she might think him forward or absurd.

Felix was sitting at the next table writing a letter and thoughtfully sipping his brandy with a soft dreamy look upon his handsome and normally so discreet features. He had been exceedingly gay at dinner. He had obviously been much more cheerful since he had decided to do the Gurkha job instead of staying in Whitehall. Hugh felt, and said so, that he was quite right. After all, if one is a soldier one had better *be* a soldier and not a wretched bureaucrat. Hugh could not see how a stay-at-home office job could tempt a man like Felix at all. Mildred had also lately confided in Hugh concerning Felix's love life, an entity which Hugh had never, he discovered, believed to exist at all. Mildred's brother was, it appeared, deeply in love with a French girl who was now in Delhi, and thither he would hasten, as soon as they arrived in India and the very dark blue Mercedes had been unloaded from the hold, to plead his case. He had, it appeared, good hopes; and Hugh took pleasure, though with a slight sigh, in the younger man's evident happiness.

"Is he writing to *her*, do you think?" he whispered to Mildred.

"Yes. I saw it was in French!"

Hugh beamed.

"Absurd Hugh!" she said. She often said this now and Hugh had stopped hearing it as something else. His hearing seemed to be altogether better lately, and the din of argument in his head had subsided to a docile murmur. He had provided himself with plenty of Dramamine for the trip but hoped that now he would not need it.

"Would you like to see Sarah's letter?" he asked Mildred. "There's nothing in it, actually."

"Does she say anything about Humpo?"

"Well, yes. She says Penn had a great spree with him, though he's a little vague about what they actually did together."

Mildred gave a little scream of laughter, startling the pen-biting Felix. "*You* aren't worrying, are you? I know my Humphrey."

"Of course I'm not worrying. Still, we hardly looked after the boy and I rather blush at Sarah's letter."

"He'll forget the bad times and remember the good," said Mildred. "We all do."

"Where's Humphrey now, anyway?" In the haste of a rather suddenly-decided-upon departure he had not managed to check on the activities of the, as usual, conveniently preoccupied Humphrey.

"Oh, he's in Rabat. I'm sure he has consoled himself quickly. We all do."

"Hmm," said Hugh. He signalled to the waiter. The bar was warm and plushy and now almost empty. Most of the passengers seemed to have opted for an early night. The beat of the engines, happily drowning his murmuring ears, surrounded him protectively as the bright cosy air-conditioned ship moved smoothly onward through the waste of black waters. It was good to be going south. When he had been at Grayhallock lately a steady east wind had been blowing a rain of rose petals down onto the sodden levels of the Marsh. It was good to be going. "Another drink, Mildred?"

"I don't think so," said Mildred. She yawned and stretched shamelessly. "I think I'll be off. I've ordered a bottle of Scotch and some milk in my cabin. Why not come and see me there before you go to bed? I'll give you a special whisky drink with cinnamon. It'll make you sleep."

"All right," said Hugh. "I'll come along in twenty minutes or so. What's the news of Beryl, by the way?"

"They're getting married next month. Humpo will go, of course."

Beryl Finch, to the general amazement, was getting married to a well-known barrister.

"I hope she'll get on with it," Mildred added. "I'm dying to have more descendants. I'll be a fizzing grandmother."

"Confess you were surprised!"

"About Beryl? Stunned. It was awfully good for me. One ought to expect life to be full of surprises."

"Ah—I've had all mine," he said sadly.

Mildred laughed. "I wouldn't be too sure! Well, be seeing you."

She picked up her pile of picture-books of India and went off, ruffling Felix's hair as she passed him. She certainly seemed quite rejuvenated.

Hugh brooded quietly. He had a sense of everything being now in order. Or rather it was not yet quite in order, but a stage had been reached, a clearance had been made, and he felt as if he had only now, at his leisure, to put each thing neatly into its place. With this there came to him a comfortable sense of being justified.

He thought about Ann. He had spent, he felt, shortly before leaving, a quite *reasonable* amount of time at Grayhallock, and had really done his best to cheer her up. He had found, in fact, that she scarcely needed cheering, so immersed was she in the mysterious world of village life which seemed to him, over such trifles, so inordinately busy. Miranda being down with the German measles also gave Ann plenty to do in the house, which was perhaps just as well. He had arrived just in time to admire her winning entry in the flower-arrangement contest, and to note, partly with relief and partly with a slightly shocked surprise, that she was doing every-thing as usual, was thoroughly back in her old bread-and-buttery routine, and seemed hardly to have noticed Randall's departure so little difference had it made to the shape of her days. Hugh thought, I wouldn't have behaved so if my spouse had left me, I'd have broken the place up. He felt almost a small resentment on Randall's behalf. But, for Ann, it doubtless did very well, and he was glad to be able to leave her with a clear conscience.

There was still no direct news of Randall. It appeared that he had left Rome, and there were rumours of his having been seen in Taormina and that he was trying to buy a villa there. Hugh felt no distress about his son, but only a sort of rather exhausted rather pleasurable feeling such as one might have after a successfully brought-off bout of illicit love-making. No one knew. It had been his own private *coup*, his own privately arranged alteration to the face of the world, the beautiful, extravagant, feckless setting of Randall free. He had been let out, like a wild bird, like a wild beast, and whatever should come of his more extended prowl his father did not feel that he would regret his act. He could be confident that Randall would slash the colour on. Happy or not, Randall would certainly *live*. And Hugh could now be demure with an untroubled heart. This crime squared him with the tipsy gods.

Yet it had been all for Emma. Or had it really? Emma. He wondered if he would ever see her again; and he thought now of the possibility of her death with a calm resignation which did justice to her own dignity. He must in the end let her be. It was impossible to remake the past. They had fashioned their own destinies and had of necessity become dream figures to each other, and there was no violence of action, no feverish grasping and flinging back of the years, which could alter that now. Emma, enthroned in her wisdom, her witchery, her illness and the sheer mystery of her own life had sufficiently given him a sign. She was, he felt, beyond him; and his humility contained its own flat cheerfulness. As he dropped his hands in resignation he felt something akin to relief. After all he had doubtless, in the old days, turned her down for some good reasons.

He had thought lately a great deal more about Fanny, a Fanny more real to him now than at any time since her death, as if the pale shade had waited its moment. He saw her, playing patience on the counterpane with Hatfield purring beside her. He saw her anxious face lifted after the doctor had gone. Poor Fanny! She had had, like Ann, her simplicities. He had indeed sometimes thought of her as a miniature Ann. Yet why miniature? Ann was not so large, after all, nor Fanny so small. Fanny had had her life, she had been something. He saw her life behind him, remoter now, like a pastel-shaded ellipse. He was glad that he had not lied to her about the swallows, though she had been, in a way, a person to be lied to. It was as if at the end he had recognised in her a dignity which she had had all along, but had kept humbly lowered like a dipped flag or a crumpled crest. He was glad, after all, that he had stayed with her. He was glad that he had been good to her.

Felix had finished his letter and got up. He passed by Hugh to say good-night, and Hugh noticed benevolently how tired, in fact, Felix looked, and how his hair was greying and receding. Being in love is an exhausting business.

Felix asked, "Is there any news of Ann? I do hope she's getting on all right."

"How very kind of you to think of her. She was quite well when I left. She has such resources."

"Not moping, you thought?"

"Certainly not. Gay, rather, in her own little way. She's quite a bouncy little person really."

"A bouncy little person," said Felix. "Yes, I'm glad she's not depressed. Well, good-night, Hugh. I hope you remembered to bring your painting things?"

"Yes. I'm looking forward to painting again. I'm looking forward to everything. I expect we shall see the sun tomorrow. Good-night, Felix."

Hugh got up when Felix was gone and wandered out of the now empty bar on to the deck. He walked to the rail. Behind the ship the pale road of the wake stretched away back into the night. The black empty water surrounded them, the old eternal preoccupied ruthless sea. Hugh worshipped its darkness, its vastness, its utter indifference. He felt lighter and happier than at any time since Fanny became ill; perhaps, he suddenly thought, lighter and happier than ever before. Yet how did one know? One forgot, one forgot. What hold had one on the past? The present moment was a little light travelling in darkness. Penn Graham would forget, and think that he enjoyed his time in England. Ann had forgotten the real Randall, Randall had forgotten the real Ann, probably by now. Hugh had rejected Emma for reasons, and forgotten the reasons. His consciousness was a tenuous and dim receptacle and it would soon be extinct. But meanwhile there was now, the wind and the starry night and the great erasing sea. And ahead there was India and the unknown future, however brief. And there was comfortable cosy Mildred and gay enamoured Felix. Perhaps he had been confused, perhaps he had understood nothing, but he had certainly survived. He was free. *O spare me a little that I may recover my strength: before I go hence and be no more seen.*

He turned back toward the lights of the ship and peered at his watch. It was time to go in now. Mildred would be waiting for him.

THE END